Between the Wild Branches

Books by Connilyn Cossette

OUT FROM EGYPT

Counted with the Stars
Shadow of the Storm
Wings of the Wind

CITIES OF REFUGE

A Light on the Hill
Shelter of the Most High
Until the Mountains Fall
Like Flames in the Night

THE COVENANT HOUSE

To Dwell among Cedars
Between the Wild Branches

© 2021 by Connilyn Cossette

Published by Bethany House Publishers
11400 Hampshire Avenue South
Bloomington, Minnesota 55438
www.bethanyhouse.com

Bethany House Publishers is a division of
Baker Publishing Group, Grand Rapids, Michigan

Printed in the United States of America

Library of Congress Cataloging-in-Publication Data
Names: Cossette, Connilyn, author.
Title: Between the wild branches / Connilyn Cossette.
Description: Minneapolis, Minnesota: Bethany House, a division of Baker
    Publishing Group, 2021. | Series: The covenant house; 2
Identifiers: LCCN 2020056580 | ISBN 9780764234354 (trade paperback) | ISBN
    9780764239144 (casebound) | ISBN 9781493431533 (ebook)
Classification: LCC PS3603.O8655 B48 2021 | DDC 813/.6—dc23
LC record available at https://lccn.loc.gov/2020056580

This is a work of historical reconstruction; the appearances of certain historical figures are therefore inevitable. All other characters, however, are products of the author's imagination, and any resemblance to actual persons, living or dead, is coincidental.

Cover design by Jennifer Parker
Cover photography by Todd Hafermann Photography, Inc.
Map illustration by Samuel T. Campione

Author is represented by The Steve Laube Agency.

21 22 23 24 25 26 27   7 6 5 4 3 2 1

Between the Wild Branches

CONNILYN COSSETTE

BETHANYHOUSE

a division of Baker Publishing Group
Minneapolis, Minnesota

For my brother, Sam.

Your arrival in our family was the very first time I saw God directly answer a prayer from my lips, but certainly not the last. No matter the physical distance between the two of us wild branches, the name I helped choose for you will always be a reminder of the blessing you are to me.

"For this boy I prayed, and the LORD has given me my petition which I asked of Him."
1 Samuel 1:27

The Great Sea

Tyre

Acco

ASHER

NAPHTALI

Mt. Hermon

EAST MANASSEH

Sea of Kinneret

ZEBULAN

WEST MANASSEH

ISSACHAR

Shechem

GAD

Jordan River

EPHRAIM

Shiloh

Beit El

Ramah

BENJAMIN

DAN

Ayalon

Mitzpah

Jerusalem (Jebus)

Kiryat-Yearim

REUBEN

Ashdod

Ekron

Eshtaol

Beth Shemesh

Ashkelon

Gath

PHILISTINES

JUDAH (Yehudah)

Hebron

Gaza

Salt Sea

SIMEON

Be'ersheva

MOAB

"If you will return, O Israel," declares the LORD,
"Then you should return to Me.
And if you will put away your detested things from My presence,
And will not waver,
And if you will swear, 'As the LORD lives,'
In truth, in justice, and in righteousness;
Then the nations will bless themselves in Him,
And in Him they will boast."

Judges 4:1–2

One

Lucio

1052 BC
ASHDOD, PHILISTIA

My fist slammed into my opponent's jaw, the collision so jarring that I felt the vibration of it all the way to my shoulder. His head snapped back, blood trickling from his mouth. Perhaps he'd bitten his tongue all the way through, like my last opponent, but I did not relent. Before he'd steadied himself, I struck again, this time with a kick to the knee. Leg buckling, he lurched sideways but somehow remained standing, shaking off my blow. With a growl he charged at me again, a sneer on his face.

Before his punch could connect, I spun, the action so ingrained in my bones that I barely had to think before I was behind him, driving my elbow between his shoulder blades. He tripped forward, nearly going down, but somehow found his balance before he landed in the dirt, where it would have been all over. No one could beat me on the ground. No one. Not even this champion of Tyre, who had a reputation that stretched all the way here to Ashdod.

Myriad voices hummed around me like the constant buzz of a disturbed hive, but I remained immune to their bidding. For years now, the cheers and chanting of my name had been little more than an irritant, not the impetus for the pulse-pounding rush of anticipation I used to crave more than anything.

The one voice that broke through the haze was Mataro's— and only then because he was at the edge of the fighting grounds, screaming at me to finish the man, as if I actually planned to let my opponent get the best of me. My cousin knew me better than that; I didn't know why he bothered goading me. I'd not lost a fight in years. Not one that counted, anyhow.

Even as I threw my weight forward, slamming full force into the Phoenician, my mouth soured at the proprietary tone of Mataro's commands, As if it was him and not me who knew the correct placement of my feet, which weaknesses to look for, and how to clinch victory. The thought almost made me laugh as I wrenched my opponent's dominant arm back. Mataro was little more than an overfed jackal these days. Nothing like the man who'd opened the door to me ten years ago—the man who had been on the verge of ruin, inebriated and unsteady on his feet as I explained who I was and that I'd come back to Philistia to build the fortune he'd promised me.

Mataro may have arranged the first of my matches and coached me to fight like the ruthless demon I was rumored to be, but the urge to wrap my fingers around his fat neck and squeeze was increasing. It seemed that the fuller his purse, the larger it grew, always making room for more. And along with the accumulation of his wealth, his mouth seemed to grow larger and larger as well, boasts gushing out like rancid wine with every ridiculous demand and every public declaration that it was *his* guidance that had made me an unmatched champion on the fighting grounds.

The Phoenician snarled a curse as I jerked his arm harder, then hissed as pain I knew well shot through his body. I took advantage of the momentary distraction and swung, grunting as I jammed my leather-wrapped knuckles into his ribs in a series of unrelenting blows. He hissed out a pained curse that told me this bout was nearly finished. A jolt of triumph surged in my chest, but instead of lingering the way it used to and curling around my bones in a delicious embrace, it burned away like mist on a summer morning. I'd claimed countless victories since I returned to Ashdod as a fifteen-year-old boy with my hopes crushed and my blood boiling with betrayal, and yet each one seemed to matter less than the last.

My opponent wavered on his feet, catching his breath from the relentless attack I'd delivered to his torso, and in that brief moment my attention flitted up to the balcony that surrounded this royal courtyard. The crowd was thick today, gathered to revel in the violence between us and the events that would follow, but somehow my gaze snagged on one face out of the multitude that were gleefully screaming for the Phoenician's downfall. Everything inside me slammed to a halt.

Surely it was only a trick of the light that familiar hazel eyes gazed down at me, their depths filled with an expression of stricken recognition that swiftly flared into panicked horror.

It could not be her. Could not be the one who'd left my heart in tatters ten years ago.

Sweat rolled into my eyes, blurring my vision for a moment, and I blinked it away, heart pounding as shock and confusion gripped me in an iron hold. But by the time I could see again, whatever illusion that had deceived me had vanished—nothing left of it but a ghost of a memory that had taunted me for far too long.

A fist hit my cheekbone, rattling my teeth as I tasted metal. Lights flashed and pain radiated across my face as I realized that I'd been far too absorbed in the absurd vision I'd seen among the raving crowd to notice my opponent had regrouped.

Cursing myself for such a foolish mistake, I shook off the blur in my sight, spat out the blood that coated my tongue, and plowed forward into him. Grunting as I rammed my knuckles directly into his side once again and felt a rib give, I let out a foul word of my own as he recoiled from the hit. He tripped back a step, chest heaving, but his eyes never lost their focus on me, even though he had to be in extraordinary pain. Although he was heavier than I was, he was younger by a few years, his face free of the many scars that marred my own, and the glint in his eyes told me he was hungry enough for this win to ignore any and all injuries.

I, however, was undefeated. A record that would remain unbroken because I refused to let the last year of planning and maneuvering go to waste, especially for the elusive memory of a girl who'd tossed me aside like a soiled garment. The Phoenician and I both braced ourselves for the next strike—panting, sweating, and bloody.

"What are you waiting for?" screamed Mataro. "This should already have been over! Stop hesitating!"

I blinked the sweat from my eyes again, every muscle in my body going still as granite. But instead of letting my cousin's taunting words crawl under my skin and steal my focus, I allowed them to burn in my belly, stoking the fire higher and higher until everything outside this match was nothing but ash. Mataro could rant all he wanted today; he could seethe and snarl and hiss out demands, but this would be the last time. Tomorrow I would cut the cord I'd too-willingly bound myself with, and he could hang himself with it for all I cared.

I unleashed the rage I'd been harnessing, giving it permission to flood my limbs and propel me forward as quick as a wildcat to grab the Phoenician's head with both hands. My fingers locked around his neck and dug into his skull as I yanked it forward to collide with a powerful knee strike. Before he'd even hit the ground, I'd turned away, not bothering to wait for the announcement that he'd been knocked insensible and my victory was secure. I left the fighting grounds, ignoring the clamoring crowd as they parted before me, the multitude of hands that slithered over my bare skin as I pressed past, and the lurid invitations that followed in my wake. I'd long ceased being flattered by the attention I'd once reveled in.

Even more bodies than I'd guessed were packed into this space, stirring up the dust with their sandals and adding their voices to the cacophony. Now that the long-anticipated fight between myself

12

and the Phoenician had been decided, the dancing and storytelling would begin. This festival, dedicated to the gods and goddesses credited with leading our forefathers across the sea, would culminate with the impossible and fascinating leaping of the bulls like our ancestors had enjoyed on the island of Caphtor so long ago. It was a celebration I'd dreamed about participating in when I was a boy, before my sister Risi forced me to leave Ashdod in pursuit of a magical golden box.

I tried to shut down the memory and the ache that never failed to build in the center of my chest whenever I gave myself permission to think of Risi or her beloved mountaintop in Hebrew territory that I'd never fully been able to call home. But whatever delusion had gripped me earlier must have forced open a door I'd been certain was nailed securely closed.

Helpless against the urge, I paused to peer over my shoulder, allowing my eyes to swiftly scrutinize the face of every dark-haired female on the balcony where I'd seen the apparition. Then, disgusted with my own weakness, I headed for the gates, shaking off the ridiculous notion that the girl I'd once thought to be my future would be here in Ashdod, among people who hated her kind so vehemently. The sooner this day was over, the better.

Two

Shoshana

I pushed my way back through the crowd on the balcony, bones vibrating and eyes burning. But I had to get away before anyone saw the grief on my face. I'd been reckless enough as it was today, slithering closer and closer to the parapet so I could catch a glimpse of him down below. Too helpless against the pull he had on me to restrain myself any longer.

When I was finally safe in the shadows, I slumped back against the wall and dropped my chin, doing my best to restrain the hot tears that glutted my throat.

Lukio. *My* Lukio was here.

After over an entire year and a half of avoiding him, of praying that he and I would never cross paths, I'd finally given in to my fierce curiosity and slipped in among the revelers, my greedy eyes feasting on the sight of the boy I'd loved since I was nine years old. But that boy was now a man. One who'd far surpassed even the superior height of his youth and whose enormous body was cut into lines that even the fiercest warrior might envy.

His golden-brown hair was nearly to the center of his back, the

14

curls I'd once adored now oiled and pulled back, secured by a series of gold clasps that ran the length of the long queue. His face was clean-shaven, revealing the sharp lines of his strong jaw, and his earlobes were studded with ornate ivory plugs. Dark tattoos in distinct Philistine shapes swirled around both of his arms and across his impressively broad chest as well. He'd been handsome as a boy, far more than any of the other young men in Kiryat-Yearim, but now he was devastating—a trait not lost on the hundreds of people in this courtyard who'd been screaming for him, their suggestions becoming more violent and more lewd as the fight went on.

And then, he'd seen me. And everything had stopped for the space of five eternal heartbeats. In those moments he was not the brutal champion of Ashdod, known for his unapologetic and emotionless method of beating men senseless on the fighting grounds, but the boy who'd taught me how to climb trees and differentiate between bird calls, who'd left sycamore figs on my windowsill as a sign to meet in our special place. For the four years that he and I had enjoyed a secret friendship, he'd insisted that I call him by his Philistine name instead of the one he'd been given by his sister Eliora and the Hebrew family that had adopted him. They'd known him as Natan, but he'd always been Lukio to me—the designation something sweet and sacred between just the two of us. So much had transpired since those quiet days when our innocent friendship had slowly shifted into something deeper as we explored the woods outside Kiryat-Yearim together under full moons. But I could not help but hope that behind that vicious façade my tenderhearted friend was still there.

However, at the same moment that his opponent regathered his wits and struck Lukio with a ferocious hit that jerked his head to the side, a woman beside me screamed encouragement to "Demon Eyes," and those hopes shattered to pieces.

Not only was he no longer using the name Natan, but he'd embraced the horrific moniker used to mock and humiliate him as a child because he had one brown eye and one green. A jeer that had been invented by none other than Medad, his former friend and my own husband. Why Lukio would use such a demeaning name to fight under, something meant to strip away his humanity and highlight the fact that he'd been an outsider in our town, was far beyond me; but it had been the reason I'd known it was him in the first place.

For months I'd heard tales of a ruthless fighter whose fame had spread throughout the Five Cities of Philistia, heard my mistress and her sisters exclaim over his dangerous beauty. But it was not until I'd heard him called Demon Eyes that I realized it must be Lukio, the young man who'd run away from my hometown after I'd trampled his heart into the dust. The one whose pleas I'd ignored as I fled our last conversation and ran toward the destiny chosen for me, even if it meant my own heart was left in pieces beside his.

An even louder swell of shouts and cries of joy from the mass of people gathered on the balcony told me that Lukio had thrown off whatever hesitation he'd had the moment our gazes met. The sounds of delight at his victory, undoubtedly achieved with the same cold-blooded execution of the final blows he was famous for, jerked me away from my childhood memories and reminded me of my true purpose here today.

My mistress had given me leave to watch the match from the upper level of the palace, and now I had only a short time to deliver a message before she sent someone to find me. I should not have paused to indulge in foolhardy curiosity. Lukio was no longer the boy he'd been, but neither was I the same girl, so it did no good to wish away the chasm between us. It was just as immovable as the mountain I'd grown up on and as deep as the valley I'd walked since he'd left Kiryat-Yearim.

Besides, for as much pain as I'd endured in my marriage to Medad, and even after I'd been enslaved by the Philistines, there were three very important reasons that I would not change the outcome of that fateful last conversation with Lukio. And right now, I had much more important things to deal with than thoughts of a man who'd likely forgotten me long ago anyhow.

Pushing away from the wall, I was glad that I'd not allowed any tears to slip down my face. To any of the revelers around me, I was nothing more than one of the many slaves in Ashdod, albeit garbed in a linen tunic that gave away my status as a maidservant to a family of means. No one would notice me spiriting through the shadows behind the vibrantly painted columns that held aloft the top story of the sprawling residence of the king of Ashdod.

Descending the wide stone stairs that led to the ground level, I strode down the shady hallway away from the central courtyard and toward the farthest corner of the palace, keeping my head down and my steps measured so as not to draw any attention. Thankfully, with all the excitement of the festival that had begun at sunrise with a series of sacrifices to the Philistines' gods and that would end with debauched rituals I'd rather not dwell upon, none of the revelers took any notice of me. I made my way toward the small storage shed on the southernmost outside corner of the palace, one that held garden tools that would certainly not be of any use in the midst of a festival and therefore a perfect place for meeting in secret today.

After a quick sweep of my gaze to ensure that no one's eyes were on me, I unlatched the door and slipped into the black room. Holding my breath, I waited, my heartbeat the only sound for a few long moments in which I wondered whether the detour to slake my curiosity about Lukio had meant that I'd missed my contact. Or whether he'd even come in the first place.

"Do you have the names?" said a low voice, one that was familiar now after a few months of meetings like this one. However, since I'd never seen the face that matched that deep voice, nothing about this encounter was safe. It was not wise to remain here any longer than I must.

"I do," I said. "The house of Kaparo the High Priest took in two young boys of perhaps ten or eleven, and that of Rumit the scribe purchased a girl of fourteen or so."

"Any others that gave you cause to worry?"

"They all give me cause to worry," I retorted. "They are my countrymen. Brothers and sisters from the tribes of Yaakov."

He paused, only his slow measured breaths reaching out to me from the blackness. When he spoke again, there was a deep note of compassion in his voice. "You know what I mean. We can only do so much, my friend."

I cleared my throat of the thick coating of remorse. I had no cause to snap at this man who risked so much to meet me and who relayed the names of recently sold slaves on to people who carried out more dangerous tasks than I could imagine for the sake of the most vulnerable.

This man I met in the dark could be anyone. I'd never seen his face, and for his sake and mine, had never even considered breaching the trust between us to tarry outside the storage shed and discern his identity. He did not sound Hebrew, so either he'd been in Philistia so long that the peculiar sound of our tongue had been washed away or he had chosen to help with this mission purely from a sense of compassion. I had no idea. But whatever his motivations and however he'd fallen in with those of us who did our best to help other slaves escape their bonds, he'd never given me cause to doubt his trustworthiness.

"From what I was told, there were not more than ten brought in before the festival, likely a raid on a small hamlet, and most of them were men," I said. "Only two were sold locally. The rest were taken to the port." They were probably already on a ship bound for some unknown destination so far from the shores of the Land of Promise that they would never return.

I had not seen the captives with my own eyes, of course, being only one link in a chain, but every time I received information about new victims of the Philistines' campaign of targeted attacks on Hebrew villages, my chest ached with empathy. I did not have to guess what it was like to be dragged from your home, to watch your neighbors and friends slaughtered, to pray that the vicious men who'd stolen everything from you would simply kill you instead of—

I pressed down those disturbing memories and the swell of nausea that always accompanied them.

"I'll pass the information on to my contact," he said. "Send word when more arrive."

And there would be more. Whatever fear had been put into the Philistines' hearts by the resulting plagues and famine from stealing the Ark of the Covenant had eroded with every passing year. By the time my husband moved us to Beth Shemesh just after we were married, raids on villages in the *shephelah* were commonplace. True, our enemy had not come at us with their collective might like they had at Afek, when the five kings of Philistia took the Ark from the battlefield and then laid waste to Shiloh, but they'd been relentless in nipping at our heels, making certain that the people of Yahweh were never able to rest in the peace we'd been promised a thousand years ago. Peace I would never have again but hoped that I might give others a chance to reclaim.

"I should go," I said. "My mistress will be looking for me now that the fight is over."

"Who won?" he asked, the question dragging me right back to that balcony when I'd looked into Lukio's eyes for the first time in ten years.

I swallowed down a sharp response. He would have no reason to know of my connection with one of the fighters in that match today and had not meant to wound me by asking.

"The champion of Ashdod," I replied, the words feeling like rusted blades in my throat.

"Of course," said the man with a chuckle. "He doesn't lose. Perhaps I should have put a piece of silver or two into the pot."

With that comment, one of my many questions about the man I'd been passing information to was answered. No kind of slave would have a piece of silver to gamble on a fight. And certainly not two. This man was free. Someone able to walk about unfettered in the city, to come and go when he pleased.

I left the room without further comment. I had no interest in discussing Lukio's violent tendencies with anyone, let alone a faceless person in the dark.

Slipping back into the palace through a rear entrance, I made my way toward the opposite side of the complex, where those with more than enough silver to waste had gathered to observe the festivities and make their own wagers. By the time I found my mistress, any evidence of the fight on the courtyard grounds was gone, replaced by a troupe of half-naked dancers who were performing a complicated sequence of movements, leaping and contorting their bodies in impossible ways. To my profound relief, Lukio was nowhere in the vicinity.

As was my duty, I took my place behind her shoulder, grateful that she was so absorbed in an animated conversation with her two sisters about the dancers that she did not seem to notice my return at all.

Once my heartbeat returned to a normal rhythm, my eyes dropped to the infant in the arms of her oldest sister. The little one gazed over the woman's shoulder toward the vibrant blue-and-red walls at my back, drawn to the ornate shapes and swirls, even though she could not yet comprehend the mural depicting the subjugation of my people by the Philistine ancestors who'd arrived on our shores hundreds of years before. Then the baby turned her eyes toward me, peering up at me with her wispy brows drawn together, and I was nearly leveled by an overwhelming wave of grief and longing.

Ten years ago, I'd lost the boy I'd thought I would marry, and at that time, it had been the most devastating thing in my life—even more than my mother slipping away after a long illness when I was eight. But nothing compared to the soul-shattering loss of my children, and nothing ever would.

Three

Lukio

Teitu scrubbed my head with a linen cloth, squeezing the water from the ends of my hair in a methodical way that had become familiar to me over the last four years.

I'd been tempted more than once to lop off the excessive length, as the effort it took to fashion it into the distinctive style expected of a fighter of my stature was tedious. But as I'd come to discover in the years since I'd put myself in the public eye, the performance was as much a draw for the crowds as my skill, and I'd learned to play up both for maximum effect, no matter that such antics made me feel dirtier than the sweat and grime that coated my skin after a match.

"There you are, Master," Teitu said, giving my shoulder a pat, his one eye meeting mine for only a moment. "All finished."

It had taken two washings with natron powder to remove the grime from my body. Between the thick olive oil used to tame my curls into a long, spiraled queue and coat my skin, the profuse sweat trailing down my face, and the dirt stirred up on the fighting grounds, I'd returned to my house looking and smelling like a wild boar. But Teitu was used to the aftermath of my matches, unflinchingly tending my wounds before I soaked my aching body in the sun-warmed rooftop bath he'd prepared hours before.

Teitu had been the first of my servants when I built this extravagant house. A couple of years older than me, he'd always been vague about his origins, other than to say that his father was Egyptian, which was evident in his bronzed skin and black hair. But he was so skilled at anticipating my needs that I did not press him about his past. I cared little where he came from and only hoped never to have to replace him.

"Shall I bind your hair again?" he asked as he ran a bone-handled comb through the tangles.

"No," I replied. "Leave it free to dry."

He nodded and spread the locks across my back, shaking more water from the length as he did so. When one of the damp golden-brown spirals slipped over my shoulder, I scowled at it. My sister's hair was so similar in color to mine, and ever since that apparition from my past life had appeared today during the fight, memories of Risi had been crowding in on me.

It had been years since I'd indulged in imagining what all had happened to her since I'd walked away from Kiryat-Yearim and left her to begin a life with Ronen, the Levite who'd once betrayed her and those she called adopted family. The fact that he'd feigned friendship with me to learn the location of the Hebrews' sacred box for the purpose of stealing it—and also to get his hands on my sister—was a sin I would never forgive. How she could do so, after he'd lied over and over to all of us, was far beyond me. But she'd made her choice and betrothed herself to Ronen. I'd heard it with my own ears before I'd made my decision to leave that place for good.

I flicked the wet curl back over my shoulder as Ekino, another of my servants, entered my bedchamber with a tray of fruit and bread, along with a jug of wine. He left the food on a table, affording me his usual silent, deferential nod as he strode from the room. All my servants were well aware that after matches I preferred lighter fare instead of full meals, and that they were expected to go about their duties as unobtrusively as possible for the rest of the day while Teitu alone tended to my needs. Unlike most other fighters I knew who celebrated victories with feasts and raucous entertainment, I preferred solitude after a day of bone-rattling collisions on the fighting grounds and ear-shattering screams from the surrounding crowds.

"Your lip is bleeding again," said Teitu, dipping a finger into a pot containing a honey-herb mixture. The moment he dabbed the ointment to the wound, its earthy fragrance caused an unexpected stab of longing in my ribs. I could almost feel the green-scented breeze trailing over my skin, hear the crunch of vegetation beneath my sandals, and taste the smoky haze that blanketed the thick forests of Kiryat-Yearim on soggy days.

Ignoring Teitu's ministrations to the other cuts and bruises on my face and body, which I barely felt anymore after so many years of constant abuse, I stared down at my hands and flexed my fingers wide. My knuckles were heavily callused and thick, having been broken many times over the years, and one small finger was permanently bent inward. It had been ten years since I'd felled a tree in that mountaintop forest, but somehow, I could still remember the sensation of gripping my ax, feel the satisfying vibration in my bones when its iron head bit into the thick bark of a tree for the first cut, and hear the crackle of branches as the giant toppled to the forest floor and shook the ground under my feet.

Annoyed that such memories had begun to rear up, I was almost grateful when Mataro strode uninvited into my bedchamber and dropped his overfed body onto my cushioned couch with a grunt. He tossed a jingling leather purse onto the small table between us, one that looked to be half as full as it would have been when Mataro collected my winnings. I knew I should count the silver inside, make certain he was not skimming off more than the amount we'd agreed upon, but frankly I didn't care. I had plenty of wealth, including olive orchards, vineyards, and rolling hills of wheat and barley outside the city, and now was not the time to question the far-too-generous portions of my earnings he helped himself to. I'd deal with that later, once my plans were implemented.

"Where did you go?" he said, flicking a commanding finger at Teitu. "There was a group from Gaza I'd arranged for you to meet after the fight."

Used to Mataro's wordless demands, my manservant poured him a cup of wine and placed it in his hand, his blank expression betraying none of the disdain that I somehow sensed he held for my cousin.

"I was done," I said with a shrug, knowing Mataro would not grasp my deeper meaning. Let him think I was merely overtired after my bout with the Phoenician.

"These men have the ear of the *seren* of Gaza, Lukio. We can't afford to brush off such connections. They were eager to meet the champion of Ashdod and interested in arranging a match with one of their best fighters, a mute Egyptian who they say is more beast than man." His eyes flared as he swept his hand through the air, heedlessly sloshing wine onto the limestone tiles. "Imagine what sort of wagers such a bout would inspire."

My cousin lived as a rich man and not because he was particularly savvy with his silver. Indeed, he gambled away nearly as much as he brought in and walked a fine line with his debtors. But when I was fifteen and wide-eyed after my return to Ashdod, it was Mataro who'd taught me the rules of this city and filled the right ears with word of my raw talent in order to arrange the fights that had started it all.

Would I have survived in Ashdod without him? Found a path to the fame I enjoyed now? Perhaps. Perhaps not. But I'd repaid him a thousand times over for any help he'd given me in the beginning. These past years he'd been little more than deadweight, and I was done pretending he held any sway over me.

He may have fooled fifteen-year-old me, acting as though he'd grieved over my loss and counted me as a son, introducing me to his drunken friends, and arranging sordid feasts that lasted for days. But it was not long before I'd realized that I was nothing more than another of his unfortunate slaves, wearing shackles that I'd willingly slipped onto my own wrists. Of course, by that time, I'd grown used to my bonds, and instead of fighting them had pretended to enjoy their weight. I consumed whatever he gave me—be it drink or women or hollow praise—and buried any regrets beneath an ever-growing pile of riches.

"What happened out there today?" Mataro tossed a handful of sweet grapes into his mouth and then spoke through the purple mess. "You nearly lost to that Phoenician—and in the middle of a festival no less!"

A flash of the vision I'd imagined earlier rose again in my mind. Looking back now, it was obvious that I had simply conjured up those enormous hazel eyes, the freckled skin, and the perfectly pink mouth rounded in shock—a product perhaps of one of the harder hits that Phoenician managed to land, along with the recent realization that this ridiculously extravagant house was far too empty and that it was time to do something about it. The futile longings that had been entangled with that decision had caused more than a few restless nights thinking about the girl who'd betrayed me, who'd walked straight into the arms of my enemy and had borne who knew how many of his children by now. I swallowed down the bile that coated my tongue at the thought of his greedy hands on her.

"I *don't* lose," I said, wishing it had always been the truth.

Mataro sneered and shook his empty cup at Teitu, who'd been at silent attention behind my shoulder. "You'd better not. My reputation is at stake."

I swallowed my disbelieving laugh. It was *my* consistent wins that kept his purse full of silver. *My* prestige as an unbeatable champion that ensured he was invited to the homes of those in high places. *My* blood and sweat that enabled him to call himself anything more than the sluggard and swindler he truly was. If only his perpetual inebriation and gambling were the least of his sins.

Just before I left Kiryat-Yearim, Risi had insisted that Mataro had killed Azuvah, the old Hebrew woman who'd cared for us after our mother died, on the night we'd run away from Ashdod. I'd scoffed at the idea, certain that our cousin would not waste the life of a valuable slave. I'd clung to the explanation even after I'd returned to the city of my birth, desperate to hold to the notion that Mataro could not possibly be as vile as Risi insisted.

But then, a few years ago, just before I'd moved into my newly constructed villa, I'd overheard two of Mataro's slaves fretting over a burned batch of stew before a banquet and whether they might be beaten to death and thrown from a window like that "old Hebrew." Immediately, the story I'd told myself about my cousin was shown for what it was—a many-layered blindfold I'd tied over my own eyes.

Not only was Mataro a lecher, a drunk, and a thief, he was a murderer. And I'd refused to believe my sister, the only person who'd ever truly loved me—with the exception of perhaps the slave he'd destroyed.

Disgusted with both myself and the man to whom I'd entrusted my future, I'd begun plotting then how to cut the ties between us. It had been more complicated than I'd hoped and taken longer than I'd anticipated, but this morning, while my cousin was occupied with aggrandizing himself to those men from Gaza, the final piece of the game I'd been playing without his knowledge had slipped perfectly into place. An opportunity provided by none other than Nicaro, the king of Ashdod himself.

"And I've been thinking," said Mataro, oblivious to my silent gloating, "that it's time to think larger."

"How so?"

He stood, pacing back and forth a couple of times. "When men from Gaza are making the journey here just to see you fight, it is plain that your reputation has far exceeded the territory of Ashdod. Even the king sees the potential or he'd not have invited that Phoenician down for the festival."

I sat back, amused by this rare and strangely vigorous burst of energy from my cousin. I took another long draft of well-aged wine from my own prolific vineyards while he blathered on about new connections he'd made and places he planned for us to travel in order to fight local champions. Little did he realize that not only had I long been considering such things and making plans to leverage the fame I'd already garnered, but that the king had indeed seen my potential—and not only on the fighting grounds.

It had been nearly four months since I'd spoken to Nicaro at an early harvest festival and subtly indicated that I had ideas for a new sort of festival in Ashdod, one that would eventually draw competitors from all over the region and bring our city unparalleled prestige among the Five Cities—and eventually, if my instincts were correct, the world. Having been very careful not to seem too ambitious but at the same time making clear that I would welcome the chance to discuss the matter further, I'd been fairly disheartened when I'd heard nothing from the king since then, other than the customary public commendations for each match I fought and won.

But then, to my great surprise, while I was being oiled head to foot and my hands wrapped in leather strips for the fight this morning, the king himself entered the chamber set aside for my personal preparations and said he expected me to come to the palace tomorrow afternoon in order to discuss the imminent retirement of the current Master of Games. Oleku had been in charge of organizing not only all fighting matches in the city but also bull-leaping, archery contests, and any other competition event that took place during the larger religious festivals ever since Nicaro's father, Darume, had occupied the throne. Although the seren had not explicitly said he'd decided to appoint me to the prestigious position, it was strongly implied. And I was more than ready to accept any appointment that would ensure my cousin no longer had any control over me.

"Think of the possibilities, my boy," said Mataro, waving his bloated fingers in the air. "There is an abundance of wealth to be had in far larger cities than this one. And with every place we travel, our purses will overflow even more. We will live like kings, indulge in all the pleasures the nations have to offer, and the entire world will know your name."

But they wouldn't, of course. Because even though I was a famous champion, Mataro had introduced me at my first real fight by the moniker my enemy had given me to mock my dual-colored eyes—a secret I'd unwittingly divulged while drowning in my cups not long after my return to Ashdod. So, instead of being known as Lukio to the crowds who screamed for me, I was only known by the curse Medad had repeatedly thrown in my face in the years after our friendship had been severed—Demon Eyes.

When I'd aired my frustrations about this to my cousin, he had dismissed them as histrionics and insisted that the name would lend me an air of mystery and madness that would enflame the imaginations of those who gambled on the bloody matches that at times ended with broken appendages, cracked skulls, and even death.

At least in that instance, he'd been right. Within only a month of that first fight, which had taken place in the same alley where I'd once rolled dice with my friends as a child, the name Demon Eyes was being whispered all over the city with reverence tinged by fear, and young men all over the region were clamoring to challenge me. It had taken far longer to get used to hearing an epithet being called out over and over in worship, and years before I stopped thinking of Medad whenever I heard it. Somehow, I had the sense that Mataro had known exactly how deep that wound went from the start and counted on it to inflame my rage.

My cousin may have outsmarted me back then, using my pride and pain to manipulate me, but tomorrow I would finally outmaneuver Mataro and shatter those shackles for good. And he would never see it coming.

Four

Remnants of yesterday's festival littered the courtyard of the king's palace as I entered through the northern gate. An army of slaves was busy sweeping up shards of drinking vessels, trampled food, bright strips of tattered ribbon and abandoned banners, and even a few odd sandals into piles.

The rich dirt I'd fought upon with the Phoenician had been hauled away, likely added to the extensive garden beds on the southern side of the palace. My blood and sweat would even now be mingling with the roots of the many vibrant blooms cultivated to fill this enormous palace with perpetual life and color.

Once I made my way up to the wide porch that led to the main hall of the palace, the guards at the entrance directed me toward one of the king's dining chambers. A buzz of nerves went through my limbs as I passed between two scarlet-painted columns, whose girth reminded me of some of the more ancient oak trees I'd felled atop Kiryat-Yearim. All the years of honing my body, of training my mind, of deferring to my cousin while my teeth dug grooves into my tongue came down to this moment.

Finally, I would become my own man, walk the path I'd cleared with my own two hands, and all the seeds I'd planted along the way would come to fruition. Any whispers of regret I may have harbored over my past choices would be nothing compared to the victory of attaining a goal I'd had in mind for so long. Not even hazel-eyed ghosts could haunt me today.

Using the skills I'd perfected after years of stepping onto fighting grounds with countless competitors of all shapes and sizes, some of whom had killed opponents without mercy, I shook off any trepidations, pulled in a slow, deep breath, and focused on every step toward my victory.

Like the courtyard, the towering hall before me remained a testament to the wild happenings from the night before. The patterned tiles were slick with wine and beer; cups and bowls and half-eaten morsels littered every available surface. I wondered how long it might take the slaves to return the palace to the pristine order I knew Nicaro demanded. Everyone I passed on my way toward the king's private dining chamber looked half-asleep on their feet as they went about their duties. I guessed that none had even slept last night. I'd attended the raucous celebrations after this annual festival for the last two years and was well aware that mountains of food and rivers of drink were served all night long. In honor of the gods, every sort of indulgence would have been partaken of around a blazing fire at the center of the chamber. Charred remains of the huge logs that had burned throughout the night atop the round stone-tiled health still glowed faintly from within, and smoke hung in the air despite the wide opening in the roof above.

Hearing voices as I approached the open door to the king's private dining chamber at the far end of the hall, I paused, hesitant to barge into a conversation.

"How many soldiers did we lose?" said a voice I recognized as the king's.

"Only fifteen," replied another man, likely one of Nicaro's commanders.

"*Only* fifteen?" snapped Nicaro. "We shouldn't have lost one. I sent you two to capture Tzorah! Not run away with your tails between your legs."

"Somehow the Hebrews knew we were coming, my lord," said

another man. "Even though we attacked in the middle of the night."

There was no reply to the pitiful explanation, and I imagined the seren's bright blue eyes boring into the man's face. There was something eerie about the way Nicaro fixed his eyes on people, as if he could see past their skin and into the very depths of the soul within. I did not envy these commanders their position defending losses to the Hebrews.

I knew that my countrymen hated the people I'd lived among from my seventh year to my fifteenth, and I was well aware that in the past few years they had stepped up attacks on the outlying Hebrew communities, determined to overtake the fertile shephelah region that lay between the coastlands and the hill country.

The five kings of Philistia made no secret of their desire to drive the Hebrews out of the territory they'd taken from the Canaanites hundreds of years ago, lusting after the rich farmland and bountiful crops, the hills that boasted thick forests of impossibly tall oak, cedar, and pine trees, and the enormous flocks of cattle, sheep, and goats tended by men they considered only little more cultured than those beasts themselves.

"It is past time for us to be rid of the remaining Danites. We should have annihilated them the moment their *champion*"—he sneered the word—"brought down the Gazan temple on my father's head."

If Azuvah, the Hebrew woman who'd raised my sister and me after the death of our mother, hadn't filled our heads with fantastical bedtime stories about that same champion—a man called Samson, who she insisted was imbued with supernatural strength—I likely wouldn't know much about him at all. But he had been a continual burr in the sandal of Nicaro's father for many years, and his final act of defiance killed not only Darume himself, but Nicaro's three older brothers, along with a vast number of other Philistines—a tragedy so devastating and humiliating it was still never spoken of in public arenas. It was a shock to hear Nicaro speak now of the incident that had handed him the throne at seventeen.

One of the slaves approached, head down and carrying an armful of tattered pillows that were leaking goose feathers—victims to the night's revelries, I guessed.

Not wanting to be seen listening in on the king's conversation, even by a slave, I took the last few steps and paused in the doorway while Nicaro and his two commanders continued discussing a second attack on Tzorah, one that would be so quick upon the heels of this last one that the Hebrews could not possibly anticipate it.

All three of the men were nearly as tall as me, with bodies honed for battle, if not built for the style of brutal fighting I was famous for. But from what I'd heard, although the seren did not go on most raids himself anymore, leaving that honor to his commanders, his gleaming chariot was always the first onto the field in larger skirmishes. No one would ever dare accuse the king of Ashdod of cowardice, of that I was certain, even if he was younger than all the other lords of Philistia.

Finally, the king caught sight of me hovering in the doorway like an unbidden child.

"Ah! The champion of Ashdod," called the king, inviting me inside his chamber with a sweep of his bejeweled hand. "In the crush, I did not have the pleasure of congratulating you on your win yesterday. You must have slipped out right after your victory was announced." His tone was faintly chastising.

That had been foolish on my part. By slinking off without making a public bow to him and not playing up my hard-won reputation for the crowd that had come to root for me, I'd wasted an opportunity. I could only hope that I'd not done anything to jeopardize his offer with my impetuous departure from the festival.

"Apologies, my seren," I said, hand on my heart as I dropped my chin in a show of submission. As tempted as I was to make excuses for my exit, I held back, knowing that it would only be seen as a sign of weakness by these warriors.

The king let his scrutinizing gaze rest on me for a few drawn-out moments, then his black brows lifted as a slow smile spread over his face. "Well, the important thing is that we are sending Tyre's champion back to the north with much less cause to boast than before." He spread his hands wide in a magnanimous gesture. "Of course I have nothing against the Phoenicians, as they've been excellent trading partners as of late, but the king of Tyre can afford to be brought down a notch or two."

The three of them laughed heartily at his jest, but I knew there was nothing casual about the reference to displaying our superior strength to our distant neighbors. I suspected that once the kings of Philistia had the Hebrews in hand, they might cast their sights to the north and the fleets of seafaring ships the Phoenicians were so famous for. Of all the lords who governed the five city-states of the Philistines, Nicaro, son of the great Darume, was the most ambitious. He made no apology for his determination to honor his father's memory by making Ashdod the most prosperous port on the Great Sea and proving himself worthy of the formidable legacy he had inherited, by any means necessary.

"Make preparations for another raid tomorrow," said Nicaro to his commanders, effectively dismissing them. "I have matters to discuss with our champion."

They bowed, both of them eyeing me with curious—but not disrespectful—glances before they silently quit the room. I'd wondered if they would cast aspersions on me for not joining the army, but it seemed they, like the rest of Ashdod, valued my role on the fighting grounds more than on the battlefield. And, if I had my way today, that would never change. My weapons of choice were my fists and feet, which had profited my purse far better than the wages of a soldier ever would—even the generous wages Nicaro offered his most trusted men.

"Come," said the king, gesturing for me to sit on one of the plushly cushioned couches built into the back wall of the chamber. "Let's you and I have a drink and talk of the future before our meal arrives."

As if they'd been hovering outside the door for just such a pronouncement, three female slaves entered the room: one with a basin of warm water to bathe my feet and hands, one with a swan-necked jug of wine, and the other with two silver-wrapped drinking horns in the shape of lions. As they set about their duties, silent as specters, Nicaro leaned back on the pillows and fixed those disconcerting eyes on me. He'd occupied the throne for nearly as many years as I had been alive but had always seemed a bit ageless to me. So I was surprised to note more silver at his temples and laced through his beard than the last time I'd spent significant time in his company.

"Tell me, Lukio," he said, stroking thoughtfully at that well-trimmed beard. "I assume you've been chewing on our discussion from yesterday."

"I have," I said evenly, then took a long draft of wine to steady myself and ensure that the explosion of excitement sizzling through my limbs did not show on my face. "Although I do have some questions."

He lifted his brows, seemingly intrigued.

"If I am appointed as the Master of Games . . ." I paused, tipping my chin curiously. "That is, if I understood you correctly and am not being presumptive . . ."

"Not at all. That *is* what I am proposing."

"I am honored to even be considered, seren," I replied, with all sincerity. "Would I be charged with coordinating all state-sponsored matches? Fights? Archery? Bull-leaping?"

"Yes, as well as the boat races," he said.

A thrill went through me. I'd not even considered that the races held between some of the smaller ships to celebrate the opening and closing of the trading seasons would also come under my purview.

My own father had been a foreign sailor from some far-flung place rumored to be covered in ice half of the year, so the call of the sea seemed to be in my blood. In my youth, I'd entertained ideas of setting sail to search for him in those unknown northern wilds, either to beg him for answers as to why he'd abandoned my sister and me after our mother died or to pay him back for doing so in the first place.

However, once I'd discovered the satisfaction of knocking a man senseless or using certain holds on the ground to incapacitate an opponent, I'd never given another thought to stepping foot on a ship. Still, the idea of organizing races between vessels stirred up a bit of that latent seawater in my blood. I could feel the rush of it as I imagined lines of bird-prowed boats bobbing up and down in the waves, banners flying, sails fluttering, and oarsmen chanting as they fought for victory against their seafaring brethren.

"I can tell the idea pleases you," said Nicaro, grinning.

"That it does." I accepted another refill of wine in my cup and tipped it back with a hum of pleasure as the perfectly aged vintage caressed my tongue.

"Excellent," said Nicaro. "It will be the first event you'll be in charge of organizing. Oleku will be discontinuing his position immediately upon your acceptance."

The temptation to press for an explanation as to why a man who'd been in charge of all such events for decades had suddenly decided to step down was strong, but the immovable expression on the king's face gave me no leave to do so. The decision had been made. Who was I to question it?

"I suppose you might be wondering why I chose you for this position."

With care born from long practice facing opponents, I remained impassive, even though that very question had kept me up half the night. There were plenty of men more qualified than I to step into Oleku's sandals.

The king surveyed me over the lip of his cup. "You heard my conversation with Virka and Grabos." My heart jolted and my gut twisted. It was not a question. He'd been well aware that I'd overheard the conversation between himself and his commanders. But I was nothing if not skilled at holding my composure, on and off the fighting grounds, so I only tipped my chin in silent agreement.

"Tzorah is not the only loss we've suffered recently." He stared into his wine, as if the disappointing images were playing out over its surface. "When we took Beth Shemesh a year and a half ago, I

35

felt certain that the rest of the foothills would fall into our hands easily. But that hasn't been the case."

I was astounded to hear Nicaro admit to defeats that were in no way common knowledge—and also to discover that the very same city to which Risi and I had followed a wagon laden with the Hebrews' greatest treasure all those years ago had fallen into Philistine hands. I knew no one in Beth Shemesh, of course, having remained on the mountain of Kiryat-Yearim the entire time I'd lived in Hebrew territory, but an unexpected pang of melancholy hit me at the knowledge that the Levitical town had been sacked.

"Timna is ours," he said, "Along with Ba'alat. But the Hebrews prevented us from taking Tzorah. They anticipated our raid somehow, and a surprisingly large force met ours. Virka and Grabos retreated after a few days, knowing it was a lost cause. But I will not give in. I want the entirety of the Ayalon Valley."

Another chill of recognition went through me. Tzorah was not far from Kiryat-Yearim. I could see the city from the hillside cave that I'd escaped to whenever I desired to get away from the disapproving scowls of the Hebrew family who'd taken in Risi and me. If Timna and Beth Shemesh were all in the grasp of the Philistines now, and Tzorah might soon follow, did that mean that Kiryat-Yearim might too be at risk? I had no way of knowing whether my sister still lived there. On the day I'd left, I'd overheard some talk between her and Ronen about moving to Ramah, which was at least two days walk to the northeast, after their marriage. But even if Risi did not live in Kiryat-Yearim anymore, the rest of Elazar's family did, of that I was certain. And regardless that I'd never been able to call Elazar and Yoela my parents like Risi did, nor accept their large brood as my brothers and sisters, I could not stomach the thought of harm coming to any of them.

The only thing that stopped me from asking about the mountainside town I'd known so well was the sacred box hidden on that summit, tended by Elazar himself. Nicaro would not dare approach the artifact after what had happened the first time the Philistines had stolen it from a battlefield. Although Ashdod had long since healed of the plagues that had killed my aunt and uncle—Mataro's parents—along with the rest of his siblings and hundreds of other people in the city, the memory of it was deeply ingrained. The golden vessel was rarely spoken of, and when it was, it was accompanied by some of the foulest curses I'd ever heard.

But what did any of *this* have to do with my appointment as the Master of Games? Nicaro must have seen the confusion play out across my face.

"There are rumors," he said. "Ones that, shall we say . . . *undermine* my reputation and have made some of the most influential people in this city nervous."

"What sort of rumors?" I dared to ask.

"They say there is a new leader among the Hebrews. One whose influence has grown steadily in the past ten years or so. From what we hear, he has been traveling throughout the Hebrew territories, destroying the ancient Canaanite high places and dishonoring the gods. And even more disturbing, he's somehow accomplished what no other Hebrew leader has done in hundreds of years—persuading some of the tribes of Israel to set aside their long-held squabbles and join forces against us. From what my commanders tell me, it was not only Danites at Tzorah, but Yehudites, Benjamites, and Efraimites who came together to protect the city. They know that I mean to take Ayalon next, and with it the road to Beit Horon."

From what I knew, that trade road cut straight through the foothills all the way to Jericho, which was a crossroads that led not only north to Damascus but to the territories of Moab and Ammon. Taking it would open up lucrative trade between Philistia and many nations to the east. No wonder Nicaro wanted to dominate that route. Ashdod had the sea and its ports, yes, but between her and an abundance of wealth lay the Hebrews. The fact that they dared remain as an obstacle was obviously a point of great frustration to our ambitious king.

"Between these setbacks, the drought that has plagued us for the past two years, and the lightning storms that set fire to the olive orchards to the south of the city a few months ago, there is concern that the gods have withdrawn their favor from my house. I cannot afford for *anyone* to question my right to this throne, Lukio. I will not tolerate any chatter among the people that has the potential to grow into a swell of support for my enemies." He leaned forward, elbows on his knees as he speared me with a look of determination. "But you, Lukio. Champion of Ashdod. You are loved by all. They scream your name. They beg for you to touch them as you pass through the crowd. They paint their eyelids brown and green in honor of Demon Eyes."

Such an odd way to honor my eye color. I'd thought at first that I'd been disoriented after a fight when I saw a group of young women with different colors of kohl on their lids, but apparently it had become quite the fashion over the past couple of years. I'd even seen a few men wearing such markings.

"With you as the Master of Games, the whispers against me will fade. Your popularity with the people, in conjunction with your public support for my kingship, will outweigh these temporary setbacks and none will dare question the power and prosperity of this city." His eyes seemed to spark blue fire as his voice rose, and I found my breaths quickening, affected by his fervor. "Together, we can lift high the name of Ashdod above all the other Five Cities and make her famous among the nations."

"You truly think that I can have that sort of influence?"

"I do," he said, his tone smooth but as impenetrable as the wrought iron our people were known for forging. "And to prove the solid bond between us and erase any doubt of where your loyalty lies, you will marry my daughter."

It was all I could do to keep my jaw from dropping into my lap. "You offer me one of your daughters?"

"Yes. The youngest, Mariada. She will make a good wife to you. She is quite young, of course, and certainly not the boldest of my daughters. But she is surpassingly beautiful and obedient. Her mother is my third wife, who has given me four sons and two daughters, so without doubt Mari will give you plenty of your own children."

"You honor me, my seren, especially when I am not of royal blood," I responded, awed that a king would offer me a marriage contract when such a thing could be used to make connections with other royal families, Philistine or otherwise.

He waved away the unspoken question. "I have five other daughters, Lukio, all who've made profitable matches. And I have full confidence that an alliance between you and I will reap unparalleled rewards in other ways. I well remember our conversation during that harvest feast, my friend. Even if both of us were four or five cups into the celebration, I heard your ideas about arranging one large festival devoted solely to games. One that would not only display the strength and prowess of our people to all the neighboring cities, but that would also draw competitors from other nations, anxious to prove their own skills, and draw even more spectators with silver and goods that they'll be eager to wager and to barter with in the marketplace."

My eyes flared wide at the revelation that he'd actually listened to my half-drunk ramblings and found my ideas worthy of consideration. So worthy, indeed, that he would offer me Mariada— a young woman I'd seen only once at that same harvest festival, who'd been so astoundingly beautiful that I'd barely been able to peel my eyes off of her. With thick, abundant black curls that flowed past her waist, smooth alabaster skin, a tantalizingly curvaceous form, and eyes that somehow were even bluer than her father's, she would be the prize of any powerful man. And Nicaro would offer her to a brute whose only value was built from pummeling other brutes with his fists? A man whose own father thought so little of him that he'd disappeared the moment he'd been born?

There was little for me to consider. Nicaro was not only offering me a bride to fill my empty home with offspring, but a place within his family, and a position of power in this city that I could never have imagined as a dirty-faced boy scuttling about in its gutters, rolling dice with other street urchins.

"Nothing would give me greater pleasure, my seren. I am at your service in all things and vow to bring honor and renown to our city and to your throne, both as Master of the Games and as your son-in-law."

His smile was nearly as brilliant as the flaring sunset over the sea just outside the window. He clapped his palms together. "I will call my scribe now to prepare the betrothal contract and the announcement about both your appointment as the Master of Games and your upcoming union with Mariada. By morning, the entire city will be abuzz with the good news."

Therefore, before Mataro laid his balding pate on his pillow tomorrow night, he would know that he no longer controlled me. I could practically hear his shrieks in my head and hoped that Nicaro would attribute the victorious grin on my face as mere delight with our agreement.

As the royal scribe prepared the document that would set both contracts in stone, that sweetly freckled face and hazel eyes I'd imagined in the crowd yesterday floated through my mind. However, with fierce determination, I forced it away for the last time. She had made her choice long ago, and now I had the chance to annihilate any leftover childhood longings by marrying one of the most desirable women in Ashdod. My old enemy Medad may have stolen Shoshana from me, but now I would marry the daughter of a king.

Five

Once the agreements had been created, with both our signet rings marking the clay of each contract as complete and irrevocable, Nicaro himself led the way toward the rooftop terrace, where some of the women of the household were partaking of a meal.

As foolish as it was for a man who spent many of his days pummeling others into submission, the closer we got to the terrace and the moment I would meet the woman who would soon be my wife, the more my limbs jittered with nervous anticipation. I toyed with the ivory plug in my earlobe, needing something to take my mind off what was to come.

"Fear not, Lukio," he said as we began to ascend the stone stairs side by side. "You look as though I am sending you into a den of lionesses." He patted my shoulder, his laughter echoing off the bright depictions of seabirds on the walls around us.

"I am merely looking forward to meeting your daughter." For the first time I wondered exactly what her reaction to all of this might be. Shock? Anger? Dismay?

"She will be pleased," he said, answering my unspoken concerns. "I have no doubt. As I said before, you are a favorite of many women in this city, my own household included."

Of course, whether or not Mariada was impressed by my skill or appearance was irrelevant. She had no choice in the matter; the deed was done. Her desires meant nothing to Nicaro, only that the alliance between us was a successful one.

"The women love to eat up here on this hidden terrace," said Nicaro, "especially when the weather is hot and the breeze sweeps off the sea. I designed it especially for Amunet, my first wife, who has a particular fondness for the water after growing up in a palace overlooking the Nile."

Nicaro had been married to Amunet when he was only fourteen. The daughter of an emissary to Pharaoh, Amunet had been offered as a means to strengthen ties between Egypt and Ashdod. The mother to five of his sons, among them his heir, she was a powerful woman in her own right and known to eviscerate incompetent slaves without remorse.

As we climbed the last few stairs, I took a deep breath to steady myself, then exhaled in slow measure in time with each step, a practice I had learned to calm my pounding heart before a match. It would certainly not do to let these women know how truly nervous I was, so I pretended that I was merely stepping forward to meet my next opponent.

Five women sat around a table at the far end of the terrace—two of Nicaro's wives and three of his daughters—with an array of delicacies spread out before them. Unaware of the arrival of myself and the king, the woman who would someday bear my children was talking animatedly with one of her sisters before she took an enormous bite of a sweet roll. Mouth full, she swiped at the honey that dripped down her chin and giggled. The sound was unexpectedly endearing and took away a small measure of my anxiety.

An infant let out a sudden and piercing squall, halting all conversation and drawing the eyes of everyone to the babe in the arms of Tela, one of the king's eldest daughters.

"Why did you bring that child up here?" said Amunet with a distinct edge of disdain. "It's obviously in need of the wet nurse."

The sharp rebuke made Tela's face go pale. "You are right, my lady. She's been in a foul mood since her teeth began coming in."

She turned to one of the slaves who was standing nearby and held out the child, her own voice a near-echo of Amunet's imperious tone. "Take her down to my room and have her fed."

Although Tela was married to Virka, one of the two commanders whose conversation with Nicaro I'd just overheard, they occupied chambers within the palace itself; an offer that was made to me during marital negotiations, but which I'd respectfully refused. I'd not spent the last five years building a well-appointed household of my own to set it aside and live in the palace, no matter how lavish the accommodations. I wondered why Virka had chosen to do so and whether he regretted being under Nicaro's watchful eye.

Catching sight of the king and me as the young slave scuttled past us with the fussy little one tucked into her shoulder, Amunet startled, her kohl-lined eyes going wide. The beautiful Egyptian woman was a few years older than her husband but was adept at hiding it, wearing black braided wigs and heavy cosmetics to hide any hints of aging. She was a daughter of the Nile to be certain and clung to the trappings that identified her as such, even though she'd now lived the majority of her life in Ashdod.

"Husband?" she said, her tone distinctly less haughty than before as her curious gaze cut to me and then back again to him. "What brings you to our table?"

At her words, the rest of the women on the terrace turned their attention to us, and one by one their mouths dropped open, the last of them Mariada herself, whose bright blue eyes were the largest of the lot. With a wine cup halfway to her lips she stared at me in blatant shock.

"I have wonderful news to share with you, my queen," said Nicaro. He placed his palm on my shoulder in a fatherly gesture that caused a surprising tightening of my throat. "You all know Lukio, the champion of Ashdod."

"Yes, of course," said Amunet, her gaze taking me in head to toe before a carefully gracious smile curved her hennaed lips. "One would have to have one's head in a posthole for the last few years to not know of the famous Demon Eyes."

"Exactly," said Nicaro, "and we are fortunate that he has just accepted an appointment as the Master of Games."

Although a flicker of surprise crossed Amunet's face, it was quickly replaced by regal composure. "Indeed? A bold choice, husband. Oleku has held that position for many years."

"That it is," he said, with the slightest edge to his tone, "and one that was not taken lightly by any means. Oleku has been well-compensated for his excellent service to the throne."

"You are most generous," she replied, with a deferential tip of her chin. "I am certain Oleku is thoroughly satisfied with your decision and that our champion will prove to be equal to the task."

Although every word between them was achingly polite, I had the distinct impression that there was an entire conversation going on beneath the surface that the rest of us were not privy to.

"Of that I have no doubt," said Nicaro. "This young man has plans that will bring glory to our city like never before."

Amunet's kohl-drawn brows lifted high as she once again swept an assessing gaze over me. "Does he?"

He ignored her question and urged me forward. "Lukio, I believe you met my wives at the harvest festival," he said, gesturing to Amunet and Savina. Orada, his second wife was rumored to be quite ill, so I was unsurprised she was not here with the others.

Murmuring a greeting, I bowed my head, first to Amunet and then to Savina, knowing full well that deference was to be given to the queen above all others.

"And these are some of my beautiful daughters. This is Tela"—he placed a palm on her shoulder—"daughter of Orada, my second wife."

Tela bowed her head slightly, keeping me in her sights as she did so. With her mother hailing from Sidon far to the north, Tela had inherited hair the color of rich red earth and deep brown eyes but bore a regal expression on her narrow face that made clear her parentage.

"And that"—he pointed across the table to the other young woman—"is Jasara, eldest daughter of Savina." Jasara, like her younger sister, had thick black curls, but she'd not inherited Nicaro's blue eyes. Instead, she fixed me with a brazen, brown-eyed stare full of meaning, but I ignored it as Nicaro tugged me by the arm to the end of the table, where Mariada sat blinking up at her father in bewilderment.

"And this . . ." He held out a palm to her, and she accepted his hand with a hundred questions playing out across her lovely face. "This beauty is my youngest daughter, Mariada."

The young woman gave me a shy but confused smile. "It is my pleasure to meet you."

She truly was one of the most exquisite women I'd ever laid my eyes on, and a surge of pride that she would soon be mine welled up in my chest. Not only would I be the most famous fighter in Ashdod and the Master of Games, but every man would envy me my wife as well. Mataro would probably swallow his tongue at the news, since there was nothing he loved more than drink except beautiful women.

"I am glad you've all finished your meal," said the king, the comment a clear command as he glanced around the table. "I need to continue my conversation with Virka and Grabos about the raid, but I do believe Lukio and Mariada have a few things to discuss. In private."

On a little gasp, Savina's hand flew to her mouth. Obviously, Nicaro had not informed his third wife of his intention to make her daughter my bride. He also seemed not to care that Mariada had gone crimson with embarrassment, nor that he was leaving me to give her the news of our marriage, alone.

As the others began to rise from their seats at the table and servants swiftly cleared the table, the king turned back to me. "We will speak again soon. I'd like to hear your plans for the boat races within the week."

"It will be my honor, my lord," I said with a bow of my head.

With no further comment, Nicaro strode away, in a rush to meet with his commanders before they returned north with renewed forces and supplies. With a pursed-mouth scowl, Amunet followed closely on his heels, and I wondered if she meant to intercept him. Something told me Nicaro's first wife was none too pleased with any of the unexpected news today but was too well trained to question him in front of others. Tela and Jasara followed soon after, but not before flashing matching frowns at Mariada as they took their leave.

Savina leaned to press a kiss to her daughter's cheek before whispering something in her ear that caused a tight and seemingly contrived smile to come over Mariada's lips.

"The breeze is cooling now that the sun is going down." She brushed a hand up and down Mariada's bare arm. "I'll send your maid up with a wrap."

"Thank you, Mother," she replied in a tone so soft it was barely audible.

With one more nervous glance toward me and a tight nod my way, Savina left the two of us with only the distant shush of waves against the rocky shoreline and the shriek of a few seabirds wheeling overhead to mitigate the silence.

"Can I offer you some wine?" Mariada said, as if she somehow knew my mouth had gone dry.

"I would be grateful," I replied and carefully sat in the chair Savina had vacated. It was so delicate that I worried it may collapse beneath my weight, so I did not relax into its cushioned hold, instead remaining at the edge of the seat, palms splayed on my knees to keep them still.

Mariada poured both of us a generous portion, and I noticed that her hand trembled as she did so. Was she afraid of me? Or perhaps just nervous, as I was? She had to have guessed the reason for this private conversation, after all.

I turned my gaze to the sea in the distance and the gold-limned horizon beyond. "This view is second to none. Do you often take meals here?" I asked, trying to set her at ease. And truly the spot was a perfect one, above everything and so quiet in its hidden location. It made me wonder why I'd built a home in the very center of town, where a constant drone of voices and animal noises entered my windows at nearly all hours.

"Yes," she replied, "when the weather agrees."

A long beat of silence vibrated between us as we both took another drink of wine, but then we spoke at the same moment.

"Do you—?"

"I saw—"

We both smiled at the awkward exchange. I'd never been so unsettled around a woman and wondered whether it was because I knew she was to be my wife or because she was the king's daughter.

"Please," I said, "go ahead."

"I was going to say that I enjoyed the match yesterday."

"Is that the first time you've seen a fight?"

"No, I've seen a few others. My mother does not care for such things though. The blood makes her ill, so it is the first time I've seen you fight up close. Usually we watch from a high balcony."

"And what did you think? Is the sport too bloody for you as well?"

She bit her lip in an attempt to hide her smile and shook her head. "I found it quite exhilarating. I could barely breathe at the end. The way you knocked that Phoenician senseless with that final blow—" She sighed. "It was all so very *exciting*. My sisters could not stop talking about you all through the rest of the festivities. They say there is no better fighter anywhere and that everyone fancies themselves in love with you."

"Do they?" I lifted a brow and then pounced on the chance to gauge her interest. "And what of you?"

Pink suffused her cheeks and her long black lashes fluttered. "Me?"

I should feel bad that I'd embarrassed her, but instead her reaction emboldened me. "Did you participate in these discussions with your sisters?"

"I . . . I . . ." she stuttered, her blue eyes going wide.

I leaned forward, giving her a little grin. "I am only teasing. Did you enjoy the rest of the festivities?"

She let out a relieved huff of laughter. "I did. I loved the acrobats, and the bull-leaping was thrilling to watch. When that last

47

man managed to flip all the way over the spotted bull with only one hand—" She pressed a hand to the base of her throat. "I felt as though my heart would pound its way right out of my chest!"

"I am sorry to have missed it all," I said. "I left after my match."

Her brows drew together. "You weren't injured, were you?"

The concern on her beautiful face made a rush of something warm fill my veins. How long had it been since anyone had truly cared about my safety? Mataro worried about injuries only because it might affect my ability to fight. And for as much as the crowds screamed for me, they seemed nearly as enthralled when I was bloodied as when I inflicted the wounding blows.

"No more than usual," I said. "I've been fighting since I was a boy."

"Truly? How old were you the first time?"

"Seven."

Her eyes went wide. "So young?"

"It was only a scuffle in the street with some older boys. Not one of the arranged matches." But I would never forget the feel of those two crumbs of silver I'd earned for beating up a boy three years older than me in my palm, even if my sister had been horrified when she found me afterward, bloodied and bruised and grinning ear to ear.

Mariada's expression remained troubled. "Was no one looking out for you? Your mother and father?"

I decided to offer enough of the truth that it would satisfy her. "My mother died in childbirth. And my father boarded a ship one day and never returned."

"You had no one?" Her gentle question unsettled me enough to say the name I'd not spoken aloud for ten years.

"My sister, Arisa." And Azuvah, but memories of the Hebrew slave woman only stirred up confusion and guilt, so they would remain where they belonged, buried deep in the past.

I allowed myself a bitter smile. "I thought perhaps Risi might thrash me herself when she realized I'd been fighting. She made me promise to never do it again."

However, I'd not kept that promise for any length of time and had continued tussling with the other boys and blaming any scrapes or bruises on climbing trees or falls during footraces. But I would never forget the day she'd seen me fighting with Medad in Kiryat-Yearim when I was fifteen and the horror on her face when I came out of the dark place I'd gone while I beat him half to death.

"I should like to meet your sister someday," said Mariada.

I stiffened, frowning. "She does not live in Ashdod."

"Oh? Did she marry someone in another city?"

The question hit me like a spear to the chest. But for as innocent as her curiosity was, I had no interest in spilling the contents of my bitter soul. I was not here to dredge up my messy past, only to build my future—a future that now included this lovely young woman in front of me.

Mariada would join my household within a few months, after the first of the intercity games we would host in Ashdod. Perhaps within a year or two, the enormous house I'd built would no longer be filled only with the gentle shushing of servants' bare feet, but with the voices of my own children. A son, perhaps, a boy I could raise to step into my position one day. Or a daughter, a sweet little girl with hazel eyes and freckles that multiplied in the sun.

No. A child of Mariada's would have blue eyes and alabaster skin, like her mother's. I blinked away the traitorous thought and brought my attention back to my soon-to-be bride.

She sat watching me with furrowed brows, and I realized I'd been so wrapped up in my own thoughts that I'd not answered her question.

"My sister is gone," I said, not willing to explain any further.

"Oh." She placed her fingers on her lips, emotion rising in her eyes as she made the exact assumption I'd intended. "I am so sorry for your loss."

I stretched a tight smile over my face, grateful she did not press upon the subject. "It was a long time ago," I said, and then to further push away all the conflicting emotions that thoughts of Risi stirred up, I decided that it was past time for me to tell Mariada about the agreement Nicaro and I had made. "I suppose you may suspect the reason for my presence here this evening."

Even though twilight had fallen and I could only see her face by lamplight now, the color of her cheeks deepened drastically. "I can only guess that you have spoken with my father about me."

"Indeed, I have."

"I did not know that you had even noticed me at the harvest festival." She lowered her gaze to where her hands were fidgeting in her lap. "There were so many desirable women around. Many far bolder than me. I cannot understand how I could have caught your eye."

That small indication of insecurity gave me pause. She seemed to have little idea of just how beautiful she was. I decided to let her think that this betrothal had been entirely my idea and not Nicaro's.

I reached for her hand, which was cool to the touch, either from nerves or the chill of the evening. "Out of all the lovely women who were at that feast, it was you who I could not keep my eyes away from, Mariada. And when I had the chance to speak to your father, to plead for your hand in marriage, I took it with great pleasure."

A noise, like the sound of someone stifling a gasp, caused me to look over Mariada's shoulder to where a maid stood in the shadows holding a length of cloth in her hands, presumably the wrap Savina had promised to send.

I wondered for a moment whether the girl had been embarrassed that she'd intruded on a private moment or simply startled to find Mariada alone with a man who looked every inch the brutal fighter. But then, with slow steps, the maid came forward into the glow of one of the lampstands flickering near the entrance to the terrace, and there was no more question as to why she'd been so stricken.

The ghost I'd seen on the balcony yesterday had not been an illusion at all. Standing ten paces away from where I sat confirming my betrothal to a Philistine woman was Shoshana, the Hebrew girl I'd loved since I was eleven years old. The girl I'd vowed to spend the rest of my life with. The girl who'd abandoned me and left me so broken and desperate that I'd run away from Kiryat-Yearim, leaving everything behind. How could she be here? Not just in Ashdod, but in the palace of the king? Blood rushed through my body in a painful torrent, my heart pounding with the same ferocity as it had during the few rare times when an opponent managed to trap me in an inescapable hold.

"Lukio?" Mariada's sweet voice broke into the thoughts careening about inside my head, drawing my attention back to her. For as much as I wanted to leap to my feet, drag Shoshana away, and demand to know everything that had happened to her since the last moment I'd seen her in the middle of a forest clearing, I'd made an agreement with the king of Ashdod. I'd pressed my own signet ring into the clay, and there was no erasing that without losing everything I'd worked for over the past ten years.

"As I was saying," I continued, making certain that none of the shock and confusion I was experiencing was revealed in my voice. "I would love nothing more than to make you my wife."

Her free hand went to her mouth as she stared at me wide-eyed. "You truly want to *marry* me?"

I nodded, not trusting my tongue and forcing myself to not dart a look toward Shoshana who was now as still as one of the columns that held aloft the roof of this magnificent palace.

"The betrothal contract has already been prepared and will be announced tomorrow," I said, then gave her an alternative that I'd not planned to offer until my past had crashed into my future. "But I certainly won't force you if it is not your desire to complete this union."

"Of course I would be honored to marry you," Mariada said, her words bubbling out like a wellspring as an enormous smile stretched across her lips. "I cannot believe this! My sisters will be so surprised! In fact, every woman in Ashdod will be faint from envy." She let out a little huff of surprised laughter. "Me—married to the champion of Ashdod!"

All the pleased anticipation I'd felt on my walk up the stairs beside Nicaro was gone. For as angry as I'd been when Shoshana had thrown me aside, I could do nothing to control the flood of memories of our childhood together. The laughter. The games in the woods. The whispers in the moonlight beneath our tree.

By appearing here now, she'd stolen what should have been the satisfaction of my most hard-won victory. I needed to find out how she'd come to be here—and I would do just that, very soon—but nothing would change what she'd done back then and what had just happened here tonight.

I stood, pointedly avoiding Shoshana's stricken gaze as she stepped forward to fold her mistress in the wrap she'd brought to the terrace; for it was clear that the girl I'd spent years with, secretly traipsing all over the mountain I'd once called home, was now the handmaiden to my betrothed.

"Your father is planning a feast to celebrate our betrothal in a few days, so I will return then." I bent to kiss the back of her hand, knowing the small affection would be expected of me now that we were to be married.

"All right," she said, obviously confused by my hasty retreat after such a significant conversation. "I'll look forward to seeing you."

I forced myself to give her a tight smile and went to take my leave, but not before I made the mistake of lifting my eyes to those of the girl I'd loved with every fiber of my being when I was young. The collision of our gazes felt like two ships ramming each other at full speed, and the shimmer of grief in her hazel eyes stripped me to the bone.

Then, just like she'd done the day she'd left my hopes in ashes beside a smoking charcoal mound, I walked away.

Six

Shoshana

Now I knew exactly how Lukio had felt the day I'd told him I was marrying someone else. How his chest must have felt like one enormous gaping wound as I'd walked away. I now fully understood why he'd taken his ax to the charcoal mound he'd spent days building with such vehemence that I'd heard his guttural cries halfway down the mountain as I fled, even above the sound of my own anguished sobs.

No wonder he'd packed a bag and run away to Ashdod a couple of days later, desperate to leave behind the pain I'd inflicted on him. If I had the ability to escape this palace right now, I would already be gone, dragging my shredded heart behind me in the dirt.

But not only was I not free to wallow in the agony of hearing Lukio profess his adoration for another woman—my mistress, no less—but I didn't even have the right to feel such things.

I'd left *him*. Married another man. In fact, the same one who'd tormented him in childhood. Lukio certainly did not have to answer to me, of all people. And even though it seemed that he had taken that same ax to my rib cage the moment he'd announced his and Mariada's betrothal, I could not let the devastation show on my face.

"Can you believe it?" Mariada said, practically vibrating with excitement as she pulled the soft woolen wrap I'd brought tighter about her bare shoulders. "Demon Eyes wants to marry *me*?"

I tried not to flinch at her choice of words. She did not know how hurtful that term had once been to Lukio. She was simply a very young woman, awed by the idea that a famous fighter had settled his affections on her.

She spun in her chair to look up at me, her blue eyes glittering. "My sisters will turn every shade of envy when they hear that he's chosen me."

I had no doubt they would. After Lukio's match yesterday, Mariada's sisters shamelessly had talked of little else than the champion of Ashdod and just how much they would welcome his attentions, regardless that Tela was married and Jasara was betrothed.

"You must be tired, mistress. Would you like to return to your chamber now?" I gave her a half-hearted smile, hoping she would not notice the abrupt change of subject. I was desperate to be away from this terrace and the memory of Lukio's beautiful mismatched eyes meeting my own and how the shock in them had so swiftly cooled into apathy before he'd turned away.

But now that he'd seen me for certain, I could breathe easier. He'd made it very clear that he wanted nothing to do with me and that was as it should be. I was determined to be content with the many wonderful memories I had with him when we were young and to remember that we were no longer children dreaming of an impossible future while tromping about the woods. He was Philistine. I was Hebrew. He was wealthy and famous. I was a slave. And nothing would ever change those facts.

Besides, I had much more important things to worry about than the boy I'd fixed my affections on when I was barely old enough to understand what transpired between men and women. I'd been summoned to a meeting tonight and needed Mariada to be asleep before I could slip away. Usually by now she was already well into her dreams so she could wake with the sunrise, a habit she'd learned from her mother, who abhorred the dark.

"I *am* tired," Mariada replied, stifling a yawn and rising. "Especially after staying up through most of the festivities last night."

I was even more weary, not only because it had been expected that I continue serving Mariada until she finally went to bed sometime before dawn, but because I'd been on edge the entire time, worrying that Lukio might reappear in the royal hall during the drunken revelries. I'd not allowed myself to relax until I lay my head down on my pallet in the corner of Mariada's room, and I had paid for such exhaustion by not being on my guard when I stumbled upon Lukio's speech to Mariada.

To hurry along the process of returning to Mariada's chamber, I began to snuff out the remaining lamps around the terrace while my mistress talked of her betrothed.

"Have you ever seen a more beautiful man, Shoshana?" she asked. "There is something so arresting about his face."

I hummed a non-response but could not disagree. I'd always been drawn to him, even when I was a girl, and could not explain what it was about him that was so interesting to me. In comparison to the other boys in Kiryat-Yearim, his skin was lighter, his curly hair was a fascinating golden-brown, and his dual-colored eyes were entrancing. But far more than the unique looks that had initially captured my attention, it had been the sweetness of his soul that had ensnared me, a hidden depth that he revealed only to me and his sister, along with the feeling that he needed my friendship as much as I needed his.

As we made our way toward her rooms, Mariada continued to talk, seeming not to notice that I hadn't answered her question. "I heard that his home is beyond compare as well. He purchased three smaller houses and had a team of men tear them down to make room for his own. There was no expense spared in the construction either. It is rumored to be the most richly appointed home in Ashdod—next to this one, of course." She giggled and grabbed my arm, gasping in delight. "I cannot believe that within a few months you and I will be living there!"

My blood went still. For all the revelations this evening had brought, the realization that I would be forced to serve in his household hadn't yet occurred to me. How could I possibly endure such torture?

Thankfully, Mariada was so caught up in dreams of her future husband that I was able to usher her down the stairs and to her chamber quite easily. I hoped that once I helped her undress and tucked her into her bed the excitement of the day would wear off quickly and she would succumb to sleep. My friends would wait for a while but certainly not all night. There was too much at stake to be careless.

"Do you think he will come to love me?" asked Mariada as she gazed into the copper mirror while I untwined the many metal beads from her long black hair. Her guileless question was like a battering ram to my chest, but I refused to let the blow show on my face.

She was only sixteen, three years older than I had been when Lukio ran away, but in some ways, she was far more childlike than I'd ever been. I'd not only had to step into the void my mother had left upon her death, tending to the house and preparing meals for my father when he was not on duty guarding the Ark of the Covenant, but I'd also had the responsibility of raising my two younger brothers, Levi and Yadon, who were so young they barely even remembered our mother. My stolen moments with Lukio, during rare times when one of the other guards' wives offered to watch the boys while my father was on duty or on nights when I was able to sneak out of the house to meet him, had been the only ones in which I'd felt the freedom to be a child.

"I don't know how anyone could help but love you," I replied, and meant it. She may be my mistress, but I'd come to care for her in these past months. She had saved me, after all. When I'd been brought to Ashdod nearly a year and half before, with the twelve other survivors of the attack on Beth Shemesh, I'd been beyond

terrified when we were herded into the royal courtyard. Mariada must have been watching from a window while the soldiers
divided us into two groups, the males to be placed on ships and
the females to be delivered to the priests in the temple, because
instead of being paraded away with the rest, I was astonished to
find myself being led to her room and assigned as her personal
maid. I did not know why she'd chosen me that day from among
the five other bedraggled and despondent women, but she'd rescued me from a far worse fate than serving one of the pampered
daughters of the king of Ashdod.

She'd never treated me like chattel the way Amunet did her
slaves. She did not hit me or scream at me or have me flogged if I
did not meet impossible standards. In fact, her compassion in the
face of my circumstances had been unbelievably generous. Out
of all the women in this awful city to choose as a wife, Lukio had
at least chosen one of the kindest.

"My mother said he is dangerous." A pinch of concern formed
between her black brows. "And that I should take care."

I paused, her thick hair held aloft since I'd been weaving it into
a sleeping braid. "Did she?"

She nodded. "She whispered into my ear before she left the
terrace and told me that I must be careful to not cross him." She
chewed on her lip as she met my gaze in the mirror. "Do you think
he might be violent with me the way he is with his opponents?"

The question dredged up the memory of the day I'd met him.

He'd been fighting, of course. Medad and a couple of his
friends had followed him through town, taunting and calling him
Demon Eyes, and he'd had enough. He'd swung an untrained
eleven-year-old fist at the older boy's face, catching a surprised
Medad in the ear before the other boys struck back and wrestled
a furious Lukio to the ground while he shouted unintelligible Philistine words at his attackers.

Two men nearby broke up the scuffle, sending Medad and his
friends toward their homes with threats of informing their fathers
about the commotion. After ensuring Lukio was unharmed, they

sent him away as well, telling him that such behavior did nothing to honor Elazar, the well-respected Levite who'd taken him and his sister in and treated them as his own children.

I wasn't certain why I followed Lukio that day. Perhaps it had been mere fascination with the older, handsome Philistine boy I'd seen around the mountain but had never spoken to. Perhaps it was concern that he'd been injured. Or perhaps it was because my father had told me to stay far away from him in the first place. But for some reason, my feet insisted on taking the same steep trail he had into the woods, and my eyes refused to stop searching until I caught a glimpse of him through the underbrush. His body, overly tall for a boy his age, was folded in on itself, tucked in a gap between the enormous twisted roots of an ancient sycamore tree.

I'd crept closer, uncertain whether to approach a strange boy who'd fought so ferociously against four others. When I'd stepped on a twig and his head had shot up to meet my curious gaze, the tearstains on his dirty cheeks had destroyed me. I'd refused to leave even when he told me to. Pretended that he hadn't been weeping over the Hebrew boys in town who'd rejected him. And by the time the sun had gone down that day, the two of us had sworn a pact of secret friendship, one born from a shared understanding between motherless children and mutual curiosity. One that had lasted for nearly four years, until I broke both of us.

I could never explain to Mariada the precious friendship I'd had with Lukio when I was young. Never speak of how gentle he was with animals. Or how whenever I would stumble to the ground during a starlit romp through the woods or catch a splinter while we were climbing trees, he would care for my bumps and scrapes with such tenderness. More than once he had carried me home on his back when I twisted an ankle. Nor could I explain the times he'd held me close in our hideaway under the sycamore when my father, mad with drink, had taken out his grief on me with vicious words and angry hands. How he'd whispered sweet words while I cried and vowed to protect me for all of my life. And truly, I had no way of knowing whether the boy I knew back then was even the same person, or if in returning to Ashdod and becoming a brutal fighter he'd tossed aside all of the traits that had caused me to trust him so completely.

So I said the only thing I could to put her mind at ease. "Your father cherishes you, mistress. I can only hope that he would not put you in harm's way."

Before she could respond, the door to her chamber burst open and both Tela and Jasara entered without waiting for an invitation, demanding to know what had happened up on the terrace and insisting that Mariada repeat every word that passed between her and Demon Eyes. Not only would I miss the meeting with my friends tonight, and have no way to send them a message, but now I would be forced to endure the agony of this evening all over again while the three of them tittered and gossiped.

Chest aching, I anticipated the desires of my mistress and her sisters and went to fetch a juglet of wine while the three of them celebrated Mariada's good fortune. But I had endured far more painful things than this in the last few years, and like I had done time and again, I would push past the hurt and survive.

Seven

Lukio

Nicaro lifted his silver drinking horn in the air. "May the gods bless this union and the Great Mother bestow the fruits of her favor upon my daughter."

A multitude of discordant but enthusiastic affirmations echoed around the hall from the guests who'd gathered to celebrate our betrothal. Although the pointed statement about Mariada's fertility made my skin feel too tight, I lifted my own wine cup in acknowledgment of his declaration, making certain to stretch a wide smile across my face.

"And may our fair city continue to be blessed by the reign of Nicaro, son of Darume, for many decades to come," I replied, having practiced the response in my head many times over. "I am certain our children's children will reap the benefits of his wisdom and strength."

Nicaro bowed his head, placing a humble palm to his chest, but his blue eyes sparkled. I'd done well with my public support of his kingship, the first of many times I would be expected to voice my favorable opinion. Although I had little problem fighting in front of crowds, it made me cringe to talk with so many eyes on me, but I must play the role I'd chosen for myself, even if over the past few days, the reasons for my ambition had become a bit hazy.

The announcement of my upcoming marriage to Mariada had been coupled with an invitation to celebrate his joy with a feast only a few nights after I'd spoken to her for the first time on the terrace. Nights that had seemed to meander into eternity, since instead of devising ways to encounter my soon-to-be bride again, I lay awake plotting ways to get her maid alone. And even as I stood here in the great hall of the king, with at least forty of the city's most elite who'd assembled to deliver their personal good wishes to myself and my betrothed, the only person I could think about was the slave girl twenty paces away with her back to the wall and head down, awaiting orders from her mistress.

I'd spent nearly every moment of these past few days wondering how long Shoshana had been here, what had occurred for her to be enslaved, where Medad was, and whether her presence meant Kiryat-Yearim had been attacked after all. Was my sister even alive anymore? Or had she been taken captive as well and was somewhere within the Five Cities, enduring the same humiliation as Shoshana?

It was all driving me to madness.

Even more frustrating was the fact that since the moment Shoshana had entered the room this evening, three paces behind Mariada, who beamed at me with the light of a thousand suns, she'd not once met my eyes.

Therefore, I barely tasted the wine Nicaro had boasted was the finest in the land of Canaan. The richly spiced boar meat that had been roasted to buttery tenderness in a cooking pot on the hearth was like leather in my mouth. And every time one of the beautifully attired people whose adulation I'd coveted for so long approached to congratulate me on both my marriage and my new position, it felt like a pointed stick jammed between my ribs.

Why had she appeared *now*? When everything I'd worked for had finally been delivered to me in a golden chalice? I'd been so successful for all these years at burying deep any thoughts of her, of Risi, and of my time at Kiryat-Yearim, and as soon as I'd seen her on that balcony above the fight every one of them had been exhumed at once.

As I stared at her, willing her to look at me, if only for a moment, I rolled the small shell I'd found on the ground outside the palace back and forth in my hand, somewhat soothed by the repetitive rhythm against my palm.

Mataro suddenly appeared at my side, his eyes on Mariada across the hall, where she was surrounded by a group of young women her age, all of them talking at once. "The king's daughter." He made a noise of lurid appreciation in the back of his throat. "You did well, cousin."

My jaw twitched. This was the first I'd seen of Mataro since the public announcement of my betrothal and my new position had been made. I'd expected him to storm into my home days ago, spewing curses on my name for keeping him out of my plans. It was odd that he'd taken until now to appear. And he was far too calm. What was he about?

"I'm glad you approve," I replied with a flat tone that conveyed just how disinterested in his validation I was.

His attention was drawn away for a moment when he lifted his empty cup to Amunet across the room in greeting, as if he were on friendly terms with the queen of Ashdod. She frowned and looked away. He was nothing if not dogged in his pursuit of influence.

"Of course I approve." Seemingly unperturbed by the swift dismissal from such a powerful woman, he gave me a yellow-toothed grin, now tipping his cup toward me in salute. "This is what I always thought you were capable of, Lukio. Even when you were a boy, I knew there was something special about you. You've only proved my foresight correct."

"Your foresight may have been right about my potential to be a champion, *cousin*," I said, leaning on the word and more than ready to be done with this conversation. With him. "But perhaps it was lacking in a few areas."

His expression went flat, his eyes narrowing.

I lowered my voice. "Whether or not you guessed that I would be a fighter someday, you had little to do with it, other than to perhaps arrange a few matches in the beginning and boast about how you discovered me as a boy. *I* did this. *I* trained my body every day for the past ten years. *I* faced opponents who outweighed me by many stones when I was barely old enough to grow a beard. *I* fought with broken bones and deep bruises that lasted for weeks. *I* endured bites, scratches, lacerations, and all manner of wounds. And *I* devised a plan that impressed Nicaro so much that he offered me his daughter in return. All you did was reach your hand into my purse and take what wasn't yours to begin with."

He spluttered, his face turning red and splotchy.

I leaned closer, unintimidated by the evidence of his brewing rage. He'd miscalculated by waiting until now to approach me, because if he exploded in front of everyone gathered here to celebrate my fame, it would only color him a fool. "From now on you'll have to find a different way to satisfy your debtors."

I took perverse pleasure in the way his eyes bulged while his face drained of color, and as I turned away, leaving my cousin speechless in my wake, I felt the weight of his ten-year hold on me slide off my back.

Nicaro caught my eye as I left Mataro behind and beckoned me to cross the room. The stone throne he was seated on at the end of the grand hall was surrounded by exquisite murals. On one side, a herd of antelope frolicked through a blossoming meadow of poppies, and on the other, a finely detailed depiction of a pack of hounds pursued a wild boar through a forest. Both scenes reminded me of Kiryat-Yearim and the plentiful wildlife that made the fertile area around the mountain their home. I pushed aside the thought immediately.

"Bring Lukio another cup," he demanded of a slave nearby. "We are only beginning to celebrate!" The girl scuttled away to fetch more drink that I would not consume. I'd learned years ago that my mind was far clearer when I limited myself to small amounts, and my early morning training sessions not nearly as painful either. The king, however, bound himself to no such restrictions, so even his smile was slightly crooked as he clapped his hands at the bevy of half-dressed women gathered about his throne—none of whom were his wives—and ordered them to give the two of us a moment to speak alone.

"Tell me," he demanded, one eye squinting briefly. "What did my daughter say when you told her of the marriage?"

The moments on the terrace flashed through my mind, making me realize that I barely remembered Mariada's reaction since Shoshana's appearance had overshadowed everything that night. But I answered as I was expected to.

"She seemed pleased, seren."

He made a raspy noise with his lips. "There's no need to call me *lord* when it is just the two of us, Lukio. I will soon be your father, after all."

The word plunged deep, its edges serrated. I'd already had two fathers. One who'd walked away when I was not old enough to remember him, and the other whom I'd steadfastly refused to call *abba*, even if my sister had been more than happy to be labeled Elazar's daughter. I was certain that it had not taken long after my disappearance for Elazar to forget me just as thoroughly as my Philistine father had done as he sailed away on his ship for the last time.

"I have wonderful news!" Nicaro said, then took another long draft from his silver horn. "We are not only celebrating your betrothal and new position tonight! Virka and Grabos have returned victorious!"

I'd seen the two commanders enter the hall earlier but had been so absorbed in boring a hole in Shoshana's downturned head with my gaze that I'd barely noted their presence.

"The raid went well, then?"

Nicaro's blue eyes shimmered, both from excitement and the wine, and his smile tilted further as he leaned closer to me. "Better than I'd hoped. Tzorah is ours now." He swished a hand through the air with a gleeful hiss through his teeth. "Nothing much left but stones and corpses."

I swallowed hard. Tzorah was far too close to Kiryat-Yearim, only a few hours' walk. I'd avoided anything having to do with the Hebrews for so long, purposefully leaving the room whenever scuffles with the tribes of Yaakov were mentioned or changing the subject with an ease I'd practiced many times over the years. But now the desire to push to my feet and barrel across the room to demand answers from Shoshana about what all had happened in my absence reared up with nearly painful urgency.

Nicaro knew nothing of my past. Mataro and I had purposefully left that part of my life in shadow, letting those missing years become rumors that had spun into legends without any help from us at all. To some, I'd been with my father, sailing to the northern lands of his birth. To some, I'd returned to the island of my mother's ancestors, learning ancient fighting techniques from one of the tribes that remained in the shadow of the crumbling palaces and temples that our forefathers abandoned so long ago. To some, I'd been living in the wild, a man without a home who'd survived by his wits alone and fought lions and bears with his bare hands.

No one knew that instead I'd been fed and clothed by our enemies, called a son and brother by people the Philistines considered little more than an uncultured blight of shepherds and Yahweh-worshipers who should be eradicated from the verdant hills and trade routes they so desired.

I lifted the cup the slave-girl had pressed into my hand and forced a smile across my face. "To the glory of our soldiers, then!"

The king returned the accolade with a grin and then absently wiped at the trickle of scarlet that dribbled down his oiled beard. "We *will* find it. We are getting closer."

"Find what?"

"That cursed box," he spat out.

I stiffened, my fingers clutching my wine cup tighter. "Box?" I echoed, although I had little doubt of the object he was referring to.

"That Ark of the Hebrews," he said, every word coated in gall and his blue eyes darkening considerably. "I should have destroyed the thing when I had it in my grasp, like I wanted to do."

The memory of plodding along behind a royal caravan of chariots was still strong after all these years. Nicaro had been young then, but he'd been one of the five kings who followed after the golden vessel as it bumped along on a wagon drawn by two bawling milk cows. To this day I did not understand why they'd hitched untrained beasts to that cart and sent back the Hebrews' treasured object. But although I'd been furious that my sister had made me leave Ashdod in the first place, I'd been fascinated by the chariot wheels flashing in the sun, the feathered headdresses of the royal entourage, and the gleaming white robes of the priests who accompanied the lords of Philistia on their strange mission. Risi had told me then that the kings agreed to rid themselves of the Ark to stop the plagues that had struck our cities but, as I well remembered, Nicaro had made no secret of his disagreement with the other kings over the plan.

Gripped by curiosity, I braved a question, hoping the wine had dulled his usual razor-sharp acuity. "Why didn't you?"

Looking over my shoulder, as if somewhere behind me the answers were written on a wall, he bared his teeth, appearing more feral than I'd ever seen the man who was lauded as the most polished among the lords of Philistia.

"The priests insisted. They divined through the entrails and visions that the only answer to stopping the plagues was to send the box back to the Hebrews. They swore over and over that the thing would be the end of Philistia if we did not return it." He cursed, taking another drink. "All it did was embolden those filthy shepherds. Give them a reason to join together and find their backbones. If the other kings had listened to me instead of those fool priests, we would already have crushed them and their powerless *One God*." He shook his head, eyes still tracking off to the side as he contemplated. Then he swung his gaze back to me. "Your uncle was Harrom, the High Priest, wasn't he?"

Even if my missing years were a mystery, my familial ties were not. Risi and I had lived at my uncle Harrom and aunt Jacame's house from the time our father disappeared until the day we followed after the very Ark Nicaro was so angry about.

"He was. He died in the plagues, along with most of his family."

"Harrom wouldn't have stood for it," he said. "He was a good man, your uncle. Far too wise to give in to the fear the other cowards did."

I had no idea what my uncle would have done when faced with the question of whether to send the Ark back to the Hebrews or not. He ignored me most of the time that we lived with his family, other than one time when he laid into me for breaking one of his precious statues of Dagon in the family sanctuary while chasing after a ball, and another time when he'd threatened to choke the life from both my sister and Azuvah after I'd accidentally barged into a room where he'd cornered one of the kitchen maids. I'd left, of course, believing his warning. But I'd also searched out my aunt Jacame and told her I'd seen a rat in the very same room and so she'd ordered two of the male servants to go catch it. I didn't know if my ruse helped the terrified young woman escape the lecher, but Harrom never did come after Risi or Azuvah. Instead, it was his son who ended up murdering the woman who'd cared for my sister and me as if we were her own.

Spurred on by both the amount of wine flowing in his veins and his newfound trust in me, the king continued his rant. "But I will not make the same mistake I did when I was younger. I will find that box and I will watch it burn. The Hebrews will pay—both for what their so-called champion did to my father and for the destruction of my city."

It did not seem to matter that both of those things had happened long ago. Nicaro had not forgotten. No wonder he'd been so driven to take all the cities in the territory of Dan. Samson, the *shofet* of Israel who'd pulled the temple of Gaza down on Darume's head, had been from the tribe of Dan. I could see now it was less about conquering the fertile lands of the shephelah and more about personal retribution.

"But enough of this," said Nicaro. "Tonight is for celebration, not talk of war."

With a lift of his bejeweled hand, his concubines slithered back from wherever they'd been hovering in wait. One sat on the floor beside the throne, draping herself across the king's lap, another leaned against the wall beside it in a way that best displayed her ample figure, and a third sat beside me, slipping a bare arm around my shoulders, pressing herself against my side. Knowing Shoshana might be watching, the temptation to push the concubine away was fierce, but the king grinned down at the girl on his lap.

"Patience, my lovelies," said Nicaro, dragging a finger over the girl's painted lips. "The wives will leave soon enough and then we can properly celebrate."

A flush of hot sickness rose in my gut, something I'd not experienced in many years of attending parties with the elite of Ashdod. I'd become immune to the debauchery. Blind to the escapades of men and women to whom marriage contracts meant little. And desensitized to the guilt that had hovered around the edges the first few months after I'd returned to Ashdod. But now, with the reminder of my life among the Hebrews standing across the room from me—a life with people who would be horrified by the things I'd both witnessed and taken part in—I was more than unsettled.

"Don't look so wounded, Lukio," said Nicaro with a laugh echoed by the women surrounding the throne. "Mariada is known for retiring to her chambers early, like her mother. You won't have to wait long to have your pick." He waved a hand over the crowd, which included many slaves—including Shoshana.

Nausea burned up my throat, and I pushed to my feet before I'd even made the decision to do so.

Nicaro looked up at me with drunken confusion on his too-handsome face. Although fury was swirling through my body, I still knew my role and it was not to argue with the king of Ashdod over things Hebrews considered abhorrent but Philistines saw as perfectly normal. For the first time in ten years, I realized just how much influence Elazar and his family had on my standards of behavior, even if I'd pretended to have forgotten the lessons I'd learned in their household.

Hoping he was too drunk to notice that my wine cup was in no way empty, I forced a grin and tilted it back and forth. "Drank my last few cups a little too fast. I'll have to take a step outside for a moment."

Nicaro guffawed loudly and waved a hand at me. "Go on, then. Don't get lost on your way back. We've stronger drink being prepared now. You won't want to miss that."

I pushed out a chuckle. "Indeed, I do not."

However, I had no intention of returning. Nor of partaking in the bitter mixture of wine and herbs that separated a man from his own mind and numbed everything, including his good sense. I had no interest in falling into soft-edged visions of false peace tonight. Not only did I need to get Shoshana away from this hall before things spun out of control, but I'd also waited long enough to talk to her.

As I turned away from the king and his concubines, I let my body sway, stumbling to the side as if I'd imbibed heavily all night. Even if he was beyond drunk, there was no use in giving Nicaro any reason to doubt my own inebriation. Hopefully he'd be distracted enough that my failure to return would go unnoticed.

To add to the ruse, I stopped a few times on my way across the room, patting shoulders of various guests I barely knew, making jokes, and laughing too loudly. With a glance over my shoulder, I ensured that Mariada was well occupied with her sycophants before lurching toward the exit of the hall, where Shoshana had hidden herself in a shadow beside the doorway, her eyes on the floor. I wondered if she was trying to block out the filth around her or simply doing her best to avoid my stare.

I acted as though I planned to stride right past a faceless, nameless slave and out of the room but then feigned a stumble and landed directly in front of Shoshana, curling my hand tighter around the shell I'd had tucked in my palm all night long, in hopes of this very opportunity.

Her head shot up and her luminous hazel eyes went wide when she realized who was towering over her. But instead of the relief that I expected when she saw it was me and not some degenerate guest here to molest her, an expression of pure terror washed over the face of the girl who once had been my entire world.

Eight

Shoshana

Lukio towered over me, making me all too aware of the overwhelming enormity of his frame. And although his brows drew together for a brief moment of seeming confusion, his expression hardened as he put out his hand, uncurling his palm to reveal a small white seashell dotted with brown spots.

"I nearly slipped on this outside the palace." His voice had deepened in the past years, making him even more of a stranger. "Most likely came from the beach I saw from the terrace the other night."

Stricken mute by both his all-consuming presence and such a bewildering statement, I pressed back farther against the wall. Had I been wrong to assure Mariada that Lukio would not hurt her? Certainly, the man who'd spent the entire evening guzzling wine, laughing drunkenly, ogling the half-naked women around him, and practically licking the soles of the king's sandals was not the same boy who'd shied away from most everyone back in Kiryat-Yearim, spent most of his time in the woods or with his animals, and comforted me in the hollow of our tree whenever my sorrows spilled over. This man was brutal, and he was a Philistine,

71

through and through, right down to the jeweled ivory plugs that winked from his earlobes.

His jaw ticked, his lips pressing so tightly they went pale. His gaze flickered away from me briefly, as if he were gauging whether anyone else was listening to his wine-driven nonsense. He stiffened when a slave whisked by us with a jug on his way into the hall but then his stare trapped me again.

"So small, aren't you, girl?" He looked down his nose at me in a mocking way. "No more than a *tesi*."

As I reeled from the Philistine word he'd just said and the realization that Lukio's eyes were completely sober regardless of his show of drunkenness, he grabbed my hand and pressed the shell into my palm. "Take care of this, *tonight*, so no one else gets hurt."

And then, before I could even gather a response to the odd command or react to the way his slightest touch made my blood race, he was gone. Swaggering out of the room with an off-kilter stride that I was no longer fooled by.

After the briefest of glances around the room, ensuring that no one had caught sight of the strange interchange between the champion of Ashdod and a slave-girl, I dropped my eyes again to the cool limestone tiles beneath my bare feet and remained in the shadows where I'd waited all evening for my mistress. Thankfully, she'd been so occupied by the group of friends that had seemed to double in the wake of the news of her marriage to the famous fighter that she'd not called for me once. I'd been left to pray that no one else noticed me and to torture myself with tiny glimpses of Lukio and his carousing.

I'd been sick for hours as I watched him covertly from under my lashes. And with every moment that had passed, the hope that my friend still lived inside the brash and arrogant champion withered further.

But then he'd called me a tesi and every conclusion I'd come to over this evening, and even before I'd encountered him up on the terrace the other night, was thrown into disarray as I was hit with the memory of the very first time he'd ever called me by that name.

Only a few months after we'd been meeting on nights when I could get away from the house without notice and the moon was bright enough to illuminate our path, I'd stepped on a broken tree limb and sliced my foot open on a sharp edge. I'd done my best to hide it from Lukio, not wanting him to think me too young or cowardly to explore the woods with him at night. But when a gasp slipped past my lips after I stepped down too hard on the injury, Lukio spun around and caught me wincing in pain.

"What's wrong?" he'd said, deep concern in his fascinating brown and green eyes.

"It's only a scratch." I'd limped forward, eager to follow him to the empty cave he'd said he found on the west side of the mountain.

He bent to examine my foot. "You're bleeding."

"I am fine," I insisted, fearing that our romp tonight was indeed over and praying that Lukio wouldn't think me an infant and refuse to meet me again.

"Come," he said, beckoning me to climb onto his back. "I'll carry you home."

Folding my arms, I jutted out my chin. "I can make it on my own. I'm big enough."

His moonlit smile was crooked as he grinned up at me. "Of course you are. But you are still no more than a tesi, so carrying you will be easy."

"What's a tesi?" I asked, eager to add another new Philistine word to the many he'd taught me over the past months.

"The smallest unit of measure," he said, holding up his thumb and forefinger with only a slight gap between. "But don't worry. Even if on the outside you are no more than a tesi, you are big inside."

I'd grinned all the way home as I rode on his back, the first of many times I did so, and he'd called me Tesi from then on.

What possible reason did he have for reminding me of the affectionate name he'd given me when we were children? I rolled the shell back and forth in my fingers as I attempted to line up

73

the seams between what I knew for certain and what I'd guessed from watching him interact with his people.

What was more than plain from his feigned drunkenness was that Lukio was skilled at pulling a mask over the truth. But less clear was why he had done so in the first place, especially only to hand me a shell and mumble something about the terrace where we'd encountered each other for the first time in ten years.

I sucked in a breath as an idea tore through the wall of my confusion. A very dangerous one

Was the shell he'd pressed into my hand a code, like the sycamore figs on my windowsill that had signaled our desire to meet whenever the moon was high and bright?

My breaths came quicker as I unspooled all that he'd said in those brief moments and found that the message had not been all that difficult to decipher after all.

I gripped the shell so tight that its sharp edges dug into my palm. Following my gut on this could be disastrous—either to my heart if I'd fabricated the entire thing, or to my position in the household if I was discovered skulking about in the night with Lukio. But even if he'd truly changed as much as I suspected, this may be my only chance to speak with him. And somehow I knew I would regret it if I did not seize the opportunity to hear what he had to say. Besides, I was nothing if not skilled at spiriting about the palace at night.

Therefore, after waiting a painfully long span while my pulse thudded in my ears, I once again peered upward to ensure that no one in this room would take note of my disappearance. I must go now, for as much as Mariada seemed to be enjoying herself, she was nearly always one of the first to leave celebrations like this one. Hopefully, being the guest of honor would encourage her to stay later and take advantage of her newfound popularity among the young and wealthy of Ashdod.

I swept my gaze over the crowd, and out of the many guests who were seated on stone benches, lounging on plush cushions, or chatting in groups, only one set of eyes met mine—the man

Lukio had been having an intense conversation with earlier in the evening.

When the balding man with the protruding belly had first approached Lukio, his demeanor had been full of confidence and his smile broad. But by the time Lukio walked away, seemingly cutting the man off mid-thought by the way his mouth gaped open, it was obvious that he was not simply one of Lukio's many admirers. And from the scrutinizing way he was staring at me now, I had a suspicion that he had seen Lukio approach me earlier.

Therefore, instead of dropping my eyes back to the floor as I was tempted to do, I continued my slow perusal of the guests, pretending to be searching out my mistress and unaffected by the strange man's stare. By the time I allowed myself one last glance at the man across the room, he'd been drawn into conversation with another guest and was turned away from me. I took hold of the moment, slipped out of the grand hall, and headed for the far end of the palace.

Thankful for my noiselessly bare feet and the deep shadows that cluttered the corridor between the lamps flickering in their wall niches, I padded my way up countless stairs until I was on the top level and made my way to the terrace where I'd listened to Lukio ask Mariada to be his wife while my insides turned to ash. The secluded spot was rarely used in the first place, and everyone, including the servants, were in the main hall for the celebration, so it truly was a perfect place for a secret meeting.

If anyone knew the best locations in this palace to meet without being noticed, it was me. Galit, one of the other Hebrew women who served in this palace, had shown me all of them within the first few weeks of my arrival here, telling me that I should make it a priority to count the steps between Mariada's room and every hiding place, especially the wine cellar where my friends and I met whenever one of us had news to share, or on the rare holy days the five of us dared to come together and worship the One Who Sees.

My heart crashing against my ribs in tandem with the rhythm of the insistent waves down on the rocky beach Lukio had mentioned,

I slipped through the entrance to the terrace, only to find nothing but an empty table, a few chairs, and the quiet night air.

Had I misinterpreted the entire exchange? Or had he merely been toying with me, relying on my fond memories to lead me on a fruitless search for someone who no longer existed? I didn't know why he would do so, but in all honesty, I did not know Lukio anymore. The man I'd seen on the fighting grounds had been ruthless and bloodthirsty, without a shred of remorse for how he'd battered his Phoenician opponent in his quest to dominate the match. The man I'd seen with Mariada had been charming, polished, and focused solely on the beautiful woman before him. The man I'd watched across the room tonight had been ambitious, grasping, and immoral. None of those men were my Lukio. The boy whose friendship had been my salvation when I was young was gone, and it was foolish to hope for anything different. Annoyed with myself for allowing girlish notions to take hold of my imagination, I let out a breathy laugh as I turned toward the black ocean and leaned on the parapet, savoring the salty night breeze on my skin.

It was rare that I had a moment to myself without someone in the palace demanding something of me, be that Mariada, other slaves, or even my friends who'd discovered I had little fear about delivering messages to faceless men in garden sheds. So instead of rushing back down to await my next order, I gave myself permission to lift my gaze to the thick scattering of stars overhead.

From the top of our sycamore, Lukio had taught me the names his people gave many of those stars, along with all the things he'd remembered about Ashdod. I'd been so fascinated, so curious about the city by the sea that he'd described. But when I'd been brought here, I realized that his memories had been painted with a softer brush, a product of both a child's understanding of the world and a misplaced loyalty to the people he'd sprung from. Fine garments, intricately crafted jewelry, soaring temples, and skillfully painted murals that decorated extravagant homes were no replacement for the goodness of living among a people whose way of life was based on the laws of Yahweh—even if many had forgotten how precious those laws truly were. As a captive here, I had witnessed the distinction all too clearly. The people of Philistia may see themselves as far above the culture of the "uncouth shepherds" who inhabited the shephelah, but they also too closely resembled the brutal, debauched, and capricious gods they worshiped.

A hand wrapped around my elbow, and I swung around, slamming my heel against the stone with a gasp of pain and surprise. The dark shadow that loomed over me slapped a palm over my mouth to cut off the scream that started to let loose.

With my heart doing its best to claw its way out of my chest, I tried to suck in a breath, but his tight grip spanned most of my face. I struggled against the arm he slipped around my waist, desperate to be free and fighting both his hold on me and the memories that swam before my eyes, threatening to drown me. All I could see was the dirt and blood-smeared face of a soldier, his feathered headdress askew and horrific intent in his eyes. I clawed at him, my small hands doing little to fight him off, but my ragged nails digging into his stony forearms, nonetheless.

"Shoshana. Hush," a voice rasped as his grip tightened. But I was so frantic that it wasn't until he spoke again that I realized whose arm I was scratching at like a wildcat.

"Tesi. You are safe," Lukio said, his mouth close enough to my ear that I felt his warm breath against my skin. "Be calm. No one will hurt you." I went stiff in his hold, humiliated for my reaction, but my galloping pulse still urged me to run. To hide. To save myself.

"You are safe," he repeated. "I won't hurt you."

The statement should have reassured me, but all it seemed to do was dredge up the sight of his fist slamming into the face of that Phoenician so hard that blood spattered over a few of the nearby spectators and remind me that I was risking far too much by meeting with him now.

Lukio might not mean to harm me in this moment, but he was anything but safe.

Nine

Lukio

Shoshana was shaking like a leaf in a windstorm, her eyes so large I could see the whites of them all around the hazel. I'd expected her to startle at my touch, but she'd been so frantic that I feared she might attempt to crawl over the parapet to free herself from my hold.

I would tear apart whoever had made her this way. Whoever had left her as this cowering, trembling creature before me.

My mind traveled to very dark places that filled my gut with bile and made my veins blaze with fury. But I could not let any of the violence thundering through my body show on my face or she might very well run and there was no guarantee I'd be able to speak with her again any time soon.

"If I let go of you, will you stay quiet?" I said haltingly, in the language I'd not spoken aloud for many years.

She nodded, her breath coming in short bursts against my palm. She was not as diminutive as she'd been at twelve, having grown at least three or four fingers more, and there were curves in places that had been girlish before, but she felt familiar in my arms.

Perfect and familiar in a way that revived so many memories that my breath hitched in my chest. However, this was not the time to let my mind wander down those pathways. Not only was she still trembling in fear, but I was also betrothed to someone else.

Although I loosened my grip, I hated to let her go fully. It felt good to be so close to her again. Even after a decade's worth of bitterness toward her and brokenness without her, her presence soothed me like it had always done, since the first day she'd appeared before me at our sycamore tree. The little girl with uneven braids, a dimpled smile, and so many freckles they reminded me of the night sky had refused to let me wallow in embarrassment and anger after my first scuffle with Medad.

Carefully I peeled my hand off her mouth and took a step backward but stayed close enough that I could still catch her if she bolted. She and I were talking tonight, whether she wanted to or not.

"Why did you sneak up on me?" she snapped.

Startled by the venomous tone, I took another step back.

"I was making certain you were alone," I said. "I waited around the corner in case you were followed up from the hall."

She folded her arms over her chest, chin jutting upward. "I'm fully capable of finding my way through this palace undetected."

Her voice was a shade lower than it had been ten years ago, yet it retained the raspy quality from her girlhood that I remembered so well. However, the sharp edges on her words shocked me. These years between us had done more than change her into a woman. They'd stripped something precious from her and left behind someone with strong fences.

I had so many questions—a decade's worth. But I began with the easiest.

"How long have you been in Ashdod?"

Her eyes tracked away from mine for a moment. "A little over a year and a half."

Her answer stunned me. Granted, I spent most of my time on the fighting grounds or at my home, but the thought that she'd been here all this time, practically under my nose, made my stomach wrench. I restrained the instinct to rail at her for not seeking me out and instead kept my voice dispassionate as I continued. "You were taken captive during a raid?"

Her lips pressed together as she swallowed hard. "Yes, they attacked Beth Shemesh, and I was one of the survivors. Or at least one of the few worth dragging back here to be sold."

"Beth Shemesh? Why weren't you at Kiryat-Yearim?"

Again, she looked away. As if it were a difficult question to answer. "Medad moved us there a couple of years after we married. He became a tanner."

"He couldn't take up the occupation on the mountain?"

She shook her head. "He'd made friends with a tanner in the valley who gave him grand ideas about selling leather to the many travelers on the trade road. He thought living in Beth Shemesh would make him rich." She huffed a softly rueful laugh. "It did nothing of the sort."

I paused, not wanting to exacerbate her wounds but desperate for the truth of everything she'd endured. "Did he survive?"

"No. Somehow he scraped together enough courage to go out and fight when the Philistines were first spotted scouting in the valley. All the men who did so were killed."

Even though I felt no pity for Medad, who'd not only tormented me for years but stole Shoshana from me, the flat tone with which she described the death of her husband was so jarring that I was stunned speechless. She had been the most tenderhearted girl in Kiryat-Yearim—even more gentle than my sister, with whom no one on the mountain could ever find fault. And yet Shoshana spoke of the slaughter of the man she'd married without a shred of emotion.

There was much more to be said about what had happened at Beth Shemesh, I was certain of it. But from the stiff set of her small shoulders and the hollow-eyed way she looked up at me, it was clear she was not ready yet. I would give her a reprieve, but not for long.

So instead, I dug into my own wounds. "And what of Risi?"

Her head snapped back, and she glared up at me. "Why do you care? You left."

I may have grappled with some of the most brutal fighters in this area of the world, but Shoshana had learned how to throw a stinging punch with only a few words.

"I did. But that does not mean that I forgot her." *Or you.*

"You left Eliora brokenhearted, Lukio. If Ronen would have allowed it, she would have searched for you herself. As it was, he and your brothers looked for you for weeks. Elazar even sent some of his men to do so as well and used every connection he had with other tribes to look for you."

My insides twisted painfully. They'd searched for me?

She lifted a brow. "You didn't think they cared when you left without a word of good-bye? Without any reason for abandoning the people who loved you?"

"I had plenty of reasons," I shot back. "You among them."

She flinched. "Whatever happened between us had no bearing on the fact that you walked away from Eliora. Someone who had you firmly at the center of her world from the day you were born. If it hadn't been for Ronen . . ." She shook her head. "Her husband was the only thing holding her together for a very long time. That, and her continual insistence that Yahweh was watching over you."

The idea that the Hebrews' God cared anything for me was beyond laughable. I was their enemy and had tossed aside their covenant like refuse. But thinking of my sister broken in her mourning for me pained me deeply. I fidgeted with the ivory plug in my earlobe.

"So, she and Ronen did marry." He initially may have been in Kiryat-Yearim for nefarious purposes, but from the conversation I'd overheard between them the day I ran away, he'd professed to care deeply for her. At least that proved not to be another lie among the rest.

She nodded. "Before we left Kiryat-Yearim, Yoela told me that they'd already had one child and another on the way. I would guess their family is much larger now."

The mention of Yoela caused a pang of melancholy in my chest. It was not only memories of Risi that had been relentlessly nagging at me lately but also the woman whose maternal affections I'd brushed off for so many years. I pushed aside the unexpected remorse to focus on the news of my sister.

"But I thought my sister moved to Ramah with that prophet Samuel?"

Surprise flashed across her features. "How would you know that? You left before anything was decided."

"I'd come to retrieve charcoal from the mound. . . ." I tripped over the words, certain she remembered what happened between the two of us in the very same clearing. "And I overheard them discussing their plans to leave Kiryat-Yearim."

I left out the shock of hearing the two of them so easily talking over their future—a future that I was not considered worthy to be a part of. I stared toward the beach in the distance, where I'd once laughed and played with the sister I adored, never knowing that one day she would choose to leave me behind with the same callousness as our father had.

Shoshana remained silent until I finally met her eyes again. "You always seemed like such an intelligent boy to me. As if you knew everything in the world. I never realized you were actually a fool."

Stunned by the jab, I folded my arms over my chest to guard against another attack from one of the gentlest creatures I'd ever known. "What do you mean?"

"They weren't going to leave you, Lukio. They'd gone to tell you of their betrothal and ask you to come with them once they were married. Instead, they found poor Yonah weeping in your cave, devastated and insisting that it was his fault you'd disappeared."

My gut clenched tight as I thought of the seven-year-old boy who'd followed me nearly everywhere—at least the places that his twisted foot allowed him to go—and considered me an older brother. True, I'd snarled at Yonah as I was packing and told him to go back home when he attempted to follow me down the mountain. But I'd been so focused on leaving, on putting distance between myself and Risi's abandonment, that I'd not stopped to consider whether he might blame himself for my disappearance. Regret bloomed in places I'd thought fallow for many years.

"Eliora never had any intention of leaving you behind," Shoshana continued, crushing nearly every excuse I'd given myself for leaving in the first place. "She'd hoped that during the years when Ronen was living in Ramah and learning from Samuel, you would be with them. But instead, you turned your back on her. On all of us."

My heart thudded out of rhythm. "You had already turned your back on me."

I remembered the last time I'd seen her with perfect clarity. I'd been so anxious to speak with her, having missed my chance a few days before when I snuck out during an eclipse of the moon and found our meeting place deserted. But when she unexpectedly appeared at the smoking charcoal mound that I'd built from the remains of an enormous burned-out cedar tree, instead of running to me with a smile on her face and a sweet embrace like she always did, her eyes had shimmered with tears as she approached with a tentative gait. Immediately I'd gone to her, worried that her father had gotten drunk and slapped her again.

But she'd put out her palms, refusing to let me draw her close, and after three deep, shuddering breaths, told me that her father had betrothed her to Medad and that she had no choice but to marry the person I hated most. I'd not been shy about my response, cursing both Medad and her father and insisting that she come with me. That I would use the woodcutting skills I'd learned to take care of her. That regardless how young we were, we would build a home and a family together.

But with tears streaming down her face, she'd said it was impossible. That her father would never approve of a marriage between the two of us. Then, on a sob, she'd turned and run from me, leaving me the most alone I'd been since the day she'd first encountered me at the sycamore tree. So I had taken my ax and destroyed the charcoal mound I'd worked on for days just as thoroughly as she'd destroyed me.

"You know I had no choice," she said, pulling me back to the present.

"Of course you did. I asked you to go with me. I could have—" I halted, letting out a breath. "You know I would have taken care of you."

"That was never in doubt, Lukio. But my father told me that if I didn't marry Medad, I would never see my brothers again. I tried. I did. I begged him to let me marry you instead, to go speak to Elazar. But after your father cut him from the guard around the Ark, he said he would have nothing to do with your family. Besides, he owed Medad's father a great deal of money for a gambling debt."

"And you were the satisfaction of that debt," I stated, the words choking me.

Her father had deserved to be cut from that guard. He'd fallen asleep during his watch and subsequently had made it possible for two men to assault my sister in their failed attempt at finding the Ark. But it also seemed to have made him desperate enough to sell his daughter and keep her compliant by threatening to cut her off from her siblings, whom she'd raised just as surely as Risi had raised me.

I let my eyes drop closed as the weight of these revelations settled onto my shoulders. "Why didn't you tell me all this?"

"Because you refused to let me, Lukio. The moment I told you my father had made a betrothal contract with Medad's father, you lost control. You . . ." she dropped her voice. "You frightened me. And then you left Kiryat-Yearim before I could talk to you again and explain everything."

An ocean of guilt washed over me. I'd spent years blaming her for walking away without remorse, thinking that she'd not put up any fight for us. And she was right that I'd lost control of my mouth, said things I never should have, especially to an innocent girl who'd borne the brunt of her father's anger too many times.

Shame flooded my bones. "I would never hurt you, Tesi."

"Don't call me that," she said, acid in her tone.

I blinked at her in confusion.

"You were wrong to leave your sister. Wrong to walk away from Elazar's family, who loved you so much, even though you fought against their affection. And no matter what my father forced me into, I could have used my—" she paused to swallow—"my friend." The sudden hurt on her face was at the same moment a kick in my gut and a window into the heart of the sweet girl I'd known so well. But then just as swiftly, that vulnerability was replaced by a renewed hardening of her jaw and stiffening of her shoulders.

"But nothing can change any of that," she said. "Nothing can replace all the years the locusts have consumed between then and now. And nothing can change the fact that I am a slave to your soon-to-be wife. So do not call me Tesi. Do not act as though you know me. Because you don't anymore."

She pressed past me, and I grabbed her hand, desperate to halt her steps. "Please don't go. I have more questions, and I . . . I want to help. Get you back home to your family."

She paused, her small shoulders tense as everything went quiet except the shushing of the waves in the distance. I could feel her indecision but still she refused to look back at me. "You can help by doing as I said. We are nothing but strangers now. And that is all we can ever be."

I'd never before heard such bleak defeat spill from her lips, even during our heart-wrenching last conversation in Kiryat-Yearim. She shook off my hold and, just like she had done that day at the charcoal mound, walked away without a second glance, leaving me even more tangled in confusion and helplessness than before.

Ten

Shoshana

I held my breath as I looked back over my shoulder for the hundredth time on my barefoot trek through the palace in the depths of the night. As I'd told Lukio two weeks ago, I was more than adept at stealing about this place like a silent wraith, but I could not grow complacent. I breathed easier at the sight of the empty corridor behind me and then peered around the corner.

As usual, there was only one guard near the stairs that led down to the wine cellar, but he had his back toward me, so I padded forward with quick steps. He'd never turned around before, always remaining in place ten paces away as he watched the opposite direction, appearing diligent in his duties, even though he knew full well that my friends and I had snuck into the room he was charged with guarding.

I had no idea how Oshai and Avel had befriended the guard, nor why he'd become our silent and nameless protector, but after months of navigating this strange and secretive routine without incident, I'd learned to trust yet another man whose face I'd never seen.

"Watch over him, Yahweh," I whispered as I carefully unlatched the door and slipped into the cool darkness. Knowing the room almost as well as I did Mariada's in the blackness, I felt my way past enormous jugs of wine, taking exactly fifteen paces from the entryway to the back wall. Just as my hand met limestone, the lock clicked on the door behind me, a sound that always made my heart stutter, but which was actually a blessing. The guard had locked us in to protect us from any intruders on our meeting, or at least to give us time to hide in the narrow space behind a row of enormous wine jars in the deep shadows while he stalled with the pretense that the lock was jammed. We'd practiced the routine together before a number of times and knew our part well.

A few moments later, a flame burst to life, throwing the cluttered room into dim outline and illuminating the face of Oshai, a Levite who'd served in the stables of the seren for almost as long as I'd been alive. Taken as a sixteen-year-old boy during a raid, he was the only one of us with enough knowledge of the sacred ways of Yahweh to lead us in worship, and he also had the ability to spy on the soldiers whose horses and chariots he tended, bringing us word of any new captives brought to Ashdod.

As Oshai lit the small oil lamp, the rest of my friends' faces were made visible. Two men and two women smiled at me from their little circle on the hard ground.

"Shalom," said Galit as I took my place on the ground next to her. The young woman was a kitchen slave who'd lived in the palace for nearly half her life after being kidnapped during a berry-picking outing with her family.

"We weren't certain you were coming," said Kina, another half-Hebrew who'd been brought along with her mistress, one of the king's concubines, to the palace a couple of years before. Only fourteen years old, her sweetly ebullient demeanor and bright brown eyes reminded me so much of Miri, Lukio's adopted younger sister in Kiryat-Yearim. Although I did not know Kina as well as I did Galit, I felt especially protective of her for that reason alone.

"Mariada took a long while getting to sleep tonight," I said.

Galit scooted closer, slipping her hand through my arm as she pressed into my side. A couple of years older than me, we'd struck up a quiet friendship during the many times I was sent to the kitchen to fetch meals or drink for my mistress, but it wasn't until I'd been in the palace for a few months that she decided she could trust me and invited me to be a part of this group—the main purpose of which was to help defenseless slaves escape abusive masters.

"Did you lace her wine again?" Galit asked.

I should feel guilty that I'd tainted Mariada's drink to ensure she would sleep quickly and deeply, but I'd used it before when I needed to slip out of her room at night.

"I did. I couldn't chance her waking up. She's been far too restless and overexcited since her betrothal to the champion." I swallowed the bitter words down and hoped no one noticed my sour expression.

It had been two weeks since I'd spoken with him under the stars, since I'd told him to leave me alone and consider us strangers, but somehow I'd felt like I'd left a piece of myself behind on that terrace. It had hurt to walk away from the man who'd once been my closest friend and leave him with no explanation for why I'd done so. But the less he knew about my complicated reasons for remaining here, the better.

Kina sighed at the mention of Lukio, her wide-set eyes sparkling in the lamplight. "What a fortunate girl. He may be a Philistine, but there's no man in Ashdod like Demon Eyes. My mistress is practically seething with jealousy."

Although her statement was guileless, I stiffened without thinking. Galit must have felt the tension in my body, the way she pinned her eyes on my profile. Even though we'd only known each other for a little over a year now, she was my first true sister-of-the-heart. Along with being an inordinately perceptive woman, she was also one of the most stubborn, so I doubted I would be allowed to leave without being thoroughly questioned about my reaction to mention of my mistress's betrothed.

"Yes, well, I think we can save palace gossip for later," said Oshai in a fatherly tone. Kina reddened and pressed her lips together, but her eyes still danced with humor as Oshai continued. "Before we begin worship, Avel has some news for us about the attempt to free that last group of slaves."

All levity dissipated as Avel cleared his throat. He was a quiet man, tall and lanky for a Hebrew due to his partial Egyptian heritage, and he was one of the many skilled gardeners who tended to the extensive gardens on the south side of the palace as well as all the many lovely plants and flowers that grew within the courtyards and in pots on all the terraces and roofs. It was he who'd taught me to make a harmless sleeping elixir for Mariada and provided me with the powder. Also, his eyes followed Galit everywhere, whether she realized it or not.

"One of the boys who was taken to the house of Kaparo was freed and by now has been returned to his family in Yehudite territory," said Avel. "However, the other child and one of our friends was caught during the escape attempt."

Our quiet gasps echoed off the limestone walls.

Avel's expression was pained. "We know nothing of what happened after that. My contact said only that our friend has disappeared."

"Will they be executed?" I asked, my throat tight. Although I did not know the name of the person who'd been involved, nor even if they were a man or a woman, grief welled up in my soul. They were one of us, doing anything they could to help free vulnerable women and children, at the risk of their own lives.

When Oshai proposed that I carry messages about new captives to a man who would pass them to others outside of the palace, he'd said that because of my position as handmaiden to a king's daughter, and the unparalleled freedoms Mariada gave me, I was the perfect person for such a task. When I asked why he or Avel could not do so, he said that the balance between secrets and risks was very delicate and everyone had their own job to perform. His was to gather information and lead us in worship. Avel's was to receive news of the repercussions of our efforts from a source whose appearances in the gardens was unpredictable. Galit's was to listen in on conversations during meals and report any pertinent news. Kina's was to do the same whenever her mistress participated in palace gatherings. And mine was to meet the anonymous man in the shed whenever Oshai summoned him. After all, it would be fairly easy to pretend that the unnamed man and I were there for personal reasons instead of nefarious ones. Few would question, or even care, if an older man took advantage of a slave in a dark room.

Of course, I'd had to trust Oshai's assurances that the man I'd been sent to meet was of the utmost character and would not actually do such a thing. The first few times I'd gone, I'd taken a small knife Galit had pilfered from the kitchen with me. But the man had never even crossed the small room while we spoke, almost as if he knew I needed the reassurance that he would not touch me and that I would have plenty of time to reach the door if he proved false.

It had taken at least four meetings before I stopped trembling when I met him and six before I stopped bringing the knife. But I'd quickly learned that he expected only swift delivery of the messages I carried. We spoke of nothing personal and did not exchange names. The last time we met, when he'd asked about the winner of Lukio's match, was the first time he'd ever spoken of anything else. And each time I left him behind with the lives of women or children in his hands, I prayed that Yahweh would protect him and guide him. It was only by Adonai's mercy that this network had not been discovered before now, and I hoped that would continue to be the case.

"An execution is possible," said Avel. "But I doubt Kaparo would bother to make it public. It would only serve to show that his household was vulnerable to intruders, anyhow."

Indeed, the High Priest in the temple of Dagon was one of the most arrogant men I'd ever seen. His vivid disdain for anyone below his status was matched only by Amunet, the king's first wife, so he would certainly not want anyone to know of a weakness in the security of his home. Nor that we'd been successful in rescuing at least one child from his clutches.

"It is more than likely," said Oshai, "that we will never know what happened to our friend."

"What of the girl?" I asked, remembering that I'd carried news to the man in the shed about three captives that day. She'd been purchased by Rumit, the king's scribe, a notoriously lecherous man whom I'd seen eyeing Mariada a number of times during his palace visits.

"She remains enslaved," said Oshai. "In fact, we have been told that the scribe's wife has been unable to bear children, so it is likely he is attempting to get a babe from her."

My heart squeezed with empathy for the poor girl's humiliation. "Is there nothing that can be done for her?"

"He's treating her as a concubine for now and therefore she is guarded well. We will keep trying to get someone inside and find a way, but it will be especially difficult if she conceives. Rumit is desperate for an heir and will go any length to protect his line. And as awful as it is, we must put our efforts toward those who are in the most danger. For now, she is well fed and cared for by his servants."

"So, we will leave her to be abused by him?" I said.

Oshai's voice was laden with remorse. "As much as it grieves me, yes. We will keep an eye on her. But for now, our focus must be on the most vulnerable ones. Our resources are limited and our friends few."

He sighed and went silent for a few moments, allowing us all to consider, once again, whether our participation was worth the cost. My own risk was great. If I lost my position with Mariada, I would be forced to leave the palace, which would tear me to pieces. But I also could not justify standing by while my fellow Hebrews—especially children of similar ages to my own—were suffering.

"Does anyone have anything else to share?" asked Oshai.

"I overheard a conversation," said Galit, "between two of the commanders the other night at the celebration. It sounds as if there is another attack planned on the territory of Dan within the next few weeks."

Oshai nodded. "I've heard whispers of this among the soldiers as well. I've passed on what I know to someone who is able to carry the message to the Hebrews. We can only pray that it reaches the right people at the right time." We all nodded in response, knowing that the only thing we could do was play our part and hope it was enough.

"However," Oshai continued, his countenance brightening, "I do have some encouraging news on that front. As I've told you in the past, although there have been a few losses to the Philistines, especially in the territory of Dan, there have been victories as well. At least three raids by the king of Gath were thwarted by the Yehudites, with the help of the Simeonites. And the tribes have been working together more in order to regain some of the ground we've lost over the past few years. It seems as though the leadership of Samuel has been increasingly effective."

I'd never heard of Samuel when I was a girl, but after he appeared at Kiryat-Yearim on the night Eliora's husband and his cousin had attempted to steal the Ark of the Covenant, I'd come to learn quite a bit about the man purported to hear directly from Yahweh. I'd been fascinated by stories of a young Samuel, who'd grown up serving within the Mishkan itself and had been directed by the voice of the Eternal One to rebuff the High Priest Eli for the wickedness of his sons.

However, Samuel's chastisements of our people for mixing worship of Yahweh with that of the Canaanite and Philistine gods and intermarrying with the idolatrous people who lived among us were divisive, to say the least. By the time I'd been taken captive, half the people were calling for Samuel to be installed as king, while the other half, especially those in the south, called for him to be silenced. From what little we heard here in Ashdod, it sounded like attitudes toward the prophet of Yahweh had been shifting among

Samuel's detractors. But it would take a miracle for the tribes to finally cease bickering amongst themselves and join together as one under his leadership.

"Will Samuel lead the tribes in war against the Philistines?" Galit asked, as if she'd heard my musings.

"That is not for me to guess. Samuel does not hold himself up as a military leader but as a seer and a priest. And there are many among the Hebrews who are still clamoring for a king who will stand strong against the kings of Philistia. However, my friends tell me that our people are turning back to the ways of Yahweh like never before. Although it has taken decades for Samuel's message to reach their stony hearts, there is an ever-growing fervor for pure worship and increasing intolerance for idolatry. Thanks to the efforts of Samuel and his disciples, many ancient Canaanite high places have been destroyed and the ground consecrated to worship of the Most High instead."

On that note of inspiration, Oshai led us in prayer for our people, pleading with the God Who Hears to listen to our cries and to rescue our brethren from increasing attacks from the Philistines, and thanking him for preserving us, even in this pagan city. By the time he recited the priestly blessing over us, tears were spilling down my cheeks. I would never have imagined finding friends like these in Ashdod when I was brought here, demoralized and broken, and I could never thank Yahweh enough for the gift.

Before I even had a chance to dry my face, Galit tugged at my elbow, wordlessly insisting that I follow her to the opposite side of the room while ignoring curious looks from the others. Of course, I'd known she would not let me walk away without explaining my odd behavior earlier, so I'd already resigned myself to the conversation.

"We don't have much time," she said, "so tell me quickly what is burdening you."

"There's nothing to say—"

She put up a palm, her dark eyes relentless. "Do not dance around it, Shoshana. I know you."

And she did. From nearly the first day I'd met her, as she helped me pick up the shards of a beer mug that I'd dropped on the floor in a corridor, I'd felt a kinship with Galit. We both had lost so much. Although she'd not been married when she was taken captive, she'd watched her parents be slaughtered by the three Canaanites who'd come across them while they picked berries on a hillside. And although she'd not said as much, I guessed she'd suffered many of the same indignities at the hands of our captors as I had.

"Your heart is written on your face as surely as if it were lined with ink, my friend. I saw it the moment Oshai lit the lamp. I do not have time to pull the truth from between your teeth, so save me the hassle."

It was useless to stall; Galit was relentless. So, in low, quick tones I told her everything. Of my childhood friendship with the champion of Ashdod. Of my stumbling into his announcement of the betrothal. Of our midnight meeting on the terrace and my resolve not to repeat it.

If I was honest with myself, I was actually glad to finally tell someone about it all. I'd spent the last two weeks wrestling over my cold dismissal of Lukio when he'd seemed truly concerned for me, a fact that had startled me so much I'd nearly given in that night under the stars and told him everything.

"And why would you not meet again with someone who means so much to you?" Galit asked.

"It's fruitless to pretend he is the same person he was when we were barely more than children. And besides, it could endanger what we are doing here."

"How so? They seem separate things to me."

"He is a Philistine, Galit. And he is dangerous." *Both to my heart and our mission.*

"But what if Yahweh brought him here for a purpose?"

I flinched at the question. "What reason would that be?"

"I don't know. Only time can make that clear if it is true."

"Knowing Lukio, he'd be determined to get me out of the palace and out of Ashdod. He never was one to sit idly by." I could not count the times I barely restrained him from crashing down the mountain to dole out retribution on my father for his harsh treatment of me.

"That would be wonderful!" she said. "You could go back home!"

"No," I said, my voice firm. "My place is here."

Galit knew very well why I could not leave.

"But your children . . ."

My hand flew to my chest in a futile attempt at keeping it from splitting wide open again. "I know in my bones that the boy I sent them away with got them to safety."

My heart throbbed as I allowed myself one excruciating moment of memory. One sight of my sweet Aaliyah, with her little arms wrapped around fourteen-year-old Yoash's neck and Asher's small hand gripping that of the young man as they fled up the narrow path behind the city and into the forest, away from a horrific fate at the hands of the Philistines. I'd begged Yoash, Medad's apprentice, to get them to safety, and he'd barely hesitated, even knowing that he would likely never see his own parents again.

If it had not been for my elderly neighbor pleading for my help in escaping, I would have followed close behind. But I could not leave the terrified woman, especially when she'd been one of the first people in town to show me kindness, even though my husband was a selfish wretch.

Once it was apparent that she could not easily traverse the rocky path, the woman had begged me to leave her behind. But I couldn't bear to leave her to be slaughtered, so I'd continued on while the city behind us burned. The fact that one of the Philistines found us before we'd even made it fifteen paces past the tree line was inevitable. That he'd immediately slit her throat, even more so.

But when he'd caught sight of the two sets of footprints, one larger and one smaller, in the mud on the trail, I'd had no choice to distract him by fighting my way out of his hold and running the opposite direction. I paid dearly for the decision, but Aaliyah and Asher had remained safe. Not that soldier, nor any other, pursued them, so I believed with every part of me that they were safe with Elazar's family in Kiryat-Yearim, where I'd sent Yoash to plead for their protection. I certainly could not have trusted my father with their care and who knew where my brothers were, or if they even remembered me.

"But what good does it do for you to stay here, Shoshana?" said Galit, calling me back to the dim wine cellar. "Nothing has changed, and nothing will. If you remain, you will serve Mariada in the house of the man you once thought you would marry. You won't even be in the palace anymore."

"She's the daughter of the king. If that's all I have, then I will take it. I won't go. I won't leave my—"

Galit slipped her hand into mine just as a firm knock rapped on the door four times and the lock clicked open to signal our time in the wine cellar was complete.

"I know," she whispered, true affection in her light brown eyes. "I know, my friend. I am sorry for pressuring you."

We parted after a swift embrace, and I slipped out of the room on soft feet, making my way through the dark palace, up two flights of stairs and into Mariada's black room without notice. Then I forced myself to sleep, while holding the faces of my precious children in my mind and begging Yahweh to give them happy and healthy lives on the mountain where his holy Ark resided.

Early the next morning, I found a gleaming spiral shell, its insides the same delicate pink as the sunrise, sitting on the windowsill. Blinking in confusion at the beautiful object in my palm, I tried to reconcile how he'd possibly gotten into Mariada's room on the second floor of the king's enormous and well-secured abode. But regardless of what Lukio had gone through to get it here, I'd already made up my mind that I would not meet him again. For as much as I had missed his friendship all these years, I was already risking enough by meeting with my friends in the wine cellar. I could not endanger them, our network, or my position by remaining in contact with the champion of Ashdod.

I held the shell in my hand, wrapping my fingers around it for only a few moments of vague indecision and irrational longing. Then, before Mariada could awaken and question why I was hovering at the window, I dropped it over the sill and to the ground far below, hoping he would receive my answer to his message and leave me alone.

Eleven

Lukio

It did not matter to me that a thousand voices were lifted in excitement all across the beach, their cheerful shouts proving that this day I'd been organizing for a month was a success. My gaze continually wandered away from the horizon, where the fleet of racing boats had disappeared a short time before, and toward the woman at the very back of the royal gathering. The canopy that shaded the king, his wives, and daughters kept Shoshana's face in shadow, and although I kept my feet planted in the sand twenty paces away in order to oversee the race and the other activities I'd planned, I was almost desperate to stride over to her and beg her for an answer to the question that continued to hound me—*Why didn't you come to see me?*

I'd paid a servant well to leave that shell in the window, and for her silence, hoping the girl would attribute the gift to the king's daughter and not her servant. Had she not done as I asked? Or had Shoshana not found it at all? Perhaps Mariada had seen it first and moved it? I had as many ideas about what had gone awry as fingers and toes, but there was nothing I could do to get an answer since I could not approach Shoshana in full sight of everyone on this beach.

I'd waited half the night for her on that terrace, after attending a meeting with the king about this boat race. By the time the moon was on the descent, I'd had to restrain myself from clumping down the stairs to search out Mariada's room and demand to know why Shoshana had ignored the summons I'd left for her.

I forced my attention back to the blue expanse, imagining the twelve boats that had set out a while ago to race toward the vessel anchored a good ways out to sea. The ships would swing around that boat and head back toward the beach, where the crowds would cheer their favorite crew to victory. A number of smaller fishing boats bobbed in the water to be as close to the race as possible, and the waves were dotted with children and adults alike, who were taking the opportunity to cool themselves while they waited for the boats to return.

Now that the weather had settled into longer periods of calm after a hectic season of storms, the men who were racing today would soon be rowing across the Great Sea, trading with the islands scattered all over the enormous body of water and the nations that ringed the blue expanse, far and near.

Few were the ships that ventured outside of the Great Sea, past the perilous straits that led to an even greater body of water. When I was a young boy and had heard of the powerful currents that dashed many vessels into the rocky shoreline, I'd felt a surge of pride that my father had been courageous enough to brave such dangers to sail to his far-northern homeland, but as I grew older, I'd wondered just how desperate he had been to chance joining the many other ships on the bottom of the sea. He must have been determined indeed to put as much distance as possible between himself and the children he left behind without explanation.

"Quite a good idea you had," said one of the men who'd helped me organize this race—one who'd formerly been quite vocal about his loyalty for Oleku and his mistrust in me. His eyes were on the commotion about a hundred paces away, where a group of children were running back and forth between the edge of the water to a collection of baskets. "Keeping people entertained with organized games while the boats are out of sight was brilliant."

"I well remember the long stretch of boredom between the beginning of the race and the end," I said. "My friends and I entertained ourselves with dice games, so I thought perhaps people might appreciate a few diversions to pass the time until the sailors return."

Not only had I organized a shell-collecting game for the children, inspired by the many hours Risi and I had spent digging about in the sand on this very beach, but there was also a competition between some of the fishermen to see who could gut the most fish as well as one between their wives over who could knot the largest nets. A number of men and women wandered about the beach with baskets of fresh bread, fruit on long skewers, and pots of various fresh delicacies to make this day enjoyable for everyone who'd gathered to take part.

Finding alternative ways to entertain the people, while also directing the men and women who were used to answering to Oleku, had been a challenge, but one that I'd found to be enjoyable. And judging from the laughter and shouted exclamations of those gathered here today, I'd accomplished my goal. No one was complaining about the sun being too hot or the boats taking too long to return. Even the king of Ashdod had not stopped smiling all day long. Whenever I caught his eye as I paced back and forth, my attention divided between the activity on the beach and the slave-girl standing in the shadows, he grinned at me and lifted his cup in salutation. He was pleased, and that should make me far more thrilled than I was.

Instead, my eyes were continually drawn to Shoshana, where she waited silently under the awning we'd had constructed for the king's family. And just like on the night of the feast, she refused to look at me. It was as if those moments on the terrace had never happened and her ridiculous statement about us being strangers was actually true. Even so, I left the other man to oversee the children's games and moved a few paces closer to the canopy, trying to think of a way to get her alone, if only for a moment.

I had to talk with her again. Tell her that I would do anything in my power to help her once I married Mariada, a prospect that no longer held the same anticipation it once did.

I'd already considered the obvious—that I'd be the one to take her back to Hebrew territory myself. But I'd burned away any chance of a return to Elazar's house. Risi had already mourned me; she had a life with Ronen in Ramah and had children of her own to care for. I would leave her in peace.

Seeing Shoshana had made me realize that I no longer held onto the bitterness I once had toward my sister, nor even for Ronen—especially knowing that he'd taken such good care of her after I left. But I could not go back. I'd caused too much damage.

Tela's baby squalled, interrupting a conversation between her and her mother. Amunet scowled at the child as if she were nothing more than a yowling cat. Anticipating whatever the queen would say next, Tela handed the baby off to the nursemaid who was hovering nearby. The young woman folded herself down in the sand to nurse the child, but still the infant continued to fuss and buck against the maid's gentle ministrations.

A slight movement in the corner of my sight caught my attention, and I noticed that Shoshana was watching the babe squirm with a pained expression. At first, I thought perhaps she was upset over the child's discomfort, but then a sickening realization took hold.

Had Shoshana had children with Medad? And if so, had they been killed during the raid at Beth Shemesh? From what I knew, Philistines had little interest in keeping prisoners of war unless they were of some value, either for selling or enforced labor. Little ones were rarely allowed to live. If she'd been married within the year after I left Kiryat-Yearim, any child to whom she would have given birth could not have been more than seven years old, perhaps eight at the most. Had she watched her children die at the hands of my kinsmen?

Every bit of joy I'd found in the success of this event leaked from my body. No wonder she'd been so guarded when I spoke to her. Whether or not we'd been childhood friends, I was her enemy. Her husband, and possibly even her children, had been killed by those of my blood. She must hate me.

Why had it never even occurred to me that she might have been a mother? Even if the thought of Medad touching her caused jealousy to ooze through my veins, a child born of her body would have been infinitely precious to her. She'd adored her younger brothers, and they'd returned that adoration. She'd been willing to give me up to protect her connection to them, after all. I had no doubt that she would have fought for her own children with everything she had.

Refusing to be comforted, Tela's infant began to wail, and then, just as the nursemaid set her clothing to rights, the little one vomited all down the front of her white tunic. The poor woman stood, red-faced and flustered, while the baby whimpered.

"Go on back and wash yourself," commanded Tela without compassion. "And find something fresh to wear before you return."

The girl nodded and made an attempt to hand the child back to her mother. Tela recoiled, obviously afraid of a reoccurrence, and looked around for someone else to step in.

"Shoshana can take her," Mariada offered with a cheerful smile. "She's not busy. I'm sure the baby would calm down if she walked her up and down the beach until her nursemaid returns."

Tela's expression went stony. "No. That filthy Hebrew isn't to put her hands on my child."

Even in the dim light beneath the awning, it was clear that all the blood had drained from Shoshana's countenance. It took every thread of restraint in my body to not barrel over to the tent and demand that Tela apologize for such hateful words. Fortunately, I was prevented from destroying everything I'd been working toward for the last ten years by the sound of a horn being blown down by the shoreline.

The boats had been spotted on the horizon. All activity on the beach paused as people turned to watch their approach, hands shading eyes and fathers lifting children onto their shoulders. Everyone stared across the blue expanse to catch sight of the bird-headed prows as they cut through the water, propelled by the collective might of as many as twenty rowers on each ship.

The closer they came to the shore, the louder the crowd grew. I'd insisted that each ship fly a bright banner atop its rigging so that the spectators would have little difficulty discerning their favorites, even while far out to sea.

Three of the ships outpaced the others. One with a saffron banner was in the lead, a ship with a green flag was close behind, and a dark brown cloth flapped in the wind atop the mast of the third, which was quickly gaining speed on the others.

By the time the ships were within fifty paces of the beach, the crowd was nearly in a frenzy, all thoughts of the games they'd been playing and the delicious food they'd been enjoying lost in the excitement.

One by one, the boats neared the shore, and a man from each vaulted off the side, a banner that matched their ship's flag in one hand as they swam through the waves. In the past, the first boat to land ashore had been declared the winner, but I'd altered the rules to make the finish more exciting. Now, the winner of the race would be the boat whose crewmember put their banner in the hand of the king.

A wide path had been cleared from the beach to the canopy beneath which Nicaro sat on a cedar throne, watching the spectacle with obvious delight.

Since I'd encouraged the crews to do anything to keep their opponents from winning, thereby making the final leg of the race even more thrilling, the three men spent the last fifty paces throwing elbows, lashing out with kicks, and tripping one another as they raced across the hot sand. The crowd was wild, so intent on the struggle in front of them that the ships now making landfall were completely forgotten. The runner with the saffron banner was in the lead, the brown banner directly behind him. The green runner was limping along after a particularly harsh kick from one of the other men. In a final effort to keep his opponent from reaching the king first, the brown-bannered runner grabbed the sodden kilt of the man in the lead and yanked hard, meaning to throw him off-balance. But the man holding the saffron banner refused to be swayed from his course, determinedly plowing ahead even when the kilt was ripped from his body. Taking the last fifteen paces completely naked, the man landed in the sand, kneeling unashamedly in front of the king with his golden banner lifted high as the spectators roared behind him.

Nicaro received the winning banner and offered the exhausted man congratulations in the form of a mug of beer and a command for someone to bring him a fresh kilt. Then, the king of Ashdod turned to catch my eye, the pride on his face unmistakable as he gestured for me to join him. This day had been a triumph. The story of this race would be gleefully told over and over again, making any recent military losses insignificant in comparison to the love of the people for a king who would provide such enthralling entertainment.

"I knew you could do this," said the king as I approached. "I knew I chose the right man for this job."

All I'd done was remember the things I'd enjoyed as a boy during celebrations, along with considering what made the crowd scream louder for me during fights. I'd known how to throw punches, how to place a kick to knock the wind from a man's chest, and how to choke an opponent until he pleaded to end the match or fainted from the effort, but I'd also given them Demon Eyes and they'd screamed for it. Begged for it. Practically threw their silver at me for my performance. The only difference was this time I'd placed the king at the center of the spectacle, and they'd lapped it up like honey dripping from the comb.

I grinned, victory surging through me with nearly the same fervor as it had after some of my very first wins on the fighting grounds. But when Mariada flounced over to congratulate me and her father, I remembered the girl in the shadows and the humiliation that had been painted across her face after Tela insulted her. The anguish in her eyes that spoke of a mother whose heart had been torn to shreds.

Spying a pure white shell half buried in the sand near my right foot, I bent to pluck it from the ground. I brushed the sand from its surface and inspected the swirling pattern on its back. I'd have to find the servant I'd paid to sneak into Mariada's room again, and then I'd find an excuse to hang about the palace late into the evening.

Even if I had to put every shell on this beach on her mistress's windowsill, I'd convince Shoshana to meet with me again, and I would get her out of this city and home to whatever remained of her family.

Twelve

Shoshana

I turned the shell in my hands over and over, glaring at the opalescent surface.

This had to stop.

It had been a month since the shells had begun appearing in the sill every few days, and it was clear that Lukio was determined to continue until I gave in. But this was the last time. I'd come here for one purpose and one purpose only—to tell him to leave me alone for good.

I did not know why he was being so persistent, but if I was to remain in my position—and I *had* to remain in my position, for many reasons—he must cease pursuing this matter.

The fact that I'd stopped throwing the shells from the window and had started nesting them inside a jar atop a high shelf made this entire endeavor even more foolhardy. It must end. Tonight.

Sitting cross-legged in the corner of the terrace, I leaned my back against the plastered parapet wall and closed my eyes. A hint of sea air tickled my nose, reminding me of the day of the boat race and the delight on Lukio's face as the people of Ashdod thrilled over the event he'd organized. Mariada had boasted for days about his hand in the events, exclaiming over the successful changes he'd made to a competition that had become dull and routine after so many years. She'd also told everyone who would listen that her betrothed had grand and exciting plans for a new Festival of Games at the summer solstice, one that would far surpass any other celebration Ashdod had ever seen.

Although a deep sense of unease lingered in me whenever my mistress spoke of him, I could not help but be glad that she esteemed him so highly. She would be a good wife to Lukio. Supportive and faithful. The kind of wife I'd once hoped to be to him. The kind of wife I'd attempted to be for Medad, even though he was none of those things for me.

At least, unlike my father, Medad had never hit me or our children, and for that I was more than grateful. But the seven years I'd spent in his household had been cold and lonely ones, serving a man whose eye wandered to any loose woman he came across in Beth Shemesh and who callously cheated others so much that his reputation gradually drove away more customers than it attracted.

I was sorry that he died at the hands of the Philistines, but I did not mourn him—only that his children would barely remember the man they once called Abba, even if he'd had little interest in them, or me, when he was alive. The only reason Medad had wanted me in the first place was to punish Lukio for the last time they'd fought, when Lukio had beaten him senseless for publicly slandering Eliora. Medad had even admitted as much to me once, crowing over the fact that it had been all too easy for him to suggest that my father satisfy the gambling debts he owed with his own young and innocent daughter.

To push away the bitter memories, I indulged myself in a few moments of hope while I waited for Lukio. I imagined Aaliyah and Asher with Elazar's family, exploring the woods with the other children who lived on the mountain. I thought of them climbing into Yoela's lap to hear stories, knowing that Eliora and Lukio's adoptive mother would treat them as her own grandchildren. And even though it hurt, I imagined their sweet voices exclaiming over all the new things they would experience on the mountain where I was born.

A tear slipped from my eye as I recalled the sound of their laughter, their voices calling me *Ima*, the feel of their arms around my neck, and their precious bodies pressed to mine while I rocked them to sleep at night. I forced myself to smile as I imagined them happy. Safe. Loved.

And it had to be enough. For now.

"It is good to see you smile," said Lukio, making the cherished images disappear behind my eyelids.

Startled, I surged to my feet, hoping in the dim starlight he hadn't noticed the tears I'd shed while dreaming of my children.

"This has to end, Lukio." I tossed the shell at his feet, where it cracked in half. "It's fortunate that Mariada hasn't seen any of these on her sill. I would be hard-pressed to explain. How did you get them in without anyone seeing, anyhow?"

He grinned, the unguarded and dazzling curve of his lips threatening to steal my breath. "I bribed one of the kitchen maids to sneak into the room, in the guise of collecting used dishes."

A streak of fear shot through me. "What if she reveals that to someone?"

He shrugged one large-muscled shoulder. "She thinks they are gifts for your mistress. She finds the gesture *delightful*."

I frowned at the flippant way he spoke of charming Mariada, even if it was not my place to be unsettled by such things. "Regardless. You cannot summon me again. It is only complicating matters."

His mismatched eyes studied me. "How is it a complication? From what I've heard, Mariada goes to bed early and sleeps like the dead. I need to speak with you, so I coincided my messages with nights that I've been meeting with Nicaro to discuss plans for the solstice festival. If someone questions my presence in the palace—which they won't—I can make it seem as though I am visiting my betrothed. None of these people would blink an eye at such an explanation. Only a Hebrew would find that sort of behavior suspicious or immoral."

My face flushed. Not only from the swipe at my heritage and my convictions but at talk of intimacies between himself and Mariada.

Ignoring whatever emotion he saw in my expression, he clucked his tongue and bent to pick up the two halves of the shell I'd destroyed, examining them and then lining up the fracture until the seam disappeared. "I liked that one. It changes colors in the sunlight." His voice dropped to a murmur. "It reminded me of your eyes."

Heat flowed into every one of my limbs in a rush, and something like panic mixed with pleasure stirred in my blood. The feeling was dangerous. Reckless.

"Lukio," I whispered with urgency, "what is it you need to say? We cannot meet again."

Curiosity moved across his furrowed brow, but then he sighed and leaned back against the wall. "I'm determined to find a way to get you home—"

"I am not going anywhere," I said, cutting off whatever plans he thought to lay out.

His eyes went wide at my adamant statement. "I'll make certain you are safe."

I shook my head, lips pressed tightly.

"I would never put you in danger, Shoshana," he said in a gentle tone, dropping all pretense of the haughty Philistine champion. Instead, he was my Lukio. The sweet boy with the tender heart who'd promised to keep me safe from every harm. Who'd chased off jackals, coyotes, snakes, and even a wildcat once during our nighttime explorations in the woods. Who'd dried my tears and caressed my hair while holding me tight under our sycamore.

The affection in the words, along with the way his deep voice caressed my name, made me want to tell him everything. To throw myself into his arms and plead with him to make it all go away. But that would do nothing more than make a precarious situation even more difficult. I had to make him understand but without revealing too much.

"I am fine where I am," I said. "Mariada is a good mistress. I have no fear for my safety. Leave me be, Lukio."

"I will not," he said, his jaw setting in that familiar way he had whenever I'd disagreed with him about which path to take in the woods. "You are vulnerable here. These people—" He paused, taking a swift breath through his nose. "These people see you as less than human, Shoshana. They would have no issues with using you. Mariada may be kind to you because she is by nature a tenderhearted girl, but you do not understand what could happen if—" He stopped to swallow hard against whatever he'd meant to say. "If you'd seen some of the things I have, the way female slaves are abused . . ." He shook his head, his expression thunderous. "I won't allow it. No. You have to go."

The proprietary way he spoke suddenly made my blood boil. He may have known me as a child, and yes, I'd made promises to him back then, but those meant nothing anymore. I'd been married and widowed and enslaved since he'd left. He'd gone back to his Philistine kinsmen and then betrothed himself to one of their women. There was nothing between us now but regret and bittersweet memories.

I gritted my teeth against the rising frustration, but the words exploded from my mouth anyhow. "You are about a year and a half too late for all that."

"What do you mean?" His words were measured and low, his eyes going narrow with menace. I'd spoken too much, but there was no retreating now.

"Do you think that your soldiers merely came to Beth Shemesh, killed my husband, and then sweetly escorted me to this place?" My chest heaved as unwelcome images of that day reared up. "No. They slaughtered most everyone. They burned the town. They slit the throat of the old woman I tried to save as if she were nothing more than a sow to be butchered. If I hadn't sent my two children off with someone before the attack, their little bodies would have been among the dead. Or worse, they would have been captured. Because your people have no mercy, Lukio. They aren't bound to Torah laws that protect prisoners of war—especially women and children—from the aftermath of battle."

My entire body was shaking. Memories of what I'd endured came at me so powerfully that I could smell the stink of my attacker's breath. Feel the pain in my scalp as he gripped my hair in his fist. Hear the sound of his mocking words while he stripped every shred of my dignity away. I held my breath, counting my heartbeats until I was able to speak again.

I let my gaze meet Lukio's. From the way his hands were balled into white-knuckled fists and the storm of rage on his face, he clearly understood what I'd been through.

"So yes, Lukio, I know the risks of remaining in this city. But I won't leave. I can't."

His response came out like the slow grind of a knife against stone. "What possible reason could you have for staying here after what happened to you? And why, when I am offering you the means, wouldn't you go back to your children?"

The truth scalded its way up my throat as it burst free. "I won't leave my daughter!"

His head snapped back. "What?"

I closed my eyes for just a moment, collecting myself. There was no use in holding any of it back now. I released a slow, shuddering breath before I spoke again.

"Nine months after Beth Shemesh, I gave birth to a baby girl."

His mouth opened, but no words came out.

"And even though Mariada is kind and was much more lenient than most mistresses would be, I was not allowed to keep my child, of course. I only held her for a few hours."

I could still feel the ghostly weight of that precious bundle. When they came to take her away, I could do nothing. Say nothing. She was in my arms and then she was just gone.

"But you said you won't leave her . . ." he began, and I could practically see his mind working through everything I'd revealed as he swiped one of his large hands down his face and over his stubbled chin. "If they took her away, then why insist on staying here?"

I dropped my chin, choking back a sob. "Tela lost a baby a couple of months before, when she was weeks from giving birth. She replaced her dead child with mine."

He let out a muted curse. "No wonder she was so hostile on the beach when Mariada suggested you hold her."

"I suspect Virka doesn't even know the difference. He was gone during that time. He missed the death of his own child and the switch Tela made for another. Only her maid, her mother, and her sisters knew about the miscarriage anyhow. If her husband is suspicious, he's given no indication that I've seen."

Lukio said nothing, only ran his hand through his long hair, which had somehow come undone from the knot at the back of his head.

"My other children, Aaliyah and Asher, are safe. I sent them to live with Elazar and Yoela." His eyes went wide at mention of his family in Kiryat-Yearim, but I pressed on, needing him to understand my reasoning. "But my baby is trapped here in this abhorrent city, and I will not walk away from her."

"So, you will endure slavery for the rest of your life, simply for a few glimpses of your daughter in the arms of a woman who treats you like an animal?"

"Trust me, I have no intention of either one of us staying any longer than we have to."

His brow furrowed. "But how—"

I put up a hand. "That is of no concern to you. I have a plan, and any further communication between us will only interfere. So, stop this, Lukio." I gestured to the broken shell in his hand. "I appreciate that you want to help for the sake of the friendship we once shared, but I need you to let it go. Let *me* go."

He met my gaze, and I allowed my own to tangle with his. An ocean of grief and regret and broken promises swirled in the chasm between us.

"I need to get back," I said as I turned my back on him and the yearnings his presence dragged to the surface. "I've spent far too long up here."

But before I took three steps, his hand wrapped around my wrist. He pulled me to a stop and then came so near I could feel the heat of him against my shoulder. My heartbeat crashed against my ribs as memories broke through the wall I'd so carefully built around the past.

Although we'd been children when our friendship began, the last year of our time together had been different. Still innocent, of course. But there had been lingering embraces, whispered words of affection, promises made, and one sweet but bone-melting kiss mere days before my father sold my future to Medad instead of the boy who held my heart in his young but ax-roughened hands.

"I should not have left," he said, his voice gruff in my ear. "I should have stayed and fought for you. I should have told Elazar about our understanding. If I had, perhaps—"

I shook my head. "My father was serious about not allowing me to see Levi and Yadon again. And as much as I cared for you, I couldn't lose them. I could not have made any other choice." Grief compounded on grief, as I mourned again that it was all for nothing, since after Medad moved us to Beth Shemesh they were lost to me after all. I'd not seen their precious faces since the day I'd left the mountain.

"I understand," he said. "I would have done the same for Risi."

"For as worthless a husband as Medad was, Aaliyah and Asher were worth all of it. And regardless of how my baby's life began, she is worth the sacrifice." I looked back up at him and pressed my free hand to my chest in a futile attempt to stop the violent twisting of my heart. "I won't abandon her, Lukio."

"You wouldn't be the girl I knew if you did," he said, his beautiful mismatched eyes glittering in the starlight.

For as much as both of us had changed between that awful moment we'd parted and now, I could see now that he was still the boy who'd been my closest friend and confidant. The one whose embrace had made me feel like nothing could ever harm me. So, I allowed myself the indulgence of leaning into his warmth one last time, laying my cheek against his broad chest, and breathing deeply of the scent of him, at once familiar and strange.

"You will come to me if you need anything," he said, the sound of his low voice reaching into the marrow of my bones while his large palm stroked down the length of my hair just one time.

I nodded and pulled out of his hold, instantly feeling chilled at the loss of his nearness and my throat aching from the urge to weep. But I forced myself to walk away, leaving him alone on the terrace with a broken shell and all my futile longings for what might have been.

Thirteen

Lukio

I'd been staring into the same half-empty horn of beer for most of the morning, seated on an intricately carved cedar chair—not unlike the one Nicaro had occupied during the boat races—in the hearth room I'd had designed to mimic the grand one in the palace.

Alone beneath the vibrant blue ceiling my craftsmen had painted to blend seamlessly with the sky, which could be seen through the large opening in the roof above the circular stone hearth, I'd not moved from this place for hours, my eyes latched to the colorful mural on the far wall. Teitu had come in a number of times in the guise of asking whether I needed more food or drink, but judging from the furrow between his black brows, he was worried about more than my stomach. However, he said nothing, wise enough to know I was in no mood to talk.

It had been three days since Shoshana had revealed what happened at Beth Shemesh, and I'd not slept more than a few hours since that conversation. Every time I closed my eyes, I saw my Tesi fighting off a monster, crying out for help—crying out for me. And almost equal to my regret for leaving her behind to endure such horrors alone was the memory of her cheek pressed to my chest and the soul-deep satisfaction of having her so close to me after all these years.

I looked around this beautiful villa I'd built—the rich furnishings, the intricate murals, the finely woven fabrics that covered the cushions on long stone couches along the walls, the fluttering white curtains over the windows that stretched from ceiling to floor—and wondered how it was that Medad, my greatest enemy, had had a richer life and hadn't even known it.

He'd had what I'd dreamed of for years. A life with Shoshana. Children with her.

I'd once imagined using my woodcutting skills to provide a home for my own family. The satisfaction of using my ax to create piles of wood to keep that family warm. Building a house with my own two hands to keep them safe and dry. I'd envisioned coming home to my Tesi and her dimpled smile and carrying my adoring children about on my shoulders like I'd seen Elazar do with his younger sons and daughters.

Medad had taken it all from me, and from what Shoshana had said, he hadn't appreciated any of it. If the man was not dead already, I would gladly find him and repay him for the way he'd treated the family that should have been mine.

He'd once been my friend, and his friendship made me feel like finally I was part of the community of Kiryat-Yearim. He'd invited me into the games he and his younger brothers played, without a question for what sort of blood flowed within my body. But when the boys' father discovered his sons with me during a raucous game of war among the trees, he dragged Medad off by the hair, leaving my ears blistered by his vicious opinion of my contemptible heritage and the strangeness of my mismatched eyes, which he deemed an indication of my inherent evil and baseborn nature.

From that day forward, Mehad had made it his mission to prove his father's words true to everyone in Kiryat-Yearim, as if by doing so he could erase the fact that he'd once been kind to a Philistine.

He took every opportunity to mock and humiliate me, naming

me Demon Eyes, which made the dual-colored eyes that Risi had told me were a special and unique gift from our parents—since our mother's eyes were brown and our father's green—into something I began to resent.

When the attacks on my appearance no longer seemed to rile me, Medad aimed for my heritage, scorning the Philistines for their habit of eating abominable things like swine, dogs, and rats before moving on to swipe at my connection to Elazar's family, saying they took Risi and me in only out of pity, and that Gershom and Iyov were not my true brothers and never would be; that I would never be anything more than a Philistine dog to them.

Medad played on every fear and insecurity I had until he made me doubt everything and everyone, including myself. After a few months, I was convinced that Risi and Shoshana were the only people in the world who cared for me at all.

And yet, if what Shoshana had said was true, Elazar's family had *all* searched for me—even the men I'd rejected as brothers. Not just for a few hours, but for weeks, all the while I was running off to chase after achievements that I was coming to see meant absolutely nothing.

I pushed to my feet and threw the ceramic horn at the hearth, feeling a hit of satisfaction at the sound of pottery shattering across the shells and river stones that swirled in the beautiful circular patterns I'd commissioned a master tile-layer to create. Every guest I'd had for the past few years had been awed by the design, and I'd been thrilled by the pleasure such admiration for my home gave me. Now I wished I could rip up the entire useless thing with my own hands and crumble each piece to dust. I wished I could lean my body against the blue and scarlet columns that held up the roof on this gaudy villa and pull it down around my ears like Samson did that temple in Gaza.

I couldn't breathe. I needed to get out of this house with all its suffocating emptiness. A house that would soon be just another prison to my Tesi. I needed to go outside, inhale fresh sea air, and think as I wandered the streets like I did when I was young.

However, everyone in the city knew my face. Whenever I left my villa, I was constantly asked about my next fight by men who could not wait to lay down their wages on me. Women giggled and batted their lashes, blatantly offering themselves up for my pleasure, and groups of children trooped along behind me, desperate for an encounter with Demon Eyes so they could tell their friends.

I needed to get out of this house, but I had to go about it unseen.

"Teitu!" My voice echoed off the vibrant walls. "Teitu!"

My manservant appeared, breathless and his one eye wide as he took in the shattered horn and the mess of beer and pottery across the hearth.

"Get me a cloak," I said.

"My lord?"

"And something to cover my head as well. And nothing made of fine fabric. Only rough and dark cloth. Threadbare, even."

His brows furrowed. "It's very hot today. Are you certain?"

"I am. Go." I guessed that the rest of my servants would be gossiping about my strange behavior within the hour, but I did not care.

He did as he was asked, and I left behind my grand and gleaming white villa shrouded in Teitu's own brown cloak and headscarf, feeling that for the first time in months I could draw a full breath into my lungs.

Determined to lose myself in the maze of the city and escape the overwhelming barrage of emotions that had plagued me since I last saw Shoshana, I ambled through the streets of Ashdod, head down and blissfully unrecognized. By the time I looked up, I'd left the part of town where everything was color and excitement and realized I was near the southern end of Ashdod, where the houses were squashed together like crumbling mudbricks. Beggars murmured from every alleyway, and the stench of waste and refuge backed up in the street drains filled my nostrils.

Just as I'd made up my mind to turn around and go back to my desolate home, a series of shouts and snarls reached my ears.

Drawn by morbid curiosity, I followed the noise and found a

large group of people surrounding some sort of commotion. It reminded me of many of my first fights—some fought right here on these same streets when Mataro challenged anyone who dared to pit themselves against a sixteen-year-old boy who was built like a man. But as I pressed through the crowd, earning more than a few curses for blocking their view with my large frame, I saw that it wasn't a fight between two men after all but between two dogs.

One, a brindled canine with nearly as many scars as me, had the other dog—a black-and-tan brute who was smaller but stockier—by the neck.

With his jaws clamped tightly at the black-and-tan's throat, the dog let out a menacing growl through drool and bloodied foam, his every muscle locked tight.

The crowd roared its approval of the brindle's attack, but my fists were clenched tight beneath my cloak and my insides in knots. I'd never been able to stomach any animal hurting, but knowing that the black-and-tan was suffering for the entertainment of this crowd was almost more than I could bear.

There was also little difference between the sound of these spectators crowing for the brindle to finish off the other dog than when they called me to destroy my own opponents on the fighting grounds. As they screamed for the dog, who was apparently named Jackal, they might as well be calling out for Demon Eyes.

For so long I'd reveled in the shouts from the crowds, felt vindicated for coming back to Ashdod because I'd achieved the fame and fortune I'd set out to grasp. But did they see me any differently than this dog at the center of the ring of rabid spectators? They wagered on my fights the same way they did this one, after all. In fact, it was my cut of those winnings that had built that luxurious house I'd once gloried in.

Mataro had certainly never seen me as anything more than an animal, a dog he could throw into a fight so he could collect his disproportionate share. More than likely, he was furious that he no longer had control of my leash.

When the black-and-tan dog collapsed, his neck bleeding

profusely and his limbs going still, celebration broke out around me. Wagers exchanged hands as someone yanked at the cord around the brindle's neck, pulling it tighter and tighter until he finally released the neck of the dead dog, but only to snap at his handler. The man twisted the cord until the brindle yelped and submitted to the choke.

It was then that I realized I recognized the dog's handler. It was Tombaal, one of the boys I used to run the streets of Ashdod with, playing endless games of sheep knuckles and getting into all manner of trouble. At seven years old, I'd fought my very first fight with Tombaal—the same one Mataro had happened to witness and found that it took little more than a dangling of silver in front of my greedy little eyes to bait me into fighting again.

Tombaal handed off the brindle to one of his companions and then lifted his hands to quiet the crowd. "I hope you've all enjoyed the bout so far. For those of you who wagered on Jackal, I congratulate you, and for those wagered on Bear, may the gods of fortune be with you next time." He grinned widely, showing a gap where one of his front teeth used to be. The very front tooth that I had knocked from his mouth during our second match.

"And now, for the last fight," he shouted, "we have a special treat for you all—a new dog."

The crowd brayed and whistled.

"That's right. This one has had no training at all. He was found wandering in a barley field not too far from here. But you'll soon see why he was brought to me." His gapped grin stretched even wider. "I ask you to wait to place your bets until you see him. But since this is the last match of the day, shall I let it go to the final end?"

The crowd went wild at the suggestion, getting so loud that my ears rang from the noise. Hadn't the last dog been killed at the end of the match? What more could they want?

Giving in to curiosity, I leaned toward the man on my left. "What does he mean by letting it go to the final end?"

Barely taking a look at me, the man responded, "It means his pack will tear apart the loser. He doesn't feed them for days before a bout like this one. The crowd loves it."

Nausea flamed up my throat. How could watching an animal be torn to pieces and cannibalized be entertaining to these people? And how had I turned a blind eye for so long to how truly vicious the people in this city were? This was no small crowd. And it was growing.

Before I could turn around and flee this bloodthirsty gathering, the new dog was led into the ring of cheering people, and now I knew why Tombaal had brought it here. The gray-coated canine was enormous. Its shoulders would be nearly to my hip—and I stood a head taller than most men in Philistia. The dog's head was also nearly twice the size as most other dogs I'd ever seen. But what I noticed next after his extraordinary size was that his muscles were quivering and his eyes were huge, wheeling about as he was half-dragged forward, paws scrabbling against the ground in his terror. Seeing his distress, the crowd began to jeer and shout, which made him tremble all the more.

And now instead of simple disgust, a swell of anger began to surge in me at this display, growing in tandem with the savage calls of the crowd for the beautiful flesh of this animal to be shredded by a pack of ravenous dogs.

When Tombaal gestured for the brindle to be brought forward, I moved forward as well, pushing past two men who snarled curses at me. Then, when two more dogs were led into the circle, I nearly lost all restraint. In fact, I was shaking nearly as violently as the gray dog.

Before I could open my mouth, Tombaal's friend released the brindle, who immediately lunged at the gray, teeth bared and blood from his last fight drooling from his jaws.

At the same moment the cur sank his teeth into the shoulder of the gray dog, I dropped the cloak from my body and yanked the scarf from my head, all caution burned away by my concern for the terrified dog.

And even before I stepped into the circle, I heard "Demon Eyes" being called out from among the crowd. I cared nothing for my lost anonymity now. All I cared about was preventing the gray dog from being annihilated.

Heedless of Tombaal's furious shouts, I grabbed for the brindle, yanking the cord around his neck the same way Tombaal had done and pulling him off his prey. The brindle turned on me, his powerful teeth clamping down on my forearm, and instinctively I kicked with my dominant leg—the same one I'd trained to deliver blows that would level a man larger than me in one hit to his gut.

With a strangled yelp, the brindle flew across the circle to land near Tombaal's feet in a pathetic heap. The crowd seemed to gasp as one and then went quiet with gape-mouthed shock.

I moved to stand in front of the gray dog, who was on the ground, bleeding from the shoulder and shaking violently. A steady trickle of blood dripped from my own arm into the dirt.

Tombaal's face was the very picture of disbelief. "Demon Eyes? What are you doing?"

I ignored the fact that someone I'd spent years climbing trees and tossing dice with would use my fighting name instead of my given one, then stretched to my full height, allowing all my anger to funnel into my furious glare. "I won't stand by and watch this animal be torn apart. This is over."

His mouth gaped like a fish on the beach. "But this is . . . wagers have already exchanged hands . . . you can't just—"

I used the full force of the intimidating stare I'd perfected, as if he were an opponent whom I was facing across the fighting grounds. "I can. And I will."

I turned to the crowd, making a swift decision that I hoped I could convince Nicaro to support. "I am the Master of Games in this city. And from now on any fighting matches, be they human or otherwise, must be sanctioned by myself, and thereby, the king of Ashdod."

I glanced over at Tombaal, who blinked at me in profound confusion. "I am taking this dog with me."

"You have no right!" Tombaal stuttered, his face the color of a pomegranate. "That animal is mine."

I narrowed my eyes at my childhood friend, setting my jaw like granite, while at the same time shifting into a relaxed fighter's stance. I lifted a hand, beckoning him with a mocking gesture. "Then come and take him from me."

Tombaal's jaw twitched, and I could practically hear the curses he must be screaming at me from behind his clenched teeth, but he made no move to engage the champion of Ashdod in a fight he could not win.

"That's what I thought." I huffed a small laugh of derision, giving in to the urge to twist the knife. "You couldn't even beat me when I was seven and you were eleven."

Ignoring the confused buzz of the crowd around me and the feeble protests of the man I'd just humiliated, I knelt beside the gray dog, which was now trembling so fiercely that his paws were shaking.

Slowly, I stretched out my hand, murmuring assurances that I would not harm him and looking him directly in the eyes. He flinched as I touched his coat, cowering, but I laid a gentle hand on his quivering back. Then I brought my other hand to his head and stroked him behind his silky ears. Although he was still tense, he pressed into my palm, taking comfort in my touch, and I felt victory in the center of my bones.

"It's all right," I said, hiding all the fury still pumping through my body in order to keep my voice soothing, "I won't leave you behind."

I stood slowly, gently tugging at the cord around his neck to urge the giant dog to stand. When I began walking, the canine hesitated for a moment but then let me lead him forward. In bewildered silence, the crowd parted for us as I strode away without looking back, the gray dog limping along beside me as if it had always been at my side as we headed for home.

Fourteen

Shoshana

Mariada and Jasara had been playing the same game for hours. Each of them had won three rounds of Hounds and Jackals, an Egyptian game that consisted of moving carved ivory pegs around a board filled with tiny holes. The set had been a gift from one of the emissaries sent by Pharaoh to Ashdod and was a favorite pastime of the royal ladies whenever they gathered in this upper courtyard in the center of the women's quarters.

My legs ached from standing in one place for so long, my muscles twitching with the need to move and also from frustration. I had a message for the man in the garden shed. One that might mean life or death for a Hebrew girl. And since I'd been forced to stand here since late morning, waiting for Mariada to finish playing her game with Jasara, I'd been unable to get away.

I'd cycled through every excuse I'd used before when Oshai had asked me to risk delivering messages during the day, trying to decide which might give me enough time to run down to the shed and back without notice. In the past, I'd offered to fetch fresh flowers to decorate Mariada's room, after pouring a small amount of vinegar in the vase the night before to make her current arrangement wither. I'd also said I needed to borrow a new bronze needle from another maid to repair a loose seam, after ensuring that the ones I'd used before had been misplaced or bent. I'd once even chanced the wrath of my mistress by spilling an entire pot of henna down the length of her favorite gown as I was painting her fingernails with the reddish dye, and after dashing to the shed to meet my anonymous friend, had to collect natron powder from Avel, who used the gritty substance for killing pests in his beautifully manicured gardens, to scrub the stain on the dress. But no matter how many ideas I came up with to take my leave, I could think of nothing today that would not be suspect.

Across the small courtyard, Tela and Amunet sat in the shade, talking quietly, their maids busy braiding their hair into intricate plaits, interspersed with carnelian and bronze beads and even a few tiny white shells. It did not matter that at the end of the day the maids would be forced to undo all their hard work; Amunet insisted on a new and unique hairstyle every day, lately even eschewing the use of Egyptian-style wigs for the complicated fashions of the Philistine women. I took advantage of her and Tela's distraction to covertly watch my daughter, who lay on a soft cushion of layered blankets nearby.

She was cooing at her nursemaid, who'd been entertaining her with a variety of carved dolls and fluttering hand motions above her head. Everything in me screamed to run across the courtyard and snatch up my precious girl, to feel her soft skin, breathe in her sweet fragrance, and bury my face in the downy thatch of dark hair that now covered her tiny head. She'd grown so much in the past few weeks. Each time I went a day or more without seeing her, she changed in some subtle way. At eight months of age, she was becoming more vocal, experimenting with various sounds and blowing bubbles with her lips as she flailed her chubby arms and legs about.

When a delighted giggle erupted from her body in response to something the nursemaid did, I was at the same time thoroughly enchanted and distraught. It should be *me* eliciting those joyful noises from her mouth, not some Egyptian wet nurse. I blinked back hot tears and swallowed down my sorrow. There was nothing I could do but watch her across the room, drink in every sound, and pray that Yahweh would protect her even when I could not. Even so, I yearned for her every moment of the day, desperate to feel the beat of her heart against my skin and wishing that the first word from her mouth would be to call me Ima instead of naming Tela as her *matare*.

"Lukio!" cried Mariada, jerking my attention away from my baby to the man taking up most of the entryway with his large frame. I wondered how long he'd been standing there but knew enough not to look too closely at him while the rest of the women were nearby. So, I tilted my chin downward and feigned disinterest as he entered the courtyard. However, when a few stifled gasps came from the mouths of Nicaro's first wife and his three daughters, I was helpless to restrain my curiosity and looked up once again to find that he was not alone.

An enormous gray dog padded into the room at his left flank, the creature so hulking that it would likely stand almost as tall as Lukio on its hind legs. It looked like an odd mix between one of the king's boar-hunting hounds and a wolf.

"What is that?" demanded Amunet with vehement disgust.

"This is Igo," said Lukio, scrubbing the dog behind its ears, unabashed that the queen of Ashdod was unsettled by the sight of such a beast in her lushly appointed abode. I could not help but be amused that the dog was named *horse* in the language of the Philistines. It was certainly almost as large as one.

"Where did it come from?" asked Mariada, whose ocean-blue eyes were trained on the dog with both awe and fear.

"I rescued him from an unfair dogfight," he said, a hard edge coming into his voice that reminded me just how partial he'd always been to the donkeys he'd tended in Kiryat-Yearim. He'd had a way of speaking to them in such reassuring tones, and always in his Philistine tongue, that calmed them and caused the stubborn animals to follow after him with complete loyalty. I had no doubt that Lukio would throw himself in front of a bronze arrow if it meant saving the life of any animal, even one that looked as terrifying as the one at his side now.

"And you thought it wise to bring such a beast here?" said Tela, who had, in a rare show of maternal protectiveness, picked up the baby.

"There is nothing to fear," said Lukio. "He's harmless. He was so terrified when the other dog was set upon him that he did nothing more than cower, even though he was nearly twice the size as his attacker. He is as gentle as a lamb, even if he looks more like a lion."

Lukio stroked Igo's back and gave him an affectionate smile, and the dog looked up at his master with boundless adoration. "He hasn't left my side since that day, even to sleep. In fact, I was concerned he might knock down my house when I tried to leave him behind this morning. He practically tore the door from its hinges to get to me after my manservant made an attempt to lock him in a room. So, it seems that for the present, wherever I go, he goes too."

Mariada let out a shuddery laugh, breaking the tension. "He certainly looks worthy to be the companion of the champion of Ashdod. No doubt he'll be as famous as you within weeks if he insists on following you all over the city."

Lukio chuckled. "Perhaps so."

Amunet looked unconvinced, still glowering at both Igo and Lukio, and Tela excused herself from the room, my daughter clutched tightly to her chest and the nursemaid trailing behind. Although I hated to see them go, jealous of every moment my daughter spent out of my sight, I was glad that Tela cared enough about her to remove her from the presence of an animal she considered dangerous.

"Come join us for a round of Hounds and Jackals," Mariada said. "Jasara had beaten me three times already, and I am determined to see her defeated. Have you played before?"

Lukio's eyes slid to the board on the couch cushion between the two women, hesitating. "I have. Although it has been a while."

Regardless of the ten-year chasm between us, I read the disgust inscribed on his face with ease. A game like Hounds and Jackals would be far too slow for Lukio. His attention waned quickly during such activities, and more than once he'd insisted that we abandon games he'd deemed tedious during our times in the woods.

Before Mariada could press her suggestion, Lukio made one of his own. "I must go meet with your father soon, so my time is limited. But what if I teach you another game instead?"

Mariada's eyes went wide with anticipation. "What sort of game?"

"One I learned in the streets as a boy." He went over to a nearby table, where a game of Senet rested on its brightly painted surface. Slipping open the small drawer beneath, where its game pieces were stored, he extracted a few dice and a handful of ivory tokens. I immediately knew exactly which game he planned to teach the two women. He'd taught me the very same one in a cave, using the sheep knuckle dice he used to carry about in a pouch around his neck and a small pile of acorns.

After inviting the two women to join him on the floor, he explained the rules of the game, tossing the dice with a practiced hand and then snatching up the corresponding number of tokens. Before long, Mariada and Jasara were laughing as they tussled over the game pieces, playfully jabbing each other to snatch them from the ground, and to my profound surprise, Lukio was laughing as well, the rich sound burrowing into my bones and the sight of a huge smile stretched across his face and reflected in his entrancing mismatched eyes making my heart ache.

How I'd loved him as a girl. He'd been my savior, my friend, my everything. And watching him now, acting as carefree as he had during our time together as children, made me admit that despite everything, the root of those feelings had never withered. It had only been dormant in the deepest part of me and then stirred up by those last impulsive moments I'd allowed myself to lean into him on the terrace. I'd told him we were strangers now, but no one had ever known me like Lukio, and I doubted anyone ever would.

Although he still hadn't looked my way and seemed caught up in the game that he was playing with Mariada and her sister, I had the sense that Lukio was as aware of my presence in the room as I was of his. He had not left me any more shells and I'd told myself it was for the best, that I was grateful he'd respected my plea to stop contact. But I could not lie and say that I'd not felt a twinge of disappointment each time I caught sight of the empty sill. Nor could I deny that hearing him laugh with Mariada caused a current of something akin to envy to course through me.

A quiet whine from nearby jerked my attention away from their affectionate banter to find that Lukio's giant dog had edged away from the raucous game of dice and was now hovering a couple of paces away from me, his paws restlessly shifting back and forth, even as his gaze was fixed on his master. But then he turned his huge head toward me, jowls quivering slightly, as if the noise of the game was actually making the huge beast nervous. No wonder Lukio had been distressed to see this dog pitted against well-trained fighters. The animal was nothing of the sort, even if his size and ferocious appearance contradicted all evidence to the contrary.

Igo met my gaze with a timid but curious silver-eyed stare, his head tilting slightly as he watched me. Knowing I could trust Lukio that the animal was harmless, I forced my body to relax and breathed in slow measure, willing the dog to sense that I was no threat to him either.

To my amazement, he took the last few steps between us, and then, after turning his enormous body around in a circle, dropped to the floor in front of me with a heavy sigh, his attention once again affixed on his master.

Through the open roof of the courtyard, I noted that the sun had moved past its highest point, reminding me that Oshai had said there was only a small window of time to meet the man in the garden shed today. If I waited much longer to slip away, I would miss him. However, Lukio had now moved on from the first game he'd taught Mariada and Jasara another that I also remembered learning on the floor of his cave as he regaled me with stories of his wild friends in Ashdod. It was a complicated game, one that I knew would take a long time to complete and which had both women half-breathless with laughter. All hopes that Mariada would return to her room for a rest during the heat of the day shriveled, making me irrationally angry both with Lukio for coming here and with Mariada for stealing smiles from him that, had our paths never diverged, would be mine alone.

Frowning at myself, I forced my eyes back down to my feet, wondering how long it would be before Oshai could arrange another meeting, or if an alternate plan would have to be worked out to pass on the important information.

A palace guard appeared at the door, announcing that the king was now ready to meet with Lukio. With apologies to the ladies for interrupting their game, he unfolded his long legs and stood. Although I continued to keep my chin tilted down, only seeing him through my lashes, I saw the moment he noticed that his dog had taken up residence near my feet and began to cross the courtyard in our direction.

Igo was sprawled on the plaster floor, eyes closed and his broad chest moving up and down in contented rhythm, but as soon as Lukio approached, he startled and lifted his head.

Lukio squatted beside his dog, reaching out to scratch him between his ears. "Of course you would find your way to Tesi," he said to Igo in a low voice that even I could barely distinguish. "Being at her side was always my favorite place to be as well." His gaze flicked up to meet mine for only a heartbeat, but it was intense enough to make me reevaluate my insistence that he stay away.

Then, before I could even dare to breathe, he stood tall and patted his thigh. "Come, Igo. Let's go see the king." The two of them left the room with nearly matching giant strides, leaving me in such a tangle of contradictory emotions that it was difficult to keep my expression blank.

To my dismay, instead of taking her own leave, Mariada invited Jasara to play one more round of Hounds and Jackals, but one round turned into two, and then into four.

"Shoshana," called my mistress, after I'd finally given up all hope of keeping my meeting. "It is so hot. Will you fetch some fresh palm fronds and move the air for us?"

Refraining from letting out a sigh of relief that she'd delivered the perfect reason to run down to the garden, I gave her a tight nod. "Of course, mistress."

"And be quick about it," snapped Jasara, without looking back at me. "I'd rather not melt into a puddle while you dally about."

Used to her prickly demands, I shrugged away my annoyance. Even if it meant my arms ached for days, I would be more than happy to fan Mariada and her haughty sister all afternoon if it gave me the opportunity to stop by the shed on the off chance that my friend had waited for me.

I strode from the room, eager to be on my way down to the first level of the palace, but just past the doorway, a hand grabbed my elbow, yanking me to a stop. With a gasp, I peered over my shoulder, half expecting Lukio to be standing behind me, but instead, Amunet had followed me from the room.

"Take care, girl," she stated. "She may not be my daughter, but I warn you—keep your eyes to yourself."

I blinked at her in mute shock. She'd never spoken directly to me before. Everything about the woman screamed royalty—not the kind enjoyed by Nicaro, who merely governed over Ashdod and its surrounding cities and towns—but the kind that ruled the entirety of Egypt for thousands of years. It was more than evident that although she was the daughter of a minor ambassador to Philistia, the blood of dynasties flowed within her.

"The only reason that child remains in this palace is because Tela begged for it. But I won't hesitate to replace it with another if need be. It would only take one word to Virka and that little abomination would be on the rocks."

Her threat confirmed my guess that Tela's husband still thought my child had come from his wife's womb but also caused suffocating terror like I hadn't felt since the day Beth Shemesh fell.

"So, keep your greedy eyes off both the baby and the champion. I care nothing for what that brute does with you after he and Mariada wed, but I won't countenance my husband being made a fool by the machinations of a *Hebrew* slave. Do you hear me?"

I nodded, knowing that Amunet did not threaten idly. Somehow she'd suspected a connection between Lukio and me, and thought I was making an attempt to steal him from my mistress. Also, from the way she sneered the word *Hebrew*, I sensed that she harbored a deep hatred for my people. But there was an edge of menace in Amunet's voice that suggested something much more personal.

The queen spun about, her intricately braided hair sparkling with gems and silver beads as she strode away from me and back into the courtyard. But far from accomplishing what she'd meant to by her threats, her words had only strengthened my determination to get my child out of this palace. Oshai had promised to help me get her out of the city when the time came, but until I was able to steal my daughter away without endangering both her and everyone in our network, I would be patient. And I would stay far away from the man whose interference might ruin any chance I had at getting my child out of Ashdod.

Fifteen

Lukio

An older man I'd never seen before was in the king's chamber with Nicaro when I arrived. Although the seren lounged on the same cushioned bench where we'd first made our agreement, a large beer mug in hand, the two were engaged in an intense discussion. I had no desire to intrude, but since I'd been summoned, I cleared my throat to make myself known. Their conversation halted at the sight of me in the doorway, Igo hovering near my flank.

"Forgive me, seren," I said. "I can return later, if need be."

"Come in, Lukio." Nicaro beckoned me into the room with a smile that was a shade cooler than the last time I'd met with him. "This is Jaru, the head of my royal guard. We three need to discuss some of the unique issues this festival might pose."

Jaru turned to take me in as I approached, lending Igo a brief glance and a frown before pinning his gaze back on me. As he did, I was struck with a strange sense of familiarity, along with the feeling that his deep-set brown eyes, so dark they were almost black, could see past the veneer of confidence I pulled on like a

133

mantle every morning. Had Jaru said something to make Nicaro question my motives?

Unnerved by both the scrutiny and the oddly detached tone of the king's voice, I took a moment to urge Igo to lie down on the floor nearby. Thankfully, the dog complied, even though he kept his luminous silver eyes on me. Someone must have trained him to obey before he was found wandering in that field. I was still in shock that he'd migrated over to Shoshana earlier and flopped himself down in front of her with ease. But then, she'd always had the same effect on me too.

"An excellent idea," I said to the king, hoping my relaxed manner would ease the tension in the room. "What concerns do you have?"

"Jaru is worried that inviting spectators from all of the Five Cities and the surrounding areas will encourage enemies and spies to sneak in among the crowd."

I nodded, contemplating. "That is a possibility, to be sure. But as a port city and one positioned on the Way of the Sea trade route, there are undoubtedly many who enter our gates with nefarious purposes."

"But not in such uncontrollable numbers," said Jaru. "If we open our gates to a flood of people without discrimination, there is a possibility we could be invaded from the inside."

"Or it could be something that brings together the Five Cities and shows everyone that Ashdod is the greatest among them. I have full confidence in both your guards and our soldiers to ensure order is maintained. There is no army like ours." I gestured toward Nicaro. "Thanks to our king's excellent leadership. A fact that will be on full display to those who come to Ashdod and see just how impressive our military might truly is. Spies sent here during the festival will only take word of our vast superiority back to our enemies."

Jaru's lips pinched in a tight line, his eyes narrowing slightly. I could see how a man in charge of the many guards who kept this palace and all of the king's properties and interests safe might be wary of such a festival. If things did not go as planned, it was his position and reputation at stake, after all. Nicaro did not tolerate weakness of any sort, nor did he offer second chances to those he deemed incompetent.

But I could not let one man's unease unravel all the plans I'd made. I'd worked too hard to see it all go to waste now. So, I looked Jaru in the eye, showing that I was in no way intimidated by his obvious skepticism. Perhaps he, like so many others I'd been dealing with over the past few weeks, was loyal to the former Master of Games. But I'd spent a great many hours lately wooing those who were suspicious of my changes. I could convince Jaru as well, I had little doubt.

"Why don't I explain how I've scheduled each event to flow one into the other?" I offered. "Then we can strategize crowd control and discuss how best to coordinate our efforts."

With a silent tip of his head, Jaru agreed to listen to what I had to say, so I laid out my plans in detail. I'd been meeting regularly with leaders and participants of the five events I'd decided to highlight over the four-day festival: footraces, archery, feats of strength, stick fighting, and my own sport of barehanded fighting. Although at first there was some resistance to my plans to invite anyone in Ashdod who wanted to participate—be they rich or poor—my years of swaying crowds to cheer for me, even when I was at a disadvantage, had served me well. I'd successfully made my case that not only would the people of the city thrill at taking part in the games, but that those who made their living by wagers on such matches, like myself, would only further benefit from excitement among the masses.

By the time I finished, I could tell that even if Jaru was not completely convinced, Nicaro was more than pleased with all I'd managed to put together. The icy demeanor with which he'd greeted me had slowly melted into one of almost paternal pride.

"Additionally," I said, eager to lay out the offering that I was certain would secure Nicaro's absolute confidence in me, "it would be my honor to gift a large piece of land that is suitable for the construction of an arena wherein the larger events can be held. The tract I have in mind is situated at the bottom of a shallow basin near my olive orchard, which would be perfect for spectators to view the games from all sides. Other than clearing some trees and digging out the fighting grounds, it should be fairly easy to prepare for the purpose. The area is also easily accessed from the trade road. Of course, we will schedule some of the smaller events inside the city walls, to encourage bartering in the market, but the ones which will draw large crowds—"

"Like the fights," supplied Nicaro.

"Yes—such as the fights—can take place in a wide-open area in the countryside, so as not to overwhelm our streets for the entire four-day festival."

"And you are willing to give up your own land for this?" Nicaro asked, incredulous.

"Of course. It is my gift to both you, seren"—I nodded my chin—"and the people of Ashdod. My wealth is a direct result of the support of the people of this city. It is, after all, their silver with which I purchased that same olive farm as an investment a few years ago."

An investment that made me far richer than fighting itself ever did and had grown to encompass a large swath of land along the river that flowed between here and Ekron, including some of the very same orchards through which Risi and I pilfered fruit to feed our snarling bellies as we fled Ashdod all those years ago. Enormous vats of oil, grains, and fine wines bearing my personal emblem were now exported all over the Great Sea. I wondered whether my seafaring father would have found any pride in my becoming a prosperous trader of goods on the water, if nothing else.

"That is quite the offer," said Nicaro.

"I am confident that Ashdod's prosperity will only increase as a result. A small piece of land is nothing in comparison to what will be gained."

"There now, Jaru," said Nicaro, with a clap of his hands. "You have nothing to fear. This is an ambitious undertaking, to be certain. But I, too, am convinced that this festival will be a success. We will coordinate with Virka and Grabos to ensure that your men have plenty of support. And we will waste no time in putting together a team to clear Lukio's land." Then he turned to me. "You've not spoken of your own participation. You do plan to fight?"

Although the words were posed as a question, they were a clear command from the king. I'd hoped to avoid doing so, since I'd have so many activities and people to coordinate, but I also knew that my presence would excite the crowd. As well, an open invitation to anyone who dared fight Demon Eyes would be an enormous draw. Thankfully, I'd not ceased my daily training, continuing to spar with other fighters, run along the beach in the early mornings, and lift heavy rocks until my muscles screamed for mercy. I would simply have to ensure that everything was well coordinated in advance of my own bouts.

"Of course, seren. It will be my pleasure to do so." If this festival proved to be a triumph, I planned to announce that my fighting days were over, but now was not the time to take my stand on that front.

Jaru respectfully took his leave, seeming only slightly more reassured about the festival than he was before I spoke, just as a young messenger padded into the room to whisper something in Nicaro's ear. With a nod of dismissal, the king drained his mug of beer and stood, slapping his palms on his thighs. "I need to go down to the courtyard and meet with Virka and Grabos, who've just returned from a raid. Why don't you"—he gestured toward Igo, who'd still not taken his eyes from me—"and your great beast walk with me?"

"It would be my honor," I replied, glad that the king had returned to his normal cordial manner of speaking with me. The sacrifice of a small portion of land was worth disproving whatever Jaru had said to cause Nicaro's odd behavior earlier. I'd come too far to let some palace guard get in the way of my plans.

⁓

Igo's nails clicked against the tile floor in perfect cadence with my steps as we headed through the great hall toward the grand entrance at the opposite end.

"How is my daughter?" asked Nicaro, as soon as we were alone. "I've been so occupied as of late that I've barely even seen my wives, let alone my children."

"She is well," I said. "She and the other ladies are entertaining themselves with games in the women's courtyard."

"Are they indeed?" He gave me an indulgent smile. "Mariada may be a sweet girl, but she is highly competitive."

I laughed, thinking of the way she'd used her elbow against Jasara. "As I saw firsthand."

His brows arched. "Did you?"

"I taught Mariada and Jasara a simple dice game that I played as a boy in the streets of Ashdod, and after a few of the tosses, I worried they might pull each other's hair out diving for tokens."

He chuckled. "An issue one deals with on a regular basis when multiple wives and concubines live in close proximity."

"I would imagine so." I'd noticed during my visits that although Amunet frequently joined his daughters for meals and amusement, his second and third wives rarely took part. And the concubines were never in attendance, likely at Amunet's request. I could not see the proud woman appreciating reminders of her husband's divided attentions, even if it was expected behavior for a man in power.

"Think twice before you take a second wife, my friend. It's expected of me as king, of course, since it is important for me to forge connections with other dignitaries, but it can be more hassle than it is worth. There are plenty of pleasures to be had elsewhere."

Deeply uneasy with my soon-to-be-bride's father giving me leave to stray from my marriage bed, I nodded and made a non-committal hum in my throat. Although I was not ignorant of the ways of the Philistines, many of whose commitment to marriage vows were loose at best, I'd spent eight years watching the mutual regard and open affection between Elazar and Yoela and had silently coveted such a deep connection. A lifelong bond that I'd once hoped to share with Shoshana.

Although my behavior over these past years was in no way blameless, and I knew Elazar would be deeply ashamed if he knew its extent, and although I was in no way enamored of Mariada the way I'd been with Shoshana when I was young, I *would* be faithful, no matter what justifications her own father might have for sharing himself with more than one woman.

"You mentioned playing dice in the street as a boy," said Nicaro. "Tell me more about your childhood."

Thrown by the odd question, I hesitated for a few moments. Was he suddenly concerned that my upbringing was not worthy of his daughter? "What would you like to know?"

"What circumstances led you to Harrom and Jacame's house?"

I relaxed, remembering that he was well-acquainted with my aunt and uncle. "My mother died shortly after my birth. My father went to sea two years later and never returned."

"Is that so?"

"He came from a far north place. I do not even know its name. But after my mother died, he returned to it. Or perhaps his ship went down on the way. I have no way of knowing."

"I see. And then your aunt and uncle died in the plagues."

I nodded. Watching the two of them suffer from the black boils that overtook their bodies was one of the most terrifying things I'd ever seen. I'd had nightmares for years after that—ones that I'd hidden from Risi because I knew how much it would upset her. The fact that she and I survived the devastation of Harrom's household, and with minimal effects, was a miracle. Risi had attributed it to Azuvah, saying she'd anointed us with oil and prayed to her invisible God to save us, but if there was such a god, he would care nothing for two foreign children. It was simply good fortune. We weren't the only ones to survive in Ashdod. Mataro had as well, and he certainly hadn't offered sacrifices to Yahweh.

"And so your cousin raised you after that?" asked Nicaro. "Taught you to be a fighter?"

There was something in his tone, a renewal of that frosty edge from earlier that unsettled me. Perhaps it was best to unspool a small measure of the mystery to allay any suspicions he might be entertaining. However, I needed to frame my words carefully, like I had with Mariada.

"For a while," I said. "But my older sister and I ran away after she had a falling-out with Mataro."

"You have a sister?"

"I do. But she's . . . gone."

He made a noise in the back of his throat, and his blue eyes became even more intense.

"And this sister helped you survive?"

By joining us to a Hebrew family, I thought. "Risi was always my champion," I hedged. "She would have done anything to protect me as a boy—even from our cousin, whose interests she insisted were less than honorable toward us."

And now that I knew the truth of who Mataro was and what he'd done to Azuvah, I was grateful that she'd done so, even though at the time I'd been angry she made us leave. She must have been so terrified that night. She'd been only twelve years old at the time and had taken on the responsibility for her stubborn seven-year-old brother.

Even as we walked through the main hall, the king was watching me closely. I wondered how much of my regret was playing out across my face.

"Where did you go," he asked, "when you ran from Ashdod?"

The truth merged with the lie so quickly, I barely had to consider my response. "Ekron," I replied, remembering the overwhelming busyness of the city just to the east of here where we'd first gone in search of the Ark, along with my fascination with an enormous man we'd encountered there. One of the giant and elusive mercenaries employed by the Philistine army had been entering the gates of Ekron that day, and I'd vowed then that I would someday rival him in strength and ferocity. "My sister found a family to take us in and worked their gardens. It wasn't until she married that I decided to return."

Of course, I did not mention that the family was Hebrew and those beautiful and prolific gardens Risi tended were atop the mountain of Kiryat-Yearim, not too far from where the Ark of the Covenant was hidden among a grove of ancient cedar trees.

Seemingly mollified by my explanation, he smiled as we emerged from the palace into the sunlight, not far from the area in which I'd fought the Phoenician the day I'd glimpsed Shoshana for the first time. "And when did you return?"

Virka and Grabos, along with a small contingent of soldiers, were waiting in the courtyard below. They were surrounding what looked to be a group of prisoners, their arms bound behind them and cords connecting their feet into a human chain.

Although I was distracted by the sight, I knew he was still waiting for my answer. "I was fifteen when I came back to Ashdod. My cousin was more than generous to take me into his home and soon thereafter to arrange my first few fights."

Nicaro paused at the top of the stairs, not looking at me as he gestured for Virka and Grabos to join us. "And yet it seems you've parted ways with Mataro."

The question sounded innocuous, but the hair on the back of my neck rose. How would he have known such a thing? I'd not aired my grievances with my cousin publicly and had remained cordial with those whose connections we shared.

"We are still family," I replied carefully. "I've merely outgrown the need for his counsel."

He stared at me for a few prolonged moments, but I kept my expression blank until he broke into another indulgent smile. "As one does, of course. You are no longer a boy by any measure. But I do hope you'll consider *my* counsel from time to time."

"Above all others," I said as Virka and Grabos reached us. Igo shuffled backward a couple of steps, a soft whine in his throat. I reached out a hand to soothe him, and he bumped against my thigh, taking reassurance in my nearness. How he'd come to trust me so completely in such a short time was astounding, but I was grateful for it. The house wasn't nearly as lonely with him breathing deeply on the floor beside me all night.

"It looks as though you've returned with victory in hand," Nicaro said to his commanders.

They both bowed in deference. "We have, seren. We've taken Zanoah."

Realizing that the captives below were Hebrews, my eyes skimmed over each of their faces. Even though the town of Zanoah was a ways south of Kiryat-Yearim, it was not outside the realm of possibility that I might know someone there. There were fifteen of them: nine men, three women, and three children—two girls of about eleven and a boy who could not be any older than nine. Although I recognized none of them, I could not help but compare the boy to Yonah, whose blue-black curls were a similar shade. But this boy did not have a foot that twisted inward, causing a halting shuffle, and the eight-year-old who used to call me a brother would now be a man.

Even though none of the captives were Hebrews that I'd known during my time in Kiryat-Yearim, I could not escape the fact that, besides being bloodied and filthy, all of the women's tunics were cut to the navel, their faces blank of expression and their eyes hollow, as if they'd been stripped of not only their hope, but of humanity itself.

Everything Shoshana had told me the other night came back in a furious rush. Had she once stood right here, breasts bared and her violation blatantly on display?

I'd done my best to quash images of what she'd endured since she revealed the truth to me, wanting to keep my focus on plotting ways to free her and her child, but there was nothing to do now but let the truth of it wash over me in a putrid wave.

She'd been raped—violently, if the condition of these women was any indication. And as she'd said, the Philistine soldiers were under no compunction to treat prisoners of war with anything resembling respect. There was no Torah law here to keep the soldiers' depravities and lust for dominance in check. If anything, such demoralizing atrocities were encouraged among them.

And yet, Shoshana had survived. For the sake of her child, she'd refused to let the darkness overcome her. I'd always known she was strong. Even as a girl her backbone was like a rod of iron, and in some ways, I wondered if she was much stronger than I was.

I had run away like a spoiled child all the way to Ashdod, wounded by my perceptions of Risi and Ronen's conversation, along with what I'd thought was Shoshana's rebuff. I'd run away instead of standing strong and acting like the man I'd insisted I was back then.

In my musings over both the past and the horrors Shoshana had endured, I'd missed most of the conversation between Nicaro and his commanders regarding the raid, but when the king asked what was planned for the prisoners, my attention snapped back to him.

"There's a transport to Egypt in a few days," said Virka. "Let Pharaoh have the men for his brickfields to replace those he lost a few hundred years ago."

They all laughed and although my entire body was strung as tightly as a bowstring, I forced a smile as well.

"If only we could send all of them back to Egypt," said Grabos. "It would make our task so much easier."

"Indeed," said Nicaro. "If I have my way, we'll eradicate the whole lot."

It was no secret that the kings of Philistia coveted the Hebrews' territories and the lucrative trade routes they now controlled. But these men were not speaking of merely subjugating the tribes of Israel and demanding tribute. They wanted the destruction of them all—which would include Elazar and Yoela's family, along with Risi and Ronen's.

For the first time since I'd returned to Ashdod, the struggle between our two peoples became very personal, as did the realization that I had been willfully blind to the truth of Nicaro's ultimate goal.

"And the rest of them?" asked Nicaro.

"A trader from Ashkelon has already asked to claim the women. The children are meant for the temple."

Cold sickness spread through my body. These innocents had no idea what horrors lie ahead, but I was not so ignorant. Fury rose in me like I'd never experienced before, even on the fighting grounds. But what could I do? If I made an attempt to fight the soldiers, it would only get me killed. And even if by some miracle I managed to best all twelve of them, and their commanders, none of us would make it past the gates of the city, where a constant guard of ten stood at the ready.

I ground my teeth together. I was the champion of Ashdod and the Master of the Games. Surely I could find *some* way to help these people!

Like a stone-tipped arrow, an idea struck me between the eyes, one that must be handled with the upmost care. Although it gutted me to accept that though there was nothing I could do for the women and children, the men were another matter.

"The land must be cleared for the Festival of Games," I said, interrupting whatever Grabos had been saying. "It seems foolish to send able-bodied slaves to Egypt when we could utilize them here first." Then, in order to throw them off whatever suspicions might be forming, I grinned, allowing Demon Eyes to bleed through my demeanor. "Pharaoh's waited hundreds of years for their return. What's a couple of weeks more?"

I didn't know what I would do once the Hebrews were in my safekeeping, or whether I could find a way to free them, but at least I could give them a reprieve while I considered my options.

Nicaro agreed to my proposal and ordered Virka to have his soldiers lock them in one of the rooms at the city gates until I was prepared to transport them to the olive farm. As well, he offered a rotation of four well-armed guards to ensure that the Hebrews complied with my orders and remained locked inside the watchtower at the center of my vineyard.

The men who were somehow now under my charge were herded

by Virka and Grabos and their men toward the courtyard gates, and behind them came the three despondent women with shoulders bowed and heads down.

A shriek burst from the mouth of one of the young girls below, followed by a wail of "Ima!" The child lurched toward the parade of woebegone captives, crying out for her mother and dragging along the other girl, whom she was tied to.

One of the women looked back over her shoulder, the blankness wiped from her expression and replaced with utter despair. She stumbled as she tried to catch a glimpse of her frantic child and was rewarded with a vicious blow to her shoulder blade by the butt of a spear.

To my horror, one of the two remaining soldiers slammed the back of his hand against the little girl's cheek, the hit so powerful that she and the other girl were both thrown to the ground in a tangled heap, sobbing and clinging to each other's bound hands, and both now screaming for their mother. Cursing the children, the men made an attempt to drag the girls back to standing and apart from one another, but the Hebrew boy suddenly entered the melee. Somehow the child had freed himself from his bonds while no one was paying attention, the cord now hanging from only one wrist. With a battle cry every bit as ferocious as a warrior, he threw himself onto the back of one of the soldiers, one arm locked around the man's neck. The other soldier could do nothing to help since he was busy wrangling the two girls.

Beside me, Igo was agitated, whining and shifting his paws side to side, even rumbling a low growl as the soldier struggled with the boy clinging to him like a barnacle, demanding that the men release the girls. His command was delivered in a voice that was trembling with both fear and ferocity, and before I'd even thought through the implications, my legs were striding toward him.

After a surprising amount of effort, I managed to pry the boy off the back of the red-faced soldier and twisted his arm back with just enough pressure that he yelped. Then, I once again dredged up Demon Eyes and began to laugh.

The harried soldier on the ground blinked up at me in confusion, and even the two little girls paused their frantic fight against their captor, looking up at me with faces streaked with tears, blood, and dirt. I turned away from the gut-wrenching sight.

If I believed that any god cared about them, I would have prayed for their lives. But nothing could save them. I could manipulate Nicaro into using the men as conscripted labor, but there was no feasible excuse for me to purchase two little girls for my household.

The boy, however . . .

"I want this one," I said, grinning up at the king.

"What possible use would you have for that?" Nicaro called to me.

The boy was trembling. With no understanding of our language, he would see me only as a fearsome enemy three times his size.

"Did you see how strong he is? He had your soldier there in a fighting hold. He's ripe for training. And young enough that I can mold him easily."

"You want to turn a Hebrew boy into a *fighter*?"

"When I'm through with him, he won't even remember he *was* a Hebrew. Only that he belongs to me." I twisted the boy's arm harder, provoking him to fall to one knee. I hated to hurt him, but I had to play the part perfectly. "I'll pay double whatever the priests offered. He's wasted in the temple."

Nicaro's brows arched.

I unleashed my most arrogant smile. "He'll make me even richer than I already am."

The king shook his head ruefully, as if he questioned my sanity. "I'll allow it. But if there's any trouble, he goes back to the priests."

I shrugged, as if the condition meant little. "That's fair."

Nicaro waved off the soldiers, giving them leave to drag the two sobbing girls out of the courtyard. It took every bit of restraint in my bones not to chase them down.

Again, I felt that strange urge to plead for mercy to the heavens but pushed the foolish idea aside for the truth. There was no one to rely on in this situation but myself, and I was only one man. I could not save them all.

"For now, he'll tend to Igo," I said, dragging him to standing with little mercy. He would have a large bruise on his arm tomorrow, but at least he'd be alive and safe.

"Your dog?" said Nicaro.

"Indeed. Someone has to clean up after the brute." I made a gesture to Igo, who'd been paralyzed halfway down the stairs, stuck between coming to his master's aid and terror for what might befall him. As if released from his panic by my summons, he bounded down the last few steps and came to my side. "The waste this animal puts out is commensurate with his size, I assure you. And who better to deal with dung than a Hebrew simpleton who needs to learn his place in my household?"

Nicaro chuckled, convinced by my performance. "I'll be out to view the land you've donated in a couple of days. I expect to see progress."

"That you shall, seren." I made a bow. "I think you'll be surprised at just how quickly it all will be accomplished. Well in advance of the solstice, that's for certain."

"Oh, I *know* you won't let me down, Lukio," he said, his smile razor-edged. "You are anything but a fool."

He waved me off and turned his back, leaving me with the distinct impression that I'd just been ever-so-politely threatened by the king of Ashdod.

Sixteen

The boy continued to struggle as I dragged him through the royal compound, filling my ears with every Hebrew curse he could think of, not knowing that I understood every word. I chuckled to myself. He was a strong child to be certain, and not just physically. But he was also frightened and had just watched people that he knew, possibly his own family, be hauled away to endure unthinkable fates.

But revealing myself to the boy was not wise until we were in a more private place, so I kept him in a strong grip and let him fuss and wrestle as we passed down the long open-air, colonnaded corridor that would lead us out of the palace.

Igo remained close to me on the other side, his attention swinging back and forth between me and the boy. The boy, too, eyed my dog anxiously, and I had the sense he was nearly as intimidated by Igo as he was me. Regardless, he kept up his litany of foul curses and clawed at my arm with his bloody fingernails. Dragging the child through the city like this would draw far too much attention, so when we were nearing the most southeastern corner of the palace, near the extensive gardens, I took advantage of a small alcove we came upon and pressed him inside.

"Stop!" I hissed in his native tongue, looming over him. "I just saved your life, and if you don't cease fighting me, people will wonder why I am not bothering to knock the teeth from your head!"

The boy's brown eyes were huge and full of confusion. "How do you speak—?"

"That is for another time. For now, you need to stop screeching like a speared boar and trust me."

A hint of defiance slipped back into his expression and his chin lifted. "You're a Philistine. Your word means nothing."

Again, I held back a laugh. This young Hebrew was so like me when I was a boy, reacting to a fearful situation with fire and spirit to cover his terror. With strange clarity, I remembered the day Ronen had come upon Risi and me in our hiding spot behind a broken-down sheepfold and how I'd wished to be as big as him so I could protect my sister and how I'd also been determined not to let the strange Hebrew man see how my entire body trembled. But Ronen had been so calm and gentle with us, vowing that we would be safe with him. And somehow, even though I had no reason to do so, I had believed him.

Therefore, I used his same words, hoping they would calm the boy as well. "In the name of Yahweh, the Holy One, I vow that I will not harm you."

From the corner of my eye, I saw the door to a nearby garden shed inch open from the inside, so I pressed farther into the alcove, hoping no one would see me standing here with a bewildered Hebrew child and an enormous dog that was nearly as frightened as the boy.

To my profound confusion, *Shoshana* emerged from the door, surveying the area carefully before she fled in the opposite direction. I'd seen her only a little over an hour before up in the women's courtyard, watching her mistress play games. What possible reason would she have for skulking about in a garden shed now?

Before I could collect my thoughts or even decide whether to call to her, the door opened again, and a male head poked out, looking in the direction Shoshana had gone and then swinging his gaze back in the other direction.

Rage shot through me as I jerked back into the alcove to prevent being seen. Because not only had Shoshana obviously been trapped in a small room with a man at least thirty years her senior, that man was Jaru, the very same captain of the palace guard I'd just met in Nicaro's chambers. And there was only one reason a Philistine man would force a young slave woman into a dark room. I didn't care if he was the head of the royal guard. If he'd hurt Tesi, he would pay.

A nearby shout from one of the garden workers to another made Jaru pull back into the shed, and the door closed again. My fists ached to plow into the lecher's face, but what could I do with a child and a dog in tow?

"You cannot move," I said to the boy, "not for anything. If you run off, the guards will consider you a runaway slave and they will not hesitate to kill you. They won't ask questions. Do you understand me?"

He furrowed his dark brows and pressed his lips together. I had no time to wait for his acquiescence, however. I needed to deal with Jaru.

"Igo," I said, pointing at the ground in front of the boy. "Don't let him move from this place." Thankfully, the dog obeyed without pause, stretching his huge gray body in front of the alcove. To keep the child from getting too brave, I added, "And if he tries to get past you, do what you do best."

From what I'd seen of Igo, what he did best was tremble and whimper at the first hint of danger, so I doubted he would chase the boy down if he attempted to run, but by the way the child's face paled, he hadn't guessed that my enormous canine was no more ferocious than a rabbit.

I left the two of them behind and strode toward the shed, allowing anticipation to flood my muscles as I readied my body for a fight. I plowed through the door with all the force of my fury, and Jaru was in my hands in the next moment, with my fingers around his throat.

"What did you do to her?" I snarled through gritted teeth, the images that had tormented me since she'd revealed the truth of Beth Shemesh slamming into me all over again, but this time with Jaru as the one assaulting her.

His dark eyes bulged, the spare light though the open shed door illuminating the confusion on his bearded face.

"Who?" he rasped.

"The girl you had trapped in here with you, you swine!"

"Nothing," he choked out with the little breath I allowed him. "I swear it is true!"

I shook him. "I saw you. Did you violate her?"

"Of course not." He grabbed my wrists in a vain attempt to pull my hands away from his throat. "I would not touch a slave-girl."

Again, I was struck by that same sense of familiarity as he struggled against me, the severe expression on his face tapping at some memory in my mind that I could not place. Then, something on his own wrist caught my eye, dragging my attention away from the man struggling to free himself from my unbreakable hold.

A worn cord was wrapped around his wrist, so dirty that its original color was obscured. But filthy as it was, I would know the distinctive knots along what used to be its blue-and-white length anywhere. It was the very same makeshift bracelet my sister had worn since the night we fled Ashdod—a Hebrew *tzitzit* given to her by Azuvah. In fact, it looked identical to the one I used to skim my finger back and forth over every time Azuvah told us stories at night. I remembered how the motion soothed me while the Hebrew woman sang us to sleep in her gentle tones.

"Where did you get that?" I demanded, another wave of fury making my hands tighten on his neck, even as they began shaking. Had this man taken Risi's bracelet off her body? Was my sister dead?

Jaru blinked in confusion, his brows pinching. "Get what?"

"Where did you get the tzitzit that is on your arm? A raid? Where is the woman who wore it?"

His mouth opened and closed a couple of times. "There was no woman," he said. "I've worn this string my entire life."

"What do you mean?"

He paused, his body tensing and his eyes searching behind me for a moment, as if he wasn't certain whether to say more. I shook him again, determined not to let him deflect the question.

"I'm already ready to throttle you for Shoshana. If you killed my sister, I won't bother to do it quickly."

"I was abandoned as an infant on the shoreline," he said. "It was wrapped around my wrist when I was found. I don't know who put it there or why, but I've always had a strange compulsion to wear it. I've never taken it off."

My head jerked back at the revelation, and I gaped at him. Surely it couldn't be . . .

A whispered conversation came back to me, from some night long ago. On the edge of sleep, I'd been curled up between Arisa and Azuvah while they spoke in hushed tones, thinking I wasn't listening as the Hebrew woman revealed her secrets.

"Azuvah?" Arisa had said hesitantly. "You had a child?"

Azuvah sucked in a pained gasp. "I did. But he was taken from me."

"Where did he go?"

"I am but a slave, sweet child," she replied, her words so sad it made my stomach hurt. "I will never know. But you know your people and their hatred of mine. He was probably left on the rocks to die, swept into the sea. I was only able to hold him once."

She paused and then sighed. "I had just enough time to wrap one of the tzitzit I'd cut from my garment around his tiny wrist before they took him away. A paltry consecration to Yahweh, but it was all I had to give him."

Suddenly, the odd sensation that I knew him from somewhere made sense. Could Jaru be that same babe taken from the woman who'd raised me from infancy, the one who'd died trying to help my sister and me escape Mataro's wrath?

"I didn't hurt the slave," he said. "And I have not killed anyone. I swear it on the life of my wife and children. And I was only meeting the girl here for . . ." His voice trailed off.

"Why? Why else would you force a young Hebrew slave into a dark shed?"

He gritted his teeth. "I did not lay a finger on the girl. I cannot say why I was here. It's too dangerous."

"She's in danger?"

"Although I have no idea why the champion of Ashdod would care about some slave-girl, I vow to you that she is in no danger from me. She merely. . . ." He took a long breath. "She merely relayed a message."

I narrowed my eyes at him. "From Mariada?"

"No."

"Then who?"

"I—I cannot say."

I leaned in close, hoping he could feel the heat of my anger. "You *will* say, or I will ask Nicaro why the captain of his guard is wearing a Hebrew tzitzit on his wrist, a distinctive marker of not only enemy heritage but also the signal of Torah law obedience for those who partake in the covenant with Yahweh."

Even in the paltry light, Jaru's face grew paler and he squeezed his eyes closed. "All right," he said. "I was attempting to help someone. A child who is in grave danger. The slave-girl . . . Shoshana, you said her name is?"

I nodded, allowing my grip on his neck to loosen a small measure.

"Shoshana brought me news about a complication in rescuing that child. That is all. We spoke for only a short while and then she left. Untouched and unharmed. You can ask her, since it seems you are acquainted. I would never harm a woman, let alone a vulnerable slave who is younger than two of my own daughters."

His explanation provoked more questions than it answered, and perhaps I was swayed by the love I'd had for Azuvah as a child, but something deep inside told me that he spoke the truth.

"How would you know about the cord?" he asked. "And why would you think it belonged to your sister?"

I released him from my grip and took two steps backward before running my hands down my face to collect myself. Since Igo hadn't wandered into the shed yet to find me, I guessed he and the boy were still waiting in the alcove. At least I hoped that was the case.

"It seems you and I have quite a few things to discuss," I said. "But this is not the place. Meet me at my home in an hour where we can talk privately."

He paused to stare at me, likely trying to determine if I was leading him into some sort of trap.

"I know who put that cord on your wrist," I said. "And why. I'll tell you everything. But first you will explain what danger Shoshana is in and what exactly she is involved with."

Teitu closed the door behind himself, giving Jaru and me the necessary privacy to speak our minds. I'd charged my head servant with guarding the door, since it was clear that whatever we said needed to go no farther than this room, and I trusted no one more than my faithful manservant.

On the other side of the room, the Hebrew boy, who'd reluctancy told me his name was Zevi, was sitting on the floor, eating the food Teitu had brought in on a wooden tray.

Beside him lay Igo, who'd decided that the tray of food was far more interesting than the conversation between Jaru and me. Somehow, during the short time I'd left the boy and the dog together, they'd struck up a friendship; probably once Zevi had discovered that Igo had no more malice in his big gray body than a feather-down pillow. But at least he'd not run away.

"Tell me," I said, the moment the door closed behind Teitu. "What is Shoshana involved in?"

"What is she to you?" he asked.

How was I to know that I could even trust this man? I'd just met him this morning in a meeting with the king—one in which Nicaro had seemed more than a bit suspicious of me for some reason.

And even if this was Azuvah's child, he was obviously raised Philistine and he'd risen in the ranks as a guard in the palace—something only accomplished by a man of extreme ambition. Was

I placing my trust in someone who could not only destroy everything I'd built but might possibly endanger Shoshana even more? But then again, if one of us did not step into the unknown and speak, neither of us would get the information we wanted. He had little reason to trust me either.

Instead of pressing the question, Jaru instead gestured toward the boy. "Why did you bring him here?"

I hesitated for another moment but then decided that we had to begin somewhere. I would crack open the door of trust, if only a sliver. "He was brought into the royal courtyard with a group of slaves. He was destined for the temple."

Jaru's lips pressed firmly together. The twitch in his eye told me that no further explanation was necessary and also that the idea of a child being treated in such a fashion was just as repugnant to him as it was to me. So, I pushed that door open further and told him the rest. About the men I manipulated Nicaro into sending to work on my olive farm. About the violated women who'd been sold to a southbound trader and the two girls who pleaded for their mother as they were led away. As I relayed how I cajoled the king into letting me have Zevi, I noticed that the suspicion had melted from Jaru's countenance.

"I cannot help but wonder what I could have done for the girls, though," I said, my eyes on Zevi, who was now feeding Igo crumbs from his bowl and talking quietly in Hebrew to the dog. Their desperate cries of "Ima" refused to stop echoing in my mind.

"You did what you could," he said. "Anything more would have caused suspicion."

"Perhaps I could go tomorrow and say I need them for—"

"Lukio," he interrupted. "You did well. Leave the girls to me."

His tone was gentle but firm, leaving me with the strangest sense that I could indeed trust him to aid the children. And now that I'd had the chance to study his face, it was even more apparent to me that he was Azuvah's child. His dark eyes were the same as hers, along with the shape of his nose and mouth.

"Tell me," I said. "What do you know of your origins?"

He took a deep breath and then released it slowly before speaking. "I could be killed for revealing this to you. And my family would suffer too. I don't know how to trust you."

I nodded, resolving in my mind what I needed to say to prove my trustworthiness to him. "When I was seven years old," I said, landing on the thing I knew Nicaro would despise the most about my past, "my sister and I ran away from Ashdod. We ended up in Hebrew territory and were taken into the home of one of their priests. I grew up speaking their language and, for all intents and purposes, living as a Hebrew. It wasn't until I was fifteen that I returned, determined to become a fighting champion. No one besides my cousin knows the truth of my past."

He scrutinized my face for a few long moments and then nodded, seeming to accept my offering as sufficient.

"And Shoshana?"

"A friend from the town in which I lived. I only recently learned she was in this city."

He hummed acknowledgment, then leaned back into the cushioned couch. "As I said, I was found on the rocks one morning by a young woman who'd come to collect shellfish at dawn. She heard my cries and had pity on me. Her husband was a guard in the home of a rich man. They raised me as one of their own but did not tell me of my origins until I was nearly a man. They told me only that the cord on my wrist was a talisman that had saved me from being swept into the sea and never to remove it.

"My father died when I was sixteen years old, and I was given the chance to step into his role. Over time, I worked my way into a post inside the palace. But then one day, I was on duty during a drunken gathering and overheard a high official bragging about the Hebrew child he'd purchased that morning and what he had planned for the girl. It turned my stomach, especially since my own daughter was of a similar age. The urge to do something was too strong to ignore. I had a friend, a good man whom I trusted, help me steal the child away the next night."

"How did you accomplish that?"

"My friend knew a servant in the official's house. She tainted his wine with a sleeping draft and helped the child climb out a window where my friend was waiting."

"And what did you do with her once she was free?"

"My friend knew of a group of Hebrew traders who were in the city. He begged them to take the girl back to their territory. I don't know what happened to her after that, but at least she was not in that house anymore.

"I thought that was the last time I would do such a dangerous thing, but Nicaro began stepping up attacks on Hebrew villages a few years ago, and although most of the captives the soldiers bring back are men to be used for labor or to be put on ships, women and children are sometimes among the prisoners." He gestured toward Zevi. "I could not turn a blind eye. Over the years, my friend and I have very carefully recruited others to take part in these rescues. We take great care in keeping all those involved safe by not revealing names or personal details. Until you told me, I did not know Shoshana's name, nor have I seen her face outside of a dim room. I only know she works in the palace. That way, if one of us is caught, they cannot reveal anything more than their own part in the larger scheme."

"How many have you saved?"

He shrugged. "Dozens, now."

"Just Hebrews?"

He worried at the cord on his wrist. "For the most part, since Nicaro harbors such hatred for them, but there have been a few others who we felt were especially defenseless."

"Do you know what that is?" I gestured to the makeshift bracelet.

"I do. I've seen a few of the Hebrews wearing these distinctive fringes on their garments."

"So, you knew that your heritage is Hebrew?"

He released a weighty sigh. "I suspected as much."

"Her name was Azuvah," I said. "She was taken captive as a young girl and brought into my grandfather's home. A few years later, she gave birth to a son. She had only the time to tie a tzitzit cord around his wrist before he was taken from her."

Jaru's breaths were shallow as he waited for more.

"When my mother died during my birth, it was Azuvah who cared for me and my sister. She taught us her language and told us her people's stories in secret. She called us her light. . . ."

For the first time since I came to Ashdod, I truly allowed myself to remember the woman who'd cared for Risi and me. Who'd been our one constant when our father abandoned us for the sea. Who'd been a mother to us until the day Mataro murdered her.

"What happened?" Jaru asked, his tone suggesting he'd guessed that her life ended tragically.

"She was killed while helping my sister and me escape a dangerous situation, the night we ran to Hebrew territory."

Jaru went silent, staring at the floor.

"She would be glad," I said.

"About what?"

"That you are trying to help rescue those who, like her, were brought here by force and mistreated."

And she would be ashamed of what I've become, I thought. Because for too many years I'd closed my eyes to those who suffered in Ashdod, be they Hebrew or otherwise.

"How much danger is she in?" I asked.

"Shoshana? Minimal, for now. Anyone who found us in that shed would make their own assumptions about what was happening, just as you did. They would likely not guess we are rescuing slaves. However, when she meets with—" He stopped abruptly, pressing his lips together with purpose.

"Please. She was my closest friend when I was young. And even though I'd not seen her for over ten years, I would wrap an anchor around my neck and jump into the sea before putting her in peril."

He scrutinized my face with an intensity that once again reminded me of the woman who gave birth to him. Whatever he saw there must have convinced him of my sincerity.

"A few of the Hebrews in the palace meet together from time to time. To worship their God. Sometimes to pass information."

"What if they are caught?" I said, my voice rising. "I thought you said no one knew each other's names."

He raised a calming hand. "My friend in the palace had been leading worship meetings long before he found his way into our confidence. He insists that they need to come together, or they will forget the words of their ancient leader. It is a risk, to be certain, but I have a trusted man who guards the door to their meeting place. He knows nothing more than to allow five people inside and then to lock the door for an allotted time."

"How can you trust him?"

"Silver is a persuasive argument for silence," he said. "As is the knowledge I hold over him. Knowledge that the king would separate his head from his neck for."

I arched my brows at the callous way he outlined the extortion.

"One must use every weapon one has when innocent lives are at stake."

I could not help but agree. I'd felt so helpless this morning, watching those women and children be dragged away to their destruction, and had wished for just such a weapon in that moment. I'd certainly never expected that one would appear in the form of the child Azuvah had been stripped of so long ago.

"Why are you so suspicious of the festival I've planned?" I asked, remembering how Jaru had glared at me when I'd first entered the king's chamber.

"I'm not," he replied with a shrug. "It was a pretense to suss out details."

"So you can use them to your advantage."

He nodded. "And it would be best if we continue to seem antagonistic toward each other."

I looked over at Zevi curled up on the rug beside Igo, his hand on the dog's shoulder, both of them exhausted from such a traumatic day. It was unlikely I could send him off with one of Jaru's friends anytime soon, since that would only garner more suspicion from Nicaro, but perhaps, in the future, I could send him home to whatever remained of his family. I wondered if any of the men on my olive farm were related to him. And in the chaos of the festival, if those men went missing . . .

"I want to help," I said, ideas beginning to take shape.

"We can't take the risk. You are too recognizable."

"Of course I am," I said. "But haven't you heard? I am *also* the Master of Games."

A slow smile built on Jaru's face, one that was so similar to his mother's that my breath hitched in my chest. "That you are, my friend. That you are."

Seventeen

Shoshana

As I followed along after my mistress and her father, my eyes tracked over the gently rolling hills all around, taking in the green fields to the north, the olive grove to the east, and the long ropes of a prodigious vineyard to the south. When Mariada asked that I accompany her this morning to where the Festival of Games would be held in less than three weeks' time, I'd been stunned when she told me that the land had been donated to the city of Ashdod by Lukio himself for the events. How could all of this belong to a boy who once told me his greatest dream was to build a house for just us with his own two hands?

I imagined what the small, oblong basin might look like when all the slopes that encircled it were covered with spectators. It was the perfect natural arena to afford nearly everyone a clear view of the events below. I'd been told that the king had invited not only the rich and powerful of the Five Cities to partake, but the rabble as well, ensuring that this valley would overflow with excitement and commerce. I could almost hear the roar of the crowd and the call of merchants and feel the tension in the air when their champion stepped onto the grounds to face his first opponent. No wonder the king was grinning so widely as he surveyed the verdant hillsides. This festival would be a triumph—something he could boast of for decades. And it was all thanks to Lukio. I was even forced to press down an unexpected swell of pride in him myself and could not help but wonder whether he would ever have been truly happy in that little house in the woods, even if he *had* built it himself.

Surrounded by a contingent of well-armed guards, a crew of about eight slaves—the tzitzit on their filthy, tattered garments setting them apart as Hebrews—was clearing rocks from the floor of the basin, using wooden tools to dig into the earth, and then stomping the softened soil flat with their feet. Did it even bother Lukio that the men forced into such heavy labors were sons of Yaakov, just like those who once called him *Brother*?

Another group of men was on the opposite hillside, their axes moving in cadence as they chopped down a stand of trees to give the spectators a clear view of the grounds. They left a surprisingly large number of stumps in their wake.

The flash of an ax-head in the sunlight caught my eye, and I was astonished to see Lukio among the workers, tattooed chest bared as he swung a double-headed ax against the trunk of an olive tree. It was an ax I remembered well from Kiryat-Yearim, one I hadn't realized he'd taken with him when he fled. However, for all the time I'd spent larking about in the woods with him back then, I'd never seen him cutting down trees with the two Gibeonites he'd once counted as friends—young men he'd told me he cared little for but who'd helped him learn woodcutting as a means to secure our future.

The immense power in Lukio's arms as he swung the ax was unmistakable, even from as far away as we were standing, as was the smile he unleashed as the tree toppled to the ground.

"Magnificent, isn't he?" Mariada murmured in my ear while her father hailed Lukio with a wave.

My back stiffened, but I could not refute the statement. His golden-brown hair was loosely braided down his back today, so the sunlight played on the strands as he crossed the basin, every powerful stride he took toward us reminding me that he was no longer a boy. Igo leapt out of the shade of one of the remaining trees to bound along beside him, tongue lolling, delighted to be out in the sun with his adored master. A small dark-haired child followed after the two of them, one whose presence I had no explanation for and who looked very small next to Lukio's overwhelmingly large build.

"I cannot believe that I'll be his wife soon," my mistress said, pulling my attention away from the boy. "My mother said it will be a wedding feast to remember. Every woman in Ashdod will envy me my handsome husband."

I made a noncommittal noise in my throat, hoping she'd take it for something like agreement, while at the same time I squelched the desire to tell her that Lukio was far more than just a handsome man in a well-honed fighter's body. He was the kind of man who would rescue a frightened dog from a vicious fight; the kind who befriended a lonely girl two years younger than himself and whose laughter and good-natured teasing had never failed to brighten the darkest of her days; and the kind whose brief embrace on the terrace had made me dangerously hungry for more. But yearning after a man I would never have was beyond madness, and I certainly had no right to resent her.

I was his past. She was his present and his future.

When Mariada and the king went forward to meet Lukio at the center of the valley, I remained where I was, grateful to be far enough away that I would not be tempted to listen. I refused to so much as lift my eyes to meet his, lest he somehow see my inner turmoil and guess its root was envy. I must push my petty jealousy aside to focus only on my daughter's rescue and on my work with my Hebrew friends.

Instead of going to his master's side, Lukio's gray dog came toward me instead, as if he'd recognized me from the other day. And behind him, black-haired and wiry, came the boy, approaching me with far more caution than the animal.

Just before they reached me, the boy reached out to tug at a leather collar around the dog's neck. "No, Igo," he said. "Stay back."

At the sound of familiar words flowing from his tongue, all my tumultuous thoughts about Lukio and Mariada vanished. The boy was Hebrew.

Unsuccessful in his attempt to keep the dog away from me, he was dragged along behind Igo, whose shoulder nearly met the boy's own. He muttered futile chastisements to a beast whose strength would outmatch his twice over.

By instinct, I reached out to allow Igo to sniff my fingers. He nuzzled them and then slipped his enormous head into my palm in obvious demand for a caress. How could anyone have pitted this sweet animal against another in a fight?

I kept my voice low as I spoke to the boy. "Of what tribe are you?"

His chin jerked up, and he met my eyes with his own, their shade a honey-brown that glowed like burnished walnut in the sunlight but was full of an ancient sadness that made me want to enfold the child in my arms. This boy had suffered—greatly—and I could not help but remember another boy whose dual-colored eyes called to me in such a way.

"You are Hebrew?" His brows drew together.

I nodded, then took a quick look around to make certain no one was paying attention. Thankfully, Lukio was gesturing toward the vineyard, drawing Mariada's and the king's gaze to the south.

"I am Yehudite," he said, his shoulders straightening in pride for his tribe.

"Of which town?"

"Zanoah," he replied, then pressed his lips together in a tight line for a moment before continuing in a small voice. "But it's gone now."

My gut twisted. His grief-stricken expression told me he was speaking of more than just the town. I sensed that this child was completely alone in the world. The longing for my sweet Asher suddenly welled up, mixing with the urge to comfort the boy in front of me. Would my son remember how much I loved him? Would Aaliyah? They'd been so small when we'd been ripped apart. . . .

Swallowing hard, I forced the agonizing thoughts away so I would not weep. "You serve Lu—the champion now?"

He shrugged. "I am in charge of Igo."

What reason would Lukio have for a slave who tended only to his dog?

"How did that come about?"

"I tried to attack a soldier and he stopped me. Then he took me to his palace."

I had no doubt that Lukio lived in a large home, but I guessed that most of the houses in Ashdod looked like palaces in comparison to the humble dwellings of the Hebrews. Many of our people still lived in tents, following their herds to seasonal pastures, and had done so since Yehoshua led us into the Land of Promise.

"He treats you well?" I asked.

His mouth twisted in half-hearted agreement. "He does not hit me."

Without meaning to, the child revealed more about himself with those few words than he meant to, revealing the source of some of that grief behind his eyes. Only someone who'd endured the same sort of abuse would hear the relief in such a simple statement.

"What is your name?" I asked.

"Zevi."

"I'm Shoshana. I am Levite."

He nodded, his gaze dropping to Igo, who bumped against Zevi's leg with an affectionate nudge. The ghost of a smile flitted over the boy's lips before he squelched the reaction to the dog's unreserved devotion.

Before I could ask more about Zevi's time in Lukio's house, a man similar in age to Lukio but dressed like a servant approached us.

He looked to be at least part Egyptian, lanky and handsome, but he possessed only one eye. The other was covered by a strip of linen tied about his head that barely hid the jagged scar from whatever violence had taken it.

"My apologies if the dog disturbed you," said the man, his low voice full of gentle apology.

"Not at all," I replied. "He simply remembered me from a visit his master made to my mistress the other day."

His brows lifted. "You are the maidservant to his betrothed?"

"I am."

"I am Teitu, Master Lukio's manservant." His one eye took in my face with a searching sweep that made me shift on my feet. "Go on back to the shade, Zevi." He gestured across the valley.

But Zevi did not understand the Philistine words and merely frowned at him.

"Go on back," I said to him in our common language. "Wait for your master."

The boy looked back and forth between Teitu and me before nodding and turning away, Igo lumbering along after him without hesitation, but my instinct to run after him and wrap my arms around him did not abate.

"Fear not," said Teitu. "He is safe."

I blinked up at him, realizing that my concern must have been written all over my face.

"I have been in this city for five years now, and I have never seen a master treat his servants with such respect as does ours. The boy is more of a guest than a slave, I assure you."

"Why is that?"

He sighed, an enigmatic expression on his face. "Master Lukio does not share his thoughts with me, even though he trusts me above all others in his home, so I cannot say for certain. But he saved me from a life of backbreaking labor when no one else considered me fit as a house slave." He touched the linen covering over his missing eye. "And there are others within his household who have similar stories. From what I've heard, Zevi was destined for the temple."

Nausea flamed up my throat. Nothing good happened in the temples of Philistia. Lukio had rescued Zevi from unthinkable abuses. A strange thought—that Yahweh had placed him in the exact right place to do so—floated thought my mind. Oshai constantly reminded those of us who met in the wine cellar that although we could not save everyone, every life was precious, formed in the image of Yahweh himself. It seemed Lukio had not forgotten some of the lessons he learned in Kiryat-Yearim after all.

Against my better judgment, my gaze was drawn to Lukio, and I startled when I saw that he was watching me over the king's shoulder while Mariada addressed her father. Warmth spread outward from my chest, tingled in my fingers and toes, as something inexplicable and weighty passed between us. When his eyes narrowed slightly, going to Teitu at my side, I had the odd sensation that he was jealous of his own manservant. But when the king spoke to him again, his attention was drawn away from us.

"I will watch out for him," said Teitu.

"Zevi?"

He hummed in response. Then, so swiftly I had no time to react, he reached out and pressed something into my hand. "Both of them," he said, then turned to walk back over to where Zevi and Igo waited in the shade.

I curled my palm around the object, not needing to look at it to know that Lukio wanted to meet with me again tonight. And risky as it was after Amunet's pointed warning, after hearing Teitu speak of Lukio's unexpected compassion toward those in need, I doubted I could stay away.

Eighteen

"Where is Kina?" I asked Galit as soon as I'd taken my place beside her on the wine cellar floor. Usually the young woman was the first to arrive, and more often than not, was brimming with secrets she was eager to share with us after spying on her mistress. Out of all of us, Kina was the most enthusiastic about her mission, taking great pleasure in her ability to be surreptitious, yet always ready with a bright smile, in spite of the dangers. Her absence made the dark cellar a bit more shadowy.

Oshai and Avel were engaged in a hushed conversation in the corner, their expressions unreadable. Although I'd been glad to attend our usual shabbat meeting, I could not help but hope that Oshai would hurry through the traditional prayers tonight. Midnight was not far off, and the terrace was on the opposite end of the palace from here.

"She's attending the king's second wife, along with both of her handmaidens," said Galit. "They've all three come down with an illness and required aid."

I'd heard that Orada had been ill as of late, but it wasn't a surprise, since she seemed to be a sickly sort and eschewed spending much time with the other women in favor of seclusion in her chambers. But to hear that others were suffering the same illness was worrisome. I'd seen entire families stricken by fever in Beth Shemesh and for weeks had been terrified that my own children would contract whatever curse had swept through.

"Has anyone else in the palace fallen victim?"

Folding her arms and leaning them forward to her knees, she nodded. "One of the cooks. She spent days in a fever calling out for her mother who died years ago. But she recovered. She's been pale and fatigued but has been back in the kitchen."

"Then perhaps it's not anything too serious."

"We can only hope." She leaned in closer to me. "Have you spoken anymore with your . . . old friend?"

I shifted on my seat and cleared my throat. "Not yet."

She arched her dark brows.

"He sent another shell," I said, twisting my fingers in my lap and avoiding her gaze.

"And you are going?"

"I shouldn't."

"But you'll meet with him anyway." There was no question in her voice.

I worried my lip with my teeth, embarrassed that she could read me so easily. "One last time. There is too much at stake to continue. Though I cannot help but wish . . ." I let my words die away, confident that she knew me well enough to read my underlying meaning.

"I understand." She frowned, something pinching between her brows as she squeezed my hand. "Perhaps more than you know."

Before I could ask what she meant, Oshai called us to order. "Let us offer up a prayer of thanks to Yahweh for these moments we have together, and then Avel will share some news about an unexpected rescue that will undoubtedly lift our spirits."

I stifled a yawn with a palm, my early morning wandering out to the festival grounds catching up to me, as Oshai began a half-whispered prayer of gratitude to the Eternal One. My mind wandered as the meeting dragged on, revisiting Lukio out in the valley, my conversation with Teitu, and the boy whose past might well be similar to my own. If this was my last time speaking with Lukio, I had quite a few questions about what he had planned for Zevi.

". . . we can be glad," Avel was saying, when my attention

shifted back to its proper place, "that somehow our friends rescued the two girls in time—"

The latch on the door juddered, halting Avel's words. Then, in the next breath, an ominous clank of metal on metal followed at the same moment Oshai snuffed out the lamp. Within the next two frantic heartbeats we were moving, just as we'd practiced.

Ten steps forward in the pitch black brought me to one of the wide, waist-high storage jars that lined the back of the cellar. Holding my breath, I squeezed between it and its enormous neighbor and tucked myself in the narrow space between the frigid limestone wall and the ample stores of wine and beer.

The lock made another terrifying grind before the door swung open, but I could see nothing more than a dim spill of light from the corridor, which illuminated the back wall far above where I crouched in the darkness.

For all the months we'd been gathering here, we'd been close to discovery twice, both times when the king's steward came to fetch a cool jar of wine, most likely to remedy a restless night of sleep. But both times the man had been unaware that five Hebrews were hiding in the deepest shadows, measuring their breaths and praying that the God Who Sees would blind the man's eyes to their presence. But tonight, whoever stood at the door carried no lamp and did not bustle in with purpose. Instead, a rasping whisper stretched across the space between the threshold and my hiding place.

"Shoshana?" said the voice.

All the hair on my neck and arms answered the call, but I was no fool. I remained pressed as close to the floor as possible while my mind whirled with all the possibilities of what my name in the mouth of a stranger at the door might mean.

I gripped my hands together while they shook like palm branches in a thunderstorm. Was my time in this palace at an end? Would I never see my daughter again after this moment?

"Shoshana" came the whisper again, the deep timbre of it more familiar this time but also more inconceivable. One of my shaking hands slammed to my mouth. Surely it couldn't be . . . ?

"Tesi?" he said, confirming the most bewildering of my suspicions. On instinct my head reared back and knocked against the wall, adding a spike of pain to my confusion.

Blinking against the rattling sting against my skull, I slithered around the jug until I could see the partial outline of a man in the doorway, one that nearly blocked the muted flicker of the lone lamp illuminating the few stairs behind him that led down into this cold cellar.

"I'm here to help. Come out." The familiar form with far-too-broad shoulders took another couple of steps forward, his movements stretching his long shadow on the back wall. "Your friend in the shed sent me. You all are in danger. You must scatter."

If this was a ruse to trap us, it was certainly a strange one. What possible reason would the man in the shed have for sending the champion of Ashdod to warn us? But for as perplexing as the situation was, I knew in my bones that one thing had not changed over the past ten years—I could trust Lukio with my life.

I scuttled out of my hiding spot and stood, but the rest of my companions remained silent and hidden.

"How did you . . ." I began.

"There's no time," he said, his features still shrouded in shadow. "Everyone needs to leave this room. One of your friends, a young woman, was taken, and there is reason to believe that she will be forced to divulge your connections."

Kina? Dread wrapped tightly around my throat. I could not fight off the image of the sweet young girl suffering the Philistines' notorious abuse of prisoners. A crowd of questions pushed forward. But as he'd pointed out, I had no time to interrogate him.

"Friends," I said, stepping forward until I could see Lukio's features more clearly. "Cover your faces and go. I know this man. I trust him."

Galit emerged first with her scarf pulled over her mouth and nose. Her dark brows arched high when she saw who was standing in the doorway but she said nothing as she walked by me. However, she brushed my hand with her free one as she passed, and I could almost hear the silent admonition to be safe as she slipped out of the room and up the stairs.

Avel came out of hiding next, his eyes wide at the sight of the champion of Ashdod standing in the center of the room, but with his hand over his face and his head bent low, he too escaped the room without a word.

"Where's the guard?" I asked Lukio, surprised that the man who'd obviously opened the locked door for him was not nearby.

"He's gone. Another is being sent to replace him," said Lukio. "One who knows nothing. That's why we must leave right now."

Oshai approached last, not bothering to hide his face. "What do you know of the girl they took?"

"She's been accused of cursing the king's second wife in the name of Yahweh," said Lukio. "Orada is dead, along with one of her handmaidens."

My knees wobbled. How could an innocent girl be blamed for the deaths of two people who'd fallen ill before she was even sent to help? "But she—"

"I'll tell you what I know, but not here." He reached for my hand and tugged me toward the door. "We need to go before the other guard comes. I don't know how long we have."

I followed Lukio up the stairs from the cellar while Oshai latched the door behind us.

Oshai paused for only a brief moment in the corridor, his gaze briefly flickering to where Lukio still gripped my hand in his. "Thank you. I don't understand any of this. But I am grateful." Then he snuffed out the one lamp that still flickered in a nearby niche and jogged away, leaving the two of us alone in the dark. I opened my mouth to let free the first of a thousand questions but instead Lukio's fingers entwined with mine, locking me in his grip as he pulled me in the opposite direction Oshai had gone.

"Come," he said as I tripped along behind him into the blackness. "I know you are perishing of curiosity. Let's find somewhere to talk."

Nineteen

To my surprise, instead of finding myself led to the terrace where we'd met before, Lukio took me to the garden shed. He tugged me inside, and after checking to make certain no one had seen us enter, closed the door.

Heart pounding from our flight through the palace, I let silence lead, waiting for him to explain himself. But all I could hear was the sound of his labored breaths.

Finally, after a long exhale, he spoke, his disembodied voice strange but comforting in the blackness. "You met Zevi."

"I did. How did you find him?"

He told me of what he'd witnessed when the latest group of captives had been dragged into the courtyard, how he'd been given permission to use the men for his building project and that he'd managed to convince the king that he wanted to teach the boy to fight.

"The women are long gone," he said, his voice rough. "There was nothing we could do once they were transported south. But Ja—" he paused—"your friend in the shed somehow managed to get the two girls out of the temple. I don't know how. It seems as though he has a wide network of others who are involved and that he will not divulge details, but he assured me they were indeed safe."

"That was *you*?" I whispered. It must have been this same story

Avel had been in the middle of explaining when Lukio had burst into our meeting. "You were part of freeing those girls?"

"Only in that I told him where they could be found."

"It is enough," I said, my eyes misting over as I breathed a prayer of gratitude that he'd been in the right place at the right time.

"But how could you possibly have known anything about what we've been doing?"

"I saw you," he said, "coming out of this very shed on the day that I purchased Zevi. When I confronted the man you were speaking with, I discovered that he was known to me. In fact, I'd had an exchange with him earlier that day."

That certainly answered the question of how he'd known the significance of this room. "You saw him in the palace?"

He took a deep breath. "I think it best to leave his identity a mystery, as well as the reason I knew him, both for your safety and that of his family."

I'd not given much thought to the man's identity outside of our secret meeting place, other than to conclude that he was a man of privilege from his talk of wagering silver on Lukio's fight. But to hear that he had a family who might suffer should our connection be revealed made my respect for him grow even more. I would include his family in my prayers for his safety from now on.

"Did you somehow coerce the information from him?" I asked.

"In a way."

I frowned, guessing he'd used his influence with the king to his advantage, perhaps had even promised to reveal him unless he explained what I was involved in.

"I did not threaten him, if that is what you are thinking," he said, with a note of amusement in his voice. "I can hear you scowling even in the dark."

He still knew me so well after all these years. He did not even need to see my face to know what went on inside my mind.

"I had valuable information to offer him in exchange," he said, "something he was as desperate to know as I was to ensure your safety."

I ignored the way my chest warmed at his words. His worry for me was only out of respect for our former friendship. "Many precautions are taken to make certain I am not in harm's way. I carry messages, that is all. For the most part, all I risk is censure from Mariada for not attending to my duties in a timely manner."

He made a soft noise of frustration. "I should think that to-night would disabuse you of the notion that you are invulnerable, Shoshana."

I brushed past the admonition. "So, this man trusted you enough to have you come warn us? Whatever you hold over him must be damaging indeed."

"Not damaging in and of itself," he said, "since the man has proven his worth in his position. But it would certainly cause Nicaro to ask questions."

"And you won't tell me what bargain the two of you made?"

"I won't tell you something that could endanger you further. The less you know, the safer you are. You should know that from your dealings in this . . . this group you are part of. The Philistines are not gentle with their methods of making enemies talk."

"So that *is* what is happening to Kina," I said, my voice warbling as I thought of the vibrant young girl and her melodic laughter. "She's being tortured?"

"I don't know. Our friend only said she'd been taken somewhere for questioning and that her heritage was at the center of the accusations. I'd known that Nicaro harbored animosity toward your people, but until that day in the courtyard, I hadn't known the extent of his hatred. He doesn't just mean to take over Hebrew territory and demand tribute, or even just to control the tradeways. He means to either kill or enslave everyone."

"Why?" I asked. "Other than lust for our land and resources like the rest of the kings, what makes him so determined to wipe us out?"

"His father and mother were both buried under the rubble of the temple in Gaza," he said, "along with the three older broth-ers who should have inherited the throne ahead of him. That left

Nicaro, at barely seventeen, with a city-state to rule. He was the only king of the Five Cities who was against the idea of sending the Ark back. He wanted to destroy it. And he means to find it now and remedy that oversight. He believes it is a rallying point for your people, one that keeps them from capitulating to his constant barrage of raids and skirmishes."

"They are your people too," I said, "in a way."

His soft laugh was rueful. "Yes, because I was so warmly embraced by the people of Kiryat-Yearim."

"There were far more people on that mountain who did accept you than did not, Lukio. And a good number of them who loved you dearly. But you refused to accept that love." I gentled my voice to speak the truth. "You outcasted yourself in many ways."

"Perhaps" was his soft response.

I was somewhat stunned to hear him make such a concession. It was one of the few disagreements he and I had during our talks in the woods. I'd told him how much I admired Elazar's family, but he'd done everything he could to downplay their kindnesses.

"When I saw Zevi in the courtyard," he admitted, "I could not help but compare him to Yonah. Perhaps it is only his age or his black curls, but whatever it was, it made my decision for me." A note of amusement leaked into his tone. "I remember how he used to follow me about. Smiling. Always smiling and chattering at me like a blackbird."

He paused again, and I was certain that, could I see his face, there would be regret in his eyes. "Was he truly so devastated when I left?"

The deep well of contrition in his voice was purely that of the Lukio of my childhood, not the arrogant champion of Ashdod. This was the man who, regardless of the way some of the townspeople treated him, secretly delivered firewood to some of the families who could not collect it themselves, either because of illness or age. Neither did anyone other than me know that some of the reason he didn't like Yonah following him about was because he worried the boy would get hurt, either by falling trees as they worked or by his Gibeonite friends who mocked the deformity of his foot. But I felt compelled to be honest with Lukio, even if it wounded him. He needed to know the damage he'd caused with his disappearance.

"He was," I conceded. "He was inconsolable for days, thinking that you'd decided he was too much of a bother. And for months after that he barely left the house. No matter what Eliora told him, he felt he'd driven you away."

"That could not be further from the truth."

"I know that. But you were anything but open with others beside me. I could never understand why, when I would have given my right hand to be part of Elazar's family, that at times it seemed you were angry with them for their kindness."

"Not angry," he said, the words so soft I barely heard them. "Jealous."

Again, his honest response surprised me. "Of their acceptance of Eliora?"

"No. I never questioned why they would love Risi so much. One cannot help but know that she is everything good in the world. It was *her* affection for them that I envied."

"But she adored you. Her heart toward you never changed. I'm certain it still has not, regardless of your foolish decision to run away."

"She was *my* sister," he said. "My everything. For my entire life it had been just Risi and me. Truly, in many ways, she was a mother to me. And when we arrived in Kiryat-Yearim, it wasn't only the two of us anymore."

"You were angry that she wanted to be part of their family?"

"I suppose so. And I was angry that she kept me from Ashdod and all the things I thought I wanted. I begged her for months to go back. But she refused to even entertain the idea. I blamed Elazar and the others for persuading her to remain. The resentment festered inside me for so long that I was unable to look at any of it without bitterness, nor was I mature enough to see that I was blaming all the wrong people for all the wrong things."

"I'm glad you did not succeed in convincing her to leave," I said. "I cherished our friendship, secret though it was."

"As did I." The intensity in those words reached through the dark and curled themselves around my heart. We both went quiet, the stillness highlighting just how alone we were.

"I . . . I missed you," he whispered.

I held my breath while my heart thumped about, wrangling with such an intimate confession.

"Lukio, you cannot say such things to me—"

"Do not misunderstand me," he interrupted. "I am marrying Mariada, as the king has asked me to do, and I have no desire to dishonor her."

My mouth dropped open as I processed the implications of his statement. "It was not your choice to marry her?"

"Although I'd hoped to marry soon, I hadn't even met her. Only seen her from afar. The marriage is tied to my position, like any other political arrangement. I spent the last few years building myself into someone the king would appoint as the Master of Games, and he made it clear that my acceptance of the appointment included joining myself to his daughter."

"Who *did* you plan to marry?" I heard myself asking before I could think better of it.

"I had no one specific in mind," he said. "I only wanted someone to walk beside me. To fill the enormous house that I occupy with new life instead of merely the echoes of my own sandals." He paused, and I heard a smile in his next words. "Although Igo has brought a fair amount of life to the place. And although he doesn't trust me in the least bit, Zevi certainly brings his fair share of energy as well."

I could not help but press into what he'd revealed. "You desire children?" I asked, hating the sickness that twisted inside of me at the image of Mariada growing round with his sons and daughters.

"I do," he said. "I've always wanted a large family of my own. Like Elazar's, in fact. I'd even once imagined that . . . with you."

The last two words were barely above a whisper, but I felt

them all the way down to my toes. My eyes stung as I dropped them shut, unable to push away the pictures they drew so vividly behind my lids. Lukio and me, together with my children—the children that should have been his. Asher would have loved to ride about on Lukio's broad shoulders, and I had no doubt that Aaliyah would have had the man wrapped around her smallest finger.

"I need to go." I forced out the words through lips that had gone numb. "I've been gone far too long, and I must get some sleep before Mariada wakes with the sun. Thank you for alerting us to the danger," I said as I moved to press past him.

But instead of letting me go, Lukio somehow found me in the dark, loosely hooked his arm around my waist, and halted me before I could reach for the door. "There was a reason I asked Teitu to give you a shell, even before I discovered that your friend had been taken. I have some ideas of how to get you out of the city. Although it may be a few weeks before I can—"

"No. I told you I won't leave without my daughter."

"I know, I don't expect you to. But you are not safe here. Either of you. And our mutual friend will help, I'm sure of it."

I gasped. "You can't tell him. What if he tells someone else? Tela could hear something and then I might lose my position." Panic welled up, tightening my throat. "I need to be near her—"

His hand tightened on my waist. "It's all right, Shoshana. I haven't said anything yet. And he would not betray us. He is a man of honor. You've had enough interactions with him to know that, even if you don't know who he is."

"Even so, there are too many guards around this place to get her away undetected. There's too much risk in attempting to smuggle an infant out without a sound. A cry from either Tela or the nurse-maid would bring death down on all of us. It's not time yet."

"It's not safe here," he said. "The arrest of your friend should be proof of that. And I could not bear it if something happened to you." There was a hum of something indefinable in the statement, something that reminded me of the piercing way his eyes

179

had held me captive this morning in that valley. "Please, Tesi," he whispered. "Let me help you. Let me help your daughter."

I dropped my chin, breathing out a warbling sigh that he took for acquiescence.

"I won't attempt anything without your permission, I promise."

"And what is it you are planning?"

"I've decided nothing just yet. But I need you to trust me. I'll let you know when the time is right."

"I have a right to know what we are getting involved in," I said, my frustration rising.

He groaned softly. "You always were a stubborn one, Tesi, nearly as much as Kalanit."

My lips twitched at the subtle jab. The old red donkey in Elazar's household had been named for a graceful poppy flower but was known for digging her hooves into the dirt at the most inopportune times.

"The boy who tended her was even more so," I responded, returning the dig. "Where do you suppose she learned it?"

He chuckled, and the sound that vibrated in his chest burrowed beneath my skin. It was so much lower than it had been back when we were friends, but it had the same ability to warm me from the inside and make me feel safe. Cherished.

Thankful that he could not see me, I closed my eyes again. It didn't matter what turbulent waters had passed between those innocent times and this fleeting moment of clandestine reconnection in a garden shed, I would never stop loving Lukio. And try as I might not to cling to false hope, I could not help but wonder if he would succeed in finding a way to get us out of the city, something I'd not been able to accomplish in all these months. Perhaps his betrothal to my mistress, and the influence his new position in the royal household afforded him because of it, would be a blessing after all.

I disentangled myself from him before I succumbed to the temptation to wrap myself around him and beg for him to run away with us too. But even if he regretted leaving Kiryat-Yearim the way he had, he'd given no indication that he wanted to return. He had wealth beyond belief here and the adulation of everyone in the city. His marriage to Mariada would secure those things for a lifetime, even if it meant remaining with the enemies of my people. What could he have in Kiryat-Yearim other than the simple life of a woodcutter, in a home that was not so much bigger than this garden shed?

Before I opened the door to escape into the night, I paused to speak over my shoulder. "I trust you. Leave me a shell when you are ready to share your plans."

Twenty

Lukio

I did not remember much of my aunt Jacame or uncle Harrom's funerals, only vague recollections of people wailing and the blood on my older cousin's arms and legs after they'd cut their skin to display their grief. But I did remember Risi standing next to me, holding my hand while she trembled. It was strange to miss my sister during the funeral procession for the king's second wife, someone I'd never met, but the wave of longing for her soothing presence came over me, nonetheless. There was so much distance between us now, both physical and otherwise, but I would never stop missing her.

Up ahead of where Mariada, her mother, and I walked among the solemn procession was a wagon led by four majestic horses and decorated with garlands of flowers from the palace gardens. In the bed of the wagon was a brightly painted ceramic coffin in which Orada's body had been placed, the second wife of Nicaro being honored by a royal burial befitting any queen. The frown on the face of Amunet when the extravagantly appointed wagon appeared in the courtyard had not escaped my notice, and I suspected it had nothing at all to do with regret over the loss of her rival for Nicaro's attentions.

By the time the procession reached the area designated for burials outside the city walls, a large number of townspeople had gathered a short distance away from the royal family, their curiosity driving them to take part in mourning for a woman who'd been so sickly in the past few years that most of them would not have known her face should they see it in the street.

As we waited for the coffin to be unloaded from the wagon and the priests and priestesses to arrange the funerary implements, including two tall incense burners and a small two-horned altar, I could not help but be aware of Shoshana's presence just behind Mariada and me. However, I did not look her way, no matter that my entire being protested the necessity of pretending she did not exist.

It had been two days since we'd spoken in the garden shed, since I'd nearly forgotten myself and hauled her into my arms right there in the dark to see if her lips were still as soft and sweet as I'd remembered from the one and only time when I'd had the courage to kiss her. It had taken a great amount of restraint to let her walk away once again, especially after admitting how I'd dreamed of having a family with her. When she returned my tease about Kalanit's stubbornness, it had reminded me just how deeply I'd cared for her and made me realize that such affections had not withered with time. In fact, seeing her now as a woman, one who'd endured such terrible tragedy and yet was still so graceful and strong, only made her that much more compelling in my eyes. But I'd given my word to the young woman beside me, and I refused to dishonor her, no matter how much my soul ached for the one at my back.

Orada's coffin lid was carefully removed and the family invited to bring forward their burial gifts. The first to approach was a loudly weeping Tela, supported by her husband, Virka. She placed what looked to be a carnelian necklace beside the linen-wrapped body before tearing the sleeve from her dress in a show of grief. Then, although Orada's face was obscured by a mask of some sort, Tela bent to place a kiss on the grotesque representation of her mother's notoriously beautiful features. One by one, the rest of the family followed Tela's example, bringing all manner of gifts to place in the coffin and on the ground beside it—bowls, cups, carvings, idols, and other trinkets meant to ease her spirit in the underworld. A bevy of flowers, including the bouquet of lilies I'd laid near her feet, perfumed the air of the cemetery with something other than the stench of death that was already emanating from the body.

Finally, Nicaro himself stepped forward, dressed in ceremonial garb that reminded us he was not only king of Ashdod but Supreme High Priest of the city as well. Kneeling at Orada's side, he bent the head he'd shaved as a sign of mourning over her death mask and remained in that position for so long that the crowd around me began shifting on their feet. However, no one dared to interrupt the king as he mourned.

The sun was nearing the edge of the horizon, falling golden over the sea, but still Nicaro did not move. Only after four priestesses lit their torches and positioned themselves to the north, south, east, and west around the king and the coffin did he stand and face the assembly. His blue eyes seemed particularly intense as he lifted his head to survey those gathered in honor of his wife.

"Orada, daughter of Sirute, born of the exalted tribe of Mijaru, one of the original clans to land on these shores, was a woman of great honor," he said, his regal voice ringing out over the crowd. "She bore me four strong sons and a daughter with whom I am well pleased. Orada's beauty will be spoken of for many lifetimes and the generations she gave birth to will endure for thousands of years."

Only time would tell if his brash predictions would come true. The strong and prosperous city that he ruled suggested it might, but I'd heard another man speak words of foreknowledge, one who claimed to be a prophet of Yahweh, and I did not believe either of them could truly know the future.

"But for as much as she will be remembered for her regal grace," he continued, "she will also be remembered as the victim of a heinous crime."

A chill swept over my skin as the implications of his announcement sank in. It was just as Jaru had said: Shoshana's friend was indeed being blamed for Orada's death.

"A murderer slithered into my house. An enemy whose entire goal was to sow discord and to curse my beloved wife in the name of her foul god."

A tense murmur went up in the crowd, especially in the townspeople. For Nicaro to state such an accusation so openly, to admit that an enemy had found a way to infiltrate the royal household, was a bold statement, one that did not cast Nicaro or his guards in a good light. But knowing how astute the king of Ashdod was, he had to have a motive for speaking so brazenly about such a failure in security.

"But fear not," he said, "the evil one was rooted out after she was caught whispering curses over both my dying wife and her maid. And she *has* been brought to justice."

I could practically hear Shoshana's heart thumping from a few paces away, but I dared not turn around to see if she was holding herself together at the announcement that her friend had most likely been killed in retribution for something she had not done.

"We can only be grateful that this plot was uncovered before the Hebrew sow did any more damage to my household. For who knows what sort of destruction she could have caused unchecked."

The fervor with which Nicaro unleashed on the innocent girl was startling. But I had the distinct sense that I was seeing the true king of Ashdod for the first time. He was ruthless. Shrewd. Willing to twist the truth into a tale that matched his purposes. Wondering if anyone else was shocked by the transformation before us, I allowed my eyes to skim over the faces around me and found my gaze crossing with none other than my cousin Mataro, who stood off to the side of the gathering. I'd only caught sight of him a few times since I'd made my break and thought him to be nothing more than a specter of my past that had quietly faded away, so I was stunned to see him here among the mourners, most of whom were either directly or indirectly related to the royal family. When he saw that I'd become aware of his presence, he raised his brows in a gesture of subtle challenge, seeming to dare me to call him out for being among the group. But as I'd determined to do weeks ago, I refused to let him have any hold over me, so I kept my face blank and turned my attention back to Nicaro.

One of the priests handed the king a small lidded pot decorated with sacred symbols that swirled over the surface in bold black and red. With both hands Nicaro lifted the vessel over his head.

"Behold," he said, his voice taking on a distinctly religious tone, "the blood of the guilty one, taken as payment for that which will never again bloom on the cheeks of my beautiful rose."

A choked sound come from behind me, and my entire body went stiff. Shoshana could *not* break down at this confirmation of her friend's death and draw attention to herself, or it may very well be her own blood spilled next.

As if she were again standing beside me now to witness this travesty, my sister's words from the past suddenly whispered into my ear. I remembered the day she spoke them to me with perfect clarity. Just before I met Shoshana, I'd come home after an altercation with some of the boys down in town, and I'd used every Philistine curse I remembered to call down destruction on their heads. Instead of chastising me for my vitriol, Risi had slipped her arm around me and pulled me close to her side. *"The gods we grew up with in Ashdod are nothing like the Hebrews' God, Natan. He is not made of stone or wood. He hears those who call on his holy name for deliverance. Ask him to rescue you."*

Even though my instinct had been to lean into her and press my face into her shoulder, I stiffened in her hold, annoyed that she'd used the Hebrew name she'd given me, instead of the one I'd been called since birth. I did not understand why she'd embraced the ways of Elazar's family so easily and without reservation.

"A Hebrew god doesn't care anything for me," I'd snapped.

"Elazar says that Yahweh holds no regard for our earthly heri-

tage. He is the Eternal One, the One who existed long before there was any such thing as a Philistine or a Hebrew."

I wished I believed her assurances now as I silently willed Shoshana to keep her grief contained. No god had ever come to my assistance, then or now. But perhaps, for Tesi's sake, he would have mercy. . . .

My half-formed thoughts were scattered when Nicaro crossed to the flaming altar and removed the lid of the pot. Slowly, he poured some of the contents over the flames, the liquid gleaming scarlet as it trickled into the fire. Another of the priests dumped a basket of what looked to be hair mixed with leaves of some sort into the blaze. I assumed it must be the same hair Nicaro had shaved from his head to display his grief when Orada died. Then a priestess approached to pour a generous libation of wine into the center of the foul-smelling offering.

Once the sacrifice was complete, Nicaro returned to stand behind Orada's coffin and placed the jar inside as the final burial gift before two of his men came forward to place the painted lid on the vessel and seal it with pitch.

I'd hoped that the closing of the coffin would signal the end of this strange and unsettling night, but instead, a number of servants wound their way through the crowd, handing out crudely formed cups before others followed in their wake with jugs, pouring a generous measure of drink for each mourner.

The strong odor emanating from the cup pressed into my hand was distinctive and familiar. This was not simply a cup of wine to lift in tribute to the dead woman, but a drink tainted with a heavy amount of nutmeg and other herbs that would dull the senses and blur the sharp edges from our thoughts.

The king raised his own goblet, one that would contain twice as much of the noxious brew. "May the spirit of my lovely Orada be at rest in the bosom of the Great Mother," he said. "And now that her murderer has been brought to justice, may she grant us the strength to pay back those who sent the woman here—the same detestable tribe from which the devil Samson originated."

A murmur went up among the crowd as this new accusation took on shape.

"Yes," he said, his voice growing stronger. "This treacherous Hebrew woman was of the same blood as he who murdered both my mother and my father, the great Darume, and we will return their villainy upon their heads tenfold."

A number of shouts of agreement went up around me, encouraging Nicaro to continue his rant.

"And we will not stop once the Danites are annihilated," he vowed. "We will deal with the rest of the Hebrews, who have killed far too many of our people and prevented us from claiming the land the gods led our forefathers to long ago."

When he lifted the goblet to his lips and tipped back his head to drink deeply of the bitter substance, the rest of the assembly did as well. I, however, had no desire to lose my wits tonight, or any other night, so I feigned the motions before tipping my cup toward the ground and praying that the deepening shadows would hide my deception. With their cups drained, the mourners smashed the vessels on the stony ground, the sound of shattering pottery seeming to inflame them as they cheered our king and his call for vengeance, adding their own calls for the Hebrew scourge to be scrubbed from the land.

If only I could spin around, gather Shoshana in my arms, and flee, so she would not have to endure such vicious hatred for her people. But I could do nothing but remain still and hope that no one remembered that one of the bodies that stood among them flowed with the blood of those they pledged to destroy. In their fervor, they just might tear her apart. My fists clenched tight, preparing to come to her defense if so much as a whisper went up against her.

The strength of my own anger surprised me, and not only for her sake. The venom Nicaro spewed toward the people I had lived with for years, those I'd known to be mostly peace-loving, simple people only interested in tending to their farms, herding their livestock, and raising their families, was so contrary to my experience.

In fact, I could not help but remember how Elazar had spoken out against the way most of the Hebrews had cut peace treaties with the Canaanites and Philistines, how they traded extensively, intermarried, and even incorporated many of their worship practices into their own. And yet here was Nicaro threatening to not just dominate them or cause them to pay tribute, but to wipe them out. He was using this contrived murder of Orada to enflame his people's hatred of the Hebrews—hatred that would be aimed at my sister, her husband, and their children. Unlike Zevi, who'd been hauled into Ashdod for the sake of being sold into horrors, Risi and I had been invited into Elazar and Yoela's home and offered the respect, kindness, and hospitality for foreigners that was mandated by Torah law. And it was becoming increasingly apparent how woefully ungrateful I'd been for such goodness, along with how willfully blind I'd been to the true nature of my own people.

Now that the sun had completely slipped into the sea, torches held aloft by a number of priests and priestesses encircled us, the flicker of which only added to the sinister atmosphere of this morbid gathering in a place where hundreds, if not thousands, of Philistines were interred beneath our feet.

While the people around us continued to chatter with animation, their tongues loosened by the drink they'd imbibed, the priests and priestesses formed themselves in a long line, some still carrying torches and a few with hand drums or beribboned sistra. The drums began to pound a slow but sensual beat and those with sistra held them aloft, shaking the metallic instruments in a cadence reminiscent of a viper-tail warning. Then the single-file procession began to move, winding its way through the group, which parted to make room for the strange parade. Distinctly serpentine, the line slithered through the crowd, both men and women unashamedly bare-chested.

Since I'd pointedly avoided temple rituals in the years since I'd returned, I'd never seen this dance performed, but from the chants coming from the mouths of the participants, this display was both in honor of the underworld and the malevolent spirits that ruled it and a supplication for Orada's soul to be received into their divine embrace.

As the chain of temple workers passed by me, I noticed that some of the women carried live serpents. A few looped the long and colorful creatures over their shoulders and others held venomous heads in careful grips, while the snakes wound around their arms in sinuous and threatening coils. Although many of the mourners shied away from the dangerous display, others reached out to stroke the deadly animals, too stupefied by the tainted wine to count the cost of such folly.

One of the famous rituals carried out by these same priestesses had been brought by our ancestors from our ancient homeland. After either allowing vipers to bite them or cutting their bodies so drawn venom could be dripped into the open wounds, the women would writhe on the ground like animals themselves and claim vivid and divine visions. After such fits, they often would be locked into frightful paralysis, sometimes for hours, until the effects of the venom wore off.

Thankfully, this unsettling dance ended before any such madness took place, but just as the day I'd foolishly followed my Gibeonite friends Adnan and Padi to one of their high places and witnessed the foul things practiced by the Canaanites, a deep sense of wrongness spread throughout my body. There was nothing good or beautiful in this. There was only malevolence and darkness that chilled me to the marrow of my bones, making me want to flee, the same way I'd done as a boy. No longer did I wish for my sister to be here with me now; she would be horrified by all of this.

Once the priests and priestesses had returned to their positions in a loose circle around the gathering, Nicaro lifted his palms over Orada's coffin. "I make this vow to you, my beloved. Not only will I ensure that your blood is thoroughly avenged, but I will make certain that what should have been done centuries ago will no longer be neglected. The Hebrews will rue the day they left Pharaoh's mud pits and mourn the moment they stepped foot in this land."

Spittle gleamed at the corners of his lips as he ranted, and the black of his eyes nearly consumed the blue. He looked wholly unhinged, and I wondered how much of it was the drink and how much was madness leaking from the deepest parts of his soul. Those fathomless eyes then moved over the crowd and landed on me for a moment that seemed to stretch into eternity. Never was I so glad for the detached and haughty expression I'd cultivated for the fighting ring over the years, as I returned the king's stare with a dispassionate one of my own. When he blinked and looked away, I could only hope that I'd been successful in concealing the maelstrom inside me, because the plans I'd been making with Jaru were far too important. The last thing I needed over the next couple of weeks was Nicaro's scrutiny, or his suspicion.

"And not only will the Hebrew's golden box soon be turned to splinters and ash," the king declared, "but the name of their worthless God will be forgotten for all time."

Twenty-One

Shoshana

Mariada had been quiet all day, not only during that terrible and sinister funeral but even earlier this afternoon, as I'd been helping her into the fitted bodice and multilayered green-and-blue skirt that seemed more suitable for a celebration than a mourning ritual. Assuming she was mourning Orada, I'd kept quiet, but by the time we'd returned from the burial grounds, where I'd discovered that poor Kina's life had come to such a horrific end, my mistress appeared nearly as distressed as I felt.

She sat on the stool in front of me, pale-faced and vacant-eyed, while I unwound the braided bun that I'd fashioned atop her head only a few hours before. It was far past the time she normally retired, so she might only have been weary, but I sensed something else was amiss. Mariada was never this reticent, always chattering to me about anything and everything as I prepared her for bed each night.

"Are you feeling ill, my lady?" I asked as I began to remove the many shells and beads that I'd woven into the braids.

"I don't feel the same way," she said, shifting to look me in the eyes. "I hope you know that."

"I'm not certain what you mean."

"I don't hate your people like my father does. Especially you." She pressed her lips together, brow furrowed deeply. "I know he is still angry about what happened to my grandfather when that temple collapsed, but that was so long ago and the man who pulled it down died anyhow. And I certainly don't understand why he would blame that maid for Orada's death when everyone knows she and her maids were sick long before the Hebrew girl was called in to help."

There was no way to easily explain to this sheltered and naïve girl about all the history that had passed between our people, and how the struggle for the Land had been going on for hundreds of years. Nor did I dare tell her that her father seemed to be afflicted with the same sort of baseless hatred that Pharaoh had—hatred that was rooted in something deep, ancient, and inexplicable to someone who knew nothing of Yahweh.

"Did you know her?" she asked, her tone compassionate.

"No," I lied, for my daughter's sake.

"All the same, I wish you'd not been there tonight. I had no idea what he had planned with the . . . altar." She swallowed hard, and I knew she was remembering the sight of the blood spilling from that pot into the flames. I'd heard rumors of such terrible things in their blasphemous temples, but to see it with my own eyes, especially when the victim of such an atrocity was someone I knew . . . It was astounding that I'd even managed to stay upright. It was a miracle that I'd refrained from throwing myself at Lukio from behind and sobbing into his back. All I'd wanted in that moment had been the comfort of his presence. I'd spent the rest of the ceremony with my eyes firmly shut, praying that Yahweh would keep me on my feet and that I would be invisible to the enemies all around me who were practically crowing for my own blood with every one of the king's pronouncements.

"I was worried that they all might turn on you right there," she said, her voice warbling. "And I would not have been able to do a thing."

How did such a tenderhearted girl come from the line of a tyrant like Nicaro of Ashdod?

"You must stay close to me, Shoshana. I don't want you hurt."

"Of course, my lady," I said, glad for the task of unbraiding her hair to keep my shaking hands occupied.

"No more sneaking out at night."

My startled gaze flew to meet hers in the large copper mirror atop her vanity table.

"You didn't think I was truly ignorant of your midnight wanderings, did you?" A sly smile quirked her mouth as she shifted to look up at me.

"But . . . but how? You are always asleep soon after sunset."

She bunched her lips to the side. "I may drift off early like my mother, but my sleep is as light as a cat. No matter how soft-footed you are, I usually wake either when you are coming or going."

All my blood seemed to drain into my feet and, leaving half of her hair still in braids, I slumped onto the nearby couch so I did not crash to the floor.

"Don't look so upset. I've never begrudged you a bit of freedom when your duties are complete. If I had, I would have said something before now. I trusted you to be discreet."

I could not wrap my mind around the idea that all these months she'd known of my duplicity. But did that mean she also knew where I'd been? I could not ask without drawing attention to the true answer.

"But you must tell your lover that it is no longer safe. Not after what my father did to that young woman." She winced at her own words.

Face blazing, I sputtered, "My . . . my lover?"

"He's the one leaving shells for you, is he not?"

My mouth gaped open. I'd truly not given this young woman enough credit. She was far more observant that I'd ever guessed, and apparently I was far less stealthy than I'd believed myself to be. I could only hope that she would never know that it had been her own betrothed I'd met on a few of the nights I'd stolen from her room.

"Not a lover," I said. "Only a friend. We . . ." I paused to clear my throat and give myself a moment to compose a believable story. "She and I are both Hebrews," I said, thinking of my rare talks with Galit in the wine cellar. "We only speak of our homes and those we miss."

Mariada frowned. "Are you truly so miserable here?"

"No. . . ." I hedged, not wanting to offend her. "You are the kindest of mistresses. I owe you so much. My life and that of my . . ." I let the words dwindle, uncertain of whether to say more.

"Of your baby," she finished for me.

I nodded, my insides twisting into the usual knots I experienced whenever I thought of my child. Mariada and I had never discussed my daughter, except for the day I'd gone into labor and she'd had a midwife quietly escorted to her room, something no normal Philistine master would do for a slave.

"If I could have done so without repercussions, I would have let you keep her," she said. "I hope you know that. But Tela was so adamant about having her. I worried they might send you away if I argued against it." Her black brows furrowed above sorrowful blue eyes. "Amunet suggested as much, and she is not one to be trifled with."

I was speechless at such revelations. I'd never guessed Mariada had been so determined to keep me with her.

"But why?" I asked, braving a question when she'd been so open with me. "Why do you care whether I stay here?"

She chewed on her lip for a moment. "The day you were brought here, I was in the courtyard," she said. "I know you did not see me, but I'd been returning from the gardens with Jasara. I saw the soldiers bring you and the others in. I'd seen prisoners of war before, of course, when my father's men brought in groups destined for the port or heavy labor, but I'd never seen them up close."

My chest ached as I was thrown back to the humiliation of that day. I had been so focused on remaining upright and not shattering into a million pieces that I likely would not have noticed had the entire royal household been watching.

"But then I saw you, and the sight made me ill. I'd never thought of women being treated thus. And it was clear what had happened to you." Her voice softened. "Your tunic was ripped and there was . . . blood on your legs." She heaved out a shuddering sigh and shook her head mournfully. "I'd lived in this beautiful palace my entire life and never comprehended the cruelty of our soldiers. But unlike the other three women who were with you that day, you did not hang your head. You are so small, almost fragile-looking, but your back was straight, as if you were determined to meet whatever came next with dignity. And I couldn't take my eyes off you. I don't even really know why—it was almost like I was compelled by something deep in my bones to take action. I had this strange feeling that I wanted to be like you—so strong and bold, even after all you'd endured—and I knew that I needed you by my side."

I almost laughed at the characterization of those moments in the courtyard. If only she'd known that my knees were knocking together as I stood in front of those awful men, one of whom had brutally violated me, trying not to lose what bile was left in my empty stomach after the long, brutal march from Beth Shemesh.

"I went straight to my father and asked for you to be my hand-maid. I told him that Makila, the servant I had before, was not to my liking and I wanted her replaced." She grinned. "And we all know that my father is partial to me since he adores my mother so much. It did not take much persuasion to have you sent to me."

"I had no idea," I said. I'd figured she'd truly needed a replacement for the woman whose position I'd filled.

"I've never regretted it. My sisters are far bolder than I, as you know, even with their husbands, and I could never be as forceful as Amunet, but having you near me has been a reminder that I should not be fearful of my own shadow." She reached out to grip my hand. "And although you are my slave, you've also been a good friend to me. You always listen to me so patiently. I could not bear to see you hurt . . . or worse." Tears formed in her crystalline eyes. "So, please, remain in this room at night."

I nodded, still too stunned to form any sort of coherent thoughts.

"Good," she said. "I hope that my father is far too distracted by the festival to remember your heritage. No matter what, I won't let him take you from me, but it's best not to take any chances, at least not until things settle down."

"Of course, my lady," I said, although I knew much better than to think the king would ever relinquish his vow of vengeance against my people. His rants had bordered on madness tonight.

"Will you call me Mariada when it just the two of us? I always search for my mother when you call me that."

A smile twitched on my lips. She was truly such a sweet and kindhearted girl, and I nodded.

"Good," she said, her answering smile making her appear every bit the radiant woman her mother was, and one who would be a fitting wife to the most handsome man in Ashdod.

I stood to resume unbraiding her hair—and to take my mind off the twinge of jealousy in my gut.

"She is beautiful," she said as I took my place behind her.

"Who, my la—? Mariada."

"Your daughter."

I held my breath to keep in the sob that surged into my throat.

"She will have your eyes someday, I think. Such a pretty and unusual mix of colors."

I'd not been close enough to my baby to know such a detail, my greedy eyes only glimpsing dark hair and a precious face from across the room.

"And now that she laughs," she said, "she has that same dimple in her cheek that I've seen on yours, during the rare occasions that you smile broadly."

I could do nothing to stop the tears that spilled over, and I was glad she was faced away from me as she innocently twisted the spear of grief deeper into my soul. But somehow she must have sensed my pain. She swiveled around on her stool and looked into my eyes.

"I wish it were different," she said, her tone strong and sincere, "between your people and mine, so we could simply be friends. Or at the least that I had enough power to have stopped Tela from taking her."

"As do I," I said. "I would count myself blessed to have a friend such as you, no matter our heritage."

She gave me another sweet but rueful smile and turned back around to let me finish my task. But before I did, I placed my hand on her shoulder. "And thank you. For choosing me that day. I will always be grateful. If you had not, I am certain that neither I, nor my child, would have lived."

Twenty-Two

Lukio

My footsteps echoed in the dark as I headed home after Orada's funeral. The streets were empty, my only companions the sort of creatures that embraced deep shadows. Although I had nothing to fear from these night dwellers, human or otherwise, I missed Igo, having become accustomed to his quiet presence at my side. But I'd been right to leave both him and Zevi at home, far away from tonight's ghoulish ritual.

The death of the Hebrew girl lay heavily on me, even though I could have done nothing to save her. Yet whenever I thought of that blood dripping onto the altar, it was not a young slave's face I saw in my mind, but Tesi's.

Mariada had turned away once to speak quietly with her mother, and for the first and only time since we'd arrived at the internment grounds, I'd allowed my eyes to drift to Shoshana. Still standing just behind us, she'd looked so small among my compatriots, the same group of people who'd just cheered for the blood of her own kinswoman. I'd expected to see terror in her expression, but when she lifted her gaze to meet mine, her abject grief was palpable enough to wash over me like a tidal wave.

She'd lost so much. Her mother, her brothers, her children, and now a friend in the most heinous of ways. I wanted nothing more than to wrap my arms around her like I had when I was a boy, to hide her away from the pain of the world beneath our sycamore tree, and to vow that I would protect her from now on—the way I hadn't done when I left her behind. It was only a moment that our gazes connected, yet it felt as though a thousand words passed between us before I was forced to turn away from the woman whom I'd thought I would marry and toward the one who would soon be my wife—something that was becoming more difficult with every brief encounter.

As I ambled through the slumbering city, trying to force thoughts of what could have been from my mind, I could not help but remember the day I'd returned to Ashdod. With a belly full of anger, I'd strode through the streets that day in awe of the bustling spectacle that was the city of my birth. Dazzled by the inspiring buildings, finely tailored garments, and beautiful women who appreciated my face and form, everything I'd laid my eyes upon that day had made Elazar's family seem backward and uncultured.

I'd sneered at the Hebrews' simple way of life in their rough-hewn homes atop the mountain. I'd thought their laws rigid and their stories of miracles and split seas ridiculous. I'd compared the God they worshiped to the many bejeweled and well-crafted ones that decorated the homes of the Philistines and ridiculed the idea of an invisible deity who cared anything for a barely confederated nation of shepherds and farmers—let alone saw them as his treasured children the way Elazar, and my sister, had insisted.

For years, Ashdod had glittered in the sun for me, like the iridescent shell I'd given Shoshana, but the shine had finally worn completely off. After witnessing what I had tonight, I could no longer deny that my sister had been right about our people.

Although the Hebrews did offer animal sacrifices to Yahweh, the prayers that accompanied such gifts were mostly in gratitude for his goodness, supplications for his protection, and pleas for forgiveness. There was no lascivious flouting of naked bodies, no sensual and unspeakable acts committed for the sake of the fertility of the land or the people. There were no offerings of human blood on the altar or infant immolations. I'd avoided the temples here for so long that I'd been able to fool myself into believing that none of it mattered, but now I was forced to admit that the reason I'd done so was because such acts reminded me of the vast differences between the life I'd walked away from and the one I'd run headlong into.

So lost in my thoughts, I did not notice the footsteps gaining on me until I was nearly at my own front door.

I swung around, fists at the ready and body tensed for a fight.

Mataro stood three paces away, hands uplifted. "It's only me."

"What do you want?"

"Can a man not visit his cousin? It's been too long since we've spoken."

Remembering the oddity of his presence at the funeral tonight, I did not relax my stance. Mataro never did anything without a hidden motive. "I have nothing to say to you."

His hands drifted down as he took another step toward me. "We're family, Lukio. The same blood runs in our veins."

The light from the nearest window, undoubtedly lit by Teitu in anticipation of my return, illuminated the blackness of Mataro's enlarged pupils. He must have drunk deeply of the laced wine tonight.

"All I've ever desired was your success, cousin. And I can still be of help to you."

"You want only to help yourself to my wealth."

He shook his head. "That's not true. I am proud of all you've accomplished. And you're all I have left of my family, Lukio. I have no sons. You alone are my legacy. Why wouldn't I want the best for you? Let me be of service to you in your new position."

I huffed a disbelieving laugh. "And how would *you* help *me*? I have plenty of men to do my bidding and the king's ample resources at my disposal."

"I have friends in important places, friends who can ensure that this new festival of yours is a success. Those men I was telling you about from Gaza, they have a new fighter—"

I put up a hand. "I don't need anything from you. Go home. Sleep off your drink."

I turned to go, wishing I could put this awful night behind me but knowing I'd likely lie awake on my bed, dreaming up ways to get Shoshana out of Ashdod safely and without detection.

"I would not be so hasty to dismiss me, Lukio." Mataro's tone had lost all pretense of cordiality. "Those same friends who can help you can also work against you. It would be a shame if they did so."

My back stiffened, but I kept my composure as I turned to look at his face, still marked with scars from the plague that had taken my aunt and uncle and the rest of our family to their graves. The shadows thrown by the lamplight caused the pitted valleys across his skin to appear even more macabre.

"That sounds all too close to a threat, *cousin*." I leaned heavily on the word.

His palms turned up in supplication. "I would never presume to threaten you. Only to make you aware that there are whispers."

I arched my brows, inviting him to continue. "About?"

"There are those who question your appointment and the king's decision to give a common fighter so much power."

I opened my mouth to refute him, to remind him that I was not just a fighter but a wealthy landowner, whose goods were traded all over the Great Sea.

"Not me, of course," he said quickly. "I always knew you had great potential. Even in your youngest years, you were remarkably cunning."

"I am not concerned about gossip," I said, with a flip of my hand to brush away his empty flattery. "The king knows he can trust me. He gave me his favorite daughter, did he not?"

"And there's no one more worthy of such a fortuitous match."

Opening the door to my house, I turned away from his false praise, too exhausted from the emotion of the day to listen to another disingenuous word from his mouth.

"I did find it interesting, however . . ." The sinister drawl of the words made me halt with one foot over my threshold. "That you seemed far more interested in your bride's maid tonight than you did the king's daughter. A Hebrew, correct? And quite a delectable little one at that. A recent mother, too, from what I hear. So she's certainly experienced."

My blood turned to ice. He must have seen that brief but silent interchange between Shoshana and me. Although I was more than tempted to turn around and choke the life from him for even laying his filthy gaze on her, instead I curled an arrogant smile worthy of Demon Eyes on my lips and shrugged at him. "Mariada will be my wife in a matter of weeks. Who is to stop me from taking a taste of what will soon be mine, after all? You?"

My stomach roiled at degrading Shoshana to a piece of property, but for her sake and that of her daughter, I barked a laugh, shaking my head in mock amusement. "Go home, Mataro. Count what's left in your purse, if anything, now that you don't have me to leech off of. And don't come back here again."

Leaving my cousin to scuttle back into the shadows, I entered my home with a pointed slam of my door and then leaned back against the wall to calm my raging pulse.

Why could I not keep my eyes to myself? I'd put her in even more danger tonight with my foolish yearnings for the past. *Please* . . . I began, but then shut down the fruitless prayer before it could take shape in my mind.

Yahweh may listen to Risi, who was everything good and kind, and perhaps even Shoshana, who took great risks to rescue her vulnerable kinsmen, but no matter what my sister said, the Hebrew god would have nothing to do with the likes of a brutal fighter who'd run away from his sacred mountain and embraced every self-indulgence Philistia had to offer.

But no matter how useless I'd been to Shoshana in the past, and no matter the sins that blackened my soul, I would not stand by and watch her suffer any more loss. I would get her and her child out of this city, even if it cost me everything.

Twenty-Three

I stood in the center of the well-packed fighting grounds, surveying the oblong area that had now been completely cleared and flattened. Already wagers were being made on some of the more prominent fights that would take place three days from now, my own included, and a large group of young men had volunteered to take part in the opening bouts that would precede the organized matches. Everything I'd planned for the festival was coming together seamlessly, and the entire city buzzed with anticipation, yet I no longer cared. The only plan that mattered was the one I would be discussing with Jaru today.

I allowed my gaze to move over the prolific olive orchard and vineyards that I owned, which, along with the fields of barley and corn, had produced far more than even my overseer had projected for the past couple of years. I was wealthier than I'd ever imagined, even as a boy wandering about the woods of Kiryat-Yearim, dreaming of returning to Ashdod and claiming the fame Mataro had promised me. But I was more than willing to risk it all if it meant that Shoshana could return to her home and her children. Her friendship had been an oasis of joy in the midst of my lonely childhood, and I owed her everything.

"Is everything ready for the festival?"

I turned to find Jaru approaching, looking as though he'd gotten about as much restful sleep as I had over these past few days.

"Almost," I said, gesturing to the group of Hebrews and their ever-present guards under one the trees that remained along the ridge. "They're taking a break in the shade for now."

Jaru grunted his approval, his eyes moving over all the progress we'd made. I'd joined in the labors a few times over the past week and could not deny that I'd enjoyed felling trees again for the first time in a decade. I'd ignored the curious looks by both the guards and the captives as I'd done so, almost reveling in the burning blisters that had formed on the hands that had grown unaccustomed to slinging an ax.

Not until recently had I realized how much I missed the smell of wood dust, the crack of a mighty tree giving way to my strength, the roar of its fall, and the shaking of the ground beneath my feet as it hit the earth. It only made me more determined to be done fighting for good. I would have my final match here on these grounds and, hopefully by then, Shoshana would already be back in Kiryat-Yearim with her little ones. I swallowed against the ache in my throat when I thought of never seeing her again, of losing her a second time, but I vowed to be content that she was safe and free.

"It is truly impressive what you've managed to accomplish, Lukio," Jaru said. "I will admit that when I heard you were replacing Oleku as the Master of Games I did not have much confidence that a young man who'd done little more than fight with his bare hands could organize a festival like this one. But you proved me wrong, and I am glad for it."

I ignored his meaningless accolades. "I need your help."

His brows arched in surprise at my urgent tone. "After the assistance you've provided my people, both with resources and information, I am at your service."

I'd not done much to aid Jaru's rescue efforts, merely provided the location of the two girls so they could be freed and donated a small cache of silver for bribes. I'd never been more grateful for my wealth and access when he told me the girls were safe. Perhaps after Shoshana escaped, I'd get more involved in his schemes. After marrying into the royal family, I'd have plenty of opportunity to do so—if, that was, my own plan did not burn my standing with the king, and therefore my betrothal to his daughter, to the ground.

"The woman you've met with in the garden shed. Shoshana. We need to get her out of this city."

He shook his head. "As much as I would like to help every slave in Ashdod, we must conserve our energies for those who are most vulnerable. Your friend lives in the palace, Lukio. She is safe. Well fed. Not being sold for her body. If she were a child in danger, it would be another matter."

Although I felt fairly confident that Jaru was trustworthy, I hesitated to reveal Shoshana's secret. I would never forgive myself if something were to happen that would keep her from her daughter. But without Jaru's help, the idea I'd been working on would fail. I needed his contacts in the palace, his network, and his expertise in such matters.

"Shoshana may not be a child, but her infant daughter is being held in the palace."

He flinched. "Her child is in Ashdod?"

I nodded, my stomach churning as I revealed all that had happened to Shoshana and how Tela had stolen her baby just after birth.

His dark eyes were sorrowful as he contemplated my revelations for a few quiet moments. "I am sorry, Lukio. I wish we could help, but it's just not possible. Even with the men I have under my influence, smuggling a baby out of the royal residence is beyond risky—it's downright suicidal. Nicaro is fiercely protective of his family. If any one of us got caught stealing a baby he considers one of his grandchildren, he would not only have our heads but those of our entire family. I cannot risk my wife and children for a babe who will grow up in lavish splendor and treated as royalty. I am sorry for Shoshana. I truly am. She is a sweet girl who has never wavered in her commitment to helping us. But it's just not possible."

I'd anticipated as much, but I'd considered every angle. "My cousin came to visit me two nights ago, after the funeral. He knows about Shoshana and me. And he did not make his threats to expose her subtle in the least. He must have some sort of connection within the palace, too, because he seemed to know about the baby."

Jaru's jaw twitched as he considered this news.

"If he exposes the child as an imposter, as a Hebrew, I fear for what Nicaro might do. You know our king. Any whisper of subversion to his power is squelched mercilessly, and any talk of a Hebrew babe being raised in his home would be a threat to his reputation for certain. In fact, he might even kill Shoshana, too, just to keep the entire thing quiet."

Jaru's gaze moved to the west, toward the seashore where he'd been found by compassionate Philistines. He was a good man. One who risked much for those who could not protect themselves. But I sensed that he was not convinced. I hated to use my last weapon, but I'd do anything to make sure Shoshana and her baby were safe.

"If you will help me with this, I vow that I will never reveal what I know of your network."

His head whipped around, his eyes piercing. "And if I don't?"

I shrugged, letting my fighter's arrogance bleed through. "I will do what I must to protect her."

There was no mistaking my veiled threat. I had no intention of revealing his rescue efforts, knowing that his entire family would be at risk if his role were uncovered, but I was desperate enough to feign such ruthlessness.

He glared at me for a few moments, assessing the hardened expression I'd fixed on my face.

"She was more than your friend, wasn't she?" he asked, reminding me again of his mother and her uncanny way of exposing artifice. More than a few times Azuvah had caught me in lies, and with little more than a pointed look, had cowed me into spilling the truth.

"We were to be married."

"You were betrothed?"

"Not yet. We were too young at the time. I'd been working

toward that future when everything crumbled to pieces. She married someone else to satisfy her father's debt."

"I see."

"So, will you help me?"

"You've given me little choice, haven't you?"

"One must use whatever weapons one has when innocent lives are at stake."

His mouth quirked at my use of his own words against him. "And how do you suggest we go about kidnapping a baby from the palace?"

I exhaled in relief, my body relaxing for the first time since we'd begun this conversation. "I have a plan, but it will take coordination. And the assistance of some unlikely participants."

"Who?"

I gestured across the field, toward the Hebrew men who'd spent the last few weeks toiling on my land in the hot sun all day and then chained up within my vineyard's watchtower at night. "It may take some work on our part to convince them."

"The transport to Egypt is scheduled for the night before the festival begins," he said. "There's no time to involve them in a rescue, nor to organize everything that must be in place."

"The festival will give us the perfect cover." I explained the entire plan that I'd dreamed up over the last couple of days and was encouraged by the wise suggestions and resources he offered to shore up weaknesses in my plot.

When I was finished, he huffed a laugh, shaking his head. "Well, I can certainly say one thing of the great Demon Eyes. He never lacks audacity."

Then he clamped his square palm over my shoulder in a fatherly gesture that made me feel that he'd forgiven me my bluff about turning him in.

"She's worth risking all of this?" His gaze took in my rich landholdings.

"She is."

"And yet you don't plan to go with her?"

The images came to me unbidden. Returning to the mountain. Seeing my sister again. Growing old with Shoshana at my side. But on their heels came the reminders that I'd thrown away everything Elazar and Yoela offered me and spent the last decade wallowing in Ashdod's every vice. There was no going back.

Besides, what sort of future would I be able to offer Shoshana? I was still an enemy of her people. Through my body flowed the blood of those who'd violated her, enslaved her, and stole her child. Regardless of the friendship we'd had in the past, none of that could be forgotten, or forgiven.

"My profile is too high. This entire plan is built around my presence at the festival. Nicaro's attention must be on me, the wealth pouring into his city, and how all of this will solidify his influence over the region—not on a paltry number of escaped slaves. If I disappeared and threw the festival into chaos, he would be livid, send a contingent after me. Shoshana is safer if I remain where I am."

He hummed in response, and I wondered if he could sense how deeply divided I was. But instead of arguing with me, he patted my shoulder one more time. "All right. Let's go talk to these Hebrews of yours."

Together, we crossed the field to where the Hebrew men sat in the dappled shade of an acacia with their guards. They looked exhausted. I'd been very careful to treat them as if they were nothing more than forced labor and had not interfered when the guards lashed out at any who lagged in their tasks. It had been a necessary evil to keep the appearance of normalcy, and it had made me ill to do so, but I hoped they had the stamina to accomplish what needed to be done.

I spoke directly to their guards. "Jaru has given me leave to reward you for all your hard work in keeping these slaves in line over these past weeks. You'll find a fresh meal prepared by my own cooks at my steward's home just over the rise, along with plenty of cool beer straight from my own cellars. Go, take a break from the heat and relax as you enjoy my thanks."

The guards looked around, casting stunned glances at each other.

"What of them?" asked one of the guards, gesturing toward the captives. "They'll scatter like beetles if we don't keep a watch on them."

I gritted my teeth. The overworked Hebrews were far more deserving of a reward than the guards who'd been calling them foul names and striking them whenever it entertained them.

But Jaru laughed heartily at the man, placing his hand on the pommel of his sheathed sword. "You don't think that I, who am heavily armed, and the champion of Ashdod can't wrangle a few shackled and half-starved shepherds? Besides, you'll be within shouting distance should any of these fools have a mind to try anything. Go on now, enjoy your meal. And when you return, bring some water back for these lazy dogs, or we'll get nothing more out of them today."

The guards laughed and did as Jaru asked, not the least bit suspicious to be sent away by the head of the royal guard.

As soon as they were out of hearing range, I stood before the Hebrews. "I know you have been mistreated here," I said in their native tongue, which caused all their eyes to go wide, "and for that I apologize. It was impossible to lessen your burden without causing the guards to ask questions."

The men divided confused looks between them. Of course they would be wary of me. Even if I'd swung my ax alongside them and had not berated them the way the guards had done, I was still their enemy.

"How do you come to speak our language with such ease?" asked one of them, a man whose thick black curls and hawkish nose reminded me of Gershom, Elazar's eldest son.

"That is a story far too long to explain now, but I will say that I lived among your people for a number of years."

Eight pairs of skeptical eyes looked up at me.

"And so, because you were a prisoner of war, we are now your slaves?" another one asked.

"No. You misunderstand me. I was not a captive. I was a . . ." I paused, wondering how to explain. No matter that Risi had counted Elazar's family as ours, I'd never done the same. "I was a guest in a household that treated me with kindness regardless of my heritage. And for *that* I am working on a way for you to escape before you are put on a ship bound for Egypt."

Shocked murmurs passed between them. They must not have been aware of their ultimate destination.

"What's his reason for aiding an escape?" asked the first man, gesturing toward Jaru.

Azuvah's son surprised me by replying in his mother's tongue, albeit halting and deeply accented. "My reasons are my own. But you would do well to listen to Lukio. He saved your lives. Along with that of the boy who was with you."

"Zevi?" called out one of the men. "He is safe?"

"Is he your son?" I asked.

"No," he replied. "An orphan. He'd been sent to live with distant relatives after his parents died of a fever."

That certainly answered some of my questions about the boy. He'd said little about his home, simply that it was gone and no one was left. I could only imagine the horrors he'd witnessed during the raid of Zanoah and guessed it would be a long while before he would sleep without the nightmares that shook him awake most nights. Each morning, I awoke to find his arm looped around Igo's neck and was glad that the dog's presence comforted him.

Although Zevi seemed to trust me more now, it was the dog he'd taken most to, tending to his duties without complaint—a ruse that had to continue for the sake of appearances. It wouldn't do for the king to somehow get word that the boy who was supposedly a slave I planned to mold into a brutal fighter was living in luxury. Although I trusted Teitu to keep that to himself, I was not as certain of the rest of those who served in my home. Therefore, Zevi slept on the floor with Igo and spent his days running

211

about the house, performing menial tasks or cleaning up the dog's ample messes.

"He is safe and will return to Hebrew territory with you," I said. A strange pang of regret prodded my ribs at the pronouncement. For as much as I'd used Zevi's impulsive attack on the soldier to manipulate Nicaro, I truly admired the boy for trying to protect the girls. Girls who I now knew were not even his kin. The house would be quiet again without him.

"If you are so full of mercy," said the first man, "why break our backs for days? Why not simply let us go now?"

"It is not as simple as it might appear," I said, "and there are other lives at stake, including Zevi's."

"And what about my daughters? Were they not worth saving?" said a man who looked to have been beaten this morning, since his eye was nearly swollen shut. I winced at both his appearance and the understandable rancor in his question. He had plenty of reasons to hate every single one of us after what had happened to his family. I was grateful that I was able to deliver news that would assuage some of his suffering.

"Thanks to my friend here and some compassionate priest-esses," I said, "the girls were rescued. They've been secreted to a safe place east of here, and you will be reunited with them after you leave."

The man's bruised face went pale. "They are safe?" His words came out in a breathless rush.

"They are," I said, my own throat tightening at the flood of emotions that moved across his face: disbelief, gratitude, relief.

"And my wife?"

The hopefulness that lifted his voice made my gut burn like a torch. I hated to lift his spirits so high and then dash them back down to earth so quickly, but I shook my head. "The two women left the city before anything could be done. We don't know where they've been taken."

His head tipped forward as one great sob came from his mouth, the sound so raw that I wondered if this was the first time that he'd actually allowed his grief to burst to the surface since the raid on his home. The men on either side of him placed their hands on his shoulders as his body shook silently, respectfully lending their support to their brother as he mourned.

"We have little time to explain," I said, my throat feeling as though I'd swallowed a knife whole. "But we have a plan to not only free all of you but also a Hebrew woman and her infant, who've been trapped here since the fall of Beth Shemesh. If we do not have your cooperation, none of this will work. But if all goes as planned, you will be back in Hebrew territory before evening falls on the second night of the upcoming festival."

My heart clenched painfully at the thought of Shoshana being gone so soon. I would never see her again.

"And if we don't agree to help you rescue this woman?" asked the leader. "Will you keep us enslaved?"

"Of course not," I said, panic squeezing my chest, "but I beg of you to help me. To help her. She . . ." I paused to organize my thoughts. "She has suffered greatly and is desperate to get her child out of Ashdod. I was not able to save your women, and I will regret that all my life, but this is a woman bound to you by covenant and the blood of your common ancestors. She and her little girl need your help."

A silent prayer slipped free of the usual control I had on my mind, one that was as startling to me as it was inevitable. *Please, Yahweh, if you care at all about Shoshana, make these men heed my plea.*

The man whose face and soul had been so battered by my people raised his head, meeting my gaze with his lopsided one. "I will help."

It took great restraint to keep my jaw from dropping open, and by the shocked expressions of the rest of the Hebrews, they were just as startled by his offer.

"If my Yedida were here, she would be ashamed of me for *not* helping," he said. "Not only would she be profoundly grateful for what you've done for our girls—" his voice cracked and he stopped to clear his throat—"but she would do anything to help a woman in need, especially, as you say, one of our Hebrew sisters. I don't know how I will breathe without Yedida and there is nothing I would not do to have her by my side again. . . ." A tear dripped from his one good eye. "But I will not dishonor my wife by running away like a coward when a woman is in danger, even if it costs me my life."

The man's words had the impact of a team of horses hitting me at full speed. This man had lost the woman he obviously loved and yet instead of breaking into pieces, he had the courage to fight for *my* Shoshana.

Something I'd been too much of a coward to do ten years ago.

Jaru explained our plan to the other Hebrews, who'd all agreed to take part. "Do not even discuss this amongst yourselves," he said, "and follow the directions I gave you to the very word, or this plan will crumble in upon itself. And although my own family is Philistine, I would beg you to think of my wife, my son, and my three innocent daughters who will suffer greatly if my part in this scheme is mentioned. The king of Ashdod is merciless with traitors."

Thankfully, all the men nodded their agreement, and I could only hope that they would keep their word. If everything went wrong, I could lose my wealth and standing in the city, but Jaru had far more to lose than I did.

As soon as the guards returned, Jaru gave them instructions for making certain that the Hebrews finished ringing the fighting grounds with hundreds of whitewashed stones by the end of the day tomorrow. Hopefully it would be the last task they would be forced to perform as enslaved men.

Jaru and I took our leave, both of us silent as we made our way back across the fighting grounds and toward the trade road. I considered the desperate prayer I'd sent up to Yahweh, a God who I'd never believed was any more real than the stone and wood ones my people worshiped. Why, in that moment, had I let myself hope that I was wrong?

My sister was adamant that not only was Yahweh real, but that he was an all-powerful being who'd breathed life into all of creation and spoke the sun, moon, and stars into place. And Azuvah had spoken of him as a deity who loved her people like children, even going so far as to rescue them from Pharaoh when they cried out in distress. How strange that her son, the very babe who had been stripped from her arms, now walked beside me. Surely that could not be a coincidence, could it? An even more unbelievable thought struck me as I glanced at Jaru from the corner of my eye. Shoshana had said that Risi believed Yahweh was watching over me. Could Jaru's impossible appearance in my life be some sort of answer to my sister's prayers?

Feeling as though I'd been pierced through with some sort of fiery arrow, I stumbled and then came to a halt.

"Are you well?" asked Jaru, again sounding so much like his mother that I could almost hear her calling me *lior* in her low, lilting voice. I'd never forgive myself for accusing her of having forced us to crawl out the window that night only for the sake of ridding herself of two bothersome children. How I ever could have believed such lies, even as a child, was beyond reprehensible. I would do everything in my power to pay my debt to her by protecting her son and his family from Nicaro's wrath if something went awry.

"I have one more favor to ask of you," I said, "in case this plan fails."

His dark brows arched in question.

"My servants will need work in good households," I said. "If I am caught, will you make certain they are safe? Especially the women and those who are not deemed of much value?"

He tilted his head to peer at me with that penetrating gaze that never failed to make me feel as transparent as fine-spun linen. "I give you my word."

I nodded my gratitude. "And no matter what I said before, I would never betray you or your family."

"I know, Lukio," he said, and I heard the faint echo of Azuvah's approval in his voice. "I never believed you would."

Twenty-Four

Shoshana

I tipped my head back to take in the impressive face of Lukio's home, awed not only by its grandeur but by the idea that my old friend, a boy who was once more comfortable among donkeys and trees than other people, lived in a place designed to impress the masses of people who strolled by this house every day.

Unlike most of the other homes we'd passed on our walk through the city, Lukio's doorway and window casings were not decorated with charms or symbols of gods, but instead painted in bold shades of red and blue.

Mariada had been overjoyed when a messenger arrived this morning with an invitation to come visit the home of which she would soon be mistress, both to familiarize herself with its workings and to suggest any changes she might desire before their wedding in three weeks. When the man said that the invitation included not only her sister and mother but her maid, my heart sank to my toes. It was awful enough thinking of being absorbed into Lukio's household before I'd realized how deep-seated my love for him was, but it was even more so now. However, as I stood at the threshold,

I had to admit that I was also deeply curious about the place that Lukio had built for himself.

We were greeted at the door by Teitu, who ushered us into the vestibule without even a hint of acknowledgment that he and I had spoken before. He immediately knelt to wash the dust of the street from Mariada, Jasara, and Savina's feet, but when he approached me with his pot of fresh water and a clean towel, I took a couple of steps backward, arguing that I could tend to my own feet. However, he insisted, saying it was his duty to tend the feet of every one of his master's guests, no matter their station. I submitted to his ministrations to avoid scrutiny but felt the stares of the other three women boring into me. As Teitu dried my feet, his one good eye flicked upward to meet my gaze. There was something speaking in that look, a communication of some sort that I could not interpret. Before I could even think to furrow my brows, the manservant rose to his feet and invited us to follow him to the main hall.

Before I'd come to Ashdod, I'd never seen a hearth such as the ones the Philistines preferred—large circular pads of stones affixed to the floor, where their covered cooking pots would simmer for hours among the flames. Families and guests gathered around these indoor hearths for meals and celebrations, much as we Hebrews did own cook-fires under the sky. But never had I seen one as intricately detailed as the one at the center of Lukio's large hall, fashioned from all manners of seashells and smooth river rocks swirling in one great pattern. At one moment, my mind was convinced the entire thing was cycling like the stars in the heavens. Above the hearth was a large opening for the smoke to escape, the ceiling painted a brilliant blue that mimicked the clear sky overhead and was held aloft by great pillars decorated in the same bold colors as the trimmings on the front of his house.

But even those intriguing details were nothing compared to the murals.

Just like in the palace and most of the wealthy homes I'd visited with Mariada, Lukio's walls boasted vivid images, some stretching from floor to ceiling. But whereas the ones I'd seen before mostly depicted scenes from the sea, vainglorious histories of the Philistines, or various gods and animals, the ones in this room were altogether different.

Lukio's walls were covered in trees.

Oaks, terebinths, cedars, and acacias all spread their branches in well-ordered and perfectly spaced grandeur, giving the illusion that one stood not within the home of a wealthy fighter but at the center of a wood with a brilliant blue sky overhead.

I'd never seen the like and was certain that nowhere in this city was its equal, for not only had Lukio created a lavishly appointed hall where the rich and pampered guests he undoubtedly entertained would be at ease, he'd also recreated the forest of Kiryat-Yearim.

Among the trees I also spied a few images of woodland creatures: a gray squirrel, a few rabbits, a herd of graceful deer, and colorful birds of all sorts. Creatures we'd come across in our mountainside wanderings.

But for as fascinating as the scenes of forested tranquility were, only one of the trees captured my full attention.

At the far end of the hall, one tree held court over the rest—an enormous sycamore fig, its abundant roots so ancient that they rose above the ground in a gnarled and knotted mass, with a dark hollow at their center, just big enough for two children to tuck themselves inside to whisper secrets and laugh together whenever the moon was full and bright.

My eyes stung as I took in the sight of the reddish clumps of figs that grew along the trunk of the tree, the rush of tears springing up with such force that I had to command myself to take in a deep gulp of air so I did not let them spill over in front of my mistress, her sister, and her mother.

For all these years, I'd assumed Lukio had forgotten me, had run off to some unknown place, grateful to leave behind those of us who cared about him, but instead he'd carried the precious memories we'd made together in those woods and put our tree on his wall where he would see it every single day.

As I stood gawking at the evidence that I'd meant just as much to Lukio as he had to me, Teitu told Mariada that his master would be joining the ladies soon, as he was attending to a household issue, but was eager to partake of a meal with them. Then the young man invited my mistress and the others to recline on well-carved chairs and plush cushioned benches and to refresh themselves with a cup of cool white wine while he went to alert Lukio to their arrival.

Once the women were situated and busy exclaiming over the sweetness of the delicate drink Teitu had poured into blue faience cups for them, the manservant swiftly took his leave, but not before giving me another speaking glance—one tinged with such sadness in his one eye that my stomach hollowed. What was happening?

"Oh, Mariada," said her mother as soon as Teitu was gone. "This house is so lovely. Your bridegroom has done extremely well for himself." She ran an appreciative palm over the arm of the ebony chair she sat upon, which was carved with long rows of lotus flowers—an import from Egypt, without a doubt. "There is nothing in this room that did not cost a fortune. You will lack for nothing, to be sure."

"I cannot believe that this will soon be my home," Mariada said, her eyes moving from the alabaster lampstands to the crimson-striped linen curtains that billowed between the pillars leading out to the courtyard.

"If this is how well appointed the main hall is, just imagine the private quarters," said Jasara. 'You'll likely be sleeping upon one of the Egyptian-style beds." She grinned slyly. "A large one, if the size of your betrothed is any indication."

Mariada choked on her sip of wine, coughing and flushing pink. "Sister! The things you say!"

Jasara laughed and leaned toward her sister with a mischievous expression. "You'll be in that man's bed soon enough, Mar. You'd best stop blushing every time it's mentioned. There'll be nothing to be squeamish about when that beautiful man wraps you in those strong arms and has his big hands on you." She let out a sigh of longing. "What I wouldn't do to have those two-colored eyes all over me. . . ."

"Jasara!" Mariada cried, her face now fully scarlet with embarrassment and frustration. "That is *my* future husband you are speaking of."

"Hush now, Jasara," said Savina. "Let Mariada be."

"I'm only saying what every other woman in this city is thinking," said Jasara, with an unapologetic flick of her black curls. "My sister is a fortunate woman."

"Indeed, she is," said their mother. "I had no idea he was *this* wealthy. Your father certainly made you an advantageous match."

Jasara learned forward again, lowering her voice. "And yet, did you notice there are no divinities depicted in this house? Not even at the threshold or in any of the wall niches we passed. A bit strange, don't you think?"

Savina frowned slightly. "The trees are interesting. I've never seen such artistry, but it's true there is nothing to revere the gods he serves. You'll have to remedy that, Mariada. Or your fertility might be in jeopardy."

"Perhaps his gods are in the sanctuary?" asked Mariada.

"That could be," replied her mother. "It is plain that the gods have blessed him with abundant wealth and fortune on the fighting grounds. I have no doubt your womb will flourish as well."

Again assaulted by images of a glowing Mariada giving birth to Lukio's child, I slumped back against the wall. No matter that he had decorated his hall with a reminder of our past, Mariada was his future, and I would enter this house not as its mistress but as a slave. I could only pray that the marriage between Lukio and Mariada would enable my sweet little girl to one day be free. And if that happened, I could only be grateful for their union—I had to be.

As the women discussed the upcoming wedding ceremony, I allowed myself to drift back to my own—a shabby and hurried affair, where my father drank more than his share of wine and Medad's family spent most of the wedding feast either snubbing me or making lewd inferences in my presence. I'd been valiant in keeping tears from rolling down my face that day but not in restraining the foolish wish that somehow Lukio would return right then and rescue me nor the impossible wish that it could be in the circle of his arms I would awake after my wedding night. But then, as now, dreams of the two of us as husband and wife were no more tangible than a spring breeze.

Teitu returned and with him another five servants, all carrying an assortment of dishes, baskets, and platters laden with delicacies: olives of every color, honeyed bread, cheeses, fruit, and fresh cuts of fish slathered in fragrant herbs. None of which I would be allowed to partake of.

I noticed that two of the servant girls who delivered the meal were disabled in some way. One had a visible limp as she entered with a large basket of fresh bread and the other had only two fingers on one of her hands. Again, I wondered about Teitu's eye, whether it was an injury he'd sustained as a slave or whether it came from some distant lifetime before he came to Ashdod.

How many of Lukio's servants were afflicted by conditions that would make them far less desirable than other household workers? A warm rush of affection came over me. It seemed that the boy who tended wounded animals in the forest and secretly delivered goods to ill townspeople had not changed so much after all.

"My master is most apologetic," said Lukio's manservant, "but the situation he is attending has become more complicated. He asks that you begin your meal without him, and he will come as soon as he can."

"Oh, I do hope all is well," said Savina.

"Of course, my lady," Teitu replied with a bland smile. "It is a delicate matter with one of the female servants who was being . . . mistreated by one of the male cooks."

"The girl isn't injured, is she?" asked Mariada, concern in her blue eyes.

"Minimally," said Teitu. "Mostly frightened. But our master is determined to ensure justice is done."

"I'm glad to hear it," said my mistress with a sincere expression. "No one should be ill used, no matter their position." A swell of pride for the girl I served rose up in me. Yes, she would be a worthy bride for Lukio and mother to his children, no matter how much it gutted me to admit it.

"However . . ." Teitu paused. "The young woman is quite distraught. Might your maid be willing to tend to her while the master finishes dealing with the perpetrator? Everyone else is busy with their duties."

Teitu's gaze flashed to meet mine, and this time I understood his message as if he'd spoken it aloud.

"Of course," said Mariada. "There is no better person to comfort her than Shoshana."

Teitu bobbed his chin in a gesture of gratitude. "Then it is even more appreciated. Please, in the meantime, enjoy your meal. The master will be with you as soon as he can." Then, without a word, he turned and headed for the door. Even if I hadn't understood that Teitu had some underhanded motive, I had no choice but to follow, since my mistress had offered my help. I padded from the room behind him, curiosity buzzing in my bones.

He led me out of the hall and through a number of smaller chambers, each one more richly appointed than the last, before walking into a large chamber wherein sat a kingly bed, its stand crafted from cedar wood and legs carved into lions' paws, adorned with fine-woven linen and pillows dyed with the costliest Phoenician purple. A flush heated my cheeks as I thought of Jasara's teasing of Mariada about this very bed, and I swallowed hard against the rush of envy that bubbled to the surface.

"Can you find your way back?" Teitu asked, startling me when he came to a stop before a curtained archway.

"I think so. But where is the servant girl?"

His smile was rueful, but a spark of mischief lurked in his one eye as he pulled back the curtain to reveal a set of stairs secreted away at the back of Lukio's bedchamber.

With an arch of my brow to question whatever charade was

being carried out here, I leaned forward to catch a glimpse at what lay beyond. Sunlight spilled down the steps, beckoning me forward.

"He's waiting for you," said Teitu. The hushed statement dispelled any notion that I'd been summoned to help a servant. The pull to ascend the stairs was unquestionable, but I also sensed that the coming conversation was linked to Teitu's earlier sadness. I'd not seen Zevi or the dog anywhere. Had something happened to the boy?

Curiosity claimed victory over trepidation, however, so I stepped beyond the curtain and placed my foot on the first step.

"I meant what I said," Teitu murmured. "I will always watch over him. I owe him my life."

Before I could respond, he was gone, the curtain behind me fluttering with the breeze of his retreat. My confusion over his parting words was soon replaced by bewilderment when I reached the top of the stairs and found myself at the edge of a lush and vibrant rooftop garden.

The space, at least twenty paces square, was enclosed by stately cedar columns on three sides but open to the sky above. Flowers of every color overflowed from pots and stone-lined beds. Tall palm bushes fanned out to provide supple shade and a large terra-cotta bath stood at the very center of the garden, afforded privacy by the prolific flowering bushes, which encompassed the area in fragrant glory.

It was a small paradise. A world unto itself in the middle of the bustling city below.

But of course, there was no young slave-girl in distress up here among the luxuriant flora. Only the green-and-brown-eyed man who'd had this perfect place created and whose simmering gaze somehow reached across the ten paces between us to steal my breath away.

With my feet nailed to the ground, I could do nothing but stare at the face I'd adored since I was nine years old. Even though there were a few more scars on his cheeks and brows, a bump near the bridge of his nose that indicated a break or two, and a dark layer of scruff on that strong jawline, it still held me hostage.

"Welcome to my sanctuary," he said with just a hint of hesitancy, as if he were seeking my approval.

I pressed my lips together and let my gaze take in the splendor. "It reminds me of Eliora's garden."

Lukio flinched at my words, which obviously touched on a nerve, but then he nodded, surveying the profusion of color that he'd surrounded himself in.

I'd always enjoyed visiting the exquisite gardens his sister had tended with such care atop the mountain of Kiryat-Yearim, where she'd cultivated exotic flowers and strange varieties of fruits and vegetables that I had no name for. Plants grew in her terraced beds with such abundance that it was widely believed that Eliora's hands were blessed by Yahweh. But Lukio's sister maintained that it was the presence of the Ark nearby that caused such bounty. I'd always guessed it was a combination of both.

"Perhaps you are right," he said. "This place does make me feel more at peace than anywhere else in my home."

He went quiet, the sounds of the street below muted by the floral buffer he'd created and the smell of jasmine sweet in my nostrils. He'd asked so little about his sister since he and I had crossed paths, but it was more than evident from this place that he missed his sister deeply. For as much as I'd loved Levi and Yadon, there had always been something special between Lukio and the sister he still insisted on calling *Risi*, a term of deep and abiding affection.

"Why am I here, Lukio?"

"I had to speak with you."

"Why didn't you just leave me a shell? I could've met you tonight. This ruse is dangerous. If Mariada or the others find out—"

"There's not enough time," he said, cutting off my worries. "I have far too much still left to organize before the festival, so I cannot visit the palace this evening. But I had to speak with you. I must tell you our plan."

My breath hitched painfully in my chest. "You can't mean— Lukio, what are you thinking? It's not time—"

"We have a way for you to escape, and the babe as well."

My mouth went dry as unbidden hope welled up. But I ruthlessly pressed it away, determined not to lose my equilibrium over vain wishes. "You've spoken to our mutual friend about this? About my daughter?"

"Yes. And you can rest assured that he would never reveal either one of you."

"How do you know that?"

His eyes dropped to the ground for a moment, but then he stared at me with a pointedly firm gaze. "Trust me. He is an honorable man, one with his own family that he loves dearly. He understands how important your child is to you."

Something told me there was more to the story, but I nodded, granting him my confidence. "Tell me more."

"This will take coordination. Not only from those we're setting in place, but from your friends inside the palace. And it must happen during the festival."

"But that's in three days! It's impossible."

"It's entirely possible. And necessary."

There was an edge to the word that raised the hair on the back of my neck. "What do you mean?"

"I have reason to believe that my cousin Mataro knows about you—both your connection to me, and your child."

Blood rushed to my temples, pounding in cadence with my galloping heart. "What will he do?"

"He insinuated that he would reveal all should I not allow him to control me like he did in the past. But do not worry, Shoshana. I've thrown him off the scent for now. And this plan will work. You and the little one will be on your way to Kiryat-Yearim within two days' time. As long as your friends are willing to help."

Fear collided with elation, the hope so powerful it was almost too painful to bear. Would I actually hold my daughter in my arms two days from now? My mind immediately spun all my implausible dreams into visions of what might be possible.

"Shoshana," he pressed. "Will they help?"

"Of course," I choked out. "What do you have planned?"

He laid out the entire scheme for me, one that depended not only upon our cooperation but Galit's position in the kitchen, Avel's skill with certain herbs, and a diversion by Oshai in the stables. After he'd described my own part, which involved little more than a well-timed bout of faintness brought on by too much sun during the first of Lukio's fighting matches, I was in awe.

He and our mutual friend had devised a plot that very well might work, one that meant freedom for not only my daughter and me, but Zevi as well. It seemed that he was all alone in this world, but I was confident that the people of Kiryat-Yearim would find a place for him.

"You've thought of everything, haven't you?" I peered up at him in awe.

"You know me, Tesi. I don't even roll dice without making certain that the odds are in my favor."

The warm affection in his tone, and the use of his nickname for me, caused something to thump unevenly inside my chest. But then I realized that he'd left out a key detail as he'd explained the scheme he'd concocted.

"And what of you?"

"What about me?"

"What happens if things do not go the way you plan? If you are caught helping a group of Hebrews escape? Kidnapping a baby everyone thinks is Tela's? You could lose all of this." I gestured to the lovely garden around us and the palatial abode at my back.

He shrugged, as if none of it mattered.

I blinked at him in astonishment. "The king of Ashdod is anything but merciful. He could very well take your life."

"He won't," he said, with brash confidence. But then his gaze grew more potent. "But you are worth the risk, Tesi."

Tears stung the back of my eyes, blurring his visage before me. He took a few steps closer. "I should always have fought for you."

I could do nothing but stare at him in bewilderment.

"I should never have walked away to let my friend face a difficult road alone. Nor should it have taken me so long to put aside my selfishness in order to get you and your daughter out of this place."

"Lukio, I—"

He continued on as if I'd not spoken, as if he'd been storing up these words for so long that he could not control their flow. "I know I don't deserve your forgiveness. Not only did I embrace all the filth of Ashdod, but I share the same blood as those who violated and enslaved you."

My chest ached at the self-loathing in his words. "You are not responsible for the evil of other men. Nor do I hold the decisions you made as a confused and hurting boy against you."

His lashes fluttered and his palm spread over his chest, as if it pained him. "Of course you would say such things. You are everything good and kind. You have been since the moment you found me under the sycamore."

"You had our tree painted on your wall," I whispered, my vision blurring.

His green and brown eyes pierced me to the marrow. "It was the only way I could keep you close to me."

I was helpless against the flow of tears now. This man threatened to break down every single defense I'd built against him since the moment I saw him down on the fighting grounds plowing his fist into a Phoenician's jaw. My knees wavered.

One of his strong arms slipped around my waist, steadying me, pulling me closer until I was a hairsbreadth from his body and could feel his warmth from head to toe. It was useless to fight him; trying to stop myself from loving him had always been a losing battle, so I surrendered, pressing myself against him and laying my hand on his thudding heart.

All the grief and hope and longing that I'd been pressing into the smallest corner of my heart poured out of me until his tunic was sodden and my body was shuddering in his arms as I wept. He stroked my back with tenderness, his cheek pressed to the top of my head.

"Don't cry, Tesi," he murmured into my hair. "I've always hated it when you cried."

His sweet words only caused me to sob harder. I'd missed him so much. Missed being close to him and dreaming of a future together. And so I dared to ask what I did not have the courage to ask before.

"Come with us, Lukio. Come home to Kiryat-Yearim."

His body stiffened. "You know I cannot."

I pulled back to look into his eyes. "Why not?"

His lips pressed tightly together. "It is far safer for you if I stay here. My disappearance in connection with yours and the baby's would only cause Nicaro to pursue us. I could not endanger you that way."

"But your family—"

He cut me off by lifting his hands to cradle my cheeks in his palms and the determination in his expression gutted me. "Too many depend on me, Shoshana. I am needed here. Even if I wanted to return to Kiryat-Yearim, it would be negligent of me to do so."

The only thread of hope I'd allowed myself to cling to snapped and floated to the ground. No matter that he'd held onto a few pieces of our childhood together, I was in the past for him and would remain there. I knew that it would be fruitless to argue. He'd made up his mind. His care for me was evident, or he would not risk any of this. But it was not enough to make him choose life with me over the one he had here. The one he would have with Mariada.

"When you see Risi . . ." His voice faltered. "Please tell her that I am sorry."

All the blood rushed from my head to my soles as I finally made sense of the invitation to his home and this secretive conversation in his beautiful garden. He'd not brought me here merely to tell me his plan. He'd brought me here to say good-bye.

This would be the last time I spoke with the man I'd loved most of my life, even when I'd thought he'd been forever lost to me.

The way we'd parted then had been so gut-wrenching, both of

us shattering as I'd walked away from that smoky clearing in the woods, and I did not want to repeat such a scene. If these were my final moments with him, I would make them count.

"You may have had our tree painted on your wall, Lukio. But I had it painted on my heart. There was nothing my father or Medad or anyone else could do to erase that. Even though these years in Ashdod have been painful, I will always be grateful that I had the chance to see you again. To know that you are safe and well and that in spite of the darkness in this city, you are a man of honor and compassion. And no matter what happens, I will always be grateful for every effort you made toward reuniting me with my children."

I swallowed hard as Aaliyah and Asher's faces appeared in my mind. How they would have adored him. . . . I shook my head against the wayward thought. He'd made his choice.

"And no matter what you've done," I continued, "and no matter what lies you've told yourself, your family loves you. They never stopped loving you."

I drank my fill of his beautiful dual-colored eyes one last time, then, knowing Mariada and the others would be suspicious if I stayed away much longer, I pulled away from him, something tearing inside me as I did so. I had the fleeting thought that he looked nearly as wrecked as I felt.

But I turned away, leaving him standing in his exquisite garden, glad that this time it would be the scent of lotus blossoms and sweet jasmine that would remain in my last memory of him instead of the bitter tinge of ash.

However, before I descended the stairs to make my way back to my mistress, I took one last look over my shoulder, seeing not only the man he'd become but the sweet boy who'd been my sanctuary from all the hurts in my childhood.

"And neither did I."

Twenty-Five

Lukio

Although I hoped to avoid the king until after my plans were set into motion, I was glad he'd called a meeting of his council to discuss the events for tomorrow. I'd not been able to concentrate on much of anything after Shoshana walked out of my garden yesterday, leaving my soul cleaved in two.

At least this time I'd been able to say good-bye properly, without the acrimony and accusations of betrayal that had characterized our first parting. I was glad she'd seen my home before she returned to Kiryat-Yearim. I'd wanted her to see that tree mural and know that I'd never forgotten her. In fact, there had not been a day that went by since its creation that I did not stand in that room and think of my Tesi. In fact, it was only my determination to be honorable to the young woman I'd made a promise to marry that had kept me from locking Shoshana in my embrace to give her one last kiss before she left me again, for good.

As I stepped into the king's chambers, I did my best to shake off the lingering regret about my decision to remain in Ashdod. But everything I'd told Shoshana was true. The people who lived in my home and worked my lands depended on me. Many of them, like Teitu, would be worth little to anyone else, and I could not simply abandon them. Besides, for as much as I missed my sister, and for all my growing regrets over the way I'd treated Elazar and his family, they were better off without me. Even though Shoshana had forgiven me for rejecting the Hebrews, running back to their enemy and embracing their ways, I did not expect Elazar, Yoela, or their children to do so. And I would not give Nicaro any excuse to follow me to their doorstep, anyhow.

As if I were reliving the day I'd met Jaru all over again, I found him standing next to Nicaro, who lounged on his throne with a wine cup in hand. But this time a variety of the king's council members were in attendance, including Virka and Grabos, his chief army commanders, and Amunet's father, who was also Pharaoh's special envoy to the region.

For all the times I'd entered the king's chambers over the past few weeks, this was the first time my palms were slick with sweat. I'd seen many sides of Nicaro in my acquaintance with him: the magnanimous king who offered the wealthy of Ashdod every indulgence at his feasts; the calculated and cool ruler who viewed me with suspicion the day I'd purchased Zevi; the amiable elder who lavished me with praise like that of a father after the boat race; and even the cruel High Priest who had spilled the blood of an innocent girl on a funereal altar. But if Mataro had made my association with Shoshana known, and in turn her connection to the child Tela had stolen from her, it may very well be an angry father who greeted me here today.

But to my great relief, it was the Nicaro who'd first offered me the position of Master of Games who welcomed me to the council meeting, his blue eyes sparkling with anticipation as he asked us all to give report on the preparations for the festival. Either my deflection from my cousin's insinuations about Shoshana had fended him off, or whomever Mataro had connections with in the palace had not yet revealed it to the king.

A few paces away, Jaru frowned at me, his dark brows drawing together as he watched me approach, and I lauded his ability to act as though we'd not spend hours plotting together and organizing a complicated scheme that would be set into motion before the sun rose again.

"Is everything in place, Lukio, for all the events?" asked the king.

"I believe so," I replied. "And my orchards are already full of tents, so I can say that there will be plenty of spectators."

"And how is the security holding up with the extra bodies already flowing into the city?" Nicaro asked Jaru.

"Fairly well," Jaru replied, speaking with calculated reluctance. "So far, we've had a few additional scuffles and thieves, but nothing that my men haven't been able to handle."

"So, it's not been as chaotic as you predicted?" asked Nicaro.

Again, Jaru frowned slightly. "I'll admit that the plan to have the bulk of the events outside the walls was a good idea, but only the next few days will prove whether Ashdod can handle a festival of this size in the future."

"Virka and Grabos have their men stationed all over the city, Jaru. Between your guards and their battle-honed soldiers, any scofflaws will think twice before attempting anything in Ashdod."

Jaru tipped his head in acknowledgment but held his posture rigid, as if still unconvinced. He knew his part well, and I could not help but be impressed. No wonder he'd been so successful in hiding his rescue efforts in this city for so long.

I stepped back to lean against the wall while Nicaro received reports from the priests about the large-scale offerings that would be performed at sunrise before the first event, which was the city-wide open invitation for those interested in vying for a chance to fight me on the third day. A few of the most powerful tradesmen touted the brisk commerce already underway in the marketplace. Even Amunet's father agreed that the atmosphere in the city was much like festivals he remembered during his childhood in Avaris.

"I've heard nothing but excitement, Nicaro," he said to the now-grinning king. "Any negative rumors have been completely proven false. I've been told that talk of this festival"—the Egyptian glanced over at me—"and your champion has been buzzing about even as far as Gaza, perhaps even to Avaris itself. Pharaoh will be pleased to hear that all is well and prosperous in Ashdod. Prolific trade in your port means that ties between Egypt and Ashdod will only grow stronger."

"I am delighted to hear it," said Nicaro. "We are ever grateful that Pharaoh gifted these beautiful shores to us in the first place and are thrilled to be worthy of such generosity."

I held back a grimace at the blatant rewriting of history, since it had been our ancestors attempted joint land-and-sea invasion of Egypt itself that had forced Pharaoh to offer the coastal region we now inhabited as appeasement. I'd always wondered if part of Pharaoh's reason for doing so in the first place might have been to create a buffer between the Egyptians and the Hebrews, who, if Azuvah's stories were to be believed, had devastated their land with ten increasingly horrific plagues before taking their leave through the depths of a parted sea.

"In fact," said Nicaro, "I have a gift for your exalted king. One I hope you will personally deliver to him with my most humble thanks for his continued friendship."

"Is that so?" replied Amunet's father.

"Yes. I have a group of Hebrews who will be an excellent addition to his labor force." He smiled broadly. "And I plan to send many more in the near future."

It took every bit of restraint I had not to meet Jaru's eyes. If all went well, those men would be free by the morning watch, not on a ship bound for Egypt.

"Speaking of which . . . Virka. Grabos," said Nicaro. "Tell me what news you have for me on the box."

Although I remained in my carefully composed posture of disinterest against the wall, my attention snapped to Virka as he addressed the king.

"We think we have the area in which it was taken narrowed down to a collection of hills not too far from Ekron," he said.

"There are any number of small hamlets in that area, so it may take a few more weeks before we find it."

"If there wasn't a surprising amount of Hebrew presence in the valleys around the area," added Grabos, "we would already have it in hand, I'm certain. Unfortunately, our chariots cannot navigate the terrain, so any reconnaissance we do must be on foot."

Nicaro's blue eyes glittered with dark intensity. "Do whatever you must. I don't care how many Hebrews you need to dismember. *Find* that cursed box."

"We will," vowed Virka. "Even if we have to set fire to those hills and smoke out those who are hiding it."

A horrific vision of Kiryat-Yearim burning made me grit my teeth and caused my blood to pound.

The king made a humming noise in the back of his throat. "Well, let's not be hasty. That lumber is worth a fortune. But we must seek out anyone who might know where that foul thing is. It did not simply vanish into the heavens. Someone *has* to know where it went eighteen years ago."

His accusing gaze roved over those in attendance, as if every Philistine in this room were deliberately concealing the truth from their king, and then his eyes landed on me, the only man who actually was doing so.

A cold wash of foreboding slithered through me as he stared. I'd worried that I might be called out for my connection to Shoshana today, but perhaps the king had other plans. Every hair on the back of my neck stood at attention.

But instead of interrogating me, he looked away, speaking to his commanders. "I have every confidence you men have it in hand. In fact, I predict that within the week we'll know exactly where to find that abomination. And after we destroy it and conquer the Hebrews for good, we will own the trade roads in all directions. Ashdod will be at the very crux of all trade between Egypt, Tyre, and Damascus, and therefore our port will be the most powerful and profitable on the Great Sea."

A cheer of agreement went up from the council, everyone draining their cups in honor of our king, so Nicaro called for another round of wine to be served as the room broke into animated conversations about the festival. I participated in a few, wishing I could escape but knowing full well that I must keep up the ruse of being interested in the politics of Ashdod. Across the room, Jaru was engaged in a discussion with the Egyptian envoy. I wondered what it would be for Azuvah to know that not only had her child been saved but that he brushed up against the most powerful men in the region, men who had no idea that he was involved with the theft of people they considered to be their property.

"Where is that great beast of yours?" asked Nicaro, who'd sidled up to me without my notice.

"Igo?"

"Indeed. I've heard he is with you at all times now. The Demon Dog, they call him," he said with a smirk.

I held back a bark of laughter. If only they knew the poor thing was scared of his own tail. "He's just outside with . . . with my young slave."

"Ah yes. The boy you purchased to tend your cur." He blinked a few times. "And how is his training coming?"

My breath stilled. "His training?"

"I do remember a boast about honing him into a fighter. Surely you've not neglected the promise you made."

I cleared my throat. "Of course not. I've been busy of late, as you can imagine, but he shows quite a bit of promise."

He clapped me on the shoulder, his fingers digging into my skin. "Show me."

"My lord?"

His smile was on the perfect line between gleeful and dangerous. "You've had nearly a month. Show me what you've done with the little wretch."

"I'd be happy to arrange a match with one of the local boys after the festival concludes."

"No. Now." He followed up the iron command with another of his sharp-edged smiles. "Jaru?" he called across the room, causing every mouth to clamp shut. "Fetch the boy who tends the fires in the kitchen. Bring him out to the courtyard."

My stomach hollowed out. I had no idea how old the boy was or what experience he had in a fighting ring, but it was more than clear to me that this was no spontaneous match conjured in the moment. I'd done my best to treat Zevi as nothing more than an expendable slave outside of my home, but somehow Nicaro had guessed that the boy was a soft spot. My instincts before had been correct. He knew something.

"Friends!" said the king, his tone bright as he addressed his council. "Let us convene outside. I've put together a bit of entertainment for you. A taste of what's to come during the festival. Isn't that right, Lukio?"

Zevi stepped forward, his bare feet in almost the same spot they'd been when I'd pulled him off the soldier that first day. I'd had no time to explain anything to the boy, since Nicaro had not left my side since announcing this match, so instead of being able to prepare him for what was to come, I'd been forced to drag him by the neck of his tunic out of the palace and push him onto the fighting grounds without even a word of instruction for how to handle an opponent.

Blinking in the harsh sunlight, Zevi looked over to where I stood about fifteen paces away with an expression of such confusion and betrayal that my stomach hollowed out. But even if my instinct was to grab him and run, I had to hold still or everything Jaru and I had set into place, including Zevi's own chance at freedom, would be ruined. My only solace was that the kitchen slave looked to be only about a year older than Zevi and almost as confused by the proceedings as he. Unfortunately, however, the other boy was nearly a handspan taller than Zevi, with longer arms and legs.

After weeks of suspicion, little of which was mitigated by my assurances that I would not hurt him, Zevi had finally been allowing me a small measure of trust. Only yesterday he'd told me that he originally came from a tiny village in Yehudite territory but that a sickness had killed nearly everyone there, including his entire family. He'd said that no one left had been able to keep him and he'd been sent down to Zanoah only two months before the attack by the Philistines. He spoke of it all in such detached tones, his small body tense and fidgeting as he did so, but I'd been thrilled that he'd even said that much. It was better than the scowls and sneers he normally gave me. His rare laughs were the property of Igo alone, and I was surprised at how jealous I was by that fact. I suspected that I would now lose any ground I'd gained with Zevi, and that pained me far more than I ever guessed it would.

"I happened to see the kitchen boy get into an altercation with one of the boys who cleans the stables," said Nicaro, standing at my side. "He did well, even untrained, so let's hope your slave is ready to defend himself."

The smugness in his voice made it clear that he in no way believed that I'd been training Zevi to fight, so I pulled up a small measure of Demon Eyes' arrogance and smiled. "That we shall."

A flicker of uncertainty flashed in his blue eyes before he narrowed them and then raised a hand in the air. He dropped it, indicating the start of the fight, but as disoriented as Zevi was by the situation and unfamiliar with our fighting traditions, he missed the signal and earned a punch to the gut before he could even react. His opponent took advantage of Zevi's shock to land another hit to his face, splitting his lip and drawing blood. Around us, Nicaro's council members cheered for the kitchen boy, thirsty for more.

At my hip, Igo growled low in his throat, his body tensing as his young friend struggled. I felt strong kinship with the dog as I slid my fingers around the cord at his neck to keep him in place, because it was all I could do to not roar at the injustice of this match, run to the child, and dash away with him in my arms. He was only ten and had suffered so much in his short life. Watching him be pummeled for his own sake, and even for Shoshana and the baby, seemed grotesque, a betrayal of a boy who depended on me.

How could Mataro have been so gleeful about throwing me into the ring all those years ago? It was true that Philistine boys began fighting around Zevi's age, but I'd been only seven, my ears itching for praise from someone I'd considered a man to model myself after. I should have been playing with boys my own age, but instead Mataro had convinced me that to be accepted by him and others, I had to be the strongest and make everyone fear me—a lesson I took with me to Kiryat-Yearim, where I employed those same tactics on those who mocked me or made me feel inferior.

Seeing Zevi out there, unprotected and being inadvertently taught the same lesson, caused my belly to burn with fury. And yet I could do nothing to help guide him in this fight because I could not yell to him in his language. I could only stand there, rooted in place, berating myself for not spending some time over these past weeks teaching him how to defend himself.

The kitchen boy followed the blow to the face with another jab toward Zevi's torso, but Zevi jerked sideways and the hit went wide. However, the kitchen boy caught his footing and came at Zevi again, head-on, landing another harsh blow to the side of Zevi's head. Zevi's hand came up to cover his ear, which was undoubtedly ringing, his small face crumpled in pain.

I was practically vibrating, the force of my anger so surprising that I could barely remain in place. How was it that my concern for this Hebrew boy was so overwhelming? I'd known him for only a few weeks, and he'd spent more time with the dog than me, and yet from the first day I'd brought him home, I'd felt an odd sort of connection to him, something undefinable that made me want to shelter him.

Like I'd told Shoshana, I'd thought many times about being a father, but I'd never suspected that I would feel such a strong paternal instinct toward a child whose blood was not my own. Was this how Elazar had felt toward *me*?

A flash of memory took hold as I shook with rage when Zevi took another blow to the stomach.

After Medad's father had dragged his sons away from me in

the woods when I was nine, the air foul with his insults toward me and my heritage, I'd walked home in a daze, dried tears on my dirty cheeks and his words filling every empty crevice in my wounded heart. Elazar had been the first to spot me when I slunk into the house, desperate to find solace with the donkeys down in the stable, and he'd immediately begun to fret over me, demanding to know whether I was hurt.

I'd rebuffed him, of course, lashing out with hurt that was actually meant for Medad's father. But instead of reacting with anger, Elazar had reached out his big palm and placed it on my shoulder.

"I would worry the same for any of my children who came home in such a state," he'd said.

I hadn't believed him, thinking he was giving me lip service and that, like Medad's father had said while he was excoriating his sons for playing with me, Elazar would come to regret his foolish decision to let me and my sister remain. But standing here now, my insides roaring with pain over Zevi's hurt, I finally believed him.

Regret choked me nearly as much as my fear for Zevi, but just as I was holding to the last shred of restraint, Zevi somehow regained the pluck that had enabled him to attack a fully armed Philistine soldier. His face went hard, his hands curling into fists, and he retaliated with a swift kick to the other boy's knee. I had to swallow my shout of victory when his opponent staggered sideways and fell to the ground with a yelp. Zevi was on him in an instant, the other boy's height no longer an issue now that they were on the ground, since Zevi's natural strength was far superior to the lanky child he'd been facing. Looping his arm around the boy's neck, just as he'd done to the soldier, Zevi caught his opponent in a chokehold.

The kitchen boy's face turned bright red, but Zevi did not release him, only tightened his grip. The boy beneath him scrabbled at the ground, eyes bulging as he rasped a call for mercy that Zevi did not understand.

"Enough," I said to Nicaro, then without pausing to wait for the king to halt the match, I released Igo's collar and strode over to the struggling pair, not caring that the dog trotted along behind me. I'd harmed more than my fair share of opponents, a few who'd been permanently maimed after our bouts and one who'd died a few days later, and I refused to let Zevi have the death of another child on his soul.

I tugged at Zevi's shoulder, hoping he would release the kitchen boy, but instead he gripped harder, making the other boy scratch at his arm with another plea in words Zevi could not decipher. Hoping that the kitchen boy was too terrified to care that I spoke in another language, I leaned closer.

"Let him go, son," I said. "You are killing him."

With a flinch, Zevi's eyes flared wide and then he glared up at me. "I am not your son," he said, his words more of a blow than a kick to the center of my chest. But he released the other child, who sobbed in relief.

Aware that I could in no way leave the courtyard without Nicaro's dismissal, I pulled Zevi along with me as I approached the king, a gut-wrenching parallel of the first time I'd done so.

"Well," said Nicaro, his tone impressed, "it seems as though your slave does have the potential to be a fighter after all. I can only imagine what he will be when you train him in earnest."

"As I said, the boy will prove to be a profitable investment."

Nicaro's blue eyes searched my own. "As you have turned out to be as well. I only hope that will continue to be the case."

I ground my teeth at the implications, but the truth of it was hard to ignore. I *was* a slave to the king of Ashdod. Only instead of silver, he'd purchased me with both my position and his daughter. My lust for power and wealth, along with my determination to free myself from Mataro's clutches, had only ensnared me in servitude to another master.

"I vow that I will prove exactly how grateful I am for your generosity, my seren."

"Indeed, you will," he replied, waving a hand to indicate my dismissal, but even as I turned away, eager to take Zevi home and tend to both the wounds he'd earned in the ring and those I'd inflicted by sending him there, the king's eyes remained pinned to me. There was no more doubt in my mind—Nicaro knew something of my past and he'd used Zevi as a warning. Shoshana's reminder that the king was merciless and may take my life if something went wrong echoed in the silent courtyard.

I waited until I was far enough away that no one would hear me speak but did not turn my face to Zevi as I did so. "I know that you hate me right now"—I gently squeezed his arm—"and I deserve your anger for not protecting you better. But I vow that you will never fight anyone again unless it is in defense of someone else."

He didn't respond, but the tension in his body lessened a small measure as we left the royal courtyard behind. If all went to plan, he'd never step foot in this place again.

"And you may not be my son, but I am *very* proud of you."

Twenty-Six

Shoshana

Since our return from Lukio's home yesterday, Mariada had been uncharacteristically quiet, electing to shun the gathering of the ladies up on the terrace for last night's meal and stay in her room—something I was all too grateful for, since I had no desire to be reminded of Lukio and the brief moments we'd had together there under the stars. My chest had not stopped aching since I'd left his garden, and neither had I ceased wondering whether I should have worked harder to convince him to come with us. But there was no use wishing for things that were not meant to be. My focus must be on the plans he'd outlined in detail, and getting my daughter out of this palace would be the trickiest part. I needed to talk to Galit as soon as possible.

While collecting the dishes of Mariada's half-eaten meal from the previous night, I set my first step into motion. "Are you hungry, my lady?" I asked. "I'd be happy to fetch you something from the kitchens."

Lounging on a pillowed couch and gazing out the window at an empty blue sky, she shook her head and did not even bother to correct me for addressing her formally. Even though I was desperate to talk to Galit, Mariada's apathetic demeanor concerned me.

"Are you ill? Shall I call for a healer?"

She sighed. "No. I am fine. Just tired. I did not sleep well last night."

Hearing a silent plea for a listening ear from a girl who'd been so kind to me, I set the basket of dishes aside and crouched beside her. "Is there something weighing on your mind?"

She looked over at me, sadness in her big blue eyes. "What if . . . ?" she began, and then paused to chew on her lip for a moment. "What if I don't want to marry Lukio?"

Seized with a spasm of surprise, and not a small amount of guilty pleasure at her question, I took a moment to collect myself before I replied, "What makes you feel that way?"

She shrugged one shoulder. "I don't know, really. Everyone is thrilled about this match—if they are not jealous, that is. But after going to his house yesterday, it all became very real. He has been nothing but cordial since the first night he announced our betrothal and even showed himself to be kind and amusing when he showed us his dice games, but other than what I've been told about his fighting and the glimpses I saw of who he might be by the way his home is appointed, I don't know anything about him. And I certainly don't love him."

As much as it coated my tongue with bile to assuage her fears of marriage to the man I loved, I placed a comforting hand on her shoulder. "You'll come to know him. You have an entire lifetime to spend learning about each other. And I have no doubt you'll eventually care for each other." My heart squeezed tight at my tongue's betrayal of its deepest desires.

She shook her head. "I don't know. The entire time we were there he would barely look at me and said no more than a few words to me during the meal he'd invited us to. How could he ever love me after we are married if he doesn't even bother to speak to me now?"

I'd noticed the same thing, even though I'd tried my best to avoid staring at him after our parting on the roof. Lukio had been pleasant and accommodating, giving a long narrative about the nonexistent female slave who'd been assaulted by a cook and how he'd dealt swiftly with the imaginary man, but he was plainly distracted and unsettled by our conversation. Yet, without divulging the truth, I was at a loss for how to comfort Mariada.

"Perhaps he is simply overwhelmed with planning the festival. Once it is finished, you'll have more time to talk with him. As I've said before, I don't know how anyone couldn't love you. The champion of Ashdod included."

The ghost of a smile came to her lips before she peered at me curiously. "You were married before you came here, weren't you?"

"I was." I'd told her that long ago, but she'd never before pressed me for details.

"And was the marriage arranged by your father?"

My throat tightened, but I managed to press out a response. "Yes."

"And did love bloom after you were wed?" Her tone was hopeful.

I swallowed down an inappropriate bark of laughter. "No. He was not a kind man." Never had a statement been more true.

Her face fell. "So, you've never experienced the kind of love that some of the Egyptian poets speak of? When a man and woman are so enamored of each other that they see no one else? Or when he calls her his morning star and she says she is the fairest in the land because *he* said it was so?"

I'd heard these poems from a group of traveling musicians invited to the palace to entertain during a feast—some that were so intimate and descriptive my face flushed with heat as I listened from my place against the edge of the main hall. I'd noticed then that Mariada had been captivated by the recitations, her wide eyes pinned to the flamboyant costumed singers, but it seemed they'd made a deeper impression than I'd realized. Still, how could I answer such a question without revealing too much? I could deny to have known such affection, but my tender heart, still throbbing from yesterday, would not allow the lie.

"I have," I said, before I could think better of it.

Her eyes grew impossibly larger. "Who?"

I took a deep inhale to steady my voice. "I met a boy in the woods when I was nine. He and I formed a secret friendship that lasted nearly four years before he . . . moved away from our town. But even as young as we were, we loved each other very much. He was indeed my morning star, and he certainly made me feel like I was the fairest in the land." I smiled ruefully. "He was everything to me, and the loss of him has never gone away."

And it never would.

"Oh, Shoshana." Tears glittered on her lashes as she pressed a palm to her chest.

"I do not know what the future holds for you, Mariada. But I do know this: the man you are pledged to marry employs servants who no one else in this city would even tolerate in their homes. A man with that sort of compassion, even if it is hidden from the world, is a man who can love deeply and love well. And I wish you nothing other than to be cherished the way you deserve, for a lifetime."

Feeling a surge of maternal affection, I gave in to my instincts and leaned forward to kiss her on the forehead. "Now, I'll go down to the kitchen and bring you back some warmed milk with honey and spices the way you like. Perhaps it will help you to rest. All right?"

She sniffled, her cheeks wet as she nodded.

For as much as I could not wait to leave this place and return home with my daughter, I would miss Mariada very much.

After a brief detour to the gardens, where I explained Lukio's plan to Avel in hushed tones and plucked a few pink and white blooms to brighten Mariada's chambers, and hopefully her mood, I took my basket full of dirtied cups and bowls and headed for the kitchen courtyard with a tiny packet of herbs tucked into my belt.

The courtyard where most of the meals consumed in the palace were prepared smelled of smoke and roasted meat, making my own empty stomach snarl with an anticipation that would remain unrequited. There were a number of fires burning on small hearths that lined one side of the open area, a few with spits above them being slowly turned by blank-eyed slaves, and most with large lidded cooking pots steaming among the low flames.

Somehow, the aroma took me back to my mother's little corner oven, where she'd taught me to make bread and we sang as we patted the sticky rounds with floured hands. I blinked away the unbidden tears that arose. I'd avoided thoughts of my ima for a long time, not because I did not miss her, but because they usually provoked a cascade of memories: her slow death, how my little brothers had cried for her afterward, and the way my father changed from my abba who called me his butterfly to a man who lifted his hands against me in anger and eventually sold me to pay his debts.

Just as I spied Galit across the courtyard, a young boy passed by with an armful of wood—one of the children who tended the ever-burning hearth fires here and hauled water daily from the well outside the city. I was momentarily distracted by the dark bruise on his cheek and the scrapes on his arms and legs. It looked as though he had been involved in some sort of scuffle, reminding me of a number of times I'd seen Lukio battered from run-ins with Medad and his brothers.

Galit approached, drawing my attention away from the boy by reaching for the basket of soiled dishes. "What are you doing here?"

"I must speak with you. Now. Can you make some excuse to come with me so we can talk privately?"

Galit's dark brows furrowed.

Unless I could speak to her now, this entire plan might never come together. "Please. It's urgent."

"I'll take care of it," she replied, needing no more explanation before she spun away.

While I waited for Galit, I begged a cup of spiced honey-milk from one of the cooks for Mariada. The woman graciously ladled out a generous portion from a lidded pot of milk among the coals on a nearby hearth and added the perfect amount of spice and sweetness. Then I stood by the doorway with the warm jug and the flowers I'd gathered for my mistress in my hands.

Galit bounded over to me with an impish grin much faster than I expected. I should never have doubted her skills of subterfuge. I'd heard Galit spin more than one tale and knew her to be a true storyteller.

"What did you say to the head cook?"

"That your mistress desires a certain type of sweet dish that you are not familiar with and that I need to go with you so she can describe it in detail."

How she came up with such an excuse so quickly I could not imagine, but I was certainly glad for it. Once again, my eye was caught by the kitchen boy and the purple mark on his cheek.

"What happened to him?" I asked, gesturing with a subtle tick of my chin toward where he was laying a new fire on a cold hearth.

Her brows arched high. "Your Demon Eyes pitted him against his young slave in the fighting ring."

"What?" I gasped as we entered through the back door into the palace.

"Indeed. Apparently, the poor boy lost badly to the other child, even though Jarepe is older and taller."

I could not imagine why Lukio would do such a thing, especially when he'd seemed so protective of Zevi. I could not see him willingly putting any child in danger. There had to be an explanation. At least I knew I would see Zevi tomorrow and could make certain he was all right.

I led Galit down the corridor and into the space between two fat columns, a shadowy place I'd noticed on my way here from the garden.

"Talk quickly," said Galit, darting her eyes down the corridor. "And quietly. Anyone could come by."

"We've found a way to get my baby and me out of the place, but we need your help."

I paused, waiting for her questions.

"And?" she pressed.

"So, you will help?"

"Of course," she replied, as if offended I would even question it. "You are my friend. I'd do anything to help you and your little one."

I held back my yelp of glee and the effusive gratitude that demanded to be lavished upon her. But, for the sake of time and stealth, I reached into my belt and pulled out the little linen-wrapped packet Avel had given me.

"The first morning of the festival, at the ninth hour, you will be summoned by a guard to take a basket of food and drink to Tela's room. The nursemaid will be there, alone, since the baby naps during this time and Tela will not want a fussy child with her during the events. You'll offer the nurse a tea with these ingredients." I handed her the packet. "It will render her senseless within only a short time. You'll carefully put the baby in the basket, making certain she remains asleep."

"How will I get out without the guards seeing me?"

"There will only be one in that area of the palace, and he's been paid to not see you. But at the same time, the stables will be set on fire, to create chaos and draw any additional guards away. You'll take the baby down to the garden shed and hand it to a woman in a yellow-and-blue headscarf, who will bring her through the city gates. Then you'll run back to the kitchen and act as though nothing has happened."

Galit's eyes grew wider and wider as I described the scheme. "How will you get away?"

"I'll feign sun sickness and ask Mariada to allow me a few moments in the shade so I can slip away to a meeting point."

"And who is the woman?"

248

"I don't know, only that she's a friend."

"You trust this plan? You'll put your child's life in a stranger's hands because your old friend told you to?"

I held my breath, considering her words, but then nodded. "I do. If there's anyone I trust, it's him."

"Then I will do as you ask," she said, then her smile turned rueful. "But I will miss you."

"I'll miss you too." I reached out to squeeze her hand. "You have been the best of friends. I need to go back up to Mariada's room now. She'll wonder what happened to me."

"Go on, then. I'll take good care of your little one. I promise." She returned my hand squeeze and turned away.

"Oh, Galit?"

She paused, looking over her shoulder.

"If the rest of you get out of here—and I pray you do—have pity on poor Avel and marry him, will you? He practically floats on air when I mention your name."

She laughed softly, her dark eyes glimmering. "Perhaps I shall. And you live a long and beautiful life with that daughter of yours."

She left me to dream about just that, and of the sound of Aaliyah and Asher calling my name when I returned to Kiryat-Yearim. But when one of Amunet's maids padded by, I broke from my stupor and slipped out of the shadows, then hurried all the way back to my mistress's chamber.

I was in the middle of re-braiding Mariada's hair before bed when they came for me.

Four guards burst into her room, knives brandished but their faces blank of emotion. Mariada jolted to her feet, her waist-length curls tangled in a half-finished plait.

"What is the meaning of this?" she squawked.

"I apologize for the intrusion, my lady, but your maid is to come with us," said one of the guards.

My young mistress stretched to her full height, her tone shifting into an imperious demand worthy of a king's daughter. "For what reason? She's done nothing!"

Amunet strolled into the room, Tela in her wake, and I felt all my blood drain into my feet.

"She's under arrest for a plot to kill a nursemaid and steal Tela's child," said the king's first wife.

"That's ridiculous," said Mariada, a slight quaver in her voice. "She would do no such thing."

Amunet put out her hand, a small linen packet in her palm. "No? Then why did she deliver these deadly herbs to one of her accomplices in the kitchen earlier today?"

Mariada blanched and looked at me, shock and confusion swimming in her ocean-blue eyes. "Shoshana?" she choked out on a whisper.

But I had no response for my bewildered mistress, whose kindness I'd willfully betrayed, not when everything had come crashing down and it was obvious that not only were Galit and the others in peril, but that I'd lost my one and only chance to rescue my child.

I would never hold her. Never kiss her face. Never hear her call me *Ima*. Never see Aaliyah and Asher again.

When the guards stepped forward to bind my hands, I went without a struggle. There was no use fighting the inevitable.

Twenty-Seven

Lukio

It felt strange to not have Zevi and Igo with me today as I walked through the palace on my way to find Mariada. No toenails clicking on the stone next to me or little-boy questions in my ears. I'd become accustomed to their constant presence at my side over these past weeks, but after what Nicaro had done, I refused to bring Zevi back here. I did not trust the king of Ashdod.

Although he'd not spoken to me all the way back to the house after the fight, Zevi had listened to my explanations about why I had to make him fight the kitchen boy, with his small jaw set and belligerence in his dark brown eyes.

"How does letting someone beat on me make me safer?" he'd asked.

I'd sighed, knowing that my back was in a corner. I had to tell him a small measure of truth in order to regain what I'd lost of his precious trust.

"We have a plan to get you back home," I'd said. "Along with my friend and her child. But it will only work if no one suspects my true reason for bringing you to my house in the first place."

His eyes narrowed. "And what is that?"

"Because I could not bear to see you hurt, Zevi. You remind me of my . . . someone I used to know. And"—I let a smile curve my lips—"a little bit of myself when I was your age."

He'd tilted his chin, skepticism written on his face. "Because I fought that soldier?"

I laughed softly. "Yes. But also because I, like you, had a hard time trusting people who offered help. And I want you to know that the two girls you tried to save that day have been rescued."

His brows flew high. "They were?"

"Yes. They did not remain with the man who purchased them for even a night."

"I am glad. I did not know those girls, but it made me so angry that they were frightened."

"You did well, Zevi. As someone once told me, my hands were made for defending those who cannot defend themselves." Although the rest of the night Risi and I escaped Mataro's home was a hazy blur, the words Azuvah spoke to me before I crawled out the window were still clear in my mind. "And I believe yours are as well."

He'd studied my face for a long while, his lips pressed together and his gaze penetrating.

"I don't have one," he'd said, his eyes dropping.

"What don't you have?"

"A home. Everyone I know is dead or gone."

Gut twisting, I'd swallowed hard, wondering if I was being hasty in sending him away, but especially after the strong emotions I'd felt when he was out there fighting, I wanted him to be safe. I had to let him go. Just like Shoshana.

"When I was a little younger than you are now, some people took me in. They cared for me, even though I was their enemy."

His eyes flared at my admission. "Why would they do that?"

I'd taken in a deep breath, contemplating for only a moment before the answer came to me in the form of my sister's voice, when I'd asked her the same question during one of my belligerent rants against Elazar's family.

"Yahweh sent us to them, Natan," she'd said. *"And Elazar and Yoela believe it is their duty to love others as they love themselves, like Mosheh told them to do. And what better way to show love to two orphans like us than to adopt us into their family so we wouldn't be alone anymore."*

"Because their kindness and generosity have no limits. And I am sending you to them, because I know they will embrace you the way they did me."

"But if they were so kind to you, why are you here?" he'd asked, cocking his chin to the side like Igo did from time to time.

"Because I was a fool, Zevi. Don't be a fool like me. Let them love you."

His nod was solemn, and I prayed he would remember this conversation when he got to Kiryat-Yearim. At least I knew Shoshana would take good care of him. Knowing my Tesi, she would enfold him into her life with ease, the same way she'd done to me when I was a wounded and confused boy.

After inquiring of one of the guards which chamber was Mariada's, I climbed the stairs to the second floor. I'd been too distracted by Shoshana and our conversation yesterday to speak to her about the festival, but for our plans to work, it was imperative that Mariada attend my first fight tomorrow morning. I figured the best way to ensure her presence would be to invite her personally and perhaps use a bit of my persuasive charm to flatter her into a promise that she would attend—with her maid.

Wondering whether I could successfully act as though Shoshana meant nothing to me while I toyed with her mistress's affections right in front of her, I knocked on the door. But the young girl who opened it a handspan to peer out did not have beautiful hazel eyes and myriad freckles at all; instead, she had dark brown eyes that went as wide as moons and a jaw that unhinged at the sight of me. Had Mariada taken on a second maid? I'd never thought of her as the type of preening royal who demanded a bevy of girls to tend to her every whim, but perhaps I was wrong.

Regardless, the girl seemed so astounded by my presence that she did nothing but stare at me wordlessly until Mariada spoke from somewhere inside the room.

"Who is it, Seko?" she asked, but there was an odd, pinched quality in her tone that I'd never heard from her before. "I am not up for seeing anyone."

The maid continued to gape at me with fluttering lashes but somehow choked out an answer. "It's . . . it's Demon Eyes . . . I mean . . . your betrothed, mistress."

Mariada responded with a muffled groan. "Tell him that I cannot—" she began, but I pressed the door open and pushed past the astounded maid, hoping her mistress was not in a state of undress.

I'd expected Mariada to be preparing for the day or perhaps breaking her fast, not still abed with the bedclothes pulled up around her head like a child hiding from the dark. And where was Shoshana?

"Mariada," I said, "I am sorry to come here like this, but I need to speak with you."

She gasped and pulled herself deeper into the blankets, until only the mess of her black curls could be seen. "Please," she said, her words muffled. "Just go. This is not the time."

"Are you ill?"

Still not emerging from her fortress of linens, she waved a hand in my direction. "I'm fine. I'll speak with you tomorrow."

Although I knew little of this young woman, she'd never come across to me as overly emotional, but her words were tinged with an edge of hysteria, and there were tears in her voice.

"What is wrong? Has someone hurt you?"

She shook her head but did not respond.

"What can I do to help? Shall I call for your usual maid?"

She sat up, her black hair a tangled nest and her eyes red and swollen. "They took her!"

A chill of foreboding swept over my skin and my voice went low. "What do you mean? They took who?"

She threw her arms wide. "Shoshana. My maid. They came last night and took her away."

254

My head went foggy and my eyes blurred for a moment as I barely restrained a snarl. "Who took her? Where is she?"

"Amunet came in here and accused her of something awful. And I don't know how to help her!" She dropped her face in her hands and let out a sob. "No one has ever been so kind to me, even my own mother."

My stomach had turned to stone the moment she mentioned the queen. Acid scorched my throat as I thought back to my spat with Mataro in the street. He'd said he had friends in the palace, friends who could do me harm.

A flash of memory flickered to life from the gathering where I'd given Shoshana the very first shell. I'd seen Mataro exchange a silent greeting across the room with Amunet, even if she'd seemed to rebuff him at the time. And he'd somehow known about Shoshana having given birth. Had his boasted connection been none other than Nicaro's first wife?

I swallowed down the bile that surged upward as I considered all the implications. If Mataro told Amunet about what he saw between me and Shoshana after the funeral, then who was to say he'd not also told her about my history with the Hebrews? But even if he'd seen my longing for Mariada's maid and shared it with the queen, what possible justification would that be to arrest her? To most in Ashdod, my future wife's slave would soon be mine to use as I willed.

"Tell me what happened," I said through gritted teeth. "What is she accused of?"

Mariada must have heard the barely leashed fury in my voice because she peered up at me in tearful bewilderment. "Amunet and Tela came in last night with some guards, accusing her of a murder plot and planning to steal the baby. They tied her hands and marched her away. But Shoshana would never murder someone. I know her. She wouldn't, even if she wanted her—" She stopped, her glistening blue eyes wide as she realized that she'd almost revealed too much. If only she knew . . .

I dug my hands into my hair as the full weight of her revelation slammed into me, each breath painful as I began to pace the floor. "This is my fault," I muttered to myself. "All my fault."

I'd thought our plan so well coordinated, so perfect, and yet Shoshana was suffering for my arrogance. I'd practically dared Mataro to make good on his threats.

I had to find her. Had to make her safe. If Nicaro hurt her, I would burn this city to the ground.

"Why would it be your fault?" said Mariada. "You don't even know her."

"You don't understand," I mumbled as I continued my pacing, my mind racing with half-formed ideas of how to undo all of this.

"If my father does to her what he did to that other girl . . ." she said, on a choked sob.

"No!" I shouted, images of blood dripping onto an altar slamming into me. "I won't let that happen to her!"

She blinked up at me, her mouth gaping open for a few long, silent moments as she took in whatever wrecked expression was on my face.

Then, without looking away from me, she spoke. "Seko," she said softly, "please leave us. Wait in the women's courtyard. I'll send word when I'm ready for you to dress my hair for the day."

From the corner of my eye, I saw the young maid flee, her face pale and no doubt carrying tales of a livid Demon Eyes screaming at her mistress.

"Lukio," said Mariada, her voice gentle and tentative, "why are you so upset about my maid's arrest?"

The tears on her cheeks made it clear that she was terrified for Shoshana as well, and she'd certainly come to her defense while explaining the arrest. But could I trust her with any part of the truth? She was Nicaro's daughter. She could ruin everything with one word. And yet the blue eyes that matched her father's were shot through with red from what looked to be a night of crying on her bed, and her face was deathly pale.

I closed my eyes, squeezed them tight, and whispered a plea for wisdom to the God my sister and Shoshana said was the One

Who Hears. My next breath came steadier as I made my decision. I had to tell the truth and take a chance that she truly cared for Shoshana. However, she spoke before I could do so.

"It was you. You are the boy."

My eyes flew open. "What?"

"She told me that she'd loved a boy in her youth. And that he'd been lost to her. It was you, wasn't it?" She gasped, a hand clapping to her mouth. "And the shells! That was you too. You've been meeting secretly."

I let out a shuddering sigh as I collected my thoughts.

"It was," she rasped, my silence having spoken for me. "Did you betroth yourself to me to get close to her?"

"No. I did not know she was here when your father and I made our agreement."

Her brows furrowed as she waited for me to clarify.

"Mariada, you must vow to me that you will not breathe a word of this to anyone else. It's not only Shoshana's life at stake if anything I tell you is revealed. Can you promise me?"

She was silent for a long while as she studied me with the same sort of intense scrutiny I'd experienced from her father. Whatever she saw on my face must have convinced her of my sincerity.

"You have my word, Lukio. I would not do anything to put her in jeopardy. She is . . ." She sighed. "She is my friend."

"Just as she is mine," I said, almost relieved to finally be able to speak the truth to this impossibly kind young woman. "And I saw her for the first time in ten years the night I told you of our marriage."

Her mouth opened slightly but nothing came out, so I continued.

"I met Shoshana when I was around eleven years old."

"But she was brought here only a year and a half ago."

"That's true. But I met her in Hebrew territory, where I lived with a Hebrew family for nearly eight years."

Being careful not to disclose details about exactly where my sister and I had lived or why we went there, I told Mariada of the past I shared with her maid, how much I'd desired to marry her one day, and how I'd lost her to both her father's greed and my own pride.

"I'd not known she was here, not until that evening on the terrace when she brought you your wrap. But I'd already made a binding contract with your father. I had no choice but to follow through."

She was quiet for a long while, contemplating everything I'd laid at her feet, and then her posture softened and her gaze turned compassionate. "She told me of how much she loved you. And how the loss of you had never dissipated."

"When I lost her, it left a hole in me and no matter how many matches I won or how much wealth I accrued, that hole was never filled."

Tears trickled down her cheeks as she pressed both hands to her chest. "And here the two of you were kept apart by me and I did not even know it. No wonder you were so distracted yesterday when we were in your home."

"You could not have known. And I'd just told her good-bye for the last time."

"But why? If you would have told me the truth, I would have refused to marry you and you could have taken her as a wife."

I huffed a rueful laugh. "If only it all could have been so simple. Your father might have a thing or two to say about that. And of course there is her child to consider."

She nodded. "True. And Tela would never willingly give up the baby."

"No. She would not."

"But why did you say that her arrest was your fault?"

I let out a heavy sigh. "Because she's not the one who planned the scheme to retrieve the baby. It was me. And if my guess is correct, my cousin Mataro may well have been the one who caused Amunet to be suspicious of her, because I refused to bow to his wishes. She likely had Shoshana followed around the palace."

"You were trying to get her back home, weren't you? With her child?"

258

I nodded. "She has two other children there."

"She does?" Again, her jaw slackened as she looked up at me with surprise. How was it that Mariada knew of our childhood together but had been ignorant of such an important part of Shoshana's life? Perhaps she'd guarded her children so deep in her heart that even talking about their loss was too painful to bear. I understood that well; I'd not even allowed myself to speak her name aloud until she appeared on the terrace the night she'd finally accepted the summons I'd delivered by seashell.

"Yes," I said, "and she is in far too much danger here. Especially after what happened to that other innocent Hebrew girl your father accused of treachery."

She flinched at the mention of that awful funeral. "What do we do? We cannot let my father kill her."

"I don't know. Everything I'd set in place is ruined."

"Amunet said Shoshana's accomplices had been arrested as well. Who did she mean?"

Another jolt of regret hit me. It was not just Shoshana I'd put in peril, but her friends as well. "I only know they are Hebrews who work in the palace."

I could certainly not share what I knew of Jaru or he, too, would be in chains. I'd have to go to him next and let him know what had happened. And then decide what to do with the Hebrew men and Zevi while I figured out how to get to Shoshana. Perhaps we could at least get them to a safe place away from Ashdod tonight, and in the meantime I could—

Mariada bolted upright, throwing her legs over the side of her bed with no regard for her mussed hair and tangled nightdress. "We must rescue her. Tell me what to do."

I rocked back on my heels, startled by her adamance. "No, it's too dangerous. I have others I can ask for aid."

Her jaw hardened, and the same sharp-edged determination I'd seen in the king when he spoke of the Ark came into those blue eyes. "She is my friend, Lukio. And I *will* help."

"What about your father? And Tela and Amunet?"

"My father will be livid, but my mother will soothe his ruffled feathers if I beg her. Leave that to me. As for Amunet and Tela, I do not care at all what they think. They've always bullied the rest of us, and Tela took Shoshana's baby without a drop of remorse." She frowned and crossed her arms. "I wish I'd been able to stop my sister."

"There was nothing you could have done, Mariada."

"Still, I should have tried to do *something*. I owe it to Shoshana to help her now since I was too weak and cowardly to do so before."

Compelled to set her mind at ease, especially since everything had now changed between us, I placed a reassuring hand on her shoulder. "I hope you understand that if things were different, I would have been proud to have you as my wife. Whomever you marry will be a fortunate man indeed. You are very brave."

She shook her head with a sorrowful smile. "Anything I learned of bravery was from Shoshana. Now, what is the plan?"

Twenty-Eight

I pressed my back to the stone wall, willing my pulse to slow. I'd already dragged two corpses behind the stables, hoping no one came across the dead guards before I added to their number, nor that anyone had heard the short scuffle that occurred when I refused to comply with their demand that I not pass through the gate into the palace complex. Although I'd permanently maimed a number of opponents on the fighting grounds, I'd never purposely killed someone before. But when one, and then the other, came at me with weapons drawn, I'd not hesitated to defend myself.

Thankfully, I'd had little problem finding my destination. Playing the part of spoiled royal daughter, Mariada had made good on the vow she'd made this morning to help with the rescue and demanded to see her maid. Although she'd not been allowed inside the storage room on the far side of the stables where Shoshana was being held, she'd been able to at least discern that the door latch and the hinges were flimsy, and that only two men were stationed inside—two more lives I would need to end in order to free Shoshana and her friends. But with their own lives in the balance, I could not take any chances.

I'd gone directly to Jaru's home after I left Mariada, making a loud show of demanding to see him under the guise of frustrations over crowd control during the first event of the morning. Although he'd been unable to reassign the guards Amunet had put in place,

261

he'd at least made certain that no one else was patrolling this area around the stables and that our plans for the Hebrew men would fit the new situation we found ourselves in.

Gripping the handle of my ax, its familiar weight a strange comfort, even if blood coated its edges for the first time, I used the same method I did before stepping into the fighting ring— slow breaths, measured heartbeats, fashioning my rage into a sharp blade so it did not interfere with my goal. I was here to save Shoshana and her friends, not to take vengeance, so I must keep my anger in check or I would lose control.

With my body and mind prepared, I lifted my ax over my shoulder and brought it down on the door with the same force I'd once used to fell trees. The hinge clanked as wood shards flew, the brittle bronze giving way to my iron ax, just as I'd hoped it would.

A shout came from inside as I swung again, the second hinge cracking just as easily as the first. Then using the muscles I'd spent the last ten years building into weapons themselves, I ripped the door away from the frame.

Two young guards stood at the ready, short swords in hand. By the bewilderment on their faces, they had in no way expected Demon Eyes to batter down the door.

I took advantage of their shock and charged. The first one received a blow with the flat of my ax, which threw him into the wall, where he crumpled into a heap, head bleeding. The second man jabbed his sword at me, but I jumped back and spun in the same way I dodged a punch in the ring. When he stumbled, I grabbed his arm and yanked it back with a sickening crunch that had him screaming in pain. Then I elbowed him in the face, and he, too, fell to the ground, unconscious.

I snatched up the one oil lamp that illuminated the room, noting the dice and tokens on the floor. They'd been so distracted by their game that they'd probably not even noticed the sounds of distress from the guards at the gate as I overcame them. At least Amunet had gifted me an advantage by assigning incompetent guards to imprison Shoshana.

I made short work of the inner door, which did not even stand up to one powerful kick, its wooden latch splintering the moment my foot made contact. Weaving past a number of enormous jugs, pots of grain, and various dried goods that filled the storage room, I called Shoshana's name, but everything was silent and still. Surely Mariada had not been mistaken about her location, had she?

I pushed back farther, called out again, and was rewarded with a small voice that seemed to be coming from belowground.

"Lukio?"

"Shoshana? Where are you?"

"We've been put down in an old well."

I took a few more careful steps and came to the edge of the well. Holding the oil lamp high, I caught sight of three forms huddled at the bottom, which wasn't nearly as deep as I'd feared but was obviously being used as cold storage for the many jugs of beer that littered the bottom and the baskets of dried meat stacked against its walls.

Shoshana's head tilted up and her lovely eyes shimmered in the lamplight. "There is a ladder somewhere up there, I think, although they threw us down here without one."

Swinging my light around, I spotted the ladder and maneuvered it so that they could crawl out of the pit.

"Come on up, Shoshana," I said.

"Galit is wounded. She needs to go first. I'll help her get up the ladder. Get her to safety and then come back for me."

"Climb up after her."

"No, I won't leave our friend down here alone. He's in even worse shape than Galit."

Frustrated with her stubbornness but at the same time proud of her strength and concern for others, I reluctantly agreed. If there was anything I knew about Shoshana, she would always put others first. "But what of you? Are you hurt?"

There was a slight pause. "I'm fine. I landed hard on my foot when they threw us down, but I don't think it's broken. Just swollen and tender."

After some shuffling and a quiet argument between the two women, Shoshana's friend ascended the ladder, using one arm to pull herself upward while Shoshana aided her from below, and I reached down to steady her from above. The woman's face was a mass of bruises, and one eye was a swollen slit. When she finally stood next to me, she swayed slightly, one arm limp at her side.

"Can you walk?" I asked her, and she nodded but didn't speak. Her jaw looked as though she'd just left the ring with a brute like me.

I ushered her to the door and then gave her directions to find Zevi and Igo, who were waiting in the shadows between two buildings about a hundred paces down the street. I hated having only a boy and a dog to rely on during this rescue, but there was no one else. Jaru was busy organizing the Hebrew men, who'd hopefully already overtaken their captors with the weapons I'd left buried beneath their watchtower prison in my vineyard. I could only hope that instead of running off the moment they were free, they would keep their commitment to helping us.

At least Zevi knew where to go if something went wrong. He'd insisted on helping once I'd informed him of Shoshana's arrest, and I knew that even young as he was, he would do everything in his power to get Galit to safety. And as devoted as he was to Zevi, I trusted Igo to watch over them both.

I kept my eyes on Galit as she walked down the street as swiftly as her broken body would allow her and then melded into the shadows. I would not let Shoshana stay down in that pit for a moment longer. She was coming up next, even if I had to carry her up the ladder. I'd deal with the wounded man once she was safe.

But when I returned to the storage room, she was already emerging from the old well, her face pale and her eyes hollow.

"He's dead," she said. "They threw Oshai down headfirst. I think perhaps he hit the stone wall. I'd hoped he would survive, but he is gone."

"I'm sorry," I said. "What of your other friend? I thought there were five of you."

264

"There was. Avel died trying to protect Galit." Her voice broke. "He refused to see her suffer, so he tried to attack, and one of the guards jammed a knife in his back."

I wished I could pull her into my arms and comfort her, but there was no time. There would be much to grieve later, and many questions to be asked about what had happened to them after their arrest, but for now I needed to get her to safety. I grasped her hand in mine and pulled her toward the exit.

However, before we emerged from the storage room, I halted in the doorway, realizing that only one body remained where I'd left two. Sometime when I'd been helping Galit and Shoshana in the back room, one of the guards I'd knocked unconscious had awakened and slipped away. I cursed myself for not ending them both when I had the chance.

"If something happens," I said, "find Zevi. He and Igo are hiding between the fourth and fifth building on the left just down the street. Use his name to alert him to your presence. He knows where to go."

"But—"

"Just in case," I said, pressing a kiss to her forehead. There was no use frightening her by pointing out the missing guard.

She nodded, and after snatching up my ax, I slipped my arm around her waist and led her out into the main room. She was limping for certain, her lips pressed together to stifle any indication of pain, but at least she was not nearly as battered as her friend Galit.

Everything was still as we emerged into the deepening twilight, and I felt a surge of hope that perhaps we could indeed reach our destination undetected. But when we were only ten paces away from the door I'd knocked down, a group of men came around the corner, two with torches in hand. Leading the way was none other than Nicaro himself.

I pushed Shoshana behind me and brandished my ax.

"I wondered if you might show up here," said the king, with a frown. "Although I'd hoped I was wrong."

"Let her go," I said.

"Amunet said you were obsessed with Mariada's slave, but is she truly worth losing everything?"

"Just let her go. You can deal with me as you will."

He tilted his chin, those blue eyes full of cunning. "I don't think so, Lukio. You've betrayed me. And she'll be the price you pay for doing so."

He gestured to his men, but before they could step toward me, I used the only tool I had to bargain with.

"I'll tell you where the Hebrews' Ark is. Just let her go free."

"No!" cried Shoshana. "You can't!"

The king's eyes were wide as he stared at me. "You know where it is?"

I nodded.

"Mataro said you were with the Hebrews and not in Ekron, but I didn't believe him. He is a notorious liar, after all, and a spineless coward with a grudge against you."

Now his odd behavior toward me—trustful at times and suspicious at others—made sense. Mataro had attempted to weasel into Nicaro's confidence, and when he did not succeed, he found his way into the queen's ear.

The king's eyes narrowed on me and then flicked to Shoshana behind me. "But you're lying about the Hebrews' box for the sake of this slave. The gods only know why you'd bother when you had my daughter already in hand." He shook his head, again gesturing to his men to take us.

"I was there!" I shouted. "I saw you on the hillside at Beth Shemesh."

Nicaro ordered his men to halt. "What did you say?"

"My sister and I followed the cow-drawn wagon in which you and the other kings sent the golden box back to the Hebrews. We hid up on the hill above you, where you and the others crouched behind boulders and waited for the Hebrews to see the wagon approach."

"But that was nearly two decades ago," he said, incredulous.

"Indeed. I was seven. But I distinctly remember that you were not in complete accord with the other kings. In fact, you tried to leave at one point, but another king forced you to remain until it was determined that the Hebrews would not be sending the wagon back here."

Nicaro's jaw went slack as I spoke. I'd never seen him at a loss for words.

"After you left, my sister and I were found by some of the Hebrew priests who were sent to deal with their box. We went to live with one of the families, where I remained until I was fifteen and decided to come back to Ashdod. And if you will let this woman go, without sending anyone to follow her, I will tell you *exactly* where it is."

I kept my expression very still as I waited for him to decide, but I did not relax my grip on my ax.

"Fine, she can go," he said. "And then you'll tell me everything I need to know."

"I will."

"No," Shoshana said, gripping my arm, "Don't tell him. He'll destroy it."

"I have no choice. You are more important than a gold box."

I glanced over my shoulder to look into her beautiful eyes, unable to do anything more than send her off with the knowledge that I had no intention of revealing the truth to Nicaro, but that instead I chose her, my sister, and the family I'd rejected in Kiryat-Yearim over my own life. "And promise me that someday you'll teach Elazar the game I taught you in my special place."

Confusion clouded her features, and I could only hope that she would somehow discern my meaning and carry the message to the man I should have called Abba.

"Go." I turned back to the men in front of me, keeping my ax at the ready. A muffled sound of distress came from her mouth, but from the corner of my eye I watched her limp away toward where Zevi waited in the shadows.

I waited until she had been completely swallowed up by the

darkness, begging Yahweh to be merciful and protect her, hoping that my sister had been right that her God would hear even the sincere call of a Philistine.

Thankfully, the hiding place Zevi would take her to was only at the end of the alley in which he and Igo had been waiting, so they did not have far to go. But still, I waited as long as I could with my weapon high, glaring at Nicaro's guards with the veneer of Demon Eyes firmly set in place. They might be armed, but they knew who I was and what I was capable of. From the looks some of them were giving me, they were still in shock that they were standing against me in the first place.

When finally I felt Shoshana had had enough time to escape, and that even if Nicaro sent men after her she'd be safely ensconced in the hiding place we'd arranged, I let the ax drop. Let the king think he'd bested me. I trusted Azuvah's son with Shoshana's life.

The guards swarmed me, picking up my weapon and binding my hands.

"If only I'd known you were the type of fool to get caught up in a slave escape," said Nicaro. "I must say you certainly had me and my daughter fooled."

I shrugged. "I was caught up in nothing."

Out of love, Azuvah had saved Risi and me the night that we'd fled Mataro's home. She'd taken the beating that ultimately had killed her, leaving behind a child she did not know had survived. And now I could repay her for that love by keeping Nicaro's eyes firmly fixed on me.

"Don't you see?" I said. "I've been doing this for years. Those two girls one of your priests purchased who happened to disappear a few weeks ago? That was me." I baited him with a smile. "Why do you think I was so determined to be the Master of Games and marry your daughter? It gave me access to the palace so I could help even more Hebrews escape. I didn't just live in their territory for all those years—I was *adopted* into a Hebrew family. You invited the enemy right into your palace."

Fury blazed across his face, and red crawled up his neck. "Tell me where it is, or I go after her now. And I won't leave enough of her to be recognized."

I glared at him. "You control Beth Shemesh now?"

"We do. Any Hebrews who remain pay hefty tribute."

"Then your commanders have been walking by it for years."

I smiled at him again, leaning into the lie. "It's under the boulder. The one the wagon stopped in front of while you crouched like cowards on that hill above the valley."

He grimaced. "Why would the Hebrews leave it there?"

"It killed seventy of their men," I said. "While my sister and I watched, they opened it, and then a storm appeared from nowhere and burned the lot of them. The priests who came the next day, the ones who found my sister and me, buried the box under the boulder, too terrified to move it for fear it would destroy more of them, especially after we told them what happened to our cities. They even pretended to hide it up in the hills in a tent, but of course no one has been inside for nearly twenty years to discover that it is empty." I laughed. "And here you've been searching all over and it was in the very place you left it all those years ago."

Nicaro folded his arms over his chest, locking on me that sharp ocean-eyed gaze that made many lesser men crumble. "If what you say is true, then it will be easy enough to determine. In fact"—he grinned—"you'll be the one digging it up. And if it's not where you say it is, it'll be your grave."

I'd guessed as much, but if a daylong trek to Beth Shemesh gave Shoshana and the others time to get back to Kiryat-Yearim via the northern route we'd planned to avoid main roadways, then my life was worth the sacrifice. My allegiance to the Philistines had been a misguided one from the start. If only I'd learned that lesson while I still lived in Elazar and Yoela's home.

Instead, I'd yearned for a place that was replete with wickedness, that worshipped death and enslaved innocent men, women, and children. I'd rejected those who called themselves my brothers and sisters for a cousin who'd used, manipulated, and ultimately betrayed me for the sake of his greed. I'd done very little in my twenty-five years that was of true worth, so this would be a fitting end, and at least one that would help ensure that the Hebrews' treasure remained hidden. It was a paltry atonement for my sins, but it was the only thing I had to offer. I'd betrayed them all before by walking away in anger. I would not do it again by revealing the truth of the Ark's location.

"But before you go dig up that abominable thing," said the king, "you'll fight."

I flinched, astounded by his words. "What?"

"I've invested far too much for this festival to fail, Lukio. It *will* be successful and make Ashdod the most powerful city in Philistia. You may be a traitor, but at least your hard work on these events won't go to waste."

"You still want me to fight?"

"Of course. They want Demon Eyes and that's who they will get."

"And if I refuse?"

His lips curled upward. "I thought perhaps you might ask that." He turned to the nearest guard. "Show our friend who we happened to come across on our way here."

The man hurried off and within only a few moments brought forward a bound and gagged Teitu.

"I do believe this is your trusted manservant. But this poor fellow only has one eye," said Nicaro, with false compassion. "It would be tragic if he lost the other."

Growling, I pulled against the three men who were holding me in place.

"So, I will make you a bargain. You will win every one of the four bouts. You will play your part as the champion of Ashdod. You will rile the crowds and smile and give *me* the glory for each match. But for every contest you lose, or every time you fail to show me the proper obeisance, he'll lose another piece of himself. Starting with that second eye."

Twenty-Nine

Shoshana

Galit was so quiet on the pallet next to me that I sat up to ensure that she was still breathing and was relieved when her chest rose and fell. I surveyed her poor battered face, heartsick at the violence she'd endured, along with the loss of Avel, who'd sacrificed himself in a vain attempt at protecting her from the guards.

I'd been so grateful that Zevi had led us from his hiding place among the shadows to a back door only about thirty paces away, since I hadn't been certain whether Galit would have made it much farther.

When the boy had knocked on the door, I'd been terrified that it was a mistake. Surely someone who lived so close to the palace would not be involved in this rescue, but the moment the door opened and a low voice spoke into the darkness, I'd known it was my friend from the shed. He'd ushered us in without question, put us in a back room with food and soft bedding, and assured us that we would leave the city first thing in the morning. He'd been so kind last night, splinting Galit's broken arm and tending to her wounds, and mine, with almost fatherly concern.

But for as grateful as I was that the three of us and the gray dog were safe for now, the thought of leaving Lukio behind to suffer an unknown fate, as well as never seeing my daughter again, was almost more than I could bear. Grief had filled every part of my body as I lay unsleeping next to Galit.

Just before dawn, the door to our sanctuary opened, and I got my first glimpse of the man I'd met in secret all those months. Dark hair, threaded with silver, deep-set brown eyes, and a thick beard. I was surprised to note that he could pass for a Hebrew, but his clothes and bearing were Philistine through and through. It was plain to see that he was a man of some influence, which made his motives for all of this even more bewildering.

A young man who looked to be about eighteen or so entered with him. Their similar appearance, the long nose and the shape of his mouth, caused me to think they were related in some way. A son, perhaps? He also looked vaguely familiar to me, but I was not certain where I'd seen him before.

At the intrusion, Igo came to his feet but remained near Zevi, who was still prone on his bed in gape-mouthed exhaustion. The poor child had been so distraught when I'd told him of Lukio's capture that I half-worried he would charge out the door and take on Nicaro himself. Igo, too, had been unsettled when Lukio did not return, his ears pricking up at every foreign sound long after Zevi had finally drifted off to sleep.

"Here are some fresh clothes for you." My once-secret friend, whose name I'd finally learned was Jaru, laid a bundle on a nearby table. "We need to get you out of the city right away. Thankfully, the festival will be starting soon so the streets will be full and the guards at the gate overwhelmed with spectators making their way to the arena for the dedication ceremony this morning."

"Are we putting your family in danger by being in your home?"

He shook his head. "I've sent my wife and daughters away for a few days, just to be safe. And my son Teo here is fully aware of what I do." He glanced over at the young man with a rueful smile.

"Since he discovered my secret by accident a few months ago, he's been involved as well."

Understanding struck as I remembered where I'd seen Teo before. "He's a palace guard, isn't he?"

"He is. He's been watching over you and your friends for a while now. In fact, he knew who you were before I did."

Astonished, my gaze went back and forth between the two of them. Just how many nameless, faceless friends had I been protected by without knowing it? But there was no time to ask about the past. I must focus only on what came next.

"The sun is already coming up," I said. "How will we escape Ashdod? Aren't the guards at the city gates looking for us?

"Have no fear." Jaru's tone was soothing but strong. "We organized this all very carefully. And even with the change in plans due to your arrest, I believe we will have little trouble. Lukio entrusted you to me, and I will not let him down."

I nodded, a glut of gratitude and grief choking off my words.

"I will do all I can for him, Shoshana." He frowned, brows pinched with regret. "If I did not have a family to protect . . ."

"You have done far more than we could've ever hoped. You've saved many women and children. On behalf of my people, I thank you."

He nodded, lips pressed into a tight line and some indeterminable emotion in his dark eyes. "There is someone here to see you. But you'll have only a few moments before we must load you all into the wagon." He turned to his son. "Go ahead and bring her in, Teo."

Teo disappeared for only a moment, then ushered in a small female figure shrouded in a linen headscarf that veiled her face and carrying a bundle against her chest.

When she removed the covering, I slapped my hands to my mouth so I would not cry out. Because not only was my mistress Mariada standing in front of me, but the bundle moved, and one tiny foot poked out. Jaru and his son left the room as I gaped at the impossible scene in front of me, Teo glancing back twice over his shoulder as if he, too, were shocked that the king's daughter was standing in his home with a baby in her arms.

My knees went weak and tears blurred my vision as the door closed behind the men.

"I could not let you leave without her," she said.

"How did you . . . ?"

She grinned. "You didn't think you were the only one skilled at sneaking about the palace, did you? I slipped into Tela's room well before dawn and took her, then strolled out the door without disturbing her sleep, or the wet nurse's. The guards did not even question me or ask to see what I was carrying—I am the daughter of the king, after all. And then I came right here."

"But, my lady . . ."

"*Mariada*," she pressed. "You are no longer my maid."

"Mariada, they will be furious. What if they—?"

She put up a palm to stop my argument. "I do not care. This is *your* child, not Tela's. I wasn't able to keep you together when she was born, but I can now. And I will never regret it, no matter what they say or do."

A squawk came from the bundle in her arms, and she smiled down at it. "I think someone is awake and ready to meet her mother."

My feet would not move for some reason, and as Mariada approached, it felt as though I was caught up in some sort of dream. And then, just as swiftly as she'd been taken from my arms, my daughter was in them again.

Her sweet little face peered up at me, a pinch of curiosity between her wispy brows but none of the fear I'd expected. I greedily drank in everything about her: her hair, which was similar in color to mine, enormous grayish eyes, and rosy lips that pushed out as she met my gaze.

"Shalom, Davina," I said, using the name I'd called her in my heart from the moment of her birth. Finally being able to call her my "cherished one" aloud permanently wiped away whatever Philistine name Tela had bestowed upon her. I tightened my hold, brushed my finger over her soft cheek, and was rewarded with a sleepy smile. Tears streaming, I pressed a kiss to her forehead.

"I can never thank you enough," I said to Mariada. "I don't even understand how you knew to come here."

"Lukio told me everything, Shoshana—that *he* was your secret childhood friend and how you came to be separated from each other in such a tragic way. I insisted on helping rescue you, as I owed you that much and more."

The idea that the girl who'd once owned me would feel as though she was in my debt had my mind reeling. It was *I* who would be forever grateful to her for her unexpected kindnesses.

"I'm just glad he trusted me enough to tell me where to deliver your little one when we planned the rescue," she said. "When I heard he'd been arrested, I nearly panicked. But I could not let you suffer one more day without your daughter."

Her smile was tinged with sorrow. "I am so sorry about what Amunet and my father have done, both to you and to Lukio. You should be together, especially after all you've both been through. I wish I could do something to free him."

But even as the favored youngest daughter, I doubted she could do anything for a man deemed a traitor by the king. And if it was revealed that she'd taken part in the kidnapping of Tela's baby, she would be punished for certain. Gratitude for her kindness, and for the risks she took to reunite me with Davina, washed over me in a powerful wave.

"Please forgive me for deceiving you," I said. "But know that Lukio and I did not mean to hurt you. He was determined to honor his promise to you."

She waved a hand in dismissal. "Had I known he loved you, I would have never even considered being his bride. I can only pray that the gods will somehow give both of us our hearts' desire."

Let it be as she says, Yahweh, I thought.

"I must go and find someplace to hide for the day, so they don't track me here. But I need to replace my precious burden with something else, just in case I'm seen. . . ." She searched around the room for a moment before snatching up one of the small pillows I'd slept on last night. "Perfect!" Grinning at her own cleverness, she wrapped the fabric she'd carried my daughter in around the pillow to create a bundle of similar size and then kissed me on the cheek. "I will miss you so much."

"Thank you for saving both of us—twice," I said. Then in my own language, I spoke the priestly blessing over her, my heart aching as I wished that Oshai were here to do it for me.

"What did you say?" She peered at me curiously.

"I asked my God, Yahweh, to watch over you, be gracious to you, and to give you peace."

She smiled at me one more time and then glanced down at the baby, her blue eyes shimmering before she lifted the linen covering over her head and headed toward the door.

"Be safe, my friend," she said over her shoulder as she disappeared from my life.

How odd that she'd ever thought herself cowardly. For the rest of my days, I would count her as one of the bravest women I'd ever known.

⌒

After Galit and I donned the new clothing provided by Jaru—fine garments that must belong to his wife or daughters—we were ushered out the back door by Teo while the sun was still low in the sky. A large wagon with a canopy of woven reeds awaited us, as did several Philistine soldiers.

Jarred by the sight and terrified we were being taken back to the palace, I hesitated crawling into the wagon bed, but one of the soldiers leaned close and whispered to me in the Hebrew tongue.

"Have no fear, sister," he said, "Yahweh is with us."

Although I had no explanation for Hebrew men dressed as Philistines, I had little choice but to allow the man to help me into the wagon, where I was instructed to crawl into an enormous wide-mouth grain pot and crouch inside as he held my child. I did as I was instructed, thankful for my small stature, but not at ease until he returned Davina to my arms, along with a jar of honeyed goat milk. Then he placed a loose-woven linen covering over the opening and secured us inside by tying it closed. I was thankful that it was still cool and hopeful that our escape from the city would not take long, or else the stagnant air would become stifling for the two of us, no matter how breathable the linen was over our heads.

I listened as Galit was carefully rolled into a linen canopy near the back of the wagon, her injuries preventing her from crouching in a grain pot like me. Zevi and Igo were made to lay flat on the wagon bed, the boy speaking gently to the dog and reassuring him as they were covered with a pile of palm fronds. If anyone could keep the animal calm, it was Zevi. He seemed to have the same way with beasts as Lukio.

Once the five of us were settled, Jaru whispered again that there was no cause to fear but reminded us to remain quiet until he announced we were free from the city. As the oxen lurched forward, I soaked the end of a twisted linen cloth in the milk and put it in Davina's mouth. She suckled at it greedily, her lashes fluttering in pleasure at the taste. Within only a few minutes, she whimpered for more, and I indulged her, hoping that it would keep her well occupied until we were past the gates. She seemed not at all bothered by the fact that she'd awakened earlier in my arms instead of the Egyptian wet nurse who'd been caring for her since birth. It was almost as if she sensed who I was, even though she'd never seen me before.

As we bumped along through the city, the sounds of excited chatter mixed with the call of vendors, everyone anticipating the competitions they would be watching today. I heard the name of Demon Eyes more than once and wondered if the people would revolt when they discovered that the fighter whom they so revered was imprisoned and would not be entertaining them today.

The wagon shuddered over a bump in the road, jostling my daughter and me within the enormous grain pot. Davina whimpered, but I shushed her and then softly hummed a gentle tune while soaking the rag with the sweet milk again. As I placed the end in her mouth, she brought her tiny hand to mine and held on, making joyful tears prick at my eyes, in spite of the precarious situation we were in. After a few more moments, her lashes fluttered heavily as she slid into milk-laden slumber, even as she continued to suck on the cloth, and I wondered if perhaps in addition to honey the milk contained something to help her sleep.

After countless stops and starts through the busy street, we were halted by guards at the gate. I took up a cycle of breathless prayers to Yahweh that we would pass through without notice amidst the chaos.

"I'm taking these supplies to my men out at the arena," said Jaru from his place at the front of the wagon.

"I understand," said one of the men, "but we've been instructed not to let cargo pass through without checking. There was a prison break last night, as you know."

Jaru laughed. "Of course I know, Paito. I'm the one who assigned you to this detail."

I sucked in a breath at the revelation, as a number of details clicked into place. My secret friend was not only an influential man in Ashdod, he was the head of the royal guard. No wonder we'd been able to meet in the wine cellar under guard and that he'd been able to come and go into the palace with ease. He'd even been the one to assign his own son to watch over us.

"Zakaro," said Jaru, sounding more annoyed than worried, "hop up here and check the cargo so Paito is satisfied, will you? We are running late. The ceremonies will begin soon and there is a long line behind us."

My pulse doubled in speed as the wagon bounced with the added weight of the man named Zakaro. What was Jaru doing? What possible reason would he have for putting all of us in danger of being discovered, especially when his own family might be accused of treachery if we were caught in his wagon?

"New men, Jaru?" came Paito's voice as Zakaro poked about, and I pleaded with Yahweh to keep Zevi and Igo still beneath the palm fronds.

"Yes," replied Jaru, his voice untroubled, "I've brought in a few recruits from a village outside of Ekron. You know how difficult it is to train some of these younger ones these days. I found a few who actually know which end of the sword hurts."

After the two of them shared a hearty laugh at his jest, they continued discussing the sad state of the younger generation and then moved on to the fights today. When I heard the rustle of a body near my hiding place, I held my breath, willing Zakaro to be blind to our obvious presence.

Suddenly, the linen cover atop my pot was peeled away, and a face hovered over the opening. All my hopes for escape were dashed to pieces. I'd only held Davina in my arms for less than an hour. How could I possibly lose her so quickly?

"Nothing!" yelled the young man above me, even as he met my startled gaze. "Just supplies back here. Roasted barley, some beer jugs, shade canopies, and such."

Then, just before he replaced the linen cover, Zakaro winked at me.

Relief poured from my eyes, and I pressed my palm tight against my mouth to muffle the sob that demanded escape. Now I knew why Jaru had been so unconcerned about being stopped at the gate. He'd assigned this young man here today for this express purpose, because Zakaro had been the same guard who'd watched over us for all those months in the wine cellar. The same guard I'd prayed over each time I'd slipped past him to meet my friends.

As the wagon lurched forward again, taking us away from the city in which I'd endured so much humiliation and sorrow, I slumped back against the side of the pot and wept silently. I may be going toward home with my daughter in my arms, but once again I was leaving Lukio behind. And this time he was in the hands of a ruthless king whose murderous ways I'd now seen with my own eyes. There was no chance that I would ever see my love again.

Have mercy on him, Yahweh, I breathed as I finally allowed grief to close in around me. *Do not let him suffer.*

Thirty

Zevi and Igo bounded ahead of us on the trail, the boy insisting that he must scout ahead as we ascended toward the summit of the mountain. Of course, I knew this trail like the back of my own hand and had since I was a girl, but I said nothing, allowing him to feel useful.

After we parted from Jaru, once the wagon could no longer traverse the terrain, Zevi had found his way to my side while we walked and, after much prodding on my part, told me the entire story of his rescue and about his time in Lukio's grand residence. My chest ached for the boy who had undoubtedly begun to look up to the man who'd saved him, perhaps even regarded him as a father figure of sorts. No wonder he'd been so grieved over Lukio's capture.

Sensing he was still uncertain of me, I'd kept my eyes trained ahead as I told him that no matter what happened, he and Igo would always have a home with me and my family. He'd not responded then, but since that conversation, he'd not gone more than a few moments without turning around to keep me in his sights, as if he worried I might disappear.

It was more than obvious why Lukio had so easily connected to him. Zevi was just like he'd been as a boy: a bit suspicious, overflowing with pain, desperate for acceptance, and deeply wounded.

If only Lukio were here to help me understand him, to teach him to be a man and guide him through the rough patches that were most assuredly to come.

A few paces behind me, Galit rode astride a donkey, one Jaru had purchased from a farmer along the journey with twice its worth in silver. The captain of the royal guard had been so kind to make certain my friend did not have to walk all the way to Kiryat-Yearim, a journey that had taken us most of yesterday and half of today. My own foot had bothered me as we walked, and Galit had offered many times for me to take a turn on her donkey, but I'd refused since she was still in so much pain. The tenderness in my foot was nothing compared to what she'd endured at the hands of the guards.

So, I pushed through the pain, determined to reach Elazar's house by midday. Once we entered the Ayalon Valley in the territory of Dan, we all breathed a bit easier. But it wasn't until we began climbing the mountain of Kiryat-Yearim that I relaxed. Enclosed by the trees I'd explored with Lukio so long ago, I finally felt safe again.

The Hebrew men who'd accompanied us out of Ashdod, dressed as Philistine soldiers, had insisted on remaining with us until we arrived at our destination, and I'd been astounded to discover that Lukio had rescued them at the same time he'd saved Zevi. One of the men spoke with such reverence about the Philistine who'd helped his daughters survive the ordeal, but who also had been visibly distressed about his inability to save the man's wife from being sold to some unknown place from which she would never return.

"I will go fetch my daughters soon, since Jaru told me where to find them," said the man. "But for Lukio's sake, I will not leave your side until you are safely home. I owe him a great debt and that is what he would have wanted."

The words were so final, sounding more like a promise to a dead man than one who still breathed. Jaru had told me before he turned his wagon back toward Ashdod that the king had not immediately put Lukio to death, as I'd feared, but instead said that he would fight all four of his matches before showing them where the Ark was hidden.

My Lukio still lived and breathed in this world for now, but if he refused to lead the Philistines to the Ark—which, after unraveling the message he'd given me for Elazar, I was convinced he would not do—there would be no mercy for him. His fierce and beautiful heart would not beat much longer.

I could not even bring myself to hope that Jaru might somehow find a way to save him. I could not expect him to put his family in more danger than they already were. All I could do was pray. *Please, Yahweh*, I repeated, for the thousandth time since leaving Ashdod, *do not let him suffer. Send him a comforter. Envelop him in peace.*

The closer we came toward the upper portion of the mountain, where Elazar's home was located, the more my heart raced. I'd spent the last sixteen months convincing myself that my children were safe here, cared for by the family that had adopted Lukio and Eliora all those years ago. It had been the hope that sustained me for all this time and helped me to survive everything I'd endured. But what if I'd been wrong? What if the young man I'd sent them with on that awful day had not been able to protect them or hadn't followed my instructions? Every step I took toward the summit caused another ripple of panic to flood my bones. What would I do if they were not at the end of this path, after I'd been through so much to get here?

Davina had stayed quiet almost the entire wagon ride, but once we'd parted ways with Jaru, she'd begun to fuss. Her world had changed so much in the past day, and regardless that I was her mother, we all were still strangers to her, so I did not fault her for being uneasy. At least she'd held off making noise until we were well past the outskirts of Ashdod.

Whenever Davina caught sight of one of the men walking with us, she pressed herself closer to my body. Although I hated that she was fearful, it did my mother's heart good to have my baby take comfort in my embrace. She rode strapped to my back now, content to gaze up at the enormous trees that lined our path and hold tight to my braid as we climbed.

A haze of smoke hung in the air, the scent of cook-fires mixed with the perfume of the trees, and greenery all around wrapped me in familiarity. How strange it was that I'd only visited this part of the mountain a number of times with my father for one celebration or another—and a few more times when I'd been in search of Lukio—and yet this place felt more like a home than my own ever had.

In fact, I'd insisted we avoid the town below and head directly for Elazar's house instead of my father's. I had no desire to see him today, or ever again, if it could be helped. I wondered if perhaps Elazar might be willing to arrange a secret meeting with Levi and Yadon once I found a place to settle—if they were even still here after all these years. So many unknowns hounded me as we walked: where we would live, how I would sustain myself and my children, and what came next for me, Zevi, and Galit. But I pushed them all aside, determined not to fret about things I had no answers for—at least until we reached the top of the mountain.

When we finally emerged from the twisting trail that led up the hillside, the small grouping of homes that housed Elazar's family and a number of the Levites who guarded the Ark came into view. My heart took up an urgent drumbeat of anticipation, mixed with pulsing dread.

Would I see the faces of my children today? Or would I never do so again? Every step closer became a prayer of supplication.

That same frantic heartbeat nearly came to a halt when I caught sight of a group of children in the clearing up ahead, tossing a small leather ball between them and screaming with laughter when someone dropped it on the ground. My greedy eyes surveyed their faces, desperately searching for those I'd loved since the moment I'd realized they were growing inside my body. My gut twisted painfully when none of the dark-haired children resembled Asher or Aaliyah.

I must have released a noise of dismay, because from her seat on the donkey's back that had caught up to me when my feet slowed, Galit reached down a hand and laid it on my shoulder.

"Breathe, my friend," she said through her swollen lips. "Just breathe."

But before I could respond to her reassurances, I heard the most exquisite sound in all of creation.

"Ima!"

Jolted violently by the word, my knees wobbled as I searched for its source. Again, the small voice called out to me, and then my beautiful son tore out of the woods nearby, followed a few paces behind by my precious Aaliyah.

My eyes blurred as I darted toward them, arms outstretched. On my back Davina whimpered at being jostled about, but I could not stop my feet from racing toward my children.

When Asher's arms came around my waist, the painful relief nearly ripped me in half. As soon as Aaliyah was within two paces of me, I reached out and dragged her to me as well, finally allowing my tears to fall in a flood of gratitude and grief.

"Ima! We've missed you so much!" said Asher, his voice still high but slightly raspier than the last time I'd heard it. "Where have you been?"

Aaliyah said nothing, her face red and her eyes squeezed tightly closed as she clung to me.

I kissed both of their foreheads. "That is a long story that I will tell you soon. But I am just so grateful you are here and safe, my beautiful children. You both have grown so much!" I pulled them tighter, glorying in the feel of their bodies against mine and thanking Yahweh over and over for watching over them.

When I finally allowed them a small measure of freedom from my hold, Aaliyah's eyes went to Davina, who was peering over my shoulder in curiosity, her little grip even tighter on my braid as she took in the sight of her brother and sister.

"I have someone for you to meet," I said, kneeling down so they could see her better. "This is Davina, your sister."

Their jaws went slack as they stared at her.

"Our sister?" Asher breathed, incredulous.

"Yes, isn't she sweet?" I reached back to tickle her toes, something I'd discovered made her forget her confusion and laugh with abandon. Asher echoed her giggle and reached out a hand. Davina grabbed his fingertips with a babbling squeal, and the instant she did, I could see my son fall in love. There was a light in his eyes that told me he would champion her all of his days.

Aaliyah had still not spoken and instead studied Davina with intense interest before looking back up at me. "She is truly my sister?" she whispered tentatively, and I could not hold back the tears that fell at hearing her sweet voice again after all this time.

"She is. And I think perhaps her eyes will one day be the same lovely color as yours. Yours used to be the same shade of gray before transforming in hazel. And I know for certain she will look up to her older sister."

A sob came from Aaliyah's mouth, and she threw herself against me again, this time with her whole body shaking. I gripped her tight to my chest as she wept.

"I thought you were dead," she cried. "I thought I'd never see you again."

She must have been so shocked by my appearance that she hadn't truly let herself believe I was real until now. I understood the feeling and did not fault her for her hesitation in accepting the truth of my return.

"Oh, my love," I said, pressing my lips to her hair. "Yahweh has brought us back together. And I will never leave you again."

Asher joined our embrace, and I felt nearly whole again for the first time in sixteen months. I looked up to find a large group gathered around us. Elazar's wife, Yoela, and his daughters, Rina and Safira, were all in tears as they watched our reunion. A few other women who I did not know were gathered around us as well, and nearly twenty children were looking on in astonishment. At least my oft-imagined hopes of Asher and Aaliyah having a place to laugh and play in safety had been fulfilled. There were plenty of children up here, of a variety of ages, to make friends with. I could not have sent them to a better place.

Movement toward the back of the group drew my eye, and I was astounded to realize that Eliora and Ronen were here as well. I'd assumed they were still at Ramah, where they'd been living near Samuel the Seer these past years. Her forest-green eyes were wide with surprise as I met her gaze and her golden-brown hair spilled over her shoulder in a thick wave that reminded me far too much of her brother and the bittersweet story I must reveal to her today.

However, Yoela came forward first, kissing my cheeks in welcome and pulling me into a motherly embrace that made my throat tighten. "We are so glad you are home, Shoshana."

"Thank you," I said on a choked whisper. "And thank you for keeping my children safe. I knew this was the best and only place to send them."

"And you did well to make that decision. Aaliyah and Asher have been a blessing to our household. The young man who brought them here stayed as well. He now works down in Kiryat-Yearim with the tanner."

"I owe him everything," I said, grateful that I would have the chance to thank the boy for being so brave and saving my children. I did not know how I would ever repay him for doing so.

"It seems you have quite the story to tell," she said, taking in the sight of Galit on the donkey, and Zevi, who had a firm grip on the cord around Igo's neck—likely more for his own reassurance than to control the timid dog pressed to his side. "And I am certain you all are exhausted and hungry. But at least tell us where you have been all this time."

I took a deep breath, reluctantly looking past her to Eliora. My heart stuttered as I spoke directly to her. "In Ashdod. Where Lukio . . . Natan has been all these years."

His sister, whom I now saw was in an advanced state of pregnancy, let out a cry. Wobbling, she was caught by her husband before she could sink to the ground.

How would I ever tell her that the hope I'd just given her was nothing more than a farce—and a cruel one at that? Lukio would be dead within the week, and there was nothing anyone could do to stop it.

⌒

"And you say he asked you to tell me of a *game* he taught you?" asked Elazar, whose hair and beard had become thoroughly gray while I'd been gone from the mountain. "What does this have to do with the Ark?"

With my children firmly planted on either side of me, Elazar, Eliora, Ronen, and I had been talking together atop the canopied roof of Elazar's home about all that had happened in Ashdod, while the women prepared a meal and Eliora's sister, Miri, tended to Galit's injuries with the skill of a seasoned healer. Zevi remained down in the courtyard with Igo, watching some of the boys play with swords they'd fashioned from sticks. The longing on his face had been evident, and I hoped it would not take long before he, too, was joyfully engaged in mock battles with the boys of Kiryat-Yearim.

"I am certain he was giving me directions about what to do with the Ark. So, even if the worst came to pass, and the king of Ashdod somehow discovered it was here, it would be protected."

"But what does this have to do with a game?" pressed the Levite, his silver brows furrowed.

"He told me he'd taught it to me in his special place. I thought perhaps he meant the sycamore tree, where we used to sneak out and meet as children, but then I realized he'd said *his* special place, which was a certain cave on the southwest slope."

I'd already told Elazar of the secret friendship Lukio and I had had when we were younger, but I'd revealed nothing of our dreams to marry all those years ago.

Eliora gasped softly, her hand clutching Ronen's. "I remember that cave. It's where I found Yonah the day Natan ran off."

"It was where he went whenever he was upset," I said. "His refuge. He only took me there a few times over the years."

"Did you know he was planning to leave?" asked Eliora, a note of uncharacteristic frustration in her voice. "That he was storing supplies in that cave?"

"No," I said, looking directly into her eyes. "I would have told you if I had any suspicions. It would have broken my heart to think of him leaving this mountain."

"I know," she said, giving me a contrite look. "I did not mean to accuse you. I know how deeply you cared for him—and he for you." I'd wondered if perhaps she'd sensed my love for her brother back then, especially after I'd come to fetch her during that last horrific fight between Lukio and Medad, when I thought they might kill each other.

"Was there something other than friendship between the two of you?" asked Elazar.

My face went warm. It was one thing to discuss it with Lukio's sister, but his stoic father was a different matter.

"Our friendship transformed as we grew older, and Lukio . . . Natan said he was determined to marry me someday. It was innocent, I assure you, but though we were young we were very attached to each other."

"And those affections have not changed?" Apparently, Elazar was determined to know all of it.

"Being in Ashdod stirred up those . . . memories. But as I said, he is . . ." I paused to take a breath. "He was betrothed to the daughter of the king." I blinked against the tears prickling at my composure, and Eliora reached over to give my hand a reassuring squeeze.

"I see," said Elazar. "So, tell me, why *this* game? Was it something you played together frequently?"

"No," I replied. "He only showed me once."

"And you know this is the game he meant for you to show me?"

I smiled. "I am. Once I show you, it will make perfect sense to you as well. However, I do need a few objects in order to do so." I turned to my son. "Asher, can you quickly run down and search out four acorns from under the trees?"

"Of course, Ima!" he said, delighted to be of help, even if it would be the first time he'd let me out of his sight since my return.

"And, Aaliyah, can you go down and ask Yoela for six drinking cups?"

My daughter hesitated, plainly unsettled to go anywhere without me.

"I will be right here when you return." I gave her a reassuring smile. She rose and did as I asked but checked over her shoulder twice before descending the stairs.

"Your little ones will be all right, Shoshana," said Eliora, after Ronen and Elazar excused themselves to confer together on the other side of the roof until the children returned. "If there is anything I've learned by having children of my own, it is that they are resilient. Once they see you are here for good, their fears will eventually fade."

I'd been told that my father and brothers had left Kiryat-Yearim soon after Medad took me to Beth Shemesh, which again left me without any family, so I found it more than comforting that Eliora assumed I would remain on the mountain. My children were obviously comfortable here, and I could not imagine ripping them away from a place that had offered them safety and stability when their mother had disappeared. Besides, I had nowhere else to go.

"How many children do you have?" I asked. "There are so many out there I don't know who belongs to who."

She laughed. "Yes, they are a small village unto themselves, aren't they? We have four now. And this one, who should make an appearance before the latter rains begin." She smoothed a hand over her rounded belly.

"And you remain at Ramah?"

"Yes, for now. Ronen has become a leader among the musicians there. Miri and her husband came with us, along with their three children. We returned for the celebration of Amina's betrothal. She is to marry a young Levite in a year."

"It is difficult to think of little Miri as a married woman."

Eliora's smile remained in place, but something in her eyes told me that Miri's past had not been an easy one. "She came to help me while I was pregnant with our eldest son, Avidan, and met a Benjamite during that time."

That surprised me. Most women married those of their own tribes, but it certainly wasn't unheard of for tribes to intermingle, even with the Canaanites and other foreigners among us. However, it did surprise me that Elazar would allow it, since all of his other daughters were married to Levites, Eliora included.

"She has a son just a few months younger than our Avidan," she said, which clarified the situation. Miri must have been already with child when the wedding occurred. "In fact, I would guess that your Zevi is similar in age to both Avidan and Gavriel. Perhaps the three of them will become friends. Although I think all the children are equal parts hesitant and enthralled with that giant beast watching over him."

I laughed. "Fear not. That beast is as gentle as a lamb. But he is devoted to Zevi. The poor child is alone in the world, from what I understand. And I think he has suffered much. Lukio . . . I mean, Natan told him that he would find a home here on the mountain, and I mean to fulfill that vow."

"I would expect nothing less. You are a wonderful mother," she said, "and Zevi will be blessed to have you take him under your wing." She paused to peer at me. "It's all right if you call him Lukio, Shoshana. I still think of him that way as well sometimes. Perhaps it is more my hope that he would someday embrace life with the Hebrews that causes me to call him Natan."

My cheeks flushed warm again. "It was a secret name, of sorts, between us. He was Lukio, and I was Tesi."

"Small one," she said, recognizing the Philistine word. "I can see why he called you that. I knew there was something between you back then, and he even admitted it to me when he discovered you were betrothed. I am not surprised that my brother still adores you after all this time. He is nothing if not loyal, which is why he was so very devastated when he thought that the three of us had betrayed him. It is his greatest strength but also his greatest weakness, I think."

"I am sorry that I don't bring better news of him," I said past the burn in my throat. "I would do anything if it meant he was here with us now."

She looked into my eyes with open affection. "I have learned to hold not only him but everything in my life with an open hand, trusting that no matter what, Yahweh is good and that he is watching over my brother, even in Ashdod. Until we know for certain that he no longer breathes, I will pray for his return."

Eliora had been a woman of grace and kindness when I left this mountain, but after years of living in the company of Samuel and those he was raising up to speak truth to the tribes of Israel, it was clear that she'd become a woman of great strength and faith as well. For someone born a Philistine, a child of our enemies, this was a miracle indeed.

"And even if I do not see him again in this life," she continued, her deep green eyes shimmering with tears, "I am consoled by his honorable actions in these past months. He may have spent the last few years as a fighter, just as I feared, but he is not our birth father. From what you've said, he defended the helpless and risked himself to save lives, just as Azuvah prophesied he would the night she saved us. And for that I will praise the name of Adonai."

Asher appeared at the top of the stairs, his face alight with glee before I could ask her more about what else their childhood maid had said about Lukio. "I found all four acorns, Ima!"

He dumped the treasures into my hand and sank down beside me, pressing close and grinning up at me with open adoration. Aaliyah, too, returned, carefully carrying a stack of six ceramic cups with slow and measured steps.

"Thank you, my loves," I said giving them both a kiss once Aaliyah settled back into her place at my side. Just the act of being able to kiss my children after all these months filled my heart with overflowing gratitude. My entire body seemed replete with joy.

The men returned to sit with us, Ronen tugging his wife closer to place his own kiss on her cheek and give a gentle brush of his palm over her middle. His adoration of Eliora and his unborn child caused a small pang of envy in my heart.

"Does anyone have a knife?" I asked, pushing away the longing for something that would never be. Ronen handed me a small bronze one from his belt that he probably used for instrument building. It was far too delicate to be a weapon.

I pried the top off one of the four acorns as everyone watched me with rapt attention. Then I placed each one beneath a cup and shuffled them—along with the two empty cups—around on the ground in an exaggerated manner. I could not keep the image of Lukio doing this very same thing on the floor of the cave from rising up, but I blinked it away, I was already at the very limits of my control; it would not do for me to burst into tears in front of everyone. Once I was certain that the players of my game were sufficiently disoriented, I slid one cup in front of each of us.

"There now," I said, "Asher, where is the acorn without a top?"

He pointed to Eliora's cup, and when I told her to lift it, there was no acorn at all. He frowned deeply.

"Aaliyah? Where do you think it might be?"

She hesitantly pointed to her own cup, but the acorn beneath it was intact.

One by one each cup was lifted, but none of them held the acorn with the missing top.

"Where did it go?" demanded Asher, bewildered and irritated that none of his guesses had been correct.

But Ronen was already grinning, having divined my trick.

"Ima! Show me!" said Asher.

But Aaliyah had guessed as well. She laid her small hand atop mine, and her hazel eyes sparkled up at me. Grinning, I unfolded my palm to reveal the missing acorn and tapped her on the nose with it.

Asher's jaw dropped. "How did you do that?"

But before I could answer, Elazar articulated Lukio's message with a note of awe in his voice. "He proposes we have false vessels constructed and marched about the territory so people will think it's been moved."

I nodded, glad that he'd not only deciphered the meaning of the game but also that he seemed intrigued by Lukio's idea. When I'd finally figured out the message within the message, I'd thought it was nothing short of brilliant.

"All it would take is a few priests carrying a linen-covered box on their shoulders," I said. "Since unconsecrated Hebrews cannot approach the Ark, they'd never know the difference."

"But in truth the Ark would remain here?"

"Yes. In the cave," I said. "It's plenty large enough, easily hidden by brush, and difficult to get to without knowledge of the mountain. Even if somehow the Philistines discovered Kiryat-Yearim to be the resting place of the Ark, they would be hard-pressed to find it. Especially if the tent it has been in for these past two decades remains standing, but empty."

Ronen seemed delighted by the idea. "We could even have a few men go into the towns where Philistines trade and spread rumors that the Ark was moved months ago, whisper that it was taken down to the Mountain of Adonai, or all the way up to Har Hermon, or to the east side of the Jordan, or even . . . that it disappeared in a fiery cloud and was taken into the heavenly realms! That should confuse our enemies plenty."

Elazar stroked his beard, his eyes on the cups and acorns. "They have been getting very close to us now that they control Tzorah and Beth Shemesh. And if they somehow break past Dan's defenses in the Ayalon Valley and take control of the eastern trade route, they will have us surrounded on three sides."

"It's a good plan," said Ronen. "Smart. Crafty. And it keeps the Ark where it should remain until the Philistine threat can be mitigated."

"Do you think that will happen?" I asked.

"Samuel believes so. Under his leadership, the tribes have defended against a number of attempted raids. And we've been seeing the people of Yahweh returning to his ways in droves—whole clans coming together to burn their idols, reaffirm their commitment to the covenant, and circumcise their males, young and old. Many of the tribes now see Samuel for what he is: a shofet chosen by Yahweh to adjudicate the Torah and to reveal his Word to the people."

"There are those who do not see him that way," cautioned Elazar. "Many of the clans of Yehudah and Simeon still see him as a usurper. They've installed their own High Priest at Hebron and refuse to submit to Samuel's authority."

"My uncle and his friends escaped justice after their attempt to steal the Ark," said Ronen. "Some of them fled south, vowing to lift up a descendent of Eleazar ben Aharon. And so they did."

"They will certainly not be happy when they hear we've moved the Ark," said Elazar.

"All the more reason to sow seeds of confusion," said Ronen. "I hope my uncle will not make another attempt at stealing it, but, knowing him as I do, I am certain he's not stopped plotting ways to get his greedy hands on it."

"I will confer with my men and send a message to Samuel. We'll need to do this carefully and correctly, and I do not want to do anything until I have his blessing."

The door opened just then, and three broad-shouldered men strode inside. Gershom and Iyov looked much the same as they had when I left Kiryat-Yearim, but Gershom's beard and hair were threaded with silver like his father's once had been. Yonah, however, had become a man. At eighteen, he stood nearly as tall as his older brothers. The only thing that set him apart from the rest was his slightly uneven gait, due to the foot that had been twisted from birth. It was likely that the three of them had been summoned from down in the valley when we returned, since none of them looked surprised to see me.

"What plan?" said Gershom, the eldest.

"Your brother sent Shoshana with a scheme to hide the Ark," replied his father. "It seems the king of Ashdod has a particular obsession with seeking it out."

My heart clenched tight at hearing Elazar call Lukio their brother. Just as I'd assured him, even after all these years his family hadn't turned their backs on him. If only he could see the distress and concern on their faces now. Their lack of surprise at their father's announcement made it apparent they'd already been told where Lukio was and some of what had happened over the past ten years.

Iyov looked down at me. "Where is he?"

I frowned, wondering if I'd been mistaken about how informed they were.

"In Ashdod still," I replied. "He bargained his life for mine."

"No, I mean, where is he now? In a prison?"

"I don't know. The only thing Jaru told me was that the king insisted he fight during the festival before leading the army to the Ark."

"When?" asked Gershom.

"There are to be four matches in total, one each day of the festival. Today is the second day. Once he is finished fighting, they will undoubtedly kill him. But why does that matter?"

"Because," said Yonah, his eyes narrowing, none of the small and uncertain boy he'd once been remaining in his iron-jawed expression, "we're bringing him home."

Thirty-One

Lucio

Teitu did not look well. The dim light from the high slits in the watchtower walls illuminated the swollen and bloodied mess that was his face and torso, and I wondered how he'd even survived this last beating. But at least he still had one eye.

I'd fought three times now, playing the part of Demon Eyes and winning each time. However, each time I returned to my prison, the one within the vineyard watchtower on my own land, where the Hebrew men had been held, Nicaro's men had beaten Teitu in front of me—a reminder of what was to come if I did not continue my streak of wins.

I'd only seen Nicaro himself out on the fighting grounds, where I was forced to bow before him in a public show of loyalty before and after each match and give glory to the king who would kill me the moment he realized I'd lied to him about the whereabouts of the Ark.

But he certainly could not fault my performance. I stirred up the crowd, prancing about with the arrogance I'd perfected over the years. I made light of my opponents, mocking them when they finally begged for mercy, and the people of Ashdod screamed for me. There was no doubt that Nicaro would be revered forever after this festival and that the people would clamor for it year after year. There was not a face in the crowd without a wide grin, except for Mariada, who looked beyond miserable as she watched me grovel to her father.

I'd made only one exception to my public display of obeisance to the king, when I came forward and made a great show of kissing the king's daughter on the cheek, since no one in the crowd yet knew that we would never marry. And while the crowd cheered and whistled and made lurid calls for more kisses, I'd quietly thanked her for rescuing the baby and asked if she was all right. She'd nodded, but the tears that filled her blue eyes hurt nearly as much as the next strike I took from my Egyptian opponent. I had no idea whether her duplicity in the kidnapping had been uncovered, but I prayed that whatever punishment Amunet insisted on for her was mitigated by Nicaro's adoration of his youngest child and his third wife. Perhaps he would count her disobedience as merely the product of girlish devotion to me or misplaced loyalty to her maid.

Although Nicaro had glared at me for my insolence as I turned my back on him to face my next opponent, there was nothing he could do in front of a crowd that was convinced for the moment that I was nearly divine—and enthralled by his beautiful daughter.

I'd almost felt sorry for the man I'd fought on the third day of the festival. He'd been the winner of the open fights on the first day and was certainly a large man, a fisherman who hefted nets in and out of boats every day, but he was in no way prepared for me. I'd stretched out the fight for as long as I could without humiliating him, but for Teitu's sake, I could not chance restraining my punches or softening my kicks.

After I'd made the man plead for mercy by locking him in a chokehold on the ground, he'd thanked me for the opportunity to go up against me, as if losing to Demon Eyes was a great honor. If only he knew how powerless I truly was. How much of a slave I'd made myself.

Teitu and I had spent much of the past three days talking about where we came from to take our minds off our inescapable prison and to pass the time. Although I'd been careful not to give him details about Kiryat-Yearim, I'd told him of my time in Hebrew territory, about my secret friendship with Shoshana, about the family that had taken me in, and even my regrets for rejecting their kindnesses.

In turn, he'd told me of how he'd been born within a wandering tribe that lived in the southern Wilderness of Paran, south of Be'er Sheva. Teitu was the son of a Yehudite woman and an Egyptian who had been rescued after a sandstorm separated him from his company and had been taken in by the woman's clan. When a band of Amalekites came across the group, they slaughtered most of them and sold the survivors to the Philistines.

It had been Teitu's first master who'd taken his eye as punishment for daring to look at his beautiful daughter and then sold him to a trader who'd brought him north, where I'd found him being auctioned off for half the price of a well-bodied slave in the marketplace.

The more I listened to Teitu's tragic experiences, the more remorseful I became. I'd never even asked my manservant where he'd come from, what his heritage was, or how he'd come to be a slave. And it had been this misjudgment that had led to his capture, since he'd admitted to overhearing me speak with Zevi in Hebrew about breaking Shoshana out of the storage room and had understood my words. No wonder he'd been so eager to help me speak with Shoshana the day I'd invited Mariada, her mother, and her sister to my home. He'd already guessed my attachment to my betrothed's maid went far deeper than infatuation with a beautiful slave. I'd underestimated him many times over and wasted years that could have been filled with friendship.

"Thank you," Teitu said. "For being a good master."

"I wish I'd never been a master at all," I said, thoroughly disgusted with myself for ever purchasing a man or woman to serve me. It was my fault he was here, chained to a wall and beaten so badly that I could barely distinguish his features anymore.

"If you did not purchase me that day, I would have been used either as labor in a brickfield, or put on a ship, or who knows what else. And without a doubt I would have been buried in some mass grave or tossed to the sea once my body was used up. Instead, you treated me with kindness and gave me a place to live and work where I had no cause to fear. Those of us who were half-blind, deaf, maimed, or had some other affliction would have been disposable to anyone else. You are a good man, Lukio."

Burning emotion clogged my throat. Of all the things I'd been called in my life, a good man had never been one of them.

"And no matter what," he said, "you must not reveal the location of the Ark. It is too precious. Too sacred."

I had to believe that Shoshana had deciphered my coded message. She was too quick-witted to let such a thing go untangled. "I've taken steps to have it hidden, in case they try to force my hand."

"You cannot tell them." His voice hardened. "No matter what."

"But if they torture you—"

He twisted his head to look at me, that one dark eye as sharp as a spear, giving me a glimpse of who Teitu would have been, had he not been enslaved. "No matter what, Lukio. You will *not* give up the Ark for my sake. Promise me this."

I did not know how I would ever withstand watching Nicaro's men cut Teitu to pieces, but I promised him, nonetheless.

My one consolation in all of this horror was that Shoshana and the others would have already arrived in Kiryat-Yearim. I'd seen Jaru only once since my capture, during a change of the guard that surrounded the watchtower. He could only give me one pointed nod, but the relief that had sluiced through me from that small gesture had been overwhelming. It told me that at the least she and Zevi had been delivered to the point just north of the Sobek River, where we'd felt they could reach Elazar's house safely within a day's walk. They must be on the mountain even now. Any other outcome was too devastating to consider.

Please, Yahweh, I thought, then wondered when I had begun

regularly pleading with the God whom my sister and Shoshana revered.

But who else did I have to supplicate? Dagon? The Great Mother? Baalzebub? None of the gods or goddesses my people worshipped had done a thing for me, but over these past few days in prison, I'd begun to ponder whether the God the Hebrews said ruled the entire universe might actually exist. How else could I explain that not only had the girl I'd loved ended up as the maid to my betrothed, and that the son of the slave-woman who raised me had come into my life at the perfect time, and that I'd also been given the opportunity to protect the very same vessel my sister and I had followed into Hebrew territory? There had to be a reason that I just happened to be crouched in the bushes on the same hill as the kings of Philistia that day I overheard Nicaro's argument with the others—the very thing that would prove to him almost two decades later that I knew the Ark's location. All of it was too much of a coincidence not to be divine appointment. Perhaps Risi's prayers over me had protected and guided me, after all, no matter what I'd done since I'd run from her precious, sacred mountain.

And if all those things were not coincidences, then perhaps the rest of the stories were true as well—the fire from the box that killed the Levites at Beth Shemesh; the strange mist that thwarted the theft of the Ark and saved Risi and Ronen's lives; perhaps even the stories Elazar and his father, Abinidab, used to tell us about the sea parting and the Hebrews walking through on dry land.

And the question I wrestled most with was, if all of that was real, did that mean that the God of the universe might actually care about *me*? A sullied Philistine who'd done everything he could to reject him and run from his presence?

So, with half my mind in the camp of disbelief and the other in the camp of desperation, I'd continued to pray for my Tesi, for Zevi, and even for Teitu. I only wished I had more than my tainted blood to offer as a sacrifice for their lives.

The door to our prison opened, and a guard stepped inside, followed by none other than my cousin Mataro.

The guard hastily checked to ensure my bonds, and those of Teitu, were secure while warning my cousin that he had only a few moments to speak with me. He then walked out and closed the door behind Mataro with a clank.

"The great Lukio," my cousin said, frowning in mock concern, "in shackles. I never thought I would see the day. When my friend told me he was guarding the famous Demon Eyes out here, I did not believe it. But thankfully for me, Paremo is easily persuaded with the promise of silver."

"What do you want, Mataro?" I asked.

He clucked his tongue. "Can I not simply visit my beloved cousin in his hour of need?"

"Don't bother to play ignorant. It is *your* fault that Shoshana was arrested and her friends killed."

He shrugged, his yellowed teeth displayed in a vicious smile. "I warned you."

"You've seen me in shackles now. Fitting punishment for the audacity of setting myself free from the ones you bound me in."

"Oh no. It's not nearly enough to merely see you brought low. You were supposed to make me rich."

"I did that. You live in luxury."

"I *did* until you dared toss me aside and my creditors came slithering out of their holes. They came for it all. The house. The jewels. If I hadn't hidden away a good amount of silver in a secret place, they'd have taken that too."

"You were unwise in your dealings, Mataro. That is not my fault."

"But you can redeem yourself now," he said. "Today. And all will be forgiven."

"And how would I do that, even if I wanted to? I am at the mercy of the king."

He withdrew a knife from his belt, a sinister grin made even more macabre by his boil-scarred face.

"I arranged a special match for you today, cousin. A champion brought here all the way from Gaza. When you lose, the bet I made against you with what remains of my silver will be multiplied ten-fold, maybe more. And when you die of the injuries you sustain during your match, I, your only living relative, will inherit all you own." That wicked grin curved over his face again. "And then, finally, I'll have recompense for all you've cost me."

Before I could respond, my cousin lunged forward with his weapon. Chained as I was to the wall and my feet bound together, I could do little more than twist sideways. His knife sliced at my side instead of stabbing into my belly, but the sharp edge of his bronze knife left a searing and bloody mark the length of my hand.

I let out a loud bellow and brought my bound legs up at an angle to swipe his feet out from beneath him. Faster than I would have expected of a man whose body was composed of ample amounts of drink and fatty flesh, he brought the knife down again and plunged it deep into the meat of my thigh.

The door flew open once again, and through the haze of pain I saw Jaru charge at Mataro, disarming him easily and locking my cousin into an unbreakable chokehold. I'd known Jaru was a captain of the guard, a position he'd earned over years of dealing with situations like these, but his skill at subduing Mataro was impressive.

"He's the one who killed your mother," I said, gritting my teeth against the ache in my leg.

Jaru's dark brown eyes flew to mine for only one fraught moment, and I met them without blinking. Then, as swiftly as he'd knocked the knife from Mataro's hand, he plunged his own dagger into the throat of the man who'd thrown Azuvah's beaten and life-less body from a window without remorse. With a horrific sound, Mataro crumpled to the floor, gurgling and twitching for only a few moments before everything went silent.

"It's unfortunate I discovered your cousin attempting to help you escape," said Jaru, with an almost eerie calmness after taking vengeance for the mother he'd never known.

I nodded. "It is indeed."

"And it's unfortunate that you were forced to engage the champion of Ashdod when he tried to disarm you as well," said Teitu, filling in the rest of the conjured explanation that would protect Jaru and his family.

Jaru knelt beside me to examine my wounds. "The slash in your side is minimal. But the one in your leg is deep. You won't be able to fight."

Wincing at the throbbing of my leg, I shook my head. "I have to fight. There is no option. Otherwise Nicaro will have Teitu blinded, or worse."

"But you are bleeding profusely, Lukio. You'll barely be able to stand in two hours, let alone be at your best."

"Bind me up," I insisted. "I've fought while injured before."

"But this is nothing like your other matches," he said, his brows deeply furrowed.

"And why is that?"

"Because your opponent is like none other," he said. "The Gazan they brought here for you to face in your final bout is one of the Rephaim. A giant."

Thirty-Two

The moment I stepped onto the fighting grounds, the crowd went rabid. Their screams and cheers echoed across the valley, swirling around me like a whirlwind. Each successive day that I'd fought here, they'd gotten wilder and wilder, calling for me to finish off my competitors the same way that vicious group did the day I saved Igo. I'd always left my opponents breathing, but I had the sense that if I *were* to tear a man apart in front of them, they would only scream for more. It sickened me to realize that if Shoshana had never come back into my life, I might have traveled down that very road.

And yet I could not help but marvel at the sight before me and compare it to the first fight Mataro had arranged when I was an untried lad. There had been perhaps ten people watching that day, but I would never forget the exhilaration of hearing them cheer my first victory and how proud I'd been that they found me worthy of adulation.

This crowd must be a least a hundred times that first one, the sound of their adoration near deafening, and I felt nothing. These people did not know me. All they saw was the famous Demon Eyes who lined their purses with silver or filled their jars with barley and olive oil. How could I have ever thought the appreciation of a thousand strangers meant anything compared with the people

304

who'd loved me in spite of my heritage? I was glad none of Elazar's household were here to see my shame.

My leg throbbed with every step I took, but Jaru had managed to not only find a surgeon to stitch my wounds but who also bound them tightly enough that I was able to walk.

However, all of us knew that the bandages around my middle and my leg were equal to a brightly painted target for my opponent and that it would not take much for those carefully sewn sutures to burst open.

But, as was my duty, I pretended that the linens were nothing more than decoration as I strutted around the field, lifting my arms to encourage the crowd to scream even louder for me. I even accepted a stick that one of the children offered me and played at sword fighting with him for a few moments, grinning with false enjoyment. With the calls of vendors winding through the crowd to hawk food and wares, the flutter of banners bearing my own insignia—a double-headed ax gripped in two powerful fists—and the scores of women sporting brown and green kohl on their lids, this final day of the festival was by all accounts a success.

Jaru had even told me that the other events I'd arranged had come together perfectly even without my oversight because I'd delegated everything so well and Oleku had stepped in where necessary. If I'd never been entangled in Shoshana's escape, this entire festival would have been a triumph. But instead of tasting victory on this culmination of my ten years in Ashdod, it all felt like ash and dust in my mouth.

I wanted to be where everything and everyone I loved lived on a high hill surrounded by the cool forest, in a small grouping of stone homes that could barely be distinguished from the landscape around them. I missed the hushed forest when the rain trickled through the leaves on misty days. I missed the feel of my ax in my callused palms. I missed the home and family I'd thrown away. I wanted to cut down trees and kiss my Tesi and hold my children in my arms. I wanted to walk with Zevi and Igo in the woods and show the boy how to wield an ax.

I wanted to go home.

Instead, I turned to the king of Ashdod with a thousand curses knocking against the back of my teeth and, for the very last time, knelt in the dirt before him for the sake of the man who should never have been a slave but instead should have been my friend.

A loud collective gasp from the crowd pulled my attention away from the king and to the far end of the field. I surged to my feet.

My opponent had arrived.

He was a full head taller than me and built like a sprawling cedar. I'd fought men taller than me on a few occasions but never a man with such expansive brawn. My only hope was that he, like the fisherman yesterday, was not trained in the methods I'd spent the past decade perfecting.

I would have to use every technique I knew, suss out his weaknesses, and find a way to get him to the ground, where my strengths lie, all while hiding the fact that I was seriously wounded.

But no matter my trepidations and my guess that this would be the one fight I had little chance at winning, I grinned at the giant and made a mocking bow. At least for Teitu's sake, I had to try.

The moment Nicaro dropped his hand, the Gazan charged as if he were coming across a battlefield at me. He was a mercenary warrior for certain, the way he came at me with a bold frontal attack.

But I had faced such men before, all brashness and little strategy, so I was able to throw him to the side with little effort. The spectators vibrated with excitement, the moniker I hoped to never again hear after this day coming at me from a thousand mouths.

The giant growled and charged again, his enormous hands grabbing for my shoulders, but again I slipped out of his grasp and threw a punch that hit him square in the corner of his jaw. He flinched but shook off the blow far faster than any other man I'd faced during a match.

And so it went for a long while, the two of us trading blows and working to knock the other off-balance, but neither of us giving much ground. If only I had use of the powerful kicks that had served me in past bouts against men larger than me. One blow to the right spot in the man's torso would have brought him to the ground, no matter his size, but I could not kick with my right leg when my injured left would not hold me steady. Mataro had made certain that my left leg was little more than a damaged prop and not the weapon it had been earlier this morning.

As it was, I was forced to rely on feinting tactics and my ability to slither out of his untrained holds in order to keep up a varied pattern of punches that caught him off-guard, hoping that I would wear the big man down enough that he would make a mistake.

Annoyed with the last hit that had caught him beneath the chin and forced him to bite his own tongue, he lunged for me, blood drooling from his mouth, and slammed his own fist into my side, directly into the place Mataro had cut me. I could not help but cry out as pain radiated up my body. Although I twisted free of him, I saw the moment he realized what I had—the sutures in my side had broken free. I could feel the trickle of blood down my side and knew the linen would already be turning scarlet.

His eyes flared, and a sneer turned his already fearsome face into something sinister when his attention flicked down to my leg. Nausea flared in my throat as I anticipated what was to come, but I could not hesitate. I lashed out with two more hits to his face, but neither had my usual power. He volleyed back with a slap to the side of my head that had my ears ringing.

Before I could rebound from the hit, he kicked me directly in the left leg, and all I could see for a few moments was stars of every hue streaking across my sight. While I was reeling, I received more blows to the face and one in the side that made me gasp in agony as a rib gave way. And then, before my mind had even caught up from the attack, I was on the ground.

The mood of the crowd had shifted drastically. No longer were they screaming my name in triumph. Instead, there were hisses and droning noises of disapproval—perhaps for me, perhaps for my opponent, but it would not be long before they turned on me. Perhaps Nicaro would even let the giant tear me apart like

Tombaal had wanted done to Igo. I was nothing more than a dog to these people, after all.

The giant had somehow gotten his thick arm around my neck and was squeezing, stealing my breath, his huge body pressing my own into the dirt so thoroughly that I could barely move. I could do nothing but grip his forearm and tear at it, making a futile attempt at pulling in a breath as my sight wavered.

How fitting that my life would end here in the very same dirt that my fame and fortune had purchased, beneath a giant like the one I'd swore I would one day rival. My one consolation as everything faded into darkness and the crowd bellowed their disappointment was that at least my family, all of it, was safe in Kiryat-Yearim. I could practically smell the sweetness of the forest air, see my sister beckoning me homeward, and hear my Tesi calling my name from under our sycamore tree. . . .

Thirty-Three

I groaned. There was no part of me that did not hurt, especially my left leg and my side, which felt like it had been stitched up again. Worst of all was the fiery brand searing my throat. I made an attempt to swallow, but it only enflamed the throbbing pain. The giant must have damaged something deep inside.

I peeled my eyes open, another painful move since the left one was swollen shut, and found nothing but blackness. I must be in the watchtower again, which made no sense at all since I should be dead in the middle of the fighting grounds. I was so broken they hadn't even bothered to bind my hands and feet.

Although I could not see anything, I felt a presence in the room.

"Teitu?" I rasped, the whisper causing another bolt of agony in my throat.

But there was no response from my friend in the dark. Only thick silence and the odd feeling that someone was there, watching me. I tried again, but when no whisper returned to me, dread began to settle into my bruised bones.

After a third time with no response, I accepted the truth. No one was here with me. I'd lost the fight and Nicaro's men had come for Teitu. Were they even now torturing him for my failure to best the giant? I could blame Mataro for his ambush, but ultimately it was my fault that Teitu would be blinded and maimed.

I let my face fall back to the ground, welcoming the throbbing pain in every one of my extremities. I deserved to hurt.

Feeling even more defeated than I'd been with my face pressed into the dirt by that Gazan, I fell into sleep again. When a burst of sunlight woke me, I cursed the fact that I was still alive.

A large man hunched through the small doorway, and I expected that he'd be dragging Teitu's mutilated body, but instead Jaru alone stood before me with an unreadable expression on his face.

"I was not certain you would awaken," he said, frowning as he took in the mangled mess of bruises and bloody abrasions that must now be my face.

"Teitu?" I managed to rasp through the fire in my throat.

Jaru's jaw worked back and forth, as if he were physically holding back his response.

"Blind?" I pressed.

"He's gone, Lukio."

I shook my head.

His response was far too gentle for a man who was supposed to be my jailor. "When I checked on him just before your fight began, he'd passed. I am sorry."

I stared at Jaru, unwilling to accept that the man who'd been so undeservedly loyal to me was truly gone.

"How?" I managed to grit through teeth that ached just as badly as every other part of me.

"His injuries were severe," he replied, but Azuvah's son would not look me in the eye.

"Tell me," I demanded, uncaring that I was aggravating the damage in my throat.

"He is gone, Lukio. Let us leave it at that."

Whatever had happened, Jaru had every intention of keeping the details to himself for some reason. And perhaps it was for the best. At least Teitu was at rest now, after all he'd suffered.

"May his memory be a blessing," whispered Jaru, in the tongue of his mother.

I kept my silence, mourning the man I'd never known was such a loyal friend until it was too late.

"The king is on his way here," Jaru said. "I am to bring you out before him."

I heaved a sigh and made an attempt to get to my feet, but my wounded leg would not hold me. Jaru slipped his arm around my torso, taking enough of my weight on him that I could stand.

"My servants?" I whispered, hoping he'd remembered my request from a few days before.

"Arrangements have been made for them all," he replied.

Overcome by gratitude, all I could do was swallow down the sharp lump in my ruined throat and nod my thanks. "And Mariada?"

"They know she took the child, but she managed to convince them that you and Shoshana manipulated her into doing so. Besides, once Nicaro found out that the babe was Hebrew, he turned his anger on Tela and Amunet. Don't fear for Mariada. My son remains as a guard in the palace. He will watch over her."

I exhaled, comforted by the knowledge that she would not suffer for her part in this and that Jaru would make certain she was safe.

"It has been an honor to know you, Lukio," Jaru said in a low tone.

I looked into the eyes that were the same as the woman who sang me to sleep when I was a child and who loved me so well that she offered her life for mine. I marveled again that her son had been brought into my life in such an extraordinary way. "You do your mother great credit, Jaru. If you ever need refuge, go to Kiryat-Yearim."

He acknowledged my words with only a silent nod, as if he were too overwhelmed to speak, then helped me squeeze through the narrow opening, something that was infinitely more agonizing than when I'd crawled through it yesterday.

The sun blinded me for a few moments as I emerged, but once my lopsided vision cleared, my lush vineyard spread out around me like a paradise, the vines soon to be heavy with fruit. My silver-leafed olive trees shivered in the distance beneath a gentle salt-air breeze. At least I would die beneath a beautiful blue sky with the smell of green in my nose.

Jaru's six men stood in a semicircle around me, with their hands on their weapons, as if I would lunge at them any moment. Even after my defeat, they feared Demon Eyes, a fact that I once would have reveled in and now meant nothing at all.

Instead, the once-revered champion of Ashdod slumped to the ground the moment Jaru released me, my legs shaking so badly they could not hold my weight. I sat there, with my back to the stone wall of the tall watchtower. Instead of thinking on what agonies lay before me, I closed my eyes and pictured my Tesi with her children, her laughter bright as she explored the woods with them like we did when we were young. Somehow, the images assuaged a small measure of the pain.

But when I opened my eyes again a short while later, the king of Ashdod was five paces away, staring at me with cool condescension.

"Where is it?"

I did not answer.

"Where?" he urged, no longer dispassionate. "Where is it? I sent someone to Beth Shemesh. You lied."

I'd wondered if he might not be too impatient to wait for me to dig the hole. I simply shrugged at him. Teitu was gone, anyhow.

"Tell me or you die."

I summoned Demon Eyes one last time and smirked at him.

His blue eyes blazed as he gestured to his men. They lunged at me almost as one, landing blows to my torso that had me gasping for air and their kicks to my legs and arms most certainly tore open the replacement sutures Jaru must have arranged while I was unconscious.

Through the barrage, I caught sight of Jaru, his fists clenched tight, as if he were barely able to keep from coming to my aid. Willing him to see the slight movement, I shook my head. If he broke now, his family would be forfeit, and for his sake—and his mother's—I would endure this. His eyes dropped closed for a brief moment before he wiped every evidence of concern from his countenance and I was satisfied that he would not intervene.

For Azuvah, I thought, *and for the God she revered.* Eager to feel the bliss of nothing once the king of Ashdod finally had his way, and holding the face of my love in my mind, I waited for the abyss to swallow me.

But to my astonishment, Nicaro barked a sharp command and the beating ceased. Then he was again in front of me, speaking so softly that I was forced to watch his lips to distinguish his words.

"Do you know the reason you are still breathing right now, Lukio? Because the people revolted. That Gazan had you in a headlock, squeezing the life from you, and the crowd flew into a fury. A few of them even charged onto the field, determined to save you." He laughed ruefully. "I've never seen anything like it. So, I had a choice to make. I could either let the brute finish you off and make you a martyr, or I could grant you mercy. And let me be very clear, if it were up to me, you would be dead right now, especially since I already knew you'd lied about the Hebrew box.

"But then my daughter reminded me that the festival you'd organized had been more successful than I'd even hoped. That you'd filled my city with fresh trade and turned every eye to my greatness. She said that if I let you perish on that field, that would be the *only* thing that would be remembered of this day—not my legacy. So, you can be grateful that my fool daughter is still infatuated with you, even if you threw her and everything else over for her slave."

He sneered, as if the thought was beyond unimaginable. But he didn't know my Tesi was worth everything, including my last breath.

"And, of course, I could kill you now. Have my men bury you without fanfare in an unmarked grave. But that would profit me nothing. Therefore, I have a better idea." He smiled, and I suddenly felt very much like a boar cornered by his hunting hounds.

"Since I assume that you are also responsible for costing me a few Hebrew slaves meant to be aboard the transport to Egypt tomorrow, you will take their place. I am certain that a famous fighter will be of far greater value to Pharaoh than a few brickmakers anyhow. That is, of course, if you survive your injuries on the voyage." His brows drew together in mock concern.

"But either way, the rumor will be that rather than face the shame of your loss, you boarded a ship just like your father and sailed away to foreign lands. I hate to give you the glory of a legend, but perhaps that is the price to pay for a festival that will be renowned the world over. However, knowing the fickle people of this city, no matter how much they screamed for you, they will forget you the moment a new champion arises."

He pressed his face so close to mine I could see the pinpoints his pupils had become and how they swam in the same madness that had seeped out during Orada's funeral.

"And while you breathe your last, enslaved and alone in some sandy wasteland, know that I will *never* stop until I find that box and destroy it. My armies will shake the ground of every corner of this land until every last Hebrew bows only to me." Spittle formed at the corners of his lips. "And any legacy you hoped for will be swallowed up by the dirt you die in like a dog."

He stood and took one last look at me, visibly shaking with fury. But then with one slow blink, the madness was gone, and nothing remained but the veneer of royal composure as he spoke to Jaru.

"Fetter him and put him on a ship."

Thirty-Four

I jolted awake, then cursed myself for doing so as the fetters cut into my skin with a fiery bite. If I made it to Egypt alive, I would be permanently scarred from the iron shackles at my wrists and ankles—more wounds to add to the multitude that leeched away my life. I'd given up trying to shift into a position that would take pressure off my injuries and now lay on my back, praying that the fever causing my entire body to shake would take me swiftly. The only difference between this prison and my last was that the hold of the ship smelled of brine and had a floor made of wood instead of rich soil. Both were just as black and bereft of hope.

The ship swayed back and forth in a gentle rhythm, which told me that it was still at port, but it would not remain anchored much longer. The Egyptian sailors had already filled the hold with jugs of olive oil and wine and barely gave a second glance to the man lauded only yesterday by Ashdod as nearly divine. As soon as dawn broke, whenever that might be, I would be carried away to sea.

I'd been swimming in and out of consciousness for an indeterminable length of time. But thankfully my bouts of lucidity were coming farther apart. Sleep was a mercy I relished. It was there I could be with my Tesi on the mountain, hold our little ones, wrap an arm around my sister, and tell Elazar, Yoela, and everyone else how sorry I was. Sometimes when I dreamed, I was with Risi on the beach, searching for shells and playing in the waves and when my head went under, I hoped that it wouldn't come back up again. But

315

then I would wake and remember that instead of beneath the sea I was atop it, and I would wait for oblivion to consume me again.

The clank of metal from around my wrists pricked at the back of my mind, trying to coax forward something I should remember. Something important from a long time ago. I'd just been dreaming of the mountain, of Risi's prolific flower and vegetable gardens, and of the small orchard where she tended a variety of trees.

The words came to me slowly, having been buried beneath the detritus of many years but determined to push their way to the surface, nonetheless.

"Do not fear the iron fetters that carry you to sea."

A vagabond had told me that once, there in those very orchards I'd been visiting in my sleep. Beside an apple tree upon which Risi had attached wild branches to the established root, making its apples taste sweeter and bloom faster than all the others.

My heart picked up its sluggish pace as more of the man's odd statement floated to the surface of my mind.

"You are a wild branch, young man. Do not despise the root to which you've been joined, for it is from this mountain, in the shadow of cedars, that your own deep roots will take their nourishment. And the branches who spring from you will spread wide to shade the helpless and reach heights you cannot imagine. So, do not fear the iron fetters that carry you to the sea, young man, only the ones you bind upon yourself."

At the time I'd mocked the vagabond whose dark brown braid trailed nearly to the back of his knees. In fact, I'd told Ronen that he was a madman and quite possibly dangerous. And yet, instead of agreeing with my assessment, Ronen had gone pale and nearly ran from the garden. Later, I'd discovered that the man was called Samuel, and he was regarded by the Hebrews as a seer and a wandering priest. Could he have truly known that I would one day be bound in iron shackles and put in this ship's hold? It seemed too farfetched to believe. But like Jaru's appearance in my life, and Tesi's, and even Teitu's, how else could it be explained?

There was something more that the seer had said to me that day, about the watchtower I'd been imprisoned in, but the chill in my body came over me again, washing away both the questions and the answers. It pulled me down like a wave Risi had once saved me from, relentlessly tugging at my exhausted bones until I succumbed to the darkness and let myself be pulled into the black sea again.

The smell of brine and wood pitch remained with me, even in my dream. But instead of being alone in my dank prison, the same presence from the watchtower filled the room with soft blue light.

Whispers surrounded me, calling my name. Then, a cool hand lay on my burning leg and another on my side, and I was so grateful for the respite from pain, even if it was only temporary. But my mouth would not move, so I was unable to speak my thanks aloud.

Perhaps some sort of spirit had finally come to carry me away to some world beyond this one. And yet, I did not want to go. There was something I had to do, somewhere I had to be. A place where my roots were to grow deep and my shade wide.

I tugged at whatever was holding my arms and legs together, making an attempt to escape whatever was to come, and found only frustration. I could not move at all. I could not fight an enemy I could not see or hear or touch.

"Fear only the fetters you place on yourself."

I don't want to be enslaved, I thought, even in my dreams feeling the track of hot tears down the sides of my face. *Please, Yahweh. I want to go home. My true home.*

Again, gentle hands moved over me, touching the bindings at my wrists and then my feet. The weight of them released, offering me the sweetest of relief before I fell into sleep once again.

Feet pounding on the deck above dragged me from the first peaceful dreams I'd had in hours, perhaps days. Blue skies. Green trees. My family. I cursed the interruption of such bliss and tried to reclaim it by squeezing my eyes tighter.

A confusing flurry of activity began inside the hold—harsh whispers and then hiss of cargo being shoved and dragged across the floor.

"He must be here," said someone. "Keep looking."

"Natan?" said another low voice that sounded vaguely familiar. "Lukio?"

Thinking I was perhaps still dreaming of home, since the voices spoke in Hebrew, I said nothing in response, only waited for whatever spirits had come for me to do what they must.

More voices overlapped, and the boards upon which I lay vibrated from the pounding of feet. A small torch hovered over me, blinding me after so long in the darkness.

"He's here!"

Once I could finally peel my one functioning eye open, I found three Philistine soldiers standing over me, none of whose dark bearded features I could distinguish clearly in the deep shadows cast by the torch.

Were they here to beat me more? Why would they not just leave me to die?

One of them knelt beside me, placing a hand on my forehead. "Fever. We'll need to find help for him soon."

"How did he escape his shackles?" said another, wonder in his voice. "He's too weak to break them like this himself."

"Can you stand?" one of them asked me. "We need to get you up the ladder."

I moaned at the thought of moving and then must have fallen into another stupor because I awoke to the sounds of axes chopping down trees. Or perhaps the ship was breaking apart and going down to the same depths that likely swallowed my father.

Before I could make sense of the distinctive sound of wood splintering, I was being dragged by two of the Philistines. I considered fighting them, but what did I care what they did with my body anyhow? So, I did not struggle, even when they, and their companions, pulled me through a hole in the side of the boat, and I braced myself to be tossed into the black sea. But instead, I landed atop a tangle of fishing nets, in the bottom of yet another small vessel.

"Throw it right in there," said another soldier, as the smell of bitumen and smoke took over my senses. "The ship is full of oil and wine. It won't take long to go up."

I turned my throbbing head just in time to see a torch arc across my sight, and in the flash of light I saw the young man beside me in the bottom of the boat. He looked familiar, with the same black hair as the other soldiers, but he was much younger, his beard not as full.

My attention strayed to the sky above me. So many stars. As many as Tesi's freckles but not nearly as beautiful.

I must have spoken aloud, because the young soldier at my side replied, "You'll see her soon enough, brother."

At his amused response to my ramblings, the haze that had swaddled me in confusion since I'd been thrown into the ship's hold began to clear. I stared up at the young man, my addled mind trying to ascribe Yonah's name to his face. But that couldn't be. Yonah was just a boy and I'd callously left him behind to hate me forever. And yet, when my wavering vision moved to the faces of the other men closest to me in the boat, I found Gershom, Iyov, and even Ronen looking back at me with matching expressions of horrified concern.

I blinked slowly, expecting the dream-fueled images to fade into the night sky, but the faces of my brothers remained on the bodies of the men dressed in Philistine garb, the ones who'd just pulled me from the depths of a ship's hold and were now rowing with all their might. With my heart taking up a painfully lopsided gallop, I flicked my one eye back to the youngest of them.

"Yonah?"

Although his gaze was tinged with worry, he gave me a wide smile, which was illuminated by the flames that were already consuming the ship that had nearly been my tomb.

"I know you always hated it when I followed after you, brother. But this time you had no choice."

Thirty-Five

My brothers and the other Hebrews rowed through the night, battling the black sea and the insistent waves in order to reach the port of Yaffa before dawn. For men who'd never stepped foot on a boat before or navigated by the stars, their success in keeping the coast in sight throughout the night and reaching Danite territory unscathed was a miracle.

While I lay on my sickbed in the house of a skilled healer in Yaffa for the next few days, struggling with bouts of fever and infection in my leg, Yonah told me the story of how they'd hurried to Ashdod after Shoshana told them of my fate, dressed in the same Philistine garb the Hebrew men had worn during their escape, and arrived just in time to watch the horrifying sight of me being vanquished on the fighting grounds. They'd watched from afar as I was hauled back, unconscious, to the watchtower, and then later that evening trailed after the soldiers as they took me in shackles up to the port.

Hanan, the man who credited me with saving his daughters, had taken the risk of approaching Jaru after I'd been rowed out to the ship, which was anchored a short way off the coast, and once again Azuvah's son had found a way to help.

He'd had a large delivery of strong drink sent out to the Egyptian sailors, a "gift of gratitude" for keeping my presence on their vessel a secret. All the time I'd been languishing down in the hold, the sailors had been enjoying their bribe, making it almost laughably easy for the men of my family to overtake them in the small fishing vessel they'd stolen under cover of darkness.

Yonah took great pleasure in describing how he'd picked three of them off with his bow before the Egyptians even realized they were under attack from their starboard side. By the time the other two men, who'd been left aboard to guard the vessel from just such an incident, shook themselves out of their drunken stupor, Ronen, Hanan, and my brothers had already climbed aboard and engaged them. Those men soon joined their compatriots in the depths before I was dragged aboard the fishing boat, half-mad with pain and fever.

If they had not found a woman who knew how to treat battle wounds so well, all of their efforts might well have been in vain. Once my fever had broken, she'd stated that I would have in no way survived the sea voyage to Egypt. While she assured me the knife injuries that I'd sustained at my cousin's hands would heal, she cautioned that I might always sustain a limp, a fact Yonah found quite amusing and jested that he'd not wait around for me while I trailed along after him in the woods.

During my convalescence, Gershom and Iyov found a spice trader willing to allow us to travel with him on his way to Damascus, so I found myself flat on my back in a wagon, among baskets of herbs and pots of spices, enduring hour after painful hour of jostling as we made our way eastward. But I refused to complain, since I could have been at the bottom of the sea instead of on my way to Kiryat-Yearim.

When night fell, camp was made on the side of the road within a small clearing of trees, and I was ushered between Ronen and Yonah to a pallet beside the fire. Over a meal of fish Iyov purchased at the port and fresh bread supplied by the kind healer before we'd taken leave of her home that morning, I pushed past the damage in my throat to tell my own story.

Determined to splay it all before them, and undeterred by the presence of Hanan and the others, I told them every ugly detail of my time in Ashdod. After leaving their families and risking everything to come for me, and after all my disrespectful and ungrateful behavior toward them, they deserved to know, and I deserved to endure the shame of the telling. I'd passed the time on my sickbed practicing just what I needed to say to these men I'd once refused to call brothers.

"I do not expect forgiveness for the way I shunned your kindnesses toward me." I cleared my throat and allowed my gaze to slowly move from Gershom, to Iyov, to Ronen, and to Yonah, so they could see the true depths of my contrition. "But I vow to spend the rest of my life atoning for being so hateful. I am determined to pay you all back for rescuing such an undeserving fool."

After a few long and painful beats of silence, Gershom leaned forward, elbows on his knees, to stare into my eyes. "We were more than ready to forgive you ten years ago when we set out to find you the day you left."

Guilt coated my tongue with bile as I prepared myself for his chastisement.

"But that has not changed, brother, no matter how long you've been gone. Yes, you were a fool to run off like that, but you were a boy. And we should have done better by you. All of us. We failed you in many ways. We should have done better at trying to understand why you were angry, instead of simply reacting to your hostility."

I shook my head. "You were more than patient with me. I was determined to have my own way, and I was so full of bitterness that I doubt I would have ever listened." Perhaps I had to endure all that I'd been through in order to see with clear eyes and understand that my sister had been right about Elazar and his family, after all.

"Regardless of your choices in the past," Iyov said, "we are proud of you."

I opened my mouth, but nothing came out.

"You saved lives, brother. And kept the Ark out of Ashdod's hands. And from what Shoshana says, you did not hesitate to risk your own life to do so."

Teitu's face hovered in my mind. "I could have done more—much more—had I not been so selfish and blind all these years."

"And Mosheh could have gotten us out of Egypt forty years earlier," said Gershom with a shrug, "had he not been the same."

In the years since I'd left the mountain, it was apparent that Gershom had stepped into his role as Elazar's successor well. He'd always been levelheaded and slow to speak, but now he was a man of deep wisdom. Or perhaps he'd always been so wise, and I'd just been too immature to recognize it. Either way, it was plain to see that he would continue the legacy Abinidab, Elazar's father and the original keeper of the Ark, had left behind. And from what I could tell, Iyov's role as an instructor to the young Levites in Kiryat-Yearim fit him well.

"Well, I am certainly no Mosheh," I said. "It was not a burning bush that opened my eyes to all I'd been willfully ignoring, but Shoshana."

"She was quite devastated to have to leave you behind," said Ronen. "She'll be relieved to see you." Then he leaned closer, a glint of mischief in his eyes. "And to think, after all these years you can finally have the girl you always wanted."

"You knew about this thing between them?" asked Gershom, incredulous, as he batted a trail of smoke that curled into his eyes.

"You never told them?" I asked Ronen.

"Of course not," he said with a furrow in his brow. "I may have hidden my intentions to steal the Ark from you and tried to manipulate you for information, but I promised I would not break your confidence about the girl."

Talk turned from my failings to the journey ahead, and I was grateful for it. The way they'd offered me such unmitigated forgiveness overwhelmed me, along with the fact that none of them seemed to even hold a grudge for all the grief I'd caused. I went to sleep that night with the stars overhead, my brothers beside me, and the deep sense that more than just my body was healing during this trek back to Kiryat-Yearim.

In the morning, just after they'd loaded me into the wagon again like a half-gutted buck, I called Yonah over to me, needing to offer him a separate apology. I asked him to forgive me for shunning him so much of the time, especially for that last day when I'd left him thinking it was his fault I'd run off.

"I won't lie to you. It took me a long while to understand," he replied, "but a few weeks later, Abba told me something that finally got through to me."

"And what was that?"

"That when you came from Ashdod you'd not truly let go of Philistia. That it had a firm grip on your heart, one that was so strong only Adonai could break it. But he also reminded me that if Yahweh could part the sea, topple Jericho, and make the sun stand still for an entire day, then he could certainly break whatever chains bound you to Philistia and bring you home."

The echo of Samuel's words in Elazar's explanation made it all the more apparent that I'd not been alone in Ashdod. Somehow, the God I'd been so dismissive of for most of my life had answered my sister's prayers on my behalf. Never was any man less deserving of such mercy.

"There was no question that we would come for you, brother," Yonah said, "only whether you would be glad to see us."

I reached up to put my hand on his shoulder, still reeling from the idea that this young man was the same little boy who used to trail after me in the woods, chattering loudly enough to scare all the birds away, and seemingly oblivious to the limp that hindered him. "Well, once I realized that you all were not evil spirits dragging me to the underworld, I was very glad indeed."

He grinned at me, mischief glimmering in his bright brown eyes. "Well, from what I hear from Shoshana, you had all the women in Ashdod falling at your feet. Now that we've kept you from rotting at the bottom of the sea, perhaps you can teach me a thing or two."

I stifled a groan as I stepped over a fallen tree branch, pain shooting into my hip and down past my knee. The winding path from Kiryat-Yearim up the top of the mountain somehow seemed to have grown to twice its length in my absence. But returning to Elazar's home a broken and contrite man was bad enough; I had no intention of being carried there atop a litter on my brother's shoulders. I would finish this final leg of our journey on my own two feet.

Gershom and Iyov, along with Hanan and the other men I'd rescued in Ashdod, had gone up ahead to herald our arrival. By now, everyone would know I'd returned. And not only would I see my sister for the first time in ten years, but I would hold my Tesi in my arms again, where I was determined she would remain for the rest of my life.

Waving away Ronen's offer to stop for a while so I could rest my leg, I leaned heavily on the staff Iyov had found somewhere on the journey and pressed forward, the anticipation in my belly far more urgent than the ache in my limbs.

An enormous beast burst from the bushes up ahead on the trail, causing both Ronen and Yonah to whip knives from their belts, their eyes wide as Igo charged for me with a yelp of joy. His entire body quivered with excitement as he pressed his big head into my uninjured hip, nearly knocking me down. I scratched behind his silky ears, nearly as glad to see him as he was me.

Zevi followed soon after, his smile as wide as the sea.

"Lukio!" he shouted as he barreled down the trail and then shocked me by throwing his arms around my waist. "You're safe!"

It did no good to swallow down the emotion that surged into my throat. My vision blurred as he pushed his face into my torso. I slid my hand into his dark curls and pressed him closer, telling him without words just what he meant to me.

Three other boys had appeared on the trail, all a bit younger than Zevi, their eyes were wide as they took in the sight of us.

The tallest of them jogged to Ronen's side. "Abba! Did you defeat the Philistines?" The boy had very clearly inherited his mother's large forest-colored eyes.

"Of course, Avidan. What did you expect?" said Ronen with a proud grin. "And look, I've brought your uncle with me."

If possible, those eyes grew even larger and his jaw went slack. "*He's* my uncle?" he half-whispered. "No wonder he has such a big dog."

Chuckling, Ronen gestured to the other two boys. "This is Gavriel, Miri's eldest, and Shalem, Iyov's youngest."

So much life had passed while I'd been in Ashdod. I did not even know who all among Elazar and Yoela's brood were married now or how many children and grandchildren had been born on this mountain during my time away. Shai and Amina, the twins, had been only around five when I left, and little Dafna, barely three. I'd missed so much because of my selfishness.

As these nephews I'd just met looked up at me with unconcealed awe, I vowed to do all I could to make up for lost time. I may have been a terrible brother to Yonah and the others, but I would pay restitution by being the most devoted uncle any of these children had ever known. And as for Zevi, who'd still not released his hold on me, Shoshana and I would need to have a discussion about his future, just as soon as our own was decided.

"Come now," said Ronen, scrubbing his son's hair with his knuckles. "Let's continue on. I'm certain your ima is beyond anxious to see her brother."

Avidan nodded his small chin. "She said if he doesn't hurry, she's going to come down this path and find him herself."

I barked a laugh. "Well, we'd best move along. Unless she's changed, your ima doesn't show her anger often, but when she does, it's terrifying."

"Especially if you wake the babies," my nephew replied, sounding as if he'd learned that lesson the hard way.

"Then you better lead the way," I said, biting back a grin, "or who knows what she'll do to me!"

Without hesitation, the three younger boys trotted off, but Zevi and Igo remained at my side as we continued on.

"Seems as though you've made some friends here," I said.

Zevi shrugged his small shoulders. "They asked me to explore the woods with them today."

"That's the best part of Kiryat-Yearim," I said. "When I was a boy here, there was nothing better. You should go."

His eyes darted up the path to where Avidan, Gavriel, and Shalem had disappeared, the yearning on his face more than plain. But he shook his head. "Maybe later. You just returned."

I paused to look down at him, glad to see that the bruises on his face had already faded. For the rest of my life, I'd never forget the horror on his face when he realized I'd thrown him into the fighting ring unprepared.

"It's all right," I said. "I am not going anywhere. Ever. And for as long as I live, you will have a home with me."

He looked up at me, and for the first time since I'd dragged him off of that Philistine soldier, the look of guardedness melted away, replaced by the sheen of tears. "Do you promise?"

I swallowed hard. "In the name of Yahweh, the Holy One, I vow that I will not leave you."

He nodded, his chin wobbling. Then he darted off to follow my nephews, who I very much hoped might be like brothers to the boy one day.

Ronen came to my side as I watched Zevi disappear around a bend in the trail. "Well, my friend, it's not much farther. Are you ready for this?"

"I am," I replied on a heavy sigh. "I only wish I could go back and undo leaving ten years ago."

"Then you wouldn't see just how much you were missed all this time. And neither would you know what it's like to be offered unmerited grace by this extraordinary family. I should know—I've been marveling over it myself for years."

Before I could respond to such a profound statement, Risi appeared at the top of the trail not ten paces away, her long thick braid reflecting the sunlight. One of my sister's hands was on her well-rounded belly and the other gripped that of a little girl who so resembled her it could be none other than her daughter. Except the golden-haired child had two different colored eyes—one brown, one green—just like me.

"I . . . I couldn't wait any longer," Risi said, tears already tracking down her cheeks.

I stumbled forward, leaning into my staff as I climbed the last incline. The years melted away as I stood before my sister, my champion, and the only words I could choke out of my ravaged throat were "I'm sorry, Risi."

The hand that was on her belly reached for me, and I let her tug me forward. I leaned down to place my forehead on her shoulder. She sifted her trembling fingers through my hair like she used to do when I was a boy, and peace washed through me like a cool stream.

And like always, even when I was at my worst as an angry and bitter young man, unconditional love flowed from within her as she said, "Welcome home."

Thirty-Six

Shoshana

"What is that one, Ima?" asked my son, his small hand cupped around his ear.

I paused to listen to the birdcall, with its long series of chirps and warbles. Asher had been so delighted when I discerned a few different types of birds by their songs on our way to Eliora's terraced gardens this morning that he kept insisting I identify each new one we heard. But as I did so, I could not help but remember the boy who'd taught me such skills all those years ago. It had been nine long days since Lukio's brothers had left for Ashdod, and each day that passed I'd grown more desperate for distractions to keep my mind occupied and not dwelling upon why we'd heard nothing from them.

The festival would have been long over by now. I could not stomach the thought that not only had Lukio been lost to me forever, but that Eliora and the other women had lost their husbands as well. Perhaps I should not have told his brothers where he was. But then again, they'd been so determined, and if there was even the slightest chance—

"Ima!" pressed Asher, breaking into the cycle of guilt and fear that had been my constant companion these past few days. "What is that bird?"

"I'm not certain. It's been so long. And most of the ones I know only sing at night."

He frowned but continued searching the bushes for the sweet berries he and Aaliyah had been gathering. Eliora—whom my children adored—had told them they were welcome to eat as many berries as they brought home in their baskets, so their mouths and fingers were already stained a deep purple.

Galit and I had simply been glad for the excuse to get away from the house, where a cloud of uncertainty had hung over the household like ash for days now. And since Yoela had insisted that she would keep Davina entertained, we'd already spent a long while exploring. Lukio's mother had folded my little one into her ever-expanding brood of grandchildren without hesitation.

"Look, Asher!" called Aaliyah. "A butterfly!"

The two of them took after the orange-and-black insect, giggling as they made an attempt to catch it mid-flight, then darting around the garden in pursuit, jumping and squealing.

Although they'd seemed to accept that I was not going anywhere, they still kept me in their sights much of the time, and I guessed they might do so for a long while. They were so happy here on this mountain. They smiled and laughed freely like they'd never really done when we lived in Beth Shemesh. Growing up here with so many children near their ages would be a blessing.

"They are so beautiful, Shoshana," said Galit, as we watched my children flit joyfully around the clearing.

"It is hard to believe that we are here together," I said on a sigh. "It seems as though any moment I will wake up and be back in Ashdod."

Galit did not respond, her eyes latched on some far distance. She'd been so quiet since our arrival in Kiryat-Yearim. Although I'd suspected Avel's adoration of her, I'd not known for certain that she'd returned that affection until he was gone. So, in addition to healing physically, Galit was deep in the throes of mourning what could have been had we all escaped.

I understood her pain, for although Lukio hadn't died when we parted the first time, it had felt very much as if he had, and now I was again suspended in the unknown, waiting to see if Galit and I would be mourning the men we loved together.

"They will bring him home," she said, as if she could hear my turbulent thoughts.

"I am afraid to hope."

"That is understandable," she said, "but you held on to hope for these sweet ones." She gestured to Asher and Aaliyah, who'd now discovered a lizard of some sort to beleaguer.

I brushed my fingers over the frothy stalks of a plant I had no name for, one of the many exotic varieties Eliora had cultivated here. "I got my children back. My baby was returned to me. It almost seems greedy to beg Yahweh for Lukio too, especially when you . . ." I let the words die away.

She breathed out a sigh. "I loved him. Even though the moments we were truly alone were rare. And if the Philistines would have allowed slaves to marry, we would have done. You may think it is terrible, and I understand if you want me to leave, but we were, in all respects, joined in as much of a marriage covenant as we could have been."

Then, to add to the revelation of what she'd admitted, she smoothed her hand over her belly. "And Yahweh saw fit to leave me with a piece of Avel, a gift in the midst of my sorrow."

I sucked in a breath, thinking of the terrible beating she'd received from the Philistine guards. "Are you certain after what happened that the baby is . . . ?"

She nodded, smiling gently. "I felt movement just this morning."

"And did Avel know?"

A tear slipped down her cheek, the first I'd seen. "He did. So, you see, there is hope, even though he is gone."

No wonder he'd been so ferocious in his defense of her and willing to risk himself. He'd been protecting two people he loved.

"Oh, Galit." I gripped both of her hands in mine. "I am so happy for you. And you are not going anywhere. You and your child are welcome here."

Her eyes glistened. "I was not certain where I would go. Everyone in my family is gone. And although I know I am from the tribe of Efraim, I was so young I don't even remember which town I lived in. It was just home."

"If there is one thing I know about Elazar's clan, it's that they welcome anyone in need of a place to belong. So Kiryat-Yearim will be your home now. And we will be your family."

"Shoshana!" Zevi's urgent call carried across the gardens. "Shoshana!"

My gut clenched tight at the urgency in his voice. "Here, Zevi!"

Igo bounded out of the woods before Zevi, tail wagging and tongue lolling. The canine seemed just as thrilled to be in Kiryat-Yearim as the rest of us, no longer cowering in the presence of strangers.

A few moments later, Zevi appeared, with three other boys in his wake. Avidan and Gavriel were a year younger than he was, and Shalem, two. I'd noticed that Zevi seemed drawn to the three of them, watching their games and following them about with his eyes, even as he continued to keep to himself. Until today, I'd not actually seen him join in with their little group. Perhaps some of the healing I'd been praying over him had already begun.

"There you are!" Zevi called the moment he saw me with Galit, beckoning me with both arms. "I've been looking everywhere. Hurry! They're back!"

Then, before I could even ask if Lukio was with them, the four boys spun around and plunged back into the trees, Igo bounding along behind.

"Wait!" I called out. But Zevi was gone, leaving me trapped between panic and the only small piece of hope I'd allowed myself to hold on to.

"Go," said Galit, her tone urgent. "I'll watch the children."

"Are you certain?" My breaths came shallow.

"They'll show me the way back. Go! You need to know."

As if I'd swallowed my own swarm of butterflies, my stomach whirled as I sped directly through the trees toward the group of homes that made up Elazar's expanded household. My thoughts, however, refused to stay in a straight line, all the fears I'd been holding at bay rushing into my mind at once.

He had to be here. I did not know how I would breathe if he was not. I needed him. Zevi needed him. My children needed him.

As I came upon the compound, my heart was an insistent drum, beating three times the speed of my legs, which were stiff with cold fear. A small crowd had gathered near the head of the trail, much like they'd been the day of our return.

I spotted Iyov and Yonah speaking to Elazar off to one side, neither of whom looked injured or upset—and the sight made a bright bloom unfurl a few hopeful petals as I slipped through the crowd of family and friends.

Although I didn't see Gershom or the three Hebrew men who'd willingly gone back—for Lukio's sake—to the very place they'd just been freed from, the lighthearted chatter all around gave me cause to pick up my pace. Surely if something terrible had happened, there would be long faces, tears, perhaps even the awful cries of mourning that accompanied tragedies.

And then I saw him. Alive. Whole. One long arm wrapped around his sister's shoulder as he stood with his back to me.

Although everything inside me screamed to run to him, to throw my arms around him and demand an accounting of every moment that had passed between when I'd last seen him and now, I held back. Eliora had endured a much longer wait to be with her beloved brother and deserved an uninterrupted reunion. I would be patient, even if it meant my hands shook and my insides quivered as I drank in the sight of him like a fresh stream.

When he turned to look down at his sister, his face was pale and there was extensive bruising that encircled both his eye and his cheekbone. My stomach bottomed out. He'd been beaten and looked beyond exhausted.

Yet even with his face battered, Lukio was breathtaking. A head taller than every other man on the mountain, the sunlight spilled over him, seeking out the golden tones of his light brown hair and newly bearded jaw. The beard made him look much less the polished champion of Ashdod and more like one of the other men who called Kiryat-Yearim their home. But still, he drew every eye in the clearing with that same entrancing magnetism that caused an entire city to be enthralled with him, and somehow I doubted that allure would ever wane.

But would he truly be happy here? He'd been so restless as a boy, wanting to be anywhere but this mountain, always scheming ways to earn a living apart from Elazar's family. Would he be unsatisfied with the life of a humble woodsman? Perhaps once he spent enough time with me, he would regret the words he'd said in his rooftop garden and realize that I was not the girl who'd once flitted about the forest in his wake. Perhaps I was too jaded now. Too changed.

Also, it was one thing to speak of being a family back in Ashdod, but would he ever look at Asher and Aaliyah and not see echoes of his enemy in their faces? Or look at Davina and not remember how she came to be? He'd always had such a difficult time surrendering the hurts of the past. Would he allow resentment to color his perception of my precious children?

As I battled my fears, Lukio's lips curled into a wide smile directed toward Eliora. Not the haughty smirk of Demon Eyes or the persuasive charm he'd used back in Ashdod, but a true and genuine grin of delight as he talked with the older sister he'd always adored.

I noticed that his massive shoulders no longer held the tension that I'd seen the first time he'd spoken with Mariada on the terrace. Instead, he looked relaxed, at peace. There may have been a long distance between him and Eliora until now, and a wagonload of bitterness on Lukio's part, but it was more than evident that there was an unbreakable bond forged by their childhood that could not be severed.

Igo barked somewhere behind me and Lukio's attention was snagged by the sound, but instead of catching sight of the dog, he saw me standing about fifteen paces away, paralyzed with anticipation and fear.

His arm dropped from around Eliora's shoulder and he turned to face me, both of us staring across a small distance that was still far, far too wide.

With a knowing grin, Eliora walked away, giving us space for our own reunion. Perhaps others did as well, but I did not care to take my eyes off Lukio to see if we were being watched.

He started toward me, leaning heavily on a staff, and I realized that it was not just his face that had been injured but his leg as well and perhaps other places, if the stiffness of his gait was any indication. My gut churned. What all had he endured to protect me? I met him, step for step, until only two paces stood between us.

"Tesi," he breathed out, with so much reverence that my knees wobbled. "My Tesi."

And then before I could even register how we came together, I was enveloped by his comforting presence and his lips were on mine. I did not care if his entire family was witnessing the collapse of my restraint. My Lukio, my dearest friend and love, was alive.

A hum of deep satisfaction rumbled in his chest as he tugged me closer, until my feet were nearly off the ground and my fingers were tangled in his long hair.

Remembering suddenly that he was injured, I tried to pull back, but his arms were iron bars around my body. I could only tip my head back and look up into his beautiful bruised face. "How?"

"Yahweh," he said, and a sweet smile tugged one side of his lips upward. "And my brothers."

For the moment, that was all the explanation I needed. There would be plenty of time for him to unroll the story of his return in the days to come. For now, I simply laid my head on his chest where it belonged and breathed him in for a long, long time.

A small hand tugged at mine, dragging me out of my Lukio-induced stupor.

"Ima?" said Asher from my side. "Who is that?"

Startled by his presence and blushing at the reminder that our first kiss in ten years had been on full display of everyone—and would be as good as a public declaration of betrothal to most—I attempted to step back. But Lukio still would not fully release me, keeping one arm about my waist.

Galit approached with Davina in her arms, an apologetic look on her face, and Aaliyah clutching her hand. "I'm so sorry," she said, "the children were worried. And Yoela said Davina has been fussing for you."

"It's all right," I said, then turned to my son, whose eyes were two full moons as he looked all the way up at the man beside me. "Asher, this is Lukio. My . . . my . . . friend." The word was woefully inadequate, but the conversation about who Lukio was to me, and who he might be to them, could wait.

Lukio squeezed my waist teasingly, obviously amused by my tangled tongue. "Shalom, Asher. Have you been exploring the woods today?"

Not one to know a stranger, Asher held up his palms, which were stained purple and red, matching the streaks of color around his mouth. "We picked berries in Eliora's garden."

"Ah," said Lukio. "There are no tastier berries anywhere in the world. Whenever my sister used to ask me to pick berries for her, I usually ate more than ever ended up in my basket. And once, early in the morning, I surprised a small bear sitting right in the middle of the patch who was enjoying Risi's berries as well."

Asher's jaw dropped open. "What did you do?"

"I quietly backed away and left him to eat his fill. It's not wise to tussle with a bear."

"But you are just as big as one—bigger even!"

Lukio tilted his head back and laughed, while at the same time pulling me closer to his side. "I wasn't always this size."

"Will I be as big as you one day?" asked my son.

Grinning, Lukio reached out and scrubbed his hand through Asher's dark hair. "We shall see."

Such a simple statement that spoke volumes. Lukio meant to stay with us, to be there to watch Asher grow into a man himself one day. And although Aaliyah remained tucked into Galit's side, her big hazel eyes watched Lukio with interest. I had no doubt that he would have her in his thrall within a day or two.

Galit handed Davina to me. "I am glad you are well, Lukio. We've all been so worried. I don't think Shoshana has slept since we parted from you."

He looked down at me with an expression so intense I held my breath until he spoke. "Have no fear. I mean to make certain we are never parted again."

With a sly smile that proved she did not in any way begrudge the return of my love when hers had been lost, Galit ushered Aaliyah and Asher back toward the house, leaving Lukio and me alone, with Davina in my arms. The baby gazed up at Lukio with curiosity but then pressed against my chest, taking comfort in my nearness, something I hoped she would never stop doing, even when she learned to spread her own wings wide.

Lukio reached up to smooth a gentle hand over my daughter's soft head, and, to my surprise, she did not recoil, allowing him to caress her wispy curls until her gray eyes fluttered closed.

"I have some things I must tend to, Shoshana," he said in a low and soothing voice that would not wake the baby, "and amends I need to make. But then I am coming for you. For the only one I ever wanted to be my bride."

A thrill went through me at the word, but I had to make certain of his intentions. "It is not only me anymore. You are certain *this* is what you want?" I asked, glancing down at Davina's sweet face pressed against the base of my throat.

That enormous palm came up to caress my cheek with the same tenderness he'd offered my daughter and then slipped under my chin so I was looking into the fascinating swirl of colors within green and brown eyes that had intrigued me from the moment I first beheld their uniqueness.

"There is not one moment since you found me under our tree

that I have not wanted to be close to you, Tesi," he said, "even when I was a fool and ran away. Your children are part of you, part of the woman that I adore, and I will not wait one day longer than necessary to make you *all* mine."

Thirty-Seven

Lukio

I gazed into the pool of water near my feet and smoothed my hand over my stubbled scalp, still unused to my newly shorn head.

"Just like a goat after a good shearing," said Iyov from beside me, then reached over and scrubbed at my beard with his fingertips. "And I've never seen you with such a full one. You've finally become a man."

I shoved his arm away. "Only took three weeks for it to completely fill in. I seem to remember yours being sparse well into your twenty-third year." I gave him a goading grin. "We'll see whose is longer within the year."

"If you two are quite done comparing beards, perhaps we can begin?" said Elazar as he slipped off his sandals and stepped into the water.

Iyov nudged me with his bony elbow, a twinkle in his eye. "He never allowed us to pester him before, Abba. I have more than a few years of harassment to make up for."

Although Elazar shook his head at the two of us, there was humor in his dark eyes. There had been such strain between myself and my older brothers during the years I spent in Kiryat-Yearim, all of it due to my refusal to believe that they accepted me as I was. I'd taken most everything they said or did as a slight of some sort, never understanding that even their gentle chastisements were offered from a place of love.

Even three weeks after my brothers had come for me, I could not fathom that they'd done so. Long ago, Ronen had said that Iyov and Gershom would go to the ends of the earth for me, and I'd not in any way believed him then. The fact that they had done just that still baffled me. There was no part of me that believed I had any right to the extravagant mercy Ronen had spoken of, but I would forever be grateful.

"Are you certain this is what you want?" asked Elazar, his expression now sober as he stood knee-deep in the stream-fed pool.

"I am," I replied, my gaze moving around the small circle of men gathered around me, including Elazar, Yonah, Iyov, Gershom, Ronen, Shai, and my sisters' husbands. "The last time I took this vow, it was only with my lips. My heart was not in it. I want all of you to know that I will never walk away from this family again."

"I should think your circumcision a few days ago would have convinced us," mumbled Yonah from my other side, and the rest of the group chuckled.

I'd made the decision on the journey from Yaffa to undergo a formal acceptance of the Mosaic covenant, something I'd only half-heartedly done as a boy to appease my sister. And back then, I'd been horrified by the idea of being circumcised and had therefore refused. Now I was determined to shed every part of my past that I could, which is why I'd even chosen to shave my head this morning. I never wanted anyone to question that my loyalties now lay fully with both the clan I'd been adopted into and the confederation of tribes that made up the nation of Israel.

When I'd approached Elazar two days after my return with the idea, I asked that it all be done as publicly as possible. Once this ceremony was complete, a sacrifice of thanksgiving would be

made, and then we would feast in celebration, and all in Kiryat-
Yearim were invited to witness my vows.

I'd even removed the ivory plugs in my earlobes, hoping that
with time and application of the right oils, the holes I'd been so
eager to inflict on myself to appear like other Philistines would
eventually close and the scars would fade. But the swirling tattoos
that banded both of my arms and covered much of my torso, as
well as the pain I'd inflicted on those who loved me, could never
completely be erased. I'd hurt myself and others in so many ways
that even were I to spend the rest of my life atoning, I wasn't sure
it would be enough. But I was determined that instead of resent-
ing those markings, I'd instead consider them reminders of what
I'd been rescued from.

"Come, then," said Elazar, gesturing for me to join him. "Let
us begin."

I stripped off my tunic, determined that nothing would remain
between my skin and the water. The moment my bare feet entered
the pool, my entire body recoiled from the cold, but I was almost
glad for the shock of it and hoped that it would help etch in sharp
clarity the memory of the day my new life truly began.

Once I was situated at the center of the pool, with the water
just past my waist, Elazar recited a blessing, his hands uplifted
as he praised the Eternal One for choosing Israel, the least of the
nations, with which to reveal his Torah, and in doing so, blessed
the world with knowledge of Himself. Once Elazar had finished
the prayer, which also thanked Yahweh for the goodness of laws
that invited strangers into the fold, he anointed me with oil and
placed both hands on my head.

"Now, Lukio, do you—"

"Natan," I interrupted.

Elazar's thick silver brows arched high. He was clearly surprised
by my declaration, but from this day on I chose to be known by
the Hebrew name my sister had given me all those years ago. I'd
already shed everything else that I could of Ashdod. I would leave
Lukio behind as well.

"I choose to be known as Natan, *Abba*," I said, emphasizing the title I had never honored him with, even during those rare times in my childhood when I'd felt somewhat connected to this man and his family.

His gaze was intense on mine as a sheen of moisture glossed over his dark eyes, yet he did not speak for so long that I wondered whether I'd offended him in some way. But then he swallowed hard and his palms slipped to my shoulders and squeezed.

"Then that is who you will be from this day forward, Natan ben Elazar, of the clan of Abinidab and the tribe of Levi."

His declaration was more than clear. Long ago he'd chosen me as his son, offered me a home and love and protection just like one of his children, but today I chose him as my father. It did not matter that Philistine blood ran in my veins. I was now and for always his child. I prayed that one day Zevi might feel the same way about me.

I sank into the water until every part of me was submerged, and then I rose again. I stretched my palms upward as I did so, asking that Yahweh would take the hands that had done so much damage and consecrate them, vowing that never again would they be lifted in anger or violence, only in defense of those who could not defend themselves.

When finally I dropped my arms, my father reached out to cup his palm around my neck and draw me close. I let my head fall to his shoulder in surrender. "My son," he murmured, kissing my temple. "I am so very proud to call you my own."

Thirty-Eight

Shoshana

It had been so many years since I took this trail that I nearly turned back a number of times, worried that I'd gotten lost and would not be able to find my way in the darkness. However, each time I considered it, I felt the weight of the object in my palm and remembered my purpose for venturing out in the night, alone.

A hoot and the flutter of wings in a nearby tree startled me, but when the shadowy form of an owl flew overhead, I had to laugh at myself. I'd survived far worse than a walk through the forest at night over these past few years, but perhaps my unease was more a product of what was at the end of this trek and less about what dangers, real or imagined, might be along the way.

I recognized a certain curve of the slope that told me I was indeed on the right path. The moon was gloriously full and the sky clear, lighting my way so well that in some gaps between trees it was almost like midday.

And then, before I could truly prepare myself, I'd arrived at my destination.

The sycamore had not changed all that much, though its boughs stretched out wider and its topmost branches reached new heights, but the same dark cave created by the thick mass of curled and sprawling roots on the eroded slope was still there—although it did appear much smaller than it had when I was twelve.

And standing before me was the boy I'd met in the shadow of that same enormous tree. One whose tear-streaked cheeks and wounded soul had called to me. Now, he was no longer a boy, and the weight of anger and resentment no longer sat heavily on his broad shoulders.

"You came," he said, a slight note of wonder in his voice.

I put out my hand and uncurled my fingers, revealing the sycamore fig in my palm. "How could I ignore such a summons?"

Earlier today, I'd been shocked to discover the fig on the sill of the small room I'd been sharing with Galit and the children in Safira's home. Although I was well aware of its meaning, I'd been stricken with the strangest attack of nerves, unable to concentrate on anything but the message I'd received. But I'd had to wait until all the children were sleeping and Galit was breathing evenly before I could slip out into the darkness and hasten to the tree.

It had been a month since he'd formally taken the name Natan and publicly declared himself not only fully loyal to the people of Yahweh and the tribe of Levi, but also as a true son of Elazar. The celebration after his cleansing in the stream had been one of the most joyous I'd ever attended, even over the marriage feasts of Elazar's sons and daughters, because no longer was there a pall of concern for Lukio hanging over the household. He was, after all this time, finally in perfect shalom with the family who loved him so much.

Since then, he'd been extraordinarily busy working alongside his brothers, cutting down trees again and tending to a multitude of tasks around the compound—usually with Zevi and Igo in tow. Of course, I, too, was occupied with my children and doing my part to help with the many duties the women who lived atop the mountain tended to on a daily basis, but I could not help but be frustrated that after all this time of separation we'd had very few moments alone. I was anxious to begin our life together, yes, but I also simply missed my friend.

"Is everyone asleep?" he asked.

"They are," I replied, "although I had to whisper orders to Igo three times not to follow me."

He laughed. "He is as much enthralled with you as he is with Zevi and me."

"You should see how patient Igo is with the children," I said. "Asher and Aaliyah can practically ride the animal like a mule and he simply stands there and lets them. Even Davina squeals and thrashes about with delight whenever he follows Zevi into a room."

"Zevi seems to be adjusting," he said.

"Asher and Aaliyah adore him already. And his new friends are helpful, for certain."

I had little doubt that Zevi, Avidan, and Gavriel were already well on their way to becoming lifelong friends. And even though Shalem was younger than the rest of them, they included him in all their romps through the woods as well. When Zevi was not with them, however, he was with Lukio.

Lukio's brow furrowed, and he slid his fingers through the short hair that was just beginning to curl on his head. "He still has not revealed all that much about the life he had before Ashdod, nor the raid that enslaved him."

"I know," I said, "but there is no doubt he trusts you. It may take some time, but I think he will eventually allow both of us into his heart."

"Now I know the frustration Abba and Ima felt during all those years I kept them at arm's length. I can only pray that Yahweh will give us wisdom with him, and that we won't have to wait until he is grown before he truly lets down his guard."

Hearing Lukio speak of looking to Yahweh for guidance was still so foreign, but it filled my heart with overflowing gratitude. The God Who Hears had been so faithful to both of us—protecting us, bringing unexpected help into our lives, and eventually drawing us back together—and I would never doubt his goodness. And the way he'd transformed Lukio from the vicious champion of Ashdod into a man who'd offered up his life for others on multiple occasions would never cease to amaze me.

In addition to the shearing of his long hair, the growth of his beard, the change in his clothing from Philistine to Hebrew, and the removal of the ivory plugs in his earlobes, it seemed as though he'd left behind the burden he'd been carrying for as long as I'd known him. And the new man who stood before me now, still breathtaking in his beauty but even more so in his spirit, was one I was more than eager to get to know.

"You did not leave me a fig only to speak of Zevi, did you, Lukio . . . I mean, Natan?"

He grinned at my stumble over his name. "As much as I want to leave all of my past behind me, I do not mind if you continue to call me Lukio in private. I will likely always call my sister Risi, after all. It's too engrained to think of her any other way. As for why I brought you here"—a twinkle of mischief sparked in his mismatched eyes—"I have waited far too long to be alone with you."

He crossed the short distance between us and took the fig from my hand, dropping it to the ground before entwining his fingers with mine. I held my breath as I met his potent gaze.

"As I said the day I returned, I had a few things to tend to— first among them joining the Covenant, so we can begin our lives together as one, not only in body but in the spirit of Yahweh's Torah. And I also needed to prepare a temporary place for our family to reside until a home can be built up here atop the mountain. Fortunately, when the Gibeonites unsuccessfully attempted to overtake Kiryat-Yearim ten years ago, they left their homes behind when they fled the mountain. I discovered that, for some reason, the one where my old friends Adan and Padi lived was still vacant, albeit in rough shape. It's not too far from here, and I've repaired it enough to make it livable."

"You made us a home?"

Our betrothal had been declared publicly, the same day that he'd joined the Covenant, but since I was as good as fatherless, nothing about it had been traditional. No *mohar*, no formal *ketubah*—only a joyful announcement and many days of anticipation as I waited for him to come for me. I'd certainly never expected him to have already prepared us a place to live.

"I have," he said. "However, I will begin building a new and better one for you closer to my family as soon as I can fell enough timber and collect enough stone. I've found a grove of oaks that will do nicely. It certainly won't be anything like my villa in Ashdod, but—"

I lifted a hand to cover his mouth. "Any home with you and my . . . *our* children will be a palace."

He pulled my hand away and kissed the center of my palm, sending warm delight through my limbs, then he tugged on my arm, pulling me fully against him. "I hoped you might say that."

I let my arms slide around his waist and laid my cheek on his hard chest, reveling in his warmth and nearness. I could never have imagined that terrible moment I heard him announce his betrothal to Mariada on the terrace that I would be here, planning my life with the man I'd loved for so long.

"Do you remember," he began, "when we made plans to live out here?"

"Of course," I said, "and you told me that you would build a fortress up in our tree so my father would never find me and that you could see Ashdod from its branches. I used to dream about staying out here with you and never going back home." With my chin still on his chest, I tipped my head back to look up at him. "You aren't going to build me a house in the tree, are you?"

He chuckled, the sound rumbling through his big body as he caressed my back. "No, but tonight we perhaps might recapture a bit of that joy we found here as children. When it was just you and me and all our far-fetched dreams. Dreams that aren't impossible anymore."

"Lukio," I said, craning to look over at the sycamore. "That cave beneath our tree was small enough when you were a boy. You will not fit in there."

He tilted his head back and laughed, startling more than a few night creatures into flight.

"I'm not certain *I* could even fit in there anymore," I said, squinting at the dark hole we used to squeeze into and talk until nearly sunrise.

"Of course you could, Tesi." He placed a kiss on my nose, making my heart flutter like one of those startled birds. "You've not changed so much."

I frowned playfully at him. "I've given birth to three children. If nothing else, my hips are more generous."

He bent to speak directly into my ear, his breath hot and teasing as his palm slid down my side and gripped one of those hips. "Hmm. I'm not certain about that. I'll have to determine that for myself."

"Lukio," I gasped out on a shuddering breath. "What are you doing?"

"I told you," he said, "that I would not wait one more day than necessary to come for my bride. And I know that it is customary for the bridegroom to come for his new wife with great fanfare, but I felt this would be much more fitting for our wedding night."

"What do you mean?"

He kissed my lips, slow and searching, as if he had all the time in the world to explore. "Come," he said, parting from me only enough to whisper against my mouth. "I'll show you."

He led me by the hand up around the other side of our tree, where the deep shadows had hidden a small tent pitched on flat ground. The narrow gap between woolen walls revealed that a lone oil lamp flickered inside, and even in the moonlight I could see garlands of flowers decorating the outside with delicate and fragrant blooms.

"Oh . . ." I breathed out, enchanted. "Oh, Lukio."

"Shoshana," he said, holding my face in his strong hands. "I have loved you since long before I understood what that meant. And although we were separated by distance and circumstances, that desire to be near you, to just be in your sweet presence, has never waned. I tease you about your freckles being stars"—he smoothed a gentle finger over my cheek, my forehead, down my nose, and around my lips—"but you have always been the brightest light in my sky. My lior, my friend, my love, and—after tonight—my wife."

"You mean for us to stay out here together?"

He nodded. "I have enough provisions for us to remain at least three days, maybe even more if I'm not ready to give up having you all to myself."

"But the children—"

"Are fine with Galit. She knows where to find us if there is a problem. And when we are ready, we'll fetch them and take them to our new home together."

I was stunned that everyone had hidden this all so well from me and wondered if Galit hadn't been asleep at all as I tiptoed through our dark room, trying not to wake her and the children.

"Well then," I said, tugging at his hand to lead him into the marriage tent he'd so sweetly prepared and feeling the last of my shattered pieces coming together into one beautiful whole. "I've wanted to call you my husband for more than a decade. Let's not wait any longer, shall we?"

Epilogue

Natan

1050 BC
MITZPAH, ISRAEL

The Philistines were almost here. Fire still burned on the watch-tower perched on the ridge high above us, the flaming signal set alight a few hours prior, when messengers had run from the Aya-lon Valley to warn Samuel that our enemies had amassed a huge number of chariots and were heading this way.

I was unsurprised that the Philistines had taken this opportu-nity to attack because, for the first time in twenty years, the Ark of the Covenant was in plain sight of the people. Removed from my cave, in which it had been hidden for the past two years, it had been carefully brought here by the priests so it would be present the first time Yom Kippur was celebrated corporately since I was fifteen and the golden box was nearly stolen.

Only yesterday we'd been fasting together, the entire assem-bly calling out in repentance to the Most High at the behest of Samuel, who'd summoned all the tribes of Israel to come together here and worship Yahweh. Over the past few years, there had been an enormous shift in the hearts of the sons of Israel. And over this past week, during which Samuel spoke to the entire company, hundreds—perhaps thousands—of idols, amulets, and other graven images had been smashed and burned. And even when word had come in the middle of the sacrifices that the Philistines were on their way here, the people insisted that Samuel continue the offerings and plead with Yahweh to deliver us.

Nicaro had not given up his quest to find the Hebrews' treasured object. In fact, we'd heard many stories of the Philistines searching for clues to its whereabouts, some even drawing them close to Kiryat-Yearim, as Nicaro's men chased down all the rumors of its movement throughout the territories. Elazar had even heard of a group from Ashdod that had been sent to seek it out in the land of Midian, near the mountain upon which Mosheh received the Torah from the mouth of Yahweh himself.

But now, the king of Ashdod had no fear of this gathering of barely confederated and pitifully armed tribes. I'd witnessed the strength of his well-provisioned army firsthand and of the many iron-wheeled chariots that would plow over our paltry defenses without mercy. It would take nothing less than a miracle from Yahweh for us to stand against him today.

I gripped my ax tight in my hand, wishing I'd not left the old one back in Ashdod two years ago. The one I used now was more than sufficient for chopping down trees, but the other would have made an excellent weapon.

I did not want to fight, especially against an enemy whose blood flowed in my own veins, but I would not tolerate any threats to my family and would defend them until my last breath. It seemed that Gershom, Iyov, and Yonah felt the same, though since they were born Levites, they were not in any way meant to join a battle. The four of us remained in place, knowing that if the Philistines broke through the mouth of the valley, all of our wives and children who'd come with us to celebrate the ingathering feast in this place were devastatingly vulnerable.

Although there was great panic when word came that the Philistines planned to attack this assembly, Ronen had suggested that all the women and children take refuge in Naoith, the community Samuel had built in the hills above Ramah. If the men of Israel were not able to hold back the enemy, at least our families could escape from Naoith north to Beit El.

And so, with my insides tied in a thousand knots, I'd sent off my pregnant wife and our five children, praying that Yahweh would give us a victory today and I'd be reunited with them before the sun went down.

"You can count on me, Abba," Zevi had said as Ronen swiftly organized the group of our loved ones who needed to flee from what would soon be a battlefield. My son had been angry that I would not allow him to stay and fight, but I'd told him that I relied on him to escort his brothers and sisters, and his mother, safely to Naoith. He'd complied, eager to protect those he'd come to love. He was only twelve, but the warrior's heart that beat in his chest grew larger every day. I watched him take the hands of Asher and Aaliyah as the group set off, with Igo trotting along in their wake, and wondered what battles he'd choose to fight in days to come.

After passing one-year-old Jaru off to my sister, and talking Davina into remaining with her aunt Eliora, Shoshana had come to me with tears in her beautiful eyes and thrown herself into my arms. The slight roundness of her belly pressed into me, and even with war looming over us, I thrilled at the thought that the second child we'd made together grew inside her.

"We have many more years together on our mountain, Lukio," she'd said. "So, bring yourself back to me, unscathed."

Her kiss still lingered on my lips all these hours later, and I would do my best to obey her command. I would not let Nicaro and the Philistines steal all the peace I'd been gifted. I may not be the champion of Ashdod anymore, but I would not go down without a fight.

With knives in hand, Gershom and Iyov stood on either side of me. Yonah had joined the archers and slingers up on the ridge.

Every one of us would defend our families, and the Land of Promise, to the death.

Blood pounded in my temples as a hush fell over those of us waiting in the valley. The few weapons of war among us had been passed from generations before, most in ill repair, and all of them far inferior to the wrought-iron swords of our foes. Some of us had no more than piles of rocks to hurl or makeshift stone spears, and those who were skilled with slings were at the ready. But instead of fleeing before the horde of Philistines that would soon spill into this valley, like Israel had done many times before, this time we would stand firm.

And so, we waited, praying that the outpouring of confession and repentance that the tribes of Israel had offered to Yahweh was sufficient, and that today he would protect his people like he'd done in times past.

A chorus of *shofarim* from the ridge above suddenly blew a call to arms. All eyes turned to the gap between the hills as the distant sound of hundreds of chariot wheels rolled like thunder on the trade road Nicaro had coveted so much. Without a doubt, the king of Ashdod himself would be at the head of the procession with his gleaming chariot and purple-feathered headdress.

But just as the archers and slingers were given the order to let fly their missiles, a louder clap of actual thunder swallowed up the sound of chariots, one that grew and expanded with incomprehensible force. The thunder seemed to be emanating from just above the ridge, where the Ark of the Covenant sat on a flat bluff near the watchtower, not too far from where Samuel had been performing the sacrifices in full view of the people below. Although the sky had been clear before, a column of cloud had gathered over that same place and was stretching farther into the air.

My skin prickled, and a strange and heavy weight pressed down on me, a weight that I suddenly remembered with clarity. I'd felt that same feeling, as if the sky itself were falling, when Risi and I had followed the Ark of the Covenant from Ekron, and it had erupted in light and fire to kill the seventy Levites at Beth Shemesh.

As the thunder began to recede, the ground beneath our feet began to shake and all of us braced against the tremors.

"Look!" someone shouted, and all eyes were drawn to the mouth of the valley. A huge crack had formed in the road, and the first few chariots that had been hurtling toward us pitched directly into the gap. Nicaro had once told me that my legacy would be swallowed up by the dust I would die in, but it seemed as if he'd prophesied his own end instead.

A shout of victory went up at the strange sight and grew even louder when the remaining Philistine chariots made a chaotic attempt at retreat, their horses tangling together and some soldiers even abandoning their conveyances to flee on foot.

"We can't let them get away," shouted one man. "Yahweh has given us this victory!"

Before I knew what was happening, a large number of Israelites surged forward, brandishing their paltry weapons and chasing after the fleeing Philistines. But I remained in place, allowing the makeshift army of Israel to stream around me, until only my brothers and a large group of Levites remained.

Since the moment the thunder began, the rest of Samuel's words from so many years ago in that apple orchard had been circling around and around in my mind. They'd meant nothing to me at the time, and I could never have predicted their exact fulfillment would happen today, but now they made perfect sense.

"And when you stand at the watchtower and hear thunder from on high, your knee will bow to the True King."

My eyes were drawn to the watchtower, from which Mitzpah itself had been named, and I fell to my knees in worship before the king who'd rescued his people time and again, who gave them this Land and all its blessings, even though they continually strayed from the Covenant, and who had graciously called two wild branches out of Ashdod to join with the root of his people. I'd seen up close what a human king was like and the corruption that filled Nicaro's soul. No matter that many of the Hebrews screamed for an earthly leader to take over the reins from Samuel, I knew for certain from

all I'd learned from my father that there could be only One True
King of Israel—Yahweh himself.

When I finally lifted my head, I found my brothers on their
knees beside me as well. We stood together and headed toward
Naoith, leaving the rest of the tribes to deal with the Philistines.
My Tesi was waiting for me, and I'd made her a promise.

A Note from the Author

When I set out to write a duology about two Philistine children who followed the Ark, I had only tiny whispers in my mind about who those children might be. I saw a girl forced to grow up too fast in order to protect her brother and a rebellious boy who was angry with the world and with one eye over his shoulder toward the place he came from. And that was pretty much it. But what a delight it has been to get to know Eliora and Lukio and to dig into the culture that formed them.

I, like most everyone, knew little about the Philistines and had no idea where their origins might lie. Discovering that recent DNA evidence placed those origins most likely to Crete (biblical Caphtor) gave me an excuse to gleefully explore as much as I could about the Mycenaean and Minoan cultures that we now know most likely gave birth to the Philistines and, later, the classical Greek culture with which we are most familiar. The art and architecture found at Knossos and other sites give us glimpses into the pre-Greek culture there and laid the foundation for part of the story line in *Between the Wild Branches*, namely, Lukio's desire to be a famous fighter.

There is a beautiful fresco from this era of two young boys, wrapped hands uplifted in a boxing stance and distinctive long hairstyles, which inspired Lukio's desire to be a street fighter when he was a boy and gradually transformed into grown-up Lukio's lust for power and wealth through fighting in well-publicized matches. Wrestling and boxing are ancient pastimes, and such matches were noted by the ancient Babylonians, Sumerians, and Egyptians. Since gambling is also one of the most ancient entertainments, they undoubtedly went hand in hand.

The type of fighting that Lukio participates in is related to the later Greek style of wrestling called *pankration*, which was basically a free-for-all no-rules style of fighting that utilized chokeholds, kicks, punches, biting, eye-gouges, and whatever other techniques fighters could use to subdue their opponents. It regularly ended in broken bones and, at times, death, and the men who took part in these vicious matches were highly revered. Pankration was actually an event in the ancient Olympics, which also inspired Lukio's position as the Master of Games in Ashdod. There was, of course, no such event to my knowledge in ancient Philistia, although it's more than feasible that the Philistines brought things like bull-leaping and no-holds-barred wrestling with them from Crete, but we'll just give Lukio credit for the idea that eventually formed into the Olympics, shall we?

Special thanks goes to my editor, Jen Veilleux, for an important portion of this storyline, because Shoshana was originally a minor character in *To Dwell among Cedars* (with a different name) who disappeared after the first book. Jen's suggestion breathed new life into the character and gave Lukio a heroine who fits him to perfection.

Shoshana's story is a good reminder of just how vulnerable women were in ancient times and why Torah law protections were so novel and necessary in this era of tribalistic and war-centric cultures who had no Judeo-Christian moral framework to rein in their base impulses. The entrance of the Word of God into human history began a ripple effect across the world, and the Word of God Made Flesh finished that earth-shaking, humanity-transforming work at the cross. I am certainly very grateful to be a woman born in this time and place, but we must remember that all over this globe there are women and children who are still suffering the same indignities Shoshana did, and that there are more slaves now than

358

have ever been in history. May we fight for them on our knees and with whatever tools we have at our disposal.

As usual, I must thank my family for their eternal patience with my chosen career path and for being my constant encouragers. I thank my father and mother, Don and Jodi, for adopting my brother and me and therefore living out the beautiful picture God gives us of being grafted into a new family by adoption and being offered the same unconditional love and rights as a natural-born child—a privilege given to those of us now joined to Abraham's family through our Messiah's blood. Being an adopted child is both a blessing and a challenge, but I am eternally grateful to both my adopted parents and my birth parents for choosing that path.

I cannot pass over my writing sisters, Tammy L. Gray, Nicole Deese, Christy Barritt, and Amy Matayo, for helping me to plot this series. And thank you to Tammy and Nicole especially for their constant help with turning my crazy imagination into something that resembles an interesting plot with strong characters that readers can root for and for their gentle honesty when things just don't work. How did I ever do this without you girls?

Thank you to my beta readers Tina Chen, Ashley Espinoza, and Joanie Shultz. I can't tell you how happy it made me to hear your enthusiasm for Lukio's story!

To all the wonderful people at Bethany House, including my editors Raela and Jen, and also to my agent Tamela Hancock Murray, thank you for continuing to champion my work and affording me the opportunity to keep writing stories that I love. And thank you once again to Jennifer Parker, who created the gorgeous covers for this series and far surpassed what I had in mind when I requested some sort of mirroring effect and something that depicted the special bond between the two wild branches, Lukio and Eliora. I'll never forget the moment I put the two covers side by side and saw how it all came together so perfectly.

And so much love to my readers. Without you I'd just be telling stories to my cats (who are not really all that interested in ancient history). Thank you for your constant support and encouragement and for hanging in there with me for the last few months until the resolution of Lukio's story was in your hands!

> May the LORD bless you and keep you. May he make his face to shine upon you and be gracious to you. May he lift up his countenance upon you and give you peace. (Numbers 6:24–25)

Questions for Conversation

1. Did Lukio's journey resemble what you guessed it might at the close of *To Dwell among Cedars*? What surprised you the most about his story?

2. Although he eventually comes to understand just who his cousin truly is, Lukio is heavily influenced by Mataro in his younger years. Have you ever been influenced by someone who had wrong motives? What helped open your eyes to the truth?

3. For Shoshana to remain in Ashdod in order to stay with her daughter meant not immediately finding a way to get back to her two older children. Do you agree with this decision? What might you have done in her position?

4. The sweet friendship between Lukio and Shoshana as children forms a foundation for their emotional bond, even after years apart. What are some of your favorite memories from childhood? Did you have any strong friendships that were formative to who you are now?

5. At times, it is difficult to see ourselves and our weaknesses objectively. In what ways do Igo and Zevi contribute to Lukio's introspection about his own choices?

6. How do you think Zevi will be affected by all that he has experienced and witnessed? What do you think some of his struggles might be when his own story is told?

7. Did Jaru's parentage surprise you? Did you find satisfaction in the justice he was able to mete out on his mother's murderer? What do you envision his life will be like after Lukio is gone? What about Mariada's life in Shoshana's absence?

8. There is a recurring theme in the COVENANT HOUSE series of sacrificial love. How do you see that playing out between the characters in this story in particular, and in what ways do their choices depict our Messiah's sacrifice? When have you been a recipient of this kind of love, or personally offered it to someone else? How did the experience change you?

9. There are multiple occurrences in the Bible of people's names being changed when their identity and purpose is altered. Why do you think it was so important for Lukio to choose to change his name? In what ways has your identity shifted since you were adopted into the family of God? What physical or symbolic changes did you make after that decision?

10. Eliora's devotion to her brother is a constant throughout the series, which is depicted both by her concern for him and also her commitment to prayer for his return, even though a decade passed with little hope. Who in your life have you committed to praying for on a regular basis? How does this story give you hope for their future?